The Little
Orphan Girl

ALSO BY SANDY TAYLOR

The Girls from See Saw Lane
Counting Chimneys
When We Danced at the End of the Pier
The Runaway Children

The Little Orphan Girl

SANDY TAYLOR

Bookouture

Published by Bookouture in 2018

An imprint of StoryFire Ltd.

Carmelite House
50 Victoria Embankment
London EC4Y 0DZ

www.bookouture.com

ISBN: 978-1-78681-648-1
eBook ISBN: 978-1-78681-647-4

This book is dedicated to Kathleen Forrest
A very special lady who is always in our hearts.

PART ONE

1901

IRELAND

CHAPTER ONE

The workhouse gates clanged shut behind us, as me and the mammy walked down the hill towards the town. I was six years old and I had lived in the Union Workhouse my whole life. I was leaving the only home I had ever known.

'Don't look back,' said the mammy.

She was holding my hand so tightly that it hurt. I tried to pull away but she yanked me back so hard that I nearly fell over.

I'd never met this woman before and I felt a bit frightened of her. How could I have a mammy? I was an orphan, at least that's what I'd been told. She didn't look at me, not once. We got to a cottage where a woman was sitting on her doorstep eating potatoes out of a bowl. She stood up as we came near.

'Well, if it isn't Moira Ryan,' she said, folding her arms over her dirty apron.

'I'll thank you to step out of my way, Bridgette McCartny,' said Mammy.

The woman ignored her. 'And is this the child?' she said, looking down at me.

Mammy glared at her. 'And what business is it of yours who she is?'

The woman knelt down in front of me. She smelled bad, like Mr Dunne who cleaned the drains.

'Would you like a potato, child?' she said, holding one out towards me.

I liked potatoes and I was hungry. I nodded and took it from her.

'She doesn't want anything of yours,' said Mammy, knocking the potato out of my hand.

The woman stood up. 'The workhouse hasn't changed you, has it, Moira Ryan? You're still the same mean-spirited cow you were when you went in. All I can say is, God help this poor fatherless child.'

Mammy didn't say a word; she just stared at Mrs McCartny until she started to go red in the face.

'You think you're better than us, don't you?' said the woman. 'Well, you're not. You ran these streets with your bare arse hanging out of your drawers the same as the rest of us. At least I was properly married in the sight of God before I let my man take liberties.'

'And he's been taking liberties with every other woman in the town ever since,' said Mammy. Then she kicked the bowl of potatoes so hard that they all rolled down the hill.

'The exercise will do you good,' said Mammy, walking away.

'And if you think that this town will welcome you home, Moira Ryan, you're sadly mistaken,' shouted the woman.

Mammy lifted her bundle up over her shoulder. 'And do you really think I care whether this godforsaken town welcomes me or not? I'd rather be welcomed by Satan himself!' she yelled back.

The mammy was getting cross again so I kept silent.

We got to the bottom of the hill and started to walk through the streets. My mammy was tall and her legs were very long, I had to run to keep up with her. My boots were too tight and they hurt my feet.

'My boots are hurting, Mammy,' I whispered.

She didn't answer but she slowed down.

A few people said hello to us and smiled at me but Mammy ignored them and kept walking.

I had never known anything but the workhouse and I looked in wonder at all the shops and houses and little alleyways, at the blue skies above the chimneys and the glisten of sunshine on the water between the humble dwellings, which were mostly white and not much taller than the mammy. Some of them had half doors.

An old woman was leaning out of one of them; she smiled at me as we walked past and I smiled back.

'When are we going back home, Mammy?' I said.

'That's not your home, that was never your home and we're never going back.'

My eyes filled with tears. 'I didn't say goodbye to Nora.'

The mammy stopped walking and shook me by the shoulders. 'Forget about Nora, forget you ever lived there, do you hear me?'

I nodded but I knew that I would never forget my best friend Nora, who had big blue eyes and yellow hair and a weak leg. Who was going to help her up the stairs now? Who was going to protect her from Biddy Duggan, who was mean and spiteful and pinched her hard on her little arm? I was going to miss Mrs Foley too; she looked after us and told us stories and taught us our prayers.

'Now stop your blathering, we're being met,' snapped the mammy.

In my dreams my mammy had a kind face and a lovely smile and twinkly eyes, nothing like this tall sullen woman. I was beginning to think that being an orphan might not be such a bad thing.

We cut down an alleyway between two rows of run-down cottages and there in front of us was the sea. I knew it was the sea because Mrs Foley had shown Nora and me a picture of it. Mammy put down her bundle and sat on a wall.

There were lots of boats, small ones with names on the sides and big ones with sails that nearly touched the sky. Men were standing around smoking pipes and young boys sat with their legs dangling over the side of the wall, fishing lines tipping the water. There were women in black shawls untangling nets and children with no shoes on, chasing each other around. I wished I could join them, I wished Nora could see the sea.

I walked over to the mammy. 'I like the sea,' I said shyly.

'It's not the sea,' she snapped. 'It's a river.'

'It looks like the sea,' I said quietly. 'Mrs Foley showed us a picture.'

Her hand shot out and she slapped me hard across the face. 'I told you to forget that place and everyone in it, or are you deaf?'

My cheek stung and I wanted to cry but I didn't because I knew that the mammy would be cross. I stood very still beside her in case she got cross again.

'I'm sorry I slapped you, child,' she said suddenly. 'I have a fearful temper at times.'

I climbed up onto the wall and sat beside her. She put her arm around my shoulder. I leaned into her. She didn't smell bad like the woman with the potatoes, she smelt nice, maybe she smelt like a mammy.

'And a sharp tongue,' she added.

I sat and watched the river flowing gently by; it was lovely. A couple of boys were jumping in. I wished I could jump in. On the opposite bank, green fields swept down to the water's edge and I could see little houses dotted about the rolling hills. I hoped that we were going to live here. If we lived here, I'd come down every day and I'd play chase with the other children and maybe I'd jump in the water and maybe I'd walk up the hill and visit Nora.

I felt a bit braver with Mammy's arm around my shoulder so I said, 'Is this where we're going to live?'

'Maybe,' she said. 'It all depends on himself.'

I didn't ask who himself was, because the mammy sounded cross again, so I jumped off the wall and ran across to the boats. I breathed in the smell of the river and it made me smile. I was hungry and thirsty and tired, and I missed Nora and Mrs Foley and Mr Dunne's dog but the smell of the river made me smile.

I heard someone calling 'Cissy'. I carried on looking at the river.

Then the mammy was towering above me. 'Are you stupid as well as deaf?' she shouted.

I didn't know what I'd done this time so I just stared at her.

'I was calling your name; didn't you hear me?'

I shook my head. My name was Martha, at least it was this morning.

She must have realised that I didn't know what she was talking about and she softened.

'Your name is Cissy, child. Can you remember that? Your name is Cissy Ryan.'

I nodded. 'Okay, Mammy,' I said.

I tried the name out: 'Cissy Ryan,' I said softly.

And then she smiled and touched my hair. 'That's right,' she said. 'Your name is Cissy Ryan.'

CHAPTER TWO

A horse and trap came into the square. Mammy picked up her bundle and walked towards it. I followed her.

There was a boy sitting up on the trap. The big brown horse was shaking its head and stamping its feet. It looked cross, like the mammy.

The boy jumped down. 'Yer not afraid of old Blue, are you?' he said, smiling at me.

'Will he bite me?'

'Not unless you give him reason to,' said the boy. 'If you're kind to him then you and he will become great friends.'

I stared at the horse and decided that he wouldn't make much of a friend. He wouldn't be able to play ball with me or chase with me. Nora was my friend and I missed her and I wanted to cry.

The boy knelt down in front of me. The sleeves of his white shirt were rolled up, showing brown arms that made the shirt look even whiter and on his head he had a blue faded cap.

'My name's Colm,' he said softly. 'Do you have a name?'

I nodded shyly.

'Her name's Cissy,' said the mammy, pulling herself up into the cart. 'Now are we going or is it your intention to stay here all day, Colm Doyle?'

The boy winked at me and grinned. He had very white teeth and brown eyes that crinkled up at the edges and his hair was very black and shiny; I thought that he was lovely.

He lifted me up onto the cart beside Mammy. 'Home then, is it?' he said.

'Today would be good,' said the mammy.

'Right ye are, Mrs Ryan. Come on, Blue, these fine ladies want to go home.'

'I wouldn't have known you, Colm Doyle, you're like a rasher of bacon.'

'Ah, but it's all muscle, Mrs Ryan.'

'How's the old goat?' said Mammy.

'I'd say he makes a career out of being hard done by. He won't even open the door to the priest unless he's brought a drop of the hard stuff with him but sure, he's harmless enough.'

'I'll keep my own counsel on that one.'

'You do right, missus,' said Colm. 'And does himself know you're coming?'

'He does, but he's in for a shock.'

'It's a pity you haven't a drop of something on you to soften the blow,' said Colm.

It was exciting sitting beside Colm, watching Blue trotting along the lanes. Every now and then the horse made a snuffly noise and raised his head as if catching the breeze. I watched his tail swishing and the way the sun shone on his back, making it shine like silk. Sometimes he turned around as if he was making sure we were still there. Maybe we could be friends? Maybe we could find different games to play.

The sun was warm on my face as we passed little cottages and farms and raced between tall trees that were bent so low they brushed the top of my head, making me giggle.

'Are you hungry, Cissy?' said Colm.

I was very hungry but I remembered how the mammy knocked the potato out of my hand. 'No,' I said.

'You can eat if you like, child,' said the mammy.

'Would you like an apple?' said Colm.

'I would,' I said shyly.

Colm took an apple from out of a paper bag. He rubbed it on his shirt and passed it to me.

I took a bite, it was sweet and juicy.

'Thank you,' I said.

'You're very welcome, Miss Cissy. What about you, Mrs Ryan?'

'No, thank you, Colm,' she said. 'I need an empty stomach for what I've got to say.'

I didn't know what they were talking about and I didn't like to ask. There were so many things I didn't understand about this strange day.

We went through an old stone archway, towards six white cottages facing each other across a kind of yard.

'Whoa, boy,' said Colm and the horse came to a stop outside one of them. Blue's long legs were still moving up and down as if he was impatient to keep going.

'Welcome to Paradise Alley, Cissy,' said Colm.

I looked at the cottage we'd stopped outside. It was small and white and there was smoke drifting out of the chimney. 'Is this where we're going to live, Mammy?'

She stared at the cottage, not saying anything, just staring at it.

Maybe she hadn't heard me. 'Mammy, is this where we're going to live?' I said again.

She looked down at me. 'Like I said, it all depends on himself.'

Colm handed Mammy the bundle. 'May God sit gently on your tongue, Mrs Ryan.'

'I don't think God will want to be anywhere near my tongue this day, Colm Doyle.'

The mammy knocked on the door and walked into a room that was so dark I couldn't see where I was going. It smelled very bad and I wanted to cover my nose but I knew that would be a rude thing to do. At first, I thought the room was empty but then I saw a black shape huddled beside the fire.

He stared at me and it was like looking into the face of the Devil. Mrs Foley told us all about the Devil; how his eyes were like two pieces of burning coal in his head and how he had the tail of a goat. I couldn't see whether the man had a tail and I wondered if he might be sitting on it.

'*That's* not staying under my roof,' he roared, pointing a bony finger in my direction.

Frightened, I hid behind Mammy's skirt.

'I told you I never wanted to see that thing and you have the nerve to bring it into my house.'

'She has a name.'

'And that name is *bastard*. Have you no shame, woman?'

'Have *you*?' spat the mammy.

'I have no call to be ashamed.'

The mammy shook her head. 'You haven't changed, have you? You're still the same bigoted old fool you've always been but don't worry, Cissy is not staying here.'

'Well, at least you have some sense left.'

'And neither am I.'

I still had the apple in my hand and I was squeezing it so hard that the juice was running down my dress.

'What are you talking about, Moira?' said the old man. 'You're here to look after me.'

'Am I now?'

'You'd still be up there if I hadn't offered you a roof over your head.'

'When I needed a roof over my head you left me and my child in that godforsaken hole to rot. You only want me now because my mother is dead and I'm useful to you. Well, thank you for your kind offer but I'd rather live with the pigs.'

The mammy seemed even taller as she glared at the old man. I peered out from behind her skirt and I hoped with all my heart that we weren't going to live here.

'Do you not fear the wrath of God?'

'Don't talk to me about God, you hypocrite. You think that laying on the church steps, roaring drunk is fulfilling your Easter duties?'

'You've turned into a bitter woman, Moira.'

'And whose fault is that? You bullied my poor mother, God rest her soul, and you worked her to the bone, while you drank away every penny that came into the house. I've never seen a woman welcome death like she did and it was because she knew she was getting away from you. And now I'm getting away too. Come on, child, we have no more business here.'

'And what am I supposed to do?' he yelled.

'You can rot in hell for all I care,' she said.

Mammy had her hand in the small of my back and was almost pushing me towards the door.

'Wait,' said the old man.

We waited.

'Get rid of her and we'll say no more about it.'

Mammy spun around. 'My child is not something to be rid of like a pile of rubbish. If you want me to stay here and look after you then Cissy stays too.'

The old man stared into the fire as if he'd find the answer in the flames and then he spoke so quietly I could hardly hear what he was saying. 'Well, if you're going to stay, make yerself useful. I want me tea.'

'Then you'll ask properly for it, I won't be bullied like my mother.'

'You've changed, Moira,' he said.

'Oh yes, I've changed alright and you'd do right to remember it. Cissy, say hello to your granddaddy.'

I looked at the old man sitting by the fire. 'Is he really my granddaddy, Mammy?'

'He is, God help us.'

'I thought he was the Devil himself,' I said, staring at him from behind Mammy's skirt.

And to the surprise of both of us, the granddaddy started chuckling.

CHAPTER THREE

A few weeks later, I was sitting on the doorstep outside the cottage when Colm and Blue trotted up the alleyway. 'What are you doing sitting there?' he said, smiling down at me.

'The granddaddy is having a wash, Mammy says he smells like a dead ferret.'

'Yer mammy's right well enough, the old man has a powerful stench about him.'

'He was cursing and swearing because he didn't want to have a wash but Mammy said no Christian man has a right to smell like he does.'

'I don't know about Christian,' said Colm, getting down off Blue's back. 'It's not often you see him darken the doors of the church unless it's a funeral and there's a chance of some refreshment on the cards.'

'He doesn't like me,' I said.

Colm sat down beside me on the step. 'Well, if it's any comfort, I'd say he doesn't like anyone very much.'

'Mammy says he's an old goat.'

'I think that's doing old goats a disservice, Cissy... I'm surprised your mother came back here.'

I stood up and stroked Blue; he shivered under my hand and turned his head. 'I like Blue,' I said. 'I like him better than the granddaddy.'

'I told you, you'd be great friends.'

'Mammy says I have to go to school. Do you go to school, Colm?'

'Sure, I'm too old for school, I'll be twelve on my next birthday. I help my father with the milk round.'

Colm didn't have a cap on today and his dark hair was falling down over his eyes. He brushed it back from his face and smiled.

'What do you have to do?' I asked.

'Well, me and Blue go all round the houses and the shops and we deliver the milk so that the people can have a grand cup of tea and the babies can suck on their bottles. Would you like to come out with me tomorrow?'

'I'll ask the mammy,' I said.

'Well, let me know and I'll call for you in the morning. Now me and Blue must get home for our dinner.'

I very much wanted to help Colm with the milk round and I hoped the mammy would let me. There was nothing to do in the cottage. Mammy said I had to keep out of the granddaddy's way and as there was only one room downstairs I never knew what to do with myself. I wished I was back in the workhouse because I had Nora to play with. Sometimes we helped Mrs Foley sort out the clothes that came in the charity bins, or we played with Mr Dunne's smelly dog. I wanted to go home. I wanted to be with Nora, sleeping in our little bed with our arms around each other, but Mammy said that the only way we would go back there was over her dead body. I wanted to ask Mammy how we could go back there over her dead body but I knew she'd get cross.

Just then Mammy came walking under the archway. She smiled at me. 'Has he had his wash?' she said.

'I haven't been in, Mammy,' I said.

She opened the door and I followed her into the room. She looked different, maybe even happy. I thought she looked beautiful when she wasn't cross.

'I can see you've managed to have a wash,' she said, looking down at the bowl of dirty water on the floor. 'Would it have killed you to tip the water away?'

'That's what you're here for,' growled the granddaddy.

'Not for much longer,' she announced. 'I have a job.'

The granddaddy looked up. 'What are you talking about, woman?' he snarled.

'I'm talking about a job,' she said.

'Your job is to look after me.'

'My job is to do as I please.'

'I'll send you back to that place,' he warned.

'No you won't because I have a job; they wouldn't take me back.'

'I'll send *her* back then,' he said, glaring at me across the room.

Mammy walked across and bent down in front of him. She put her face so close to his that they were almost touching. 'You just try,' she said very quietly. 'And I'll slice the nose off ya while you're asleep.'

I knew she meant it because she had a fearful temper and a sharp tongue. The granddaddy touched his old red nose and glared at her but he knew she meant what she said.

'Yer a wicked woman, Moira Ryan,' he said.

'I intend to be,' she said, taking off her shawl and hanging it behind the door. 'I have a grand job down at the laundry and I'll have my own money to spend as I wish.'

'You'll give your money to me,' snarled the granddaddy.

'I will in me eye,' said the mammy. 'I'll feed ya and I'll give you money for the baccy and a pint of Guinness on a Saturday night but I intend to keep the rest of it for me and my child.'

'Go boil yer head,' said the granddaddy, picking up a stick and poking at the peat in the flames.

I could tell that the mammy was happy today, even though she was being mean to the granddaddy, so I took a deep breath and said, 'Can I go with Colm on the milk round tomorrow please, Mammy?'

'You can of course, my love,' she said, smiling at me.

I felt like crying because she'd called me her love. Maybe she liked me, maybe my mammy might even love me one day. I ran up to Colm's house. He lived at the top of Paradise Alley in a big grey house. It was bigger than all the cottages and there was a yard round the back with a stable for Blue to go to sleep in. When I got there Colm and his daddy were in the stable, shovelling out the hay.

'Hello, Miss Cissy,' said Colm's daddy, grinning at me.

I liked Colm's daddy. His name was Jack and he looked like Colm, with the same black hair, brown eyes and smiley face.

'Have you come to help us clear out Blue's shite?' he said.

I knew that shite was a bad word but I liked it. 'Shite, shite, shite,' I muttered under my breath. I liked the sound of it on my tongue and I giggled.

'What are you so happy about?' said Colm.

'The mammy said I can come on the milk round tomorrow,' I said.

'Well now, we'll have to dress Colm in his good suit and tie and his black top hat if he has a lady up in the trap with him,' said Colm's daddy, winking at me.

I laughed and ran back down the alley and into the cottage.

'And who's going to look after me?' the granddaddy was saying as I walked through the door, 'when you're up in the town at your grand job?'

'I'll get your breakfast and then Cissy will see to you.'

'I'll not have her waiting on me,' he growled.

'She won't be waiting on you, she's not your servant, but if you can keep a civil tongue in your head, she'll bring you a cup of tea and run any errands you need. If you don't want her help then you can get your own tea and run your own errands.'

'I'm a sick man, you know I can't do that.'

'Yer not as sick as you think you are, old man. And isn't it a miracle that your legs manage to take you to the pub but can't seem to take you anywhere else? The choice is yours. Cissy will bring you your tea or you'll go without, it makes no odds to me.'

He glared at her. 'Well, don't expect me to talk to her.'

'I'm sure she has no desire to talk to *you*.'

But Mammy was wrong: I *did* want to talk to him. It was better than talking to meself and oh, I had so much to talk about and as the granddaddy had no wish to talk to me, he wouldn't be answering me back.

That night in bed I thought of the three lovely words I'd heard today: 'shite' and 'my love'.

They stayed in my head as I dropped off to sleep.

shite, shite, shite, my love, my love, my...

CHAPTER FOUR

Mammy woke me very early the next morning so that I could go on the milk round with Colm. I rolled over in the little bed and lay in the warm space that she had left behind. Weeks had passed since the day I'd left the workhouse, and I still missed sleeping beside Nora but I liked sleeping next to Mammy now too. Sometimes I'd wake in the middle of the night and feel her arms around me. I'd lay there all warm and safe and listen to the noises of Paradise Alley outside the little window. I liked having a mammy, even if she was cross most of the time, because some days she would smile at me or ruffle my hair or tell me I was a good girl for sweeping the floor. I still wasn't sure that she was really my mammy because she didn't look like me. The mammy's hair was very dark and so were her eyes. My hair was fair, almost white and my eyes were blue. I thought that maybe there'd been a mistake and she was someone else's mammy. Perhaps one day a girl with dark hair and dark eyes would knock on the door and tell me to give her back her mammy. I used to think that Mrs Foley was my mammy and that I had lots of brothers and sisters.

Sometimes me and Nora would go up to the top of the house where the poor demented souls lived. We'd climb up on a chair and look out of the window. We'd watch the people trudging up the hill and wonder if today was the day that the mammy would come to collect us. The trouble with this was that we didn't know what our mammies looked like so we wouldn't know if it was them that were coming anyway.

We weren't supposed to go up to the floor where the poor demented souls lived because Mrs Foley said you wouldn't know what some of them were going to do next. She said it wasn't their fault, God had just decided to make them that way.

'Have they not got mammies who could take them out the strand for an ice cream?' said Nora.

'I'll tell you what I think, Nora,' said Mrs Foley, smiling fondly at her. 'I think they wouldn't want to go for an ice cream even if a mammy did come to see them.'

'Why not?' said Nora.

'Because they've been here so long, they'd be afraid to go outside.'

'That's sad,' said Nora.

Mrs Foley smiled at her, but it was a sad sort of a smile. 'This is their home, Nora, and this is where they feel safe,' she'd said.

One day we were looking out of the window when Mrs Perks, a desperate mean woman, caught us.

'Get away downstairs to your own quarters,' she yelled. 'You have no right to be up here.'

'We were doing no harm,' I said quietly.

'We were just looking for our mammies,' said Nora.

Mrs Perks laughed but it wasn't a kind laugh. 'You have no mammies,' she spat at us. 'You're a pair of scruffy little orphans. Now get away out of here.'

Me and Nora jumped down from the chairs and ran out of the room.

Halfway down the stairs we sat down. 'What's an orphan?' said Nora.

'I haven't a clue,' I'd said. 'But I have a feeling it's not a great thing to be.'

'Will we ask Mrs Foley?'

'That's a good idea, Nora.'

Mrs Foley sat Nora on her knee and I sat on the floor in front of her. 'Now who told you that word?' she said.

'That mean old woman on the top floor,' I said.

'Oh, Mrs Perks?'

'That's her,' said Nora. 'She said we were a pair of scruffy little orphans.'

'What's an orphan, Mrs Foley?' I asked.

Mrs Foley gently brushed Nora's hair away from her eyes. 'An orphan is someone who doesn't have a mammy or a daddy. But sure, we all know that's not true, don't we? Because we have a loving Father in heaven and don't we all have to have a mammy to be brought into this world?'

I smiled at her. 'So do you think she was talking a load of shite?'

'Where did you hear language like that, child?'

'Mr Dunne, he has a grand collection of them.'

'Well, I shall be having a stern word with Mr Dunne.'

We both kissed Mrs Foley's soft cheek. 'Now off you go and get some good fresh air into your lungs,' she said.

Nora and I decided to visit the poor little children who were buried at the top of the graveyard.

'What do you think?' said Nora, pulling at the grass and making it into little piles.

'I think we're orphans.'

'That's what I think too,' she said.

'But we'll always have each other, Nora,' I said, putting my arm around her thin little shoulders.

I tried to forget about the workhouse because this was a happy day and not a sad one. I was going out with Colm on the milk round. I washed quickly because the water was freezing cold, then I got dressed. There was a curtain between the granddaddy's bed and ours and I could hear him snoring his old head off.

'Isn't it a miracle that his conscience is so clear that he can sleep like a baby?' said Mammy.

After I'd had my porridge, I waited on the doorstep for Colm. There wasn't a soul about because it was very early. The only sound was the seagulls sitting in rows on the roofs of the cottages, screeching and squawking as if they were cross with each other. Colm said they were dirty old things and not deserving of the time of day. I wouldn't mind being a bird, it must be lovely to fly over the town and the river and never have to go to work or go to school. I could fly up the hill and visit Nora and Mrs Foley and play with Mr Dunne's smelly dog. I might even visit the poor demented souls at the top of the house.

As I was thinking all this, Blue trotted up and stopped outside the cottage.

'Ready?' said Colm.

'I am,' I said, smiling up at him.

'You might need a shawl, it can get chilly up on the cart.'

I went back into the cottage. 'Colm says I need a shawl, Mammy.'

'You don't have a shawl,' said the mammy. She walked across to the granddaddy's chair and picked up his old blanket.

'You can have this,' she said, handing it to me.

'Do I have to, Mammy?' I said. 'It's desperate smelly.'

'Well, it's that or get cold.'

'I think I'd rather get cold, Mammy,' I said.

'As you wish,' said Mammy.

Just as I was going back out the door the mammy said, 'Have a nice time, Cissy.'

I was smiling as Colm helped me up onto the cart. 'I think the mammy might be getting to like me,' I told him.

'And why wouldn't she?' said Colm, wrapping a blanket around my knees. 'You're a grand little girl, so you are.'

Blue trotted all the way through the town, out to the beach and along beside the sea – at least I thought it was the sea. It went on and on right to the edge of the world and it was grey and green with little tips of white on the tops of the waves. 'Is that the sea, Colm?' I asked. 'Or is it a river?'

'It's the sea, Cissy. Have you never seen the sea?'

I shook my head. 'I've seen pictures of it.'

'Sure, the sea is a wondrous thing, Cissy. I'd love to be a sailor, maybe even a captain. Imagine being the captain of a grand big ship sailing across the oceans and travelling to foreign parts. Wouldn't that be a mighty thing to do?'

'Oh, it would, Colm. I'd go with you but I have to make the granddaddy's tea. But you could tell me all about it when you came back home.'

'And what would you like me to bring you back?'

'What sort of things do they have in foreign parts?'

'Well, I'm not altogether sure about that as I've never actually been to a foreign part but I'd say it would be something exotic, would that do?'

I nodded. 'Something exotic would do fine, Colm, and I'd be glad to have it. Do you think you could stretch to two exotic things? Because I think Nora would like one as well.'

'It would be my pleasure, Cissy.'

'Colm?'

'Yes.'

'What's the difference between a river and a sea?'

'Now I couldn't tell you that, Cissy, because I took no mind to me lessons when I was at school but you'll soon be starting school yourself so I'd ask your teacher. Teachers know everything and I'd say they'll be able to answer your question.'

'Didn't you like school then?'

'The teacher told my father that the only way I could be educated would be to nail me to the chair.'

'They didn't do that, did they?'

'No, I'd say they just gave up on me. School doesn't suit everyone, Cissy, and it wasn't for me. I wasn't one to be sitting on a chair all day when the sun was shining outside the window and I could be riding over the hills on old Blue. I kind of regret it now though because I'm thick as mud. When you go to school, Cissy, you must mind the teacher and pay attention to your lessons. You won't want to be ending up like meself.'

I looked at Colm with his black hair and lovely face and I looked at his strong brown arms as he held the reins. I knew that he was still a boy but he seemed so grown-up, there were times when he seemed more like a man.

'I wouldn't mind ending up like you, Colm,' I said.

Colm laughed. 'You're a funny little thing,' he said.

We trotted happily along beside the sea and on past the lighthouse. Blue started to slow down as we started up the hill.

'Come on, Blue,' said Colm. 'You can do it, boy.'

When we got to the top, Colm jumped down from the cart and pushed open a pair of big iron gates. It reminded me of the workhouse and I felt a bit sad and I wondered what Nora was doing and whether that spawn of the Devil Biddy Duggan was still pinching her little arm.

'You've gone very quiet,' said Colm.

'I was thinking of my friend Nora, back in the workhouse, and how much I missed her.'

'Maybe you could visit her one day.'

'I don't think so. The mammy said it would be over her dead body before I ever went back there and I don't want the mammy to die.'

'Leave it with me, Cissy, and I'll have a bit of a think,' he said, very seriously.

I felt cheerful again because Colm was having a bit of a think and I might see Nora again one day and I might be able to kick Biddy Duggan hard in the shins and break her two legs then she might stop pinching Nora.

Blue trotted up a long drive between tall trees that swayed in the breeze and there in front of us was a house the like of which I'd never seen before. It had rows and rows of windows twinkling away in the early morning sunshine. It took my breath away.

'Welcome to Bretton Hall, Cissy.'

'How many people live here?' I asked.

'Just the Honourables.'

'Who are the Honourables?'

'Mr and Mrs Bretton. They live in this grand big house at the top of the hill and they look down their noses at the rest of us.'

'What's an Honourable, Colm?'

'I don't have a clue but I'd say you have to be mighty rich to be one.'

'But they still need milk?'

'Oh yes, and I'm the only one left that will deliver to them.'

'Why's that?'

'For all their wealth they have very bad memories when it comes to paying their bills,' he said, hopping down from the cart.

'Money must be a terrible curse then,' I said.

'I think it's more of a curse to be poor, Cissy, and apart from the Brettons, I'd say that applies to most of the town.'

'You'd think they'd share it out a bit, wouldn't you?'

Colm laughed. 'I can't see that happening any time soon.'

'They'll have trouble when they reach the Pearly Gates then,' I said.

'And how do you work that out?'

'Well, it says in the Bible that it is easier for a camel to go through the eye of a needle than for a rich man to enter the kingdom of heaven.'

'We'll go flying through then,' said Colm, giggling.

I grinned at him.

'Now, Cissy, you must never go to the front door, you must always go round the back to the kitchens. The likes of us aren't good enough to be seen at the front door.'

I looked down at my clothes and my old boots. 'I don't think I'm dressed for the Honourables, Colm.'

'Yer grand, Cissy. Now all you have to do is knock on the kitchen door and ask for the jug. You bring that back to me and I'll fill it with milk.'

'Okay, Colm,' I replied. My old boots crunched on the pebbles as I walked towards the back door. I was just about to knock when two children came running round the side of the house. They stopped dead when they saw me. They both looked a bit older than me. The girl was very beautiful with golden curls bouncing on her shoulders and very blue eyes. She had on a fine grey woollen dress and lovely warm boots. We stared at each other.

'What do you want, girl?' she said, looking me up and down.

'I'm helping Colm with the milk round,' I answered.

'I'm helping Colm with the milk round,' she mimicked in a sing-song voice. 'Isn't she an absolute riot, Peter?' she said, laughing.

The boy didn't speak, he just smiled at me. He looked nice, nicer than his sister anyway. I tried to hide my dirty old boots. I suddenly wanted to be wearing a fine woollen dress and lovely warm boots, like the girl with the golden hair.

'How can you prove you're helping this Colm person with the milk round?' she sneered. 'How do I know you're not a thief? You look like a thief, doesn't she, Peter? Doesn't she look like a thief?'

'Stop it, Caro,' said the boy.

'I'm not a thief,' I said angrily.

'You address me as Miss Caroline when you speak to me, *girl*, and you address my brother as Master Peter.'

I could feel my face going red.

'Well?' she said.

'I won't be calling you Miss Caroline,' I shouted. 'I'd just as soon be calling you Miss Baggy Knickers!'

Her eyes looked like two angry little slits as she advanced towards me and grabbed hold of my arm. 'How dare you speak to your betters like that, you little guttersnipe! Peter, I order you to give her a good thrashing.'

Just then the kitchen door opened and a young woman stood there glaring at us. She was wearing a white apron and she was drying her hands on a towel. 'What in the name of all that's holy is this racket about?' she said.

'This is none of your business, Bridie,' said the girl.

'It's outside my kitchen door so it is my business.'

'She called Caroline Miss Baggy Knickers, Bridie,' said Peter, grinning.

'And we're going to give her a good thrashing,' said the girl.

'You'll be giving no one a good thrashing, Miss Caroline, and I suggest you get back to your own part of the house and stay there.'

Miss Caroline glared at her.

'Be gone before I set the dog on ya.'

'You wouldn't,' said Miss Caroline.

'Try me,' said Bridie.

'I'll tell my father.'

'You can tell God Almighty Himself for all I care, now get along with you.'

Miss Caroline stomped off, followed by the boy, who turned around and winked at me. I grinned and winked back.

'Right then,' said Bridie, 'and what are you wanting?'

'I'm helping Colm with the milk round, Miss. And I've to collect the jug.'

'I'll get it for ya and you don't need to call me Miss, Bridie will do just fine. And what's your name, child?'

'It's Cissy,' I said. 'Cissy Ryan.'

'Well, wait there, Cissy Ryan, and try not to get into any more trouble while I fetch the jugs.'

I waited at the door, looking around me, ready to run, in case the horrid girl came back and gave me a thrashing. 'Don't you be worrying about Miss Caroline,' said Bridie, handing me two jugs. 'She's a little madam and no mistake.'

'Thanks,' I said.

I took the jugs back to Colm, who was standing by the cart. He dipped a big ladle into the churn and filled the two jugs with creamy white milk.

'I'll take these back to the house, you wait for me here, Cissy.'

I stroked old Blue and he nuzzled me with his nose. I'd been frightened of Blue when I'd first made his acquaintance but now I loved him. Blue didn't care what I was wearing, he was a true friend. I stroked his back and leaned into him.

'I don't like the Honourables, Blue,' I whispered.

Colm came back and I climbed up onto the cart beside him.

'You've gone awful quiet again, Cissy,' he said as we sped along.

'I did an awful bad thing, Colm,' I said.

'Did you now?'

'I did, and I think you're going to be terrible cross with me and I don't think you'll let me help you with the milk again.'

'Well, that sounds mighty serious to me.'

'It is.'

'And could you be telling me what this awful thing is?'

I hung my head and stared down at the floor of the cart. 'I called Miss Caroline Miss Baggy Knickers.'

Colm didn't say anything so I knew he must be very angry but then I saw his shoulders moving up and down and realised that he was laughing fit to bust. 'You called Miss Caroline "Baggy Knickers"?'

'I did, Colm.'

He was almost choking with laughter, tears were rolling down his face and then we were both laughing and we laughed all the way round town and people must have thought the two of us were mad. I loved everything about Colm and I wanted to be his friend forever.

CHAPTER FIVE

Months had passed and I was beginning to enjoy living in Paradise Alley. My life in the Union Workhouse seemed a long time ago and although I still missed Nora, I had no desire to go back.

One morning, I'd dragged the bucket of water back to the cottage from the pump at the end of the alley and I was busy washing the little window and talking to the granddaddy. I'd been talking to the granddaddy for the past week. It had felt a bit odd to start with because the granddaddy never talked back but now it didn't bother me and I was having a great time telling him everything I'd been doing.

'I helped Colm with the milk round,' I said, dipping the rag into the bucket and giving the window a good rub. 'And I called the Honourable Miss Caroline Miss Baggy Knickers because she was mean and nasty even though she was an Honourable and she was wearing a lovely woollen dress and she had grand stout boots on her feet… I thought Colm was going to be cross with me but he laughed, Granddaddy, he laughed so hard he was crying and that made me laugh as well.' I gave the window another good rub and carried on talking. 'I'd like a little dog, Granddaddy, just a small little dog, and if I had a little dog, I'd call him Buddy. Don't you think that Buddy is a grand name for a dog? Yes, I do, too. I'd take him for walks across the fields and down to the quay. You could come too, Granddaddy. We could walk across the fields, just you and me and Buddy. It would be good for your old legs to go walking and it would make a welcome change for them to walk over the fields instead of walking to the pub. You could lean on me and we could stop now and then to give your old legs a bit of a rest. I wouldn't mind stopping for a rest, Granddaddy. We could sit on a wall and watch the boats and get an ice cream. Do you like ice cream, Granddaddy? I thought you might because I like it too. The only trouble is we'd need some money, so I'm thinking you could save up your baccy money for a few weeks and then we'd be grand altogether.'

I stopped talking and stood back to look at my handiwork. The little window was bright and shiny, although I'd have to do the outside in a minute because it was still a bit smeary. I felt my eyes filling up with tears. 'The mammy says I'm not allowed to mention the workhouse, Granddaddy, but I miss it sometimes. When I was in there my name was Martha and I had no mammy. And then I was Cissy and I had a mammy. Don't you think that's awful strange, Granddaddy? I miss my friend Nora, I miss playing with her in the yard. I worry about Nora, Granddaddy, because that spawn of the Devil Biddy Duggan pinches her little arm till she cries.' I gave a big sniff and wiped my eyes on the sleeve of my cardigan. 'I used to think you were the Devil, Granddaddy, and I'm sorry about that because I can see you haven't got a tail and your eyes don't burn like two red coals in your head. It was wrong of me to think you were the Devil but I'm only six and I make lots of mistakes. I'll know better when I grow up.' I dipped my rag into the water. 'I saw the sea, Granddaddy, and it went on forever, way out past the lighthouse and over the edge of the world. I thought it was a river but Colm said it was definitely the sea. I asked Colm if he knew the difference between a river and the sea and he said he didn't know and I'd have to ask my teacher when I went to school.'

'Colm Doyle is an eejit,' said the granddaddy suddenly. I got such a shock to hear him talking that I nearly jumped out of my skin.

'And so was his granddaddy before him. A couple of eejits, the pair of them.'

I stared at him hard.

'Colm Doyle is an eejit,' he said again, 'if he doesn't know the difference between a river and the sea.'

'He paid no mind to his teachers at school, Granddaddy.'

'Then he's a bigger eejit than I gave him credit for. You don't need a teacher to tell you the difference between a river and the feckin' sea. It's common feckin' sense.'

I knew the granddaddy was saying curse words but I didn't mind, at least he was finally talking to me.

'A river is fresh water, it comes down from the hills and it joins other rivers and streams and brooks and then it meets the sea. A river always meets the sea and then the river and the sea become one. Another thing that eejit Colm Doyle should know is that the sea is full of salt. Has the boy never been for a feckin' swim?'

'I didn't ask him, Granddaddy.'

He didn't speak again so I said, 'Can I get you a grand cup of tea, Granddaddy?'

'You can, child,' he said and then to my surprise he added, 'And thank you.'

I was so pleased I thought I'd burst. 'I'll get you a grand cup of tea, Granddaddy, and I'll put piles of sugar in it.'

The granddaddy looked up at me and nodded his old head.

CHAPTER SIX

When I was seven years old, I started school at the convent, which was at the other end of the town. I liked school and I loved my teacher, Sister Bridgette, who had a lovely kind face and carried sweeties in her pocket for the good girls. I got a sweetie every day. You couldn't see Sister Bridgette's hair because it was tucked under her black veil but I imagined it to be the colour of sunshine, all shiny and yellow. I would have enjoyed school a lot more if I didn't have the granddaddy to worry about. Who was going to get his tea and run his errands and make sure he got a proper wash so that he didn't smell like a dead ferret while I was out all day? I'd grown to love the granddaddy and I think he loved me too.

The mammy said I wasn't to worry about him because he was more than capable of getting his own tea and it would do him a pile of good to look after himself but I still worried about him, because his old legs didn't work so good and he'd miss our conversations. Mammy said he'd probably be glad of the silence but I thought he liked listening to me even if he didn't talk much.

'I'll look in on him,' said Colm, when I told him of my worries. 'I'll make him a grand cup of tea and bring the water up from the pump.'

'He likes piles of sugar,' I said, 'but not too much milk. He says milk upsets his old war wound.'

'And what war would that be, the Crimean?'

'He didn't say which war it was, Colm, he just said that talking about it upsets his system and so does too much milk.'

Colm grinned, showing his lovely white teeth. 'I'll go careful on the milk then, Cissy.'

'Don't forget the sugar, just pile it into the cup. That's what he likes best, it makes him lick his old lips.'

Once I knew that Colm would look in on the granddaddy I felt happier and began to enjoy going to school more. I sat next to Mary Butler. Mary was very beautiful; her hair was thick and brown with bits of red in it and her eyes were green like the sea. She became my second best friend. I told her that Nora would always be my best friend and she said she didn't mind one bit about being second because her best friend was her dog Eddie.

Sister Bridgette taught us all about the Saints and the Martyrs who died for their faith. She showed us pictures of them being tortured on big wheels. One day, Breda Daley got sick all over Maureen Casey, who was mighty fierce and didn't take kindly to getting sicked all over and whacked her over the head with a copy of *Lives of the Saints*. Sister Bridgette sent her to the Mother Superior for her trouble.

After school, I'd run home to check on the granddaddy. I'd get his tea and put more peat on the fire because he said there was no blood left in his body only water and his old bones suffered from the cold. After I made sure he was settled, I'd meet Mary and we'd walk out the strand and run along the beach with Eddie. We both loved the sea very much. We'd take our boots off and stand at the edge and let the cold water run over our toes and Eddie would run into the waves. You never knew what the sea was going to look like; some days it would be calm with little waves lapping the shore but other times it would race right up the old stone wall and splash over the top, making us run back, squealing, as the spray soaked our clothes.

One afternoon we walked up the hill to the workhouse. I hoped that maybe Nora would be looking out the window and then maybe she would see me and come outside. We stared through the gaps in the big gates but there was no one in the yard.

'Did you really live here, Cissy?' said Mary, pulling a face.

I nodded.

'Was it awful? It looks awful.'

'No, it was nice.'

'Well, it doesn't look very nice,' said Mary. 'It looks like a prison.'

I was feeling sad and angry because I'd felt sure that if I came up here I'd see Nora.

'What do you know?' I yelled at her. 'You didn't live here, did you? I was happy here and I wish I was back, so there.' I flounced down the hill ahead of her.

'Wait, Cissy,' shouted Mary, running after me.

I slowed down and waited for her to catch me up.

'I didn't mean to upset you, Cissy,' she said. 'I'm really sorry, don't be cross with me. I shouldn't have said it looks like a prison.'

I smiled at her. 'I'm not cross with you, it's just that I miss it sometimes and I thought I'd see my friend Nora.' I looked back at the tall building that was once my home. 'I suppose it does look a bit like a prison, Mary, but I didn't want to leave it –and I didn't want to leave Nora.'

'You're happy enough with your mammy and granddaddy, aren't you? They're not mean to you, are they?'

'No, they're not mean to me, they're kind to me, even the granddaddy. I didn't think he liked me at first but I think he likes me better now.'

'We'll come again. We'll come every day if you want to.'

We linked arms and walked back into town. Past all the little cottages whose doors opened straight onto the lane. 'Thanks, Mary,' I said.

It was nearly Christmas and we were sitting at our desks all snug and warm, listening to Sister Bridgette telling us the story of the Nativity. It was cold and windy outside. A branch from a big old tree was banging on the window as if it was asking to be let in. Sister had just got to the bit about the Wise Men travelling from the East when Maureen Hurley put up her hand.

'Yes, Maureen?' said Sister Bridgette.

'How did the Wise Men know which way to go?'

'They followed the star. Sure, you know that, Maureen.'

'But how did they know which star to follow?'

'Because it was the biggest and the brightest.'

'But wouldn't that same star be over the top of loads of stables? How did they know which was the right one?'

Sister Bridgette was going red in the face and pulling at her wimple.

'Maureen Hurley, why are you interrupting our lovely story with questions you already know the answers to?'

'My father told me to always question things, Sister.'

'Well, you can tell your father that good Catholics don't question the Holy Bible.'

'I'll tell him that, Sister.'

'You do that, Maureen. Now where was I?'

'You were telling us about the three kings who travelled to Bethlehem on their camels,' I said.

'Thank you, Cissy,' she said, smiling at me. I loved it when Sister Bridgette smiled at me, it made me feel all warm inside.

Maureen Hurley had her hand up again.

'What is it this time?' said Sister. 'And it better be a sensible question.'

'What's a virgin, Sister?'

I thought Sister Bridgette was about to explode. 'Go and stand in the corridor this instant, you little barbarian,' she snapped.

Sister Bridgette looked around the classroom. Her face looked like Mammy's when she was cross. 'Does anyone else want to join Maureen in the corridor?' she said.

'No, Sister,' we all chorused.

'Right then, let us continue with our story.'

Just then I had a dig in the ribs from Breda Coyne, who sat on the other side of me.

'What?' I mouthed.

'I know what a virgin is,' she whispered. 'It's someone who has a liking for the hard stuff.'

I put my hand up.

Sister Bridgette sighed. 'What is it, Cissy?'

'Did the Virgin Mary have a liking for the hard stuff, Sister?' I asked.

Sister Bridgette slammed the book down on the desk. 'Blasphemy,' she shouted. 'Go and join Maureen in the corridor and say ten Hail Marys while you're out there. I'm surprised at you, Cissy Ryan.'

I got up from my seat and went out into the corridor, hot tears scalding the backs of my eyes. Sister Bridgette had never been angry with me before. I hated Breda Coyne. I hoped she'd die a martyr's death on a big wheel and I hoped she'd die roaring.

'What did you do?' asked Maureen.

I wiped my eyes on the sleeve of my cardigan and sniffed. 'I asked Sister if the Virgin Mary had a liking for the hard stuff.'

'Jesus, Cissy!'

'I have to say ten Hail Marys.'

'You're lucky you weren't excommunicated. Who in the name of God put that thought into your head?'

'Breda Coyne.'

Maureen raised her eyes up to the ceiling. 'And you were daft enough to believe her?'

I nodded.

'My advice to you, Cissy, is don't believe everything you're told and only half of what you see.'

'I'll remember that, Maureen, and thank you for the advice.'

'You're very welcome, Cissy Ryan.'

I had to stay in the corridor all afternoon and so I missed the end of the lovely story and I didn't get a sweetie.

I was very quiet on the way home. I was angry at Breda and cross with myself for being daft enough to believe her.

'Breda Coyne's an eejit,' said Mary, linking her arm through mine.

'But Sister Bridgette is cross with me.'

'Ah sure, she'll get over it.'

I wasn't convinced and continued to dwell on it.

'I'll tell you what,' said Mary. 'Do you want to go to Mr Collins's farm and see the new puppies?'

'Puppies?'

She nodded. 'There's piles of 'em. Mr Collins's dog borned them a few weeks ago. We can go and see them if you like.'

'That would be grand, Mary, but I'd be awful sad to leave them there.'

'Maybe we shouldn't go then,' said Mary. 'I wouldn't like to see you sad, Cissy.'

'Sometimes you just have to be sad,' I said. 'I was sad when I left the workhouse but it turned out fine because then I got to have a mammy and a granddaddy and I got to meet Colm and Blue.' I smiled at her: 'And you,' I added.

'We'll go, then,' said Mary. 'And trust in Jesus to make it a happy occasion.'

Collins's farm was out by the old bridge that crossed over the River Blackwater.

'Will he not mind us visiting?' I said, as we trudged along in the rain.

'Ah sure, no,' said Mary. 'He's an old slob and he likes visitors. I think he's lonely since Mrs Collins was taken up to heaven in the arms of the angels. My mammy said that she was only a child herself when she died and Mr Collins lost his faith for a while but he got it back, thanks be to God.'

'Then I'm glad he has a pile of puppies to keep him company, even if they have no conversation,' I said. 'The Granddaddy doesn't have much conversation but he's great company.'

We were both soaked to the skin by the time we got to the farm and my boots were all muddy. I hoped the mammy wouldn't be cross when she saw the state of them.

We walked into the yard just as a man walked out of the barn.

'Hello, Mary,' he said.

'Hello, Mr Collins,' said Mary.

'And who's your little friend?' he said, smiling at me.

'This is Cissy Ryan, Mr Collins.'

He stared at me. 'Is your mother Moira Ryan, child?' he said.

'She is, Sir.'

'The prettiest girl in town she was,' said Mr Collins. 'It was a terrible thing that devil of a father did to her, he'll have a lot of explaining to do when he reaches the Pearly Gates.'

'If he gets that far,' I said. 'But he's not the Devil, Mr Collins. I made the same mistake meself. You see, he hasn'' got a tail, because I looked.'

'The Devil comes in all shapes and forms, Cissy.'

'Does he?'

'He does.'

'We've come to see the pile of puppies, Mr Collins,' said Mary.

'They're in the barn. Go in, go in! They'll be mighty glad to see you both.'

We walked into the barn. It was pitch-black in there and me and Mary hung onto each other until our eyes grew used to it and then we saw the little animals shuffling around in the hay.

There was a big black dog in there with a load of little puppies climbing all over her. She raised her head as we looked down at her. I'd never seen anything so beautiful in my whole life. Mr Collins walked into the barn and stood behind us.

'And which one do you like, Cissy?' he said.

My eyes landed on the smallest one. He was the only brown one and he had a white patch over one eye.

'I like that feller, Mr Collins,' I said, pointing to the little dog.

'Sure, he's the runt of the litter, Cissy. You wouldn't be wanting him, he might not even survive. His mammy will probably ignore him and he'll just die.'

My eyes filled with tears as I looked at the poor little dog. 'Please don't let him die, Mr Collins,' I said. 'Oh, please don't let him die. He's done no harm to anyone and he's one of God's creatures after all.'

'Well, Cissy, as your mother is Moira Ryan, I'll take the little dog into the house and I'll rear him meself. Will that make you happy?'

'Oh, it will, Mr Collins, and thank you. I'll remember you in me prayers.'

Mr Collins lifted the little dog out of the hay and smiled at me. 'Do you have a name for him?'

'Buddy,' I said.

'Buddy it is then, Cissy, and you must come and visit him again.'

'Oh, I will, Mr Collins,' I said. 'And I'll be glad to do it.'

'Remember me to your mother,' he said.

'I will, Mr Collins.'

When I got home I told the granddaddy all about the poor little dog and then I burst out crying because he would never be mine.

CHAPTER SEVEN

It was almost Christmas when Father Kelly paid us a visit. I liked Father Kelly; he was gentle and kind and he had fine white hair and pale blue eyes and he was a cheerful man.

'If you're wanting me to go to Mass, you're wasting your time, Father,' said the mammy, ushering him into the room.

'Sure, now why would I be wanting that, Moira? Haven't I just found myself passing the end of Paradise Alley and thinking I'd call in for a cup of tea to help me on my way?'

'You're very welcome to a cup of tea, Father, as long as the tea doesn't entail having to listen to a sermon about what a terrible Catholic I am.'

'You have a very suspicious mind, Moira Ryan.'

'You're right, I have,' said the mammy.

'And how are you, Malachi?' said the priest, looking across at the granddaddy.

I didn't know that the granddaddy's name was Malachi, I thought it was a grand name altogether.

'Oh, you know, Father,' said the granddaddy. 'I try to be patient with what God has given me to bear.'

'And what has He given you?'

'The curse of old age, Father. I'm not the man I was.'

'But sure, you have plenty to thank the Lord for. Hasn't He sent your daughter and your granddaughter back home to look after you?'

'He has, Father.'

'Do you take sugar, Father?' said the mammy.

'I do for my sins, Moira. I have a desperate sweet tooth.'

'Like meself,' said the granddaddy, licking his old lips.

'As I'm here, Moira, I was wondering why little Cissy doesn't come to Mass. Me and the Lord would love to see her there.'

I really wanted to go to Mass because the folk from the workhouse went and so did Nora and I might get to see her there.

'If the child has a mind to go, I'll not be stopping her,' said the mammy.

'Oh, thank you, Mammy,' I said. 'I do have a mind to go.'

'That's settled then,' said the priest, 'and perhaps you might accompany her to the Christmas Mass?'

'God wasn't there when I needed him, Father Kelly, and now I need no one.'

'Sure, don't we all need someone, Moira? Even Jesus Himself needed friends.'

'And where were they when he was hanging on the cross? I'll tell you where they were, Father, they were running for their lives.'

'We are only human, Moira, and we all have frailties.'

'I know what I know, Father – and I know I won't be darkening the doors of the church in this lifetime.'

'I won't give up on you, Moira,' he said gently.

'Cissy can go, Father, but she'll be going on her own.'

'And what about you, Malachi?' said the priest.

'I would,' said the granddaddy, 'but I'm a martyr to me legs.'

'So we won't be seeing you down at Murphey's pub, then?'

'I have good days and bad days, Father.'

'And isn't it a mystery that the good days never seem to fall on a Sunday?'

The granddaddy shook his old head as if it was a mystery to him as well. 'It's a terrible curse, Father.'

On Christmas Eve, me and Colm walked out to the woods and gathered armfuls of holly to decorate the cottage. I loved being with Colm. I never grew tired of looking at him. I wondered if maybe one day me and Colm would get married and live in the nice house at the top of Paradise Alley with his daddy and old Blue.

'How old do you have to be to get married, Colm?' I said as we walked back home.

'Why do you want to know that?'

I shrugged my shoulders. 'I was just interested,' I replied.

'Well, you'll have to grow up first, Cissy. How old are you now?'

'I think I'm nearly eight; I'll ask the mammy.'

'Well, you have a long way to go then before you can think about getting married.'

'How long?'

'I'd say a good few years.'

'And what about you?'

'I'm only thirteen, Cissy, and I have no mind to be getting married just yet.'

We'd reached the cottage. 'Will you wait for me, Colm?' I said.

'What do you mean?'

'Will you wait ten years until I've grown up?'

He smiled and ruffled my hair. 'You come out with the strangest things, Cissy.'

'But will you?'

'If it makes you happy, Cissy, I will.'

'Good,' I said, grinning.

On Christmas morning, I walked up the back streets to St Peter's church. On the way, I called for Mary. There was a baby sitting on the front step and two of her sisters were playing ball up against the wall. The door was open so I walked in.

'Happy Christmas, Cissy,' said Mary's mammy.

'Happy Christmas, Mrs Butler,' I said. 'And may the Lord look kindly on you this blessed day,' I added for good measure.

'You have lovely manners, Cissy,' said Mrs Butler. 'It wouldn't do you any harm to take a leaf out of Cissy's book, Mary.'

Me and Mary leaned against the wall of the church, waiting for the workhouse folk to come down the hill.

'They might already be in there,' said Mary.

'No, we were always late on account of the poor demented souls playing up.'

'Weren't you afraid of them, Cissy?'

'Not at all, sure they're harmless enough as long as you keep your distance.'

'Do you think they're happy?'

'Mrs Foley says that they are.'

'Well, as long as they're happy.'

We sat on the wall and watched all the people going into the church.

'Here they come now,' said Mary.

A long line of people were walking down the hill, two by two towards the church. At first, I thought Nora wasn't among them and then I saw her limping along at the back, holding onto Mrs Foley's hand. I ran up the hill and put my arms around her.

'Oh, Martha,' she said, her eyes filling with tears. 'I thought you had forgotten me.'

'I'll never forget you, Nora, because you're my best friend in the whole world and I love you.'

'I love you too, Martha,' she said through her tears.

'My name is Cissy now, Nora.'

'Cissy,' she said trying it out. 'Oh, that's a lovely name.'

'Can Nora sit with me and Mary, Mrs Foley?'

'She can of course, Cissy.'

Me and Mary each held one of Nora's hands as we walked across to the side altar. The Baby Jesus was lying in the manger with Mary and Joseph gazing down at Him. The angels and shepherds were grouped around them and the Three Wise Men were kneeling in front of them.

I looked at Nora, kneeling beside me. The light from the candles lit up her sweet face. I was filled with joy, because it was Christmas morning and I was with my friend again.

'Happy Christmas, Nora,' I whispered.

'Happy Christmas, Cissy.'

Father Kelly told us the story of Jesus's birth. He told us how Mary and Joseph had been turned away from all the inns and how they had to sleep in a stable, where the Baby Jesus was born. He told us of the star that had guided the Three Wise Men through that Christmas night to the manger where the Baby Jesus lay. Then we sang carols and I thought this was the happiest day of my life, with Nora on one side of me and Mary on the other; my two good friends. I joined my hands together and thanked Jesus for all His blessings and then I said a prayer for the mammy, the granddaddy, Colm and Blue. And then I added a special prayer for Mr Collins, who was looking after the little dog because I was the child of Moira Ryan.

CHAPTER EIGHT

When we came out of the church I was surprised to see the mammy waiting for me.

'That's my mammy,' I said to Nora.

'She's very beautiful, Cissy.'

'Is she?'

'Oh yes, she's like a film star.'

I felt so proud that Nora thought my mammy was beautiful.

'Thank you, Nora,' I said.

'You're very welcome, Cissy.'

I watched the folk from the workhouse lining up and the nurses trying to encourage the poor demented souls to hold hands with the person next to them. Nora was still standing next to me. 'Shouldn't you be lining up, Nora?' I said.

Nora smiled at me. 'Not today,' she said.

Just then the mammy and Mrs Foley came walking towards us.

'Now be a good girl, Nora, and I'll see you tomorrow.'

'Oh, I will, Mrs Foley,' said Nora.

'Thank you for having her, Moira. It's very good of you.'

'You're welcome, Kate,' said the mammy.

'Is Nora coming home with us, Mammy?'

'I thought you would like to be together on Christmas Day.'

My eyes filled with tears. I threw my arms around her. 'Oh, thank you, Mammy! Thank you, thank you!'

'One thank you is enough, Cissy. Now let's get away home.'

I said goodbye to Mary and then Nora and I held hands as we walked through the town beside Mammy. I wanted to skip and jump and shout with happiness but I knew that would make the mammy cross and I didn't want anyone to be cross on this special day.

People were calling out 'Happy Christmas, Moira! Happy Christmas, Cissy!' as we walked through the town and Mammy was returning the greeting. I remembered back to the day we'd left the workhouse. People were saying hello to Mammy that day but she hadn't said hello back. Maybe the mammy was happier these days.

When we got back to the cottage, I ran inside to tell the granddaddy that Nora was going to spend the day with us but he wasn't in his chair. The fire burnt brightly but there was no Granddaddy sitting beside it.

'Where's the granddaddy?' I asked.

'Sure, how would I know?' Mammy said. 'Haven't I been up at the church with you?'

'He might still be in his bed,' I said, running up the stairs – but he wasn't. I ran down again. 'He's not there, Mammy. Shall I ask Colm if he's seen him?'

'You do that, child,' she said.

'Come on, Nora, you can see Blue.'

Nora couldn't run so good on account of her poorly leg so we walked slowly up to the end of Paradise Alley. Colm's daddy was around the back, brushing out the yard.

'Happy Christmas, Cissy,' he said, when he saw me.

'Happy Christmas, Mr Doyle.'

'And what brings you here?'

'We've lost the granddaddy.'

'Is that so?'

'It is,' I said. 'He's not sitting beside the fire and he's not in his bed.'

'Perhaps you should call the guards out, Cissy,' he said.

'Do you think I should?'

'I'm only kiddin' ya, child,' he said, grinning. 'Colm has taken your granddaddy out for a bit of a spin, so you've no need to be worrying yourself.'

'Well, that's a weight off my shoulders, Mr Doyle. I was beginning to think that he was lost forever.'

'You have a vivid imagination, girl,' he said, laughing.

'That's what Mrs Foley used to say.'

'And imagination is a great thing altogether. Do you like to read, Cissy?'

'I do, Mr Doyle.'

'Then come and see me sometime and you can borrow one of my books. I'm a desperate great reader.'

'Oh, thank you, Mr Doyle, I'll definitely do that.'

'You're very welcome, child.'

'Can I take Nora to see Blue?'

'Well, you could, but isn't he out pulling the trap with your granddaddy in? Sure he wouldn't get much of a spin without old Blue pulling him along now, would he?'

'He wouldn't, Mr Doyle.'

'Now why don't you come back up after you've had your dinner and then your little friend can see Blue and you can choose a book?'

'Thank you, Mr Doyle,' I said. 'Come on, Nora.'

'Okay,' she said, following me.

When we got round to the front of the house I could see Blue and the trap standing outside our cottage.

I opened the door and we went inside. The mammy and Colm were standing beside the fire smiling at me and the granddaddy was sitting in his chair. He had something on his lap, something brown and furry; something that looked like Buddy. My eyes filled with tears. The granddaddy gave me a crooked little smile. I went across and knelt beside him. I put my head on his old knee. 'Oh, thank you,' I said. 'Thank you for getting Buddy for me.'

'Happy Christmas, Cissy,' he said.

I took Buddy in my arms and stroked his soft fur. He licked the tears that were running down my cheeks.

'I love you, Granddaddy,' I said softly. 'I love you with all my heart and I don't mind that you smell like a dead ferret. I still love you.'

The granddaddy stroked my hair. 'And I love you, Cissy. I love you too.'

'I want you to remember what has just happened this day, Colm,' said the mammy, 'because a miracle has just occurred.'

Everyone started to laugh but I didn't laugh because then it wouldn't be special, it would be ordinary. And I didn't want it to be ordinary. There was no star above our little cottage and there were no Wise Men outside our door but to me it was as special as that other Christmas so long ago, when the Baby Jesus was born. I wanted to take this day and put it in a box, so that if I ever felt lonely or scared, I could look inside and see it again and feel the way I felt today and I could remember. I looked around the room at all the people I loved and I thought that I was the luckiest girl in the whole world.

CHAPTER NINE

I loved to read at school but there were no books in the cottage; the mammy couldn't afford things like that. One day, I walked up the alley to Colm's house.

'And what can we do for you, Cissy?' said Mr Doyle, opening the door.

'I've come for a book,' I said shyly.

'Come in, come in,' he said.

I followed him.

'I love to read, Mr Doyle.'

'I can't think of a finer way to spend a few hours than to bury yourself in a good book,' he said. 'Who taught you?'

'Mrs Foley up at the workhouse. She taught me and Nora.'

'Ah, the little friend you brought up here?'

I nodded. I followed him into a room next to the kitchen. Against one wall was a dresser full of books.

'Have a good look, Cissy, and choose one you like the look of. The children's books are on the bottom shelf.'

'Were they Colm's books?'

'No, Colm has never been much of a reader, he was more of an outside feller. He couldn't abide being cooped up indoors. They belonged to a little girl called Ellen and just like you, she loved to read. This was her favourite,' he said, picking out a book and handing it to me.

'*The Water Babies*,' I read.

'She loved that book,' said Mr Doyle.

I opened the book and inside the front cover it said, '*To Ellen on your eighth birthday with love from Mammy and Daddy*'.

'Who's Ellen, Mr Doyle?'

'She was my little girl and Colm's sister,' he said.

'Colm's got a sister? Where is she?'

'She passed away when she was nine,' he said sadly. 'She was a lovely little thing, bright as a button and full of life.'

I didn't know what to say, because Mr Doyle was staring away into the distance as if he was remembering his little girl.

'I'm sorry, Mr Doyle,' I said softly.

He looked at me with some surprise as if he'd only just realised that I was standing there, then he shook his head as if trying to clear it. 'It was a long time ago, Cissy,' he said, 'but I kept these books and now I'm glad that I did, for it will give me pleasure to know that they will be enjoyed again.'

'I'll take really good care of it.'

'I know you will and when you've finished it, you can bring it back and choose another one.'

I walked back down the alley holding the book very carefully. It felt solid in my hands. My tummy twisted with excitement at the thought of what lay within its pages and I thought of the other little girl who had held it before me.

Every day after school I ran home to get the granddaddy his tea, then I'd take Buddy for a walk over the fields. Buddy was a year old now and it was hard to remember a time when he hadn't lived in the little cottage with us. He had made Paradise Alley his home and he was as happy living there as I was.

Sometimes Granddaddy came with us. The more we walked, the stronger his legs became.

Our favourite place was a rough old field filled with cowpats and weeds. It wasn't the prettiest place in the world, in fact, people called it the slob, because a sewer trickled through the middle of it. But it was close to Paradise Alley and it wasn't far for the granddaddy to walk. It ran alongside the Blackwater River and on the opposite bank, the cottages tumbled down to the river's edge.

'Your old legs are doing great altogether, Granddaddy,' I said as we walked along. 'I think they're getting used to passing the pub.'

The granddaddy nodded his old head. 'I've no mind for the drink these days, child.'

'Aren't you thirsty any more?'

'I have a desperate thirst, Cissy, but not for the drink.'

I couldn't understand that because if you had a desperate thirst, you'd be needing a drink.

'These days,' he said, 'I have a thirst for God's good clean air and the green grass beneath my feet and the changing of the seasons and the flowing of the river. I've sat in that chair for so long that I'd forgotten there was a world outside those four walls.'

'That was a grand bit of talking you just did, Granddaddy.'

'I've more to say these days.'

'I think you're a bit like Buddy. Mr Collins said he wouldn't come to much because he was the munt of the litter.'

'*Runt*, Cissy, he was the *runt*.'

'Oh, sorry. Yes, because he was the runt of the litter, but Mr Collins saved him and now he's the best dog in the whole world. Not that I'm saying you're the runt of the litter, Granddaddy,' I said quickly.

'Buddy was saved because of *you*, Cissy, because you cared about him and I think you saved me too, with your constant chattering. Even when I didn't answer, you never gave up on me, just like you never gave up on Buddy.'

The little dog was running ahead of us, poking his head into holes and sniffing at things only he found mysterious. Every now and then he'd run back with bits of twig in his mouth or a dried wing from a dead bird. He'd lay them at our feet and wag his tail as if to say, 'Look what I've brought you, aren't I the clever one?' then he'd be off again, looking for the next offering. Buddy was getting stronger every day; he wasn't a poor little thing any more. I loved him so much and I could tell by his warm wet kisses that he loved me too.

'Now I think we should head home,' said the granddaddy, rubbing at his old legs. 'I need to get a lot stronger before I can keep up with you and that dog.'

We walked back home with the granddaddy's hand in mine. His hand felt rough and bony and cold, but I liked the feel of it there: it made me feel safe. 'Shall I tell you a secret, Granddaddy?' I said.

'Go ahead.'

'You won't tell a living soul, will you?'

'I won't even tell a dead one.'

'I'm going to marry Colm Doyle when I grow up.'

'Are you now?'

'I am, and I'm going to live in Colm's house at the top of Paradise Alley and then I can still get you your tea.'

'And does Colm know about this?'

'He does, he says he'll wait for me to grow.'

'Don't grow up too fast, Cissy.'

'I'll try not to, Granddaddy.'

I liked school a lot. I liked learning about new things, reading the Bible and playing with Mary, but I missed Buddy and the grand-daddy. I wanted to be out of the classroom and walking by the river with them and then I remembered Colm telling me that he hadn't liked school one bit and would rather be galloping over the fields on Blue's back. He didn't learn his lessons and I think that now he wishes he had because if he'd listened to his teachers, he would have known the difference between a river and a sea. So I listened to the nuns and I worked hard, just like Colm told me to. I wanted to make Mammy and the granddaddy proud of me; I wanted to get a good job so that I could take care of them both.

I still went on the milk round with Colm but only on a Saturday when I didn't have school. I enjoyed getting to know all the people in the town and collecting the jugs for Colm to fill with the good creamy milk. I never went to the Honourables' door again though, because I didn't want to run into Miss Baggy Knickers who had made fun of me and threatened to thrash me.

'You don't want to be frightened of her, Cissy,' said Colm. 'She's nothing but a stuck-up little madam who's not fit to wipe your boots.'

'But she's an Honourable,' I said. 'She's a class above me.'

Colm pulled on Blue's reins and stopped the trap. 'You're as good as she is, Cissy, better even and don't let anyone tell you any different, okay?'

I thought Colm was wrong but I nodded my head and said, 'I won't.'

Colm kept his word and a week later, he informed me that he had changed the day that he delivered the milk to the workhouse, so that I could go with him. I wanted the week to fly past, I was so excited. I didn't tell the mammy about it because I knew in my heart that she wouldn't let me go and I didn't want her dead body to be on my conscience.

At playtime on Friday, I informed Mary that the next day I was going to the workhouse to deliver the milk.

'Are you sure you want to go back, Cissy?' she said. 'They might keep you in there.'

'Sure, why would they do that? They're packed to the rafters already, they wouldn't want another body in the place.'

'Well, keep an eye on the door, Cissy, just in case you have to make a quick getaway.'

'I will, Mary.'

'Because I'd miss you if you went back there.'

'Thank you, Mary, but you've no need to worry and it's not as bad in there as you think it is. Maybe one day Colm will let you come as well and you can see for yourself.'

'I'd be terrible afeared to go in there, Cissy,' she said, shivering. 'I've heard desperate tales about the place.'

'Maureen Hurley said don't believe everything you hear and only half of what you see.'

'When were you talking to Maureen?' said Mary.

'That day I was sent to stand beside her in the corridor after the terrible instance of the Virgin having a liking for the hard stuff.'

'God, Cissy! When I told my mother she said it was the funniest thing she had ever heard, especially coming from you with your fine ladylike manners.'

'It wasn't funny at the time and I'll thank you to not be making fun of me behind my back. The memory of that day will haunt me for the rest of my life.'

'You're terrible dramatic, Cissy Ryan, but I am sorry that we had a bit of craic at your expense. You have to admit though, it was funny.'

'It might have been funny to you, Mary, but I still have nightmares about it.' I smiled at my friend. 'I accept your apology, Mary Butler,' I said. 'You and your mammy.'

'Thank you, Cissy.'

'You're very welcome, Mary.'

'Cissy?'

'Yes?'

'You know the boy who serves on the altar on a Sunday morning?'

'Lots of boys serve on the altar.'

'The one with red hair?'

I nodded.

'Do you think he's nice?'

'Why? Do you?'

Mary scratched behind her ear. 'I do,' she said shyly.

'Do you want to marry him?'

'Jesus, Cissy! I only said he's nice.'

'I'm going to marry Colm Doyle when I grow up.'

'Sure Colm's ancient.'

I wanted to convince Mary that I was serious about this. 'He promised to wait for me,' I stated.

Mary made a face, wrinkling her nose up and looking as if she knew something that I didn't.

'Don't you think he'll wait for me, then?'

'I'd say he said it just to keep you happy.'

Was Mary right? Wasn't Colm going to wait for me after all? Maybe I'd got it all wrong, maybe he was playing with my feelings?

'Ah sure, I could be wrong. Don't look so sad.'

'But I *am* sad, Mary. This is my future husband we're talking about.'

'Maybe you should ask him again.'

'I'd be too ashamed to do that,' I said.

'Well, best leave it in God's gentle hands and pray a lot.'

That made me feel happier. 'I'll do that, Mary, for I know that God has my best interests at heart.'

'Best do the Stations of the Cross to be on the safe side,' said Mary.

Just then the bell rang and we linked arms and went back into school.

CHAPTER TEN

When I woke up the next morning I was so excited, I couldn't eat the good breakfast that the mammy had made for me.

'What in God's name is wrong with you this morning, Cissy Ryan?' said Mammy. 'You're jumping around like a flea on a dog.'

'I'm excited to be going on the milk round with Colm,' I said.

'Is the milk round that exciting, then?'

I tried to force down a bit of bread so that the mammy wouldn't get suspicious.

'I just like going out with Colm.'

I heard the trap pull up outside. 'There he is now, Mammy. I'd best be going.'

'Well, I hope your day is as exciting as you're hoping for.'

'It will be, Mammy,' I said, running outside.

I'd been looking forward to this morning all week but now the time had come, I felt a bit sick.

'You're very quiet,' said Colm as Blue started trotting down Paradise Alley.

'Mary said they might keep me in the workhouse if I go back.'

'Mary's an eejit, then.'

'She's not an eejit, Colm, she's just afeared for me.'

'Well, she has no need to be. Why would they be wanting a scrawny little thing like you back?'

Colm was grinning at me so I knew he didn't mean what he had said but his words hurt me. Was that what he saw when he looked at me? A scrawny little thing?

Colm pulled on Blue's reins and we stopped moving. He turned to me and held my face in his hands. 'I've hurt your feelings, haven't I?' he said.

I looked down at the floor and he put his arm around my shoulder. 'I was only codding you. Hasn't anyone told you yet, Cissy, that you are beautiful?'

I looked up at him and frowned. Was he making fun of me again?

'Because you are,' he said gently.

'Am I?' I said.

'You're the most beautiful girl in Balleybun, so now you know and you will always remember that it was Colm Doyle who was the first to tell you, because you can be sure that I won't be the last. Now let's go and pay a visit to your friend Nora,' he said, ruffling my hair.

I was smiling all the way up the hill. Colm didn't think I was scrawny at all. Colm Doyle thought I was beautiful, which meant that Mary was wrong and he would wait for me. I felt like my heart was singing.

When we got to the workhouse, Colm jumped down from the trap and rang the big old bell beside the gate. Then he got back up beside me and we waited for someone to come.

What if Mary was right? What if they did keep me in? I'd never see the mammy again or the granddaddy or Buddy or Colm or… As I thought about all the people in my life that I loved, I realised that, even though Nora was still in there, I didn't ever want to go back, especially not over the mammy's dead body.

As Mr Dunne walked towards us, I whispered, 'Don't let them keep me in, will you, Colm?'

'Never,' he said. 'I'd fight to the death for you.'

'Really?'

'Really.'

Then I felt more cheerful and I couldn't wait to see Nora.

'Well, hello there, Cissy,' said Mr Dunne, opening the big iron gates. He looked just how I remembered him from when I'd lived in the workhouse. 'Are you coming back to us, or just paying a visit?'

'Paying a visit,' I said very quickly.

THE LITTLE ORPHAN GIRL

'Well, I'm happy to see you, child, and you are very welcome. I'll get the churns, Colm,' he said, starting to walk away.

'I'd like to see Nora, Mr Dunne,' I called after him.

'I'll see if I can find Mrs Foley,' he shouted over his shoulder.

I stared up at the workhouse. I could see why Mary thought it looked like a prison. It was tall and grey, with rows and rows of windows that looked like beady eyes staring down at me. I had to remind myself that I'd been happy there but I began to think that maybe the mammy hadn't and that was why she didn't like me to talk about the place.

Eventually, Mr Dunne came back, carrying two big churns. Walking behind him were Nora and Mrs Foley. I went over and put my arms around my friend.

'Wait a minute,' I said.

I ran back to Colm, who was standing beside Blue. 'Could we take Nora for a spin, Colm, so that she can see the sea?'

'We can, of course,' he said, smiling.

I went back to Nora. 'Can me and Colm take Nora out on the strand for a bit of a spin?' I said to Mrs Foley.

She smiled down at Nora. 'Would you like that, Nora?' she asked.

Nora's little face lit up with joy. 'Oh, I would,' she said.

'Be sure to have her back for her dinner, Cissy.'

'I will,' I promised, taking Nora's hand.

As we walked over to Colm, I said, 'Where's Mr Dunne's dog?'

'Oh, Cissy,' Nora said gently. 'He was taken up to heaven only last week. Mr Dunne was desperate sad about it.'

I felt sad as well, because I'd grown to love that smelly old dog. I held Nora's hand and we went over to Mr Dunne. 'I'm sorry for your loss, Mr Dunne,' I said.

'Ah sure it was a sad day, Cissy. He might have smelt like a tinker's arse, but he was a good pal.'

'I'll light a candle for him on Sunday if the mammy will give me a penny.'

'Thank you, Cissy, you're a good girl.'

Me and Nora held hands as Blue trotted through the town and out towards the strand.

'Oh, Cissy,' she said, when the sea came into view. 'Is that really the sea?'

'It is, Nora, and don't you think it's beautiful?'

Nora didn't answer me at once; she just stared and then she said, 'It makes you believe there's a God, doesn't it?'

'Have you ever doubted it, Nora?'

She looked down at her poorly leg and sighed. 'Sometimes,' she said.

'Oh, Nora, you must always believe in God and the saints and the angels, otherwise they'll never let you in and when we die, we'll never see each other again.'

She stared out at the sea. 'No one but God could make that,' she said, smiling.

'Do you want to go down to the shore?'

'Oh, yes.'

'Colm?'

'You go ahead. I have no notion to get my feet wet.'

I took Nora's hand and helped her down from the trap and then we walked to the water's edge. We took off our boots and placed them side by side on the wet sand. Nora squealed as the cold water ran between her toes. 'Oh, Cissy,' she said, 'this is the happiest day of my life.'

I looked at my best friend and for no reason at all I felt like crying.

When I got home the granddaddy was nodding off by the fire. Buddy was curled up on his lap. He wagged his tail when he saw me but he stayed with the granddaddy.

I coughed and the granddaddy opened one eye.

'Do dogs go to heaven, Granddaddy?' I said.

He shuffled himself up in the chair and Buddy jumped off his lap.

'What's that you say?'

'Dogs, Granddaddy, I was wondering if they go to heaven when they die.'

'Well now,' he said, lighting up his pipe and puffing smoke into the room so that I couldn't see his face any more. 'Do you have a particular dog in mind?'

'Mr Dunne's dog, up at the place that Mammy doesn't want me to mention.'

'Then I'd say it all depends on the dog,' he said.

'How do you mean?'

'Well, it depends whether he was a good dog or a bad one.'

'I think he was a good dog, Granddaddy. He smelt like a tinker's arse but sure that wasn't his fault, was it? I mean, you smell like a dead ferret but you're nice and kind and I'm sure you'll go to heaven.'

'Thank you, Cissy,' he said. 'I shall rest easy in my bed tonight, knowing St Peter won't be slamming the door in my face because of my lack of hygiene.'

I smiled at him. 'I'm glad I've put your mind at rest, Granddaddy.'

CHAPTER ELEVEN

Colm Doyle started walking out with Alana Walsh. Alana was very pretty; she had long dark hair that she wore in a plait that reached down to her waist. The other thing that worried me was that she was a lot closer to Colm's age than I was.

Mary and I were sitting on the slob bank overlooking the river.

'They were strolling along past the lighthouse, Cissy,' she said. 'Holding hands, they were.'

'Are you sure it was my Colm?'

'It was your Colm alright, walking along as brazen as you like as if he hadn't promised himself to you.'

'Maybe he only said it to keep me happy, Mary, just like you said.'

'A promise is a promise, Cissy, and not to be taken lightly.'

'She's very beautiful, isn't she?'

'If you like that sort of thing.'

'What's not to like?'

'She's very blowsy, don't you think?'

'Blowsy?'

'Yes, she was posing mad, walking along beside Colm as if she owned the feller.'

'Maybe Colm likes blowsy. Maybe I'm not blowsy enough?'

'Yer fine as you are, Cissy. You wouldn't want to be getting all blowsy just to please Colm Doyle and anyway, he doesn't strike me as the sort of boy who would be impressed by blowsy.'

'I hope not.'

'Anyway, fellers don't go around marrying blowsy types, their mammies wouldn't approve. Maybe you should ask Colm if the contract between the two of you has been severed.'

'I couldn't ask him that, Mary.'

'Then you'll just have to wait until he tires of her. I'm sure that won't be long. Now don't be looking so sad, Cissy. It's not the end of the world and didn't Colm say that you were the prettiest girl in Balleybun?'

'He did.'

'Well, there you are then. I'd say he's just passing the time with Alana Walsh while he's waiting for you to grow up. My daddy says that men have their needs and I think that has something to do with blowsy types like Alana Walsh.'

I hoped that Mary was right but it didn't stop me from feeling terrible sad. I had a word with the granddaddy, who was very wise and knew the difference between a river and the sea.

'Do you think Colm will come back to me, Granddaddy?' I said.

The granddaddy scratched his old head. 'I'm no expert in the ways of the heart, Cissy. I had a fine woman and I treated her badly, may God forgive me. If I had her with me now it'd be a different story altogether. I'd treat her like gold dust, so I would. If me old legs would get me as far as the church, I'd get down on me knees and ask God's forgiveness.'

Just then Mammy came in from the lane.

'Be prepared to be on your knees a long time then, old man,' she said, winking at me.

No matter what Mary said about Alana Walsh being blowsy and that Colm was only going out with her while he was waiting for me I still felt desperate sad, like there was a dead weight lying on my heart. I took to sitting by the window, hoping for a glimpse of him as he went by with Blue.

Mammy noticed that I was off my food.

'Are you sick, child?' she questioned.

I shook my head.

'Then why the glum face?'

I didn't know whether to tell the mammy or not. I feared she would laugh at me and I had no idea if she was an expert in the ways of the heart.

'Has someone upset you?' she went on.

My eyes filled with tears. 'Colm Doyle is walking out with Alana Walsh.'

'And what has Colm Doyle's courting habits got to do with you?'

'He said he'd wait for me,' I said softly.

'Speak up, Cissy,' she snapped. 'I can't hear a word you're saying.'

I could tell that the mammy was getting cross and I wished I had kept my mouth shut.

'Colm said he'd wait for me,' I said, louder.

I could see that the mammy was losing her patience. 'Wait for you to do what?' she said.

'Wait for me to grow up so that we could get married.'

'If you say one word to ridicule the child, Moira Ryan,' shouted the granddaddy from his chair beside the fire, 'I'll, I'll…'

'You'll what?' said the mammy. 'You've done your worst, old man, what more can you do?'

'I'm just saying don't make her look foolish. What is foolish to you is the God's truth to her. I won't have her hurt.'

'It's a pity you didn't have the same sympathy for me when I needed it,' spat the mammy.

'Don't be dragging all that up, Moira. That was then and this is now.'

I stared backwards and forwards at the two of them arguing. 'Please don't argue,' I said. 'It really doesn't matter about Colm, it really doesn't. I'll get over it, I will, and anyway, Mary says Alana Walsh is very blowsy and Colm will tire of her and come back to me.'

There was silence in the little room but for the peat crackling away in the grate. Then the mammy spoke.

'All I can say, Cissy, is don't rely on someone else for your happiness. Plant your own garden and don't be waiting for someone to bring you flowers.'

'That's good advice, Moira,' mumbled the granddaddy.

'Mammy?' I said quietly.

'Yes, Cissy?'

'We haven't got a garden.'

The granddaddy started to chuckle. 'We haven't got a garden,' he spluttered. 'Did you hear that, Moira? We haven't got a garden.' He wiped away the tears that were rolling down his old cheeks. 'I don't know who fathered that child of yours, Moira Ryan, but I'd say he had a fierce sense of humour.'

And then the mammy was laughing and I felt a big lump of happiness well up in my throat.

I realised that although Mammy wasn't a great one for talking, she was wise and what she said made sense to me and it made me feel a bit different about things. I liked the idea of planting my own garden even though we didn't have one.

I started avoiding Colm. I didn't want to be passing the time of day with him when he was going through his blowsy period. On Saturday morning, he knocked on the door.

'Tell him I'm not here, Mammy.'

'Tell him yourself, Cissy. You're old enough now to see to your own business.'

The mammy opened the door and let him in.

'Ready?' he said.

'I'm not going on the milk round today, Colm,' I said.

'Are you ill?' he asked.

'The only thing Cissy's suffering from this day is a heavy heart,' said the mammy.

'A heavy heart, eh?' said Colm, winking at Mammy.

'Don't be making fun of me, Colm Doyle. I've as much right to a heavy heart as the next person.'

'You have indeed, Cissy, but I get the feeling that this heavy heart of yours has something to do with me.'

'And what if it has?' I said sharply.

'Then I'd like the opportunity to defend myself. Shall we go for a little ride and you can tell me what I have done?'

'I wish you would,' said the mammy. 'I've no stomach for affairs of the heart at this time of the morning.'

I went outside with Colm and he helped me up onto the trap.

'Where would you like to go?'

'I don't care where I go.'

'We'll go out the wood road then,' he said. 'The trees are something to behold.'

We trotted along in silence. Colm was right about the trees – they were beautiful. The sun shone through the branches, making them look as if they were on fire.

'Autumn is my favourite season, Cissy,' said Colm. 'What's yours?'

Mine was autumn too but I had no mind to be agreeing with him. 'Summer,' I said.

We turned off the road and Blue followed a track into the woods. The colours of the leaves took my breath away – reds and golds and browns falling from the branches and lying on the ground like a multi-coloured blanket beneath Blue's feet. I wished I wasn't cross with Colm, because I wanted to tell him that everything was magical and that autumn was my favourite season as well and that this moment with him in this magical place would stay in my heart forever.

Colm helped me down from the trap and sat down on an old log. 'Will you sit beside me, Cissy?'

'I will not,' I said.

'How can I put this right if you won't tell me what's wrong?'

I turned my back on him and walked a bit away.

'Cissy?' he said.

I turned around and it all came out in a rush of words: 'You promised to wait for me and now you're walking out with Alana Walsh, who's blowsy, when you said you'd wait for me to grow up so that we could get married... and now my heart is broken because I believed you and you lied to me.'

Colm got up from the log. 'Oh, Cissy,' he said.

'You didn't mean it, did you? Mary said you only said it to please me.'

He tried to take my hand but I pulled away.

'Please, Cissy.'

'Please, Cissy what?'

'I'm sorry I've hurt you,' he said gently. 'We were very young, you were only about seven years old, Cissy, and I was only thirteen meself. Maybe Mary is right, maybe I was just trying to please you. I suppose I didn't take it seriously.'

'Well, I did, Colm.'

'I can see that now,' he said sadly, 'and I can see that I haven't been careful enough of your feelings. No one knows what the future is going to bring. You're still a child.'

I could feel the blood rush to my face. 'I am not!' I shouted. 'I'm almost fourteen.'

'And I'm almost twenty, Cissy. That's a good bit older than you. We're good friends, you and I. I hope we always will be, you are very important to me.'

Tears were running down my cheeks as I listened to him.

'Come here,' said Colm gently and he took me in his arms and I breathed in his smell and I felt safe.

'One day, Cissy Ryan, some young stud of a feller is going to knock you off your feet and you'll forget all about some eejit of a bloke called Colm Doyle and that's as it should be. Now we must deliver this milk before we have a revolution on our hands.'

I looked up at him. 'I won't ever forget you, Colm Doyle.'

'And I will never forget you, Cissy Ryan.'

'Colm?'

'Yes?'

'Autumn is my favourite season too.'

CHAPTER TWELVE

The granddaddy was getting older and frailer and these days his legs wouldn't even take him as far as the pub. I used to think that Buddy was *my* dog but I came to realise that his loyalty was to the granddaddy. That little dog never left his side; it was as if he knew that the granddaddy needed him more than I did. He slept curled up on his bed at night and he sat at his feet beside the fire in the day. He changed his lonely old life. The mammy had put a chair outside the door and, every day, the granddaddy sat there and let Buddy run around Paradise Alley. Neighbours that he hadn't spoken to in years came over to say hello and to pass the time of day with him. Now he had plenty of people to talk about as he told me and Mammy about the goings-on in the lane. He'd even taken to having a good old wash every day so as not to put off his friends by smelling like a dead ferret.

It turned out to be a good job that Buddy loved the granddaddy so much because it looked as if I might be going away. I knew that I would miss my little dog but I was glad that the granddaddy would have him for company when I was gone.

I didn't want to leave the little cottage where I had been so happy but I knew it was time to find work. I loved school and I loved seeing Mary every day but I needed to bring in some money to help Mammy buy the food for me and Granddaddy. I couldn't wait to hand her my first wage packet. And Mammy said she had been told of a great job that would suit me very well. 'Colm came to see me today,' she said. 'Bridie up at the Hall said they are looking for a girl and she thought of you.'

'You mean the Honourables' house?' I said, shocked.

'I do indeed,' she said.

'But I can't work there, Mammy.'

'And why not, may I ask?'

'Miss Caroline hates me because I called her Miss Baggy Knickers. She'll give me a good thrashing if I show my face up there again.'

'Don't be so fanciful, Cissy. She's a lady now, I shouldn't think she's thought of you once. She probably won't even remember the incident, you were just a child then.'

'Oh, I think she will, Mammy. Do I *have* to work there?'

'Not if you don't want to but there's very few jobs in the town and the ones that there are hold no future for you. This is a job with prospects, Cissy. If you work hard and do as you are told, you could do very well.'

'It's not that I don't want to work, Mammy. I want to do my bit, I want to make things easier for you.'

'I know you do, love. You're a good girl.'

'Can I think about it?'

'You can of course, but don't think too long or the job will be taken.'

I went outside and stood beside the granddaddy's chair, watching Buddy running around the alley.

'Did the mammy tell you about the job up at the big house?'

'Do you want to work up there?'

'Would I have to sleep there?'

'I'd say you would.'

'I'd miss you and Mammy and Buddy.'

'And we'd miss you, child, but you have to think of your future and I'd say that working in the big house is better than sweating away in the laundry like your mother.'

'But Miss Caroline hates me.'

'Sure, you were both children then. I'd say you weren't important enough to have been on her mind all these years.'

'What will you do without me, Granddaddy?'

'I'll miss you child, but Colm will look in on me and I have Buddy. In fact, since I've been sitting outside the cottage, I think I could call on one of the neighbours if I need help.'

I rubbed my hand over the granddaddy's old head. He had a fine head of hair and it felt nice and clean. 'You smell different,' I said sadly.

'I thought you'd be pleased.'

I looked down at the ground. 'Everything is changing.'

Granddaddy nodded. 'That's life, Cissy, If everything stayed the same you'd still be up in the workhouse.'

'I suppose so.'

'Why don't you go and see Colm? See what he thinks about this job of yours.'

I called Buddy, who looked at me and then ran back to the granddaddy. Even Buddy had changed.

I walked up the alley to the grey house and knocked on the door.

'Have you come for a book, Cissy?' asked Colm's daddy.

'No, Mr Doyle, I've come to see Colm.'

'I think he's around somewhere, unless he's out with that girl of his.'

Just for a moment I hated Colm Doyle and I hated Alana Welsh. She was welcome to him, I thought angrily.

I walked away. 'It doesn't matter,' I said.

Nobody wanted me, not the granddaddy, not Buddy and not Colm, and I had a feeling that the mammy wouldn't even notice if I wasn't there. *I'll take the bloody job up at the big house and if Miss Baggy Knickers says anything to me, I'll... I'll...* What could I do? Nothing, that's what. I stomped back down Paradise Alley and into the cottage, slamming the door behind me.

'Jesus Mary and holy Saint Joseph, are you trying to take the door off its hinges?' said the mammy.

I could feel the hot tears behind my eyes and a lump in my throat. I tried to swallow it down but I couldn't and I started to cry, great gulping noisy sobs that threatened to take the breath out of my body.

Mammy came across and put her arms around me and I cried as if my heart was breaking.

'For heaven's sake, child, what's wrong with you?'

I took a big breath and rubbed at my eyes. 'Nobody wants me, Mammy. No one cares if I go away, no one will miss me,' I sobbed.

'Ah, Cissy, where has all this come from?'

'It's true, Mammy. Colm's walking out with Alana Walsh, Buddy prefers the granddaddy to me, the granddaddy has a pile of new friends and you…'

'What of me, Cissy?'

I looked into the mammy's eyes. I'd never really known whether she loved me or not. I'd had no experience of mammies when I'd first met her but I'd seen other mammies and they were different somehow; they weren't so cross all the time.

Mammy stroked my hair. 'You don't think I'd miss you?'

I shrugged my shoulders.

The mammy tipped my chin up and smiled a sad kind of smile. 'You're my world, Cissy Ryan. I may not show it very often but I love you with every breath in my body.'

I threw my arms around her and nestled my head in her shoulder. I stayed in her arms for a very long time until Colm knocked on the door and walked into our house but I wouldn't look at him.

'Shall I leave you?' he said, looking worried.

'We have a sad girl here, Colm,' said the mammy.

'I can see that, Mrs Ryan. Is there anything I can do for the pair of you?'

I shook my head but the mammy ignored that. 'You can take her for a spin, Colm. She needs taking out of herself.'

'I'll do that gladly. Will we take a ride out the strand? I find that the sea soothes the soul and I'm thinking your soul is in need of some soothing, Cissy.'

'Go on,' said the mammy.

Reluctantly, I unwound myself from Mammy's arms and nodded at Colm. I was quiet all the way through town and out towards the strand. Colm didn't seem to mind but every now and then he touched my arm, which felt nice. I wanted to be cross with him but I didn't feel cross any more, just sad.

We left Blue and the trap at the side of the road and walked down the pebbly beach. It was a beautiful summer's day and the sea was like glass. I began to feel calmer. There were some big rocks underneath the lighthouse and we sat down and looked out over the ocean.

'And what was all that about, Cissy?' he said.

'Everything's changing, Colm,' I said.

He smiled and nodded his head. 'Ah, life sure it has a habit of doing that.'

'I don't like change,' I said, looking up at him.

Colm took my hand in his. 'The daddy told me you'd been up at the house looking for me.'

'He said you were out with Alana Walsh.'

'I was in the stable giving Blue a bit of a rub down. Now don't tell me that's what put you into a mood.'

'Not just that, Colm. No one seems to need me any more.'

'Do you really believe that?'

'I did a while ago.'

'And now?'

'Now I feel like an eejit.'

'I'd say we all feel like eejits now and again. It's allowed.'

There was a warm breeze that gently lifted the hair from the back of my neck. It felt lovely. I wished Nora could be here beside me, feeling the good clean air on this beautiful day instead of being stuck in the workhouse. Maybe if I worked really hard and earned lots of money I could buy a little cottage and me and Nora could live together. Wouldn't that be a wonderful thing?

'Have you given any thought to the position up at the house?'

'I'm worried about Miss Caroline and what I called her.'

'I shouldn't worry about that one. She's away at school.'

'And her brother, Master Peter?'

'He's away too.'

'Do you think I should work there?'

'I'd say you could do worse, Cissy.'

He put his arm around my shoulder and we sat in silence, listening to the little waves lapping the shore and tumbling the pebbles.

I looked out over the calm sea, Yes things were changing and the little girl who'd thought she was an orphan was growing up.

CHAPTER THIRTEEN

The mammy was gently brushing my hair. 'You have nothing to worry about, Cissy. You're well turned out and you have a fine brain in your head.'

'But what if Mrs Bretton takes against me and doesn't give me a job?'

'Now why would she take against you? What have you ever done to her? You go up to the big house with your head held high and always remember who you are.'

'Who am I, Mammy?'

'You're Cissy Ryan, daughter of Moira Ryan and granddaughter of Malachi Ryan. You're as good as the next girl and don't you forget it.'

'I won't, Mammy.'

'And if the almighty Mrs Bretton can't see that you are the finest girl in Ballybun then it's her loss. Now stand back and let me look at you.'

I knew that I was looking great altogether with my new boots and shawl that the mammy had bought for me.

She smiled and nodded her head. 'You look lovely, Cissy. There's just one thing missing.' She walked over to the dresser and opened a drawer, then she handed me a little paper bag.

I put my hand inside and pulled out a ribbon. It was the colour of the sea – a sort of greeny blue – and as soft as velvet. 'Oh, Mammy, it's the most beautiful ribbon I ever saw, thank you.'

'Turn around, Cissy,' she said.

I knelt down in front of her and let her place the ribbon in my hair. I loved the feel of her hands against my skin; they were rough from working in the laundry but I didn't care. The mammy didn't fuss over me very often and I could have sat at her knee all day as she gently smoothed my hair, gathering in the stray wisps from the back of my neck as she tied the ribbon in a bow. It was so quiet in the little room, just the crackle of the peat settling in the grate and the feel of Mammy's breath soft as a feather on my cheek.

'There now,' she said, smiling. She took my face in her hands and kissed my forehead. 'Go and show your granddaddy.'

I went outside and stood in front of the granddaddy's chair.

'I'm ready for my interview up at the big house, Granddaddy, and I have on my good boots and my new shawl and I have a fine ribbon in my hair.' I spun around so that he could see it.

The granddaddy smiled at me and his old eyes looked glassy as if he was about to cry. 'You'll do,' he said.

I saw Colm and Blue coming down the alley so I ran inside the cottage to say goodbye to Mammy. I put my arms around her waist.

'You'll be fine,' she said.

'All ready for the big day?' said Colm as he helped me up into the trap.

'I'm terrible scared, Colm.'

'Sure, why would you be scared? You look grand altogether and is that a fine ribbon I see in your hair?'

'The mammy bought it for me.'

'Well, you look lovely, Cissy, and I'd say you have nothing to worry about.'

'Have you ever gone for a job?'

'No, I always knew I'd help my father with the milk.'

'Have you ever had a mind to do something else?'

'I've done a bit of daydreaming in my time but my father has no one else, so I feel it's my duty to remain in Paradise Alley and help him.'

'You never told me that you had a sister, Colm.'

'She died when I was a baby, God rest her soul. I don't remember her. I wish I did, it would have been nice to have had a big sister.

My mam died shortly after. People in the alley said she died of a broken heart but my father said she had a weakness in her lungs. It's always been me and him and luckily, we've always rubbed along fine.'

'Well, that's a blessing anyway.'

Before I knew it, we were climbing the hill up to the Hall and I suddenly felt awfully sick. 'I feel sick, Colm,' I said.

Colm pulled on the reins and stopped. 'Take some big deep breaths, Cissy,' he said, 'and you'll be grand.'

'I don't feel grand, I feel terrified.'

'You're tougher than that, girl. If you're not feeling brave then pretend you are, it works every time. Deep breaths and a brave face.'

'It's alright for you to be telling me to be brave, Colm Doyle. It's not you that has to go in there.'

'That's true, Cissy. I was just trying to help.'

'If you've a mind to be helpful then you can turn the trap around and take me home.'

'If that's what you want then I will, but I don't think it is.'

I took a deep breath. 'Okay, let's go.'

We continued up the hill and through the big gates.

'I'll be here when you come out. Now remember, deep breaths and a brave face.'

I climbed down from the trap and started to walk up the drive. I turned back to look at Colm and he waved to me.

I knocked on the kitchen door and it was opened by Bridie.

'Come in, Cissy,' she said.

I walked into the kitchen. It was a huge room – bigger than the whole of our little cottage. It had a long table running down the length of it and there were shiny pots and pans hanging down from the ceiling. If Mrs Bretton took me on, this is where I would be working.

'You look terrified,' said Bridie, grinning at me.

'I am,' I said.

'Well, you've no need to be and Mrs Bretton is okay, she won't eat you. Just be polite and you'll be fine. Come on, I'll take you up to her.'

I handed my shawl to Bridie and followed her up the stairs. We walked through a wide hallway, my boots making a clattering sound as we walked across the shiny wooden floor. In front of me was a beautiful curved staircase and on the walls were huge paintings in ornate frames. This was another world. This was where the Honourable Miss Caroline had been brought up; it was no wonder she'd looked down her nose at me. Talk about knowing your place. Well, if I hadn't known before, I certainly did now.

'Okay, this is it,' said Bridie and knocked on the door.

'Come in,' said a voice.

We walked into the room.

'Cissy Ryan to see you, Mrs Bretton,' said Bridie, bobbing down.

Was I supposed to bob down too? No one had told me anything about bobbing down.

Mrs Bretton was sitting in a high-backed chair beside a marble fireplace. A lovely fire burned in the grate and the walls were lined with hundreds of books reaching up to the ceiling. She was wearing a beautiful cream dress and there were pearls around her neck. Her fair hair was piled high on her head, held away from her face with silver slides that sparkled in the glow of the fire. The room was large and square; a gold velvet sofa sat below the long windows. More pictures hung from the walls and everywhere smelt of lavender and soap. It must be a wonderful thing indeed to be this rich – Mrs Bretton must be a very happy woman.

'Thank you, Bridie,' she said.

Bridie bobbed down again and left the room.

'Come and sit down, Cissy,' said Mrs Bretton, beckoning towards the chair opposite her.

I sat down; the chair felt soft and squishy and the fire warmed my legs.

She seemed to look at me for a long time. I began to feel awkward and out of place.

'Have you been in service before, Cissy?' she asked.

'I'm still at school, Madam.'

'At the convent?'

'Yes, Madam.'

She continued to stare at me and I could feel beads of sweat gathering under my armpits. I hoped I wouldn't start to smell.

'I hear from Bridie that you live in the town.'

'Paradise Alley, Madam.'

'With your mother?'

'And the granddaddy.'

'Your grandfather?'

I could feel my face going red. 'Yes, my grandfather.'

'Your mother is Moira Ryan?'

'Yes, Madam.'

'And I believe you came from the workhouse, is that right?'

I could feel my face redden.

'Yes, Madam.'

'I have just taken on a young girl from the workhouse. Her name is Annie.'

I didn't know if I was supposed to respond to that so I kept quiet.

'You are aware that I will need you to live in?'

'Yes, Madam.'

'You will work from five thirty in the morning until eight in the evening and you will have every Wednesday off and every other Sunday. Will that suit you?'

'Oh yes, Madam, thank you.'

'When do you finish at the convent?'

'In two weeks' time, Madam.'

'Then I shall expect to see you in two weeks, Cissy. Your uniform will be provided, so you can tell your mother that she has no need to worry about that.'

'I will, Madam.' I stood up. 'Thank you, Madam,' I said and did an awkward sort of bob.

Mrs Bretton looked as if she was stifling a giggle. 'Goodbye, Cissy,' she said.

'Well?' said Bridie, as I walked back into the kitchen. 'Did she take you on?'

'She did,' I said, smiling.

'She's not so scary, is she?'

'Why didn't you tell me about the bobbing thing? I just tried it and nearly fell over.'

'I'll teach you. Sure you'll be a grand little bobber after a few lessons.'

Just then a young girl came through the door, carrying a bucket that looked too heavy for her.

'Annie, this is Cissy. She's going to be working here so we'll have more help.'

Annie put the bucket down and grinned.

'Pleased to meet you, I'm sure, Cissy,' she said. 'We could do with a bit more help.'

'And I'll be glad to be of use,' I said, grinning back.

'I'll show you the ropes, Cissy. You'll soon get the hang of it. Annie here helps Mrs Hickey with the food and the running of the kitchen and you and me look after the house. I've been doing it myself since Rosie left. It'll be grand to have some help again.'

'Who's Mrs Hickey?'

'She's the cook and a bit of a banshee when the kitchen isn't running to her taste but she won't bother us, just poor Annie.'

'She won't be unkind to her, will she?'

'No, she's a fair person, she just suffers from her nerves.'

'And Rosie?'

'It's Rosie you'll be taking over from.'

'Why did she leave?'

'Lady up-her-own-backside Caroline caught her kissing the groom in the stables and told her father. Poor Rosie was out on her ear.'

'That was mean of her, she could have just told her off.'

'I'll tell you what I think, Cissy. I think she was jealous for she had her eyes on the groom herself.'

'I was hoping she'd changed.'

'That one will never change. She has a mean streak running through her and it's been there since birth. Master Peter, on the other hand, is a lovely lad. I have a soft spot for him, so I do.'

I liked Bridie and I liked the look of Annie and Mrs Hickey didn't sound too bad either. Now all I had to hope for was that Miss baggy-knickers-up-her-own-backside Caroline Bretton didn't remember me.

CHAPTER FOURTEEN

'You're really going to work for the Honourables?' said Mary, when I told her about my new job. 'What's it like up there?'

'It's the most beautiful place I ever saw in my life. I only saw the drawing room and the kitchen but it's mighty fine. Mrs Hickey seems to run the kitchen with the help of a young girl called Annie who came from the workhouse and Bridie runs the house. The last girl was sent home for getting caught kissing a young feller in the stables. What sort of eejit loses a grand job like that on account of a feller?'

'Blowsy types,' said Mary.

'Like Alana Walsh?'

'Just like Alana Walsh.'

'I'd say you're right but that's not going to happen to me. Anyway, I promised the mammy I'd be a good girl.'

'That might go out the window when you're in the arms of some handsome lad.'

'No, I'm definitely going to keep my promise, however handsome he is.'

'Have you severed the contract between yourself and Colm Doyle yet?'

'Like you said, Colm only said he would wait for me to please me and anyway, I have a fine job now. I won't have time to be pining over Colm Doyle.'

'I think that's very wise, Cissy.'

'What about you, Mary? Where are you going to work?'

'My mother is enquiring about a job in the workhouse but I'd be afeared to work there.'

'What would you be doing?'

'I don't know. I just hope it wouldn't be looking after the poor demented souls. I'd be terrible scared, Cissy.'

'It's not as bad as you think, they are more to be pitied than feared and if you didn't like it, you could always leave.'

'That's true but my mother says it's a good steady job and if they take me on, I should be grateful.'

'Where would you rather work?'

'I think I'd rather work out at the Green Park Hotel and meet all the swanky people in their swanky carriages. I'll never see the light of day up at the workhouse.'

'Have you never considered going into service like meself?'

'Jesus, I couldn't be coping with that! Cleaning up after people and washing their dirty clothes when there's no reason why they can't be cleaning up after themselves.'

'Honourables couldn't clean up after themselves, Mary. They're far too high-born for that.'

'But sure, they're only people, with two good arms and two good legs like the rest of us.'

'Oh, Mary, they are definitely not like the rest of us. They've not been brought up to look after themselves like we have.'

'Well, you wouldn't catch *me* looking after them.'

'I don't mind. I like cleaning up and it's all so lovely.'

'When are you starting?'

'When school finishes in two weeks' time.'

'Don't you feel as if it's the end of our childhood?'

'I think my childhood ended the day I left the workhouse. I was a child until that day.'

'It must have been awful hard for you, Cissy, having to leave the only home you'd ever known.'

'When I was there, Nora and me would play all day, roaming about the place and helping Mrs Foley with the little ones. It never once occurred to either of us that it was a strange place to live, it was just home and then I got up one morning and I was told that

I would be leaving that day with a mammy that I didn't know. No one said I'd be leaving forever, I thought it was just going to be a day out. I didn't even get to say goodbye to everyone. It was a very confusing day, Mary.'

'You weren't sad for long, though?'

'No, I wasn't sad for long because I grew to love the mammy and the granddaddy and I had no mind to go back. One day, when I have a pile of money and house of my own, I shall take Nora out of that place and bring her home to live with me.'

Mary nodded and smiled at me. 'It's good to have a dream, Cissy. I think that everyone should have one.'

'What's your dream, Mary?'

'To go to America.'

'Really? You'd really leave Ballybun and live in that pagan land?'

'Sure it's not all pagan, Cissy. I have an uncle who went over there and he says you can always find your own people, mostly in the nearest pub, and there's a priest on every corner. He said that half the population of Ireland went there when the potato crops failed.'

'You'd think they could have found something else to eat ,wouldn't you?' I said. 'I mean, there's fish in the rivers and birds in the trees and rabbits and all sorts of life that they could have eaten.'

'You should ask your granddaddy, for he lived through it and he would know.'

'What will you do in America?'

'I haven't thought that far ahead but America is my dream and one day I shall go there on a big ship and marry a rich man and live in a fine house and have two children who will mind what I say and we'll all live happily ever after.'

'That sounds like a great dream, Mary, and I wish you well.'

'Thank you, Cissy. Now all I've to do is save up like mad, even if that means I'll have to work up the hill.'

'Wouldn't you miss your family?'

'Jesus, Cissy, it's like living in a mad house! There's always a baby screaming its head off or peeing on the floor. There's always someone's dirty arse to clean or a snotty nose to wipe. The only one that's house-trained is the dog. You can't move in there for bloody kids. I don't even get any peace at night 'cos there's a pile of them in the bed with me. I do love them, Cissy, but I envy you living in your little cottage with just your mam and the granddaddy.'

'It can't be easy,' I agreed.

'It's not, but when I go to America and get married I shall just have two children, a boy and a girl, and that will be the end of it.'

'But how do you stop having children?'

Mary thought for a minute: 'Single beds,' she said, grinning.

'You'll need a mighty placid man to put up with that.'

'And I'll find him.'

'Then I hope it goes well for you, Mary.'

'It will.'

When I got home I asked the granddaddy about the Potato Famine.

'It was a terrible time, Cissy. I was fifteen when the crops began to fail. The stench of rotting potatoes coming off the fields made you sick to your stomach. To this day, I can smell it. It's not a smell that is easily forgotten. The crops failed for four years. Me and my older brother were the only ones in the family to survive.'

'Did you have a big family?'

'I had six sisters and four brothers.'

'And they *all* died?'

'Some of them starved, some died from the typhus, the rest from eating diseased potatoes.'

I felt tears welling up in my eyes as I listened to the granddaddy telling his story. He'd lost his family and that was the saddest thing. I was glad that now he had me and the mammy and Buddy to love; I was glad he wasn't alone.

'It made me a bitter man, a hard man. Where was God when His people needed Him? That's what I wondered.'

'Sister Bridgette used to say that we must have faith and not question the ways of the Lord.'

'When your baby sister dies in your arms, Cissy, faith goes out the window.'

I rested my head on his old knee. 'Oh, Granddaddy,' I said.

He gently stroked my hair. 'They were bad times alright.'

'Was there nothing else that you could have eaten?'

'The potato was an easy thing to grow. It didn't matter what the ground was like, the potato thrived. A single acre of stony ground could feed a family of six.'

'What about fish? Couldn't you have taken the fish from the sea?'

'Ireland was, and still is, a poor country, Cissy. The people had neither the skills nor the equipment to fish these rough Irish seas and by the time things became desperate, they hadn't the strength.'

'Why didn't you go to America?'

'We owned a small cottage and a piece of land. It was ours; there was no English landlord to throw us into the streets, it was the only thing we had. Our mother and father urged us to go with them but if we'd left for America, we'd have lost it for sure. Tales reaching us were that many never even made it there, they died on the journey. Those ships came to be known as "coffin ships". We never heard from our parents again. We never knew if they had reached America or not but I think that if they had, we would have had word from them. So me and my brother stayed and survived on the soup kitchens until the potato thrived again.'

'I'm glad you didn't die, Granddaddy,' I said.

Granddaddy didn't say anything, he just stared into the fire.

'If you'd died, I wouldn't be here and the mammy wouldn't be here.'

'And I don't deserve either of you,' he said.

'Sure, why would you be saying that?'

'Because I wasn't there when you needed me. I sent you up to that godforsaken place and then God forgive me, I called you a bastard. It would be easy to blame what I did on the drink, but maybe I just had a black heart.'

'It's not black now, Granddaddy. Sure it's as white as snow and don't worry about that name you called me. I didn't know what it meant, so it didn't upset me one bit and don't worry about God, He'll forgive you alright. He's a very forgiving person. He forgave that robber who was hanging on the cross next to him. He even invited him to dinner.'

'Did He?'

'Oh, He did, so you have nothing to be fretting about.'

'I don't think He'll be inviting me to dinner, Cissy. I've been a terrible bad man in my life.'

'But you're not bad now, are you, Granddaddy? You're as good as gold and I'd say He'd be glad to have you. You'll be sitting on a lovely white cloud with your old legs hanging over the side and you'll be grand altogether. He might even give you a harp and a pair of wings if you're lucky.'

Granddaddy started chuckling. 'Where on earth did you come from, child?'

'I haven't a clue but I'd say it had something to do with the Angel Gabriel.'

'And how do you figure that out?'

'Well, the angel came down from heaven and told the Virgin Mary she was having a child, so I think that's how it works. That angel must have visited the mammy.'

'I have a feeling it wasn't an angel that visited her, but we won't go into that,' replied the granddaddy.

CHAPTER FIFTEEN

I didn't bother going back to school once I got the job and the mammy didn't mind.

'Enjoy your freedom while you can, Cissy,' she'd said.

Some days I'd meet Mary after school and we'd spend time down on the quay or up at Collins's farm with the animals. Buddy and Eddie loved chasing the chickens around the place.

One afternoon, we were sitting on the wall watching the boats. The two little dogs were sniffing round the fresh catch of fish on the dock and being shooed away by the fishermen.

'You could always work on a farm in America, Mary. You love animals.'

'I might love animals but I've no intention of mucking out pigs for a living. I'm going to marry a rich feller. I intend never to work again.'

'What will you do, then?'

'I'll order the staff about and I'll eat fancy food and go to posh hotels with my handsome husband.'

I giggled. 'And if that doesn't work out you can always work on a farm and marry a big old farmer with a hairy chin and a red old face.'

Mary pushed me off the wall. 'You wait and see, Cissy Ryan. My dream's going to come true, so there!'

'I was just codding ya, I have no doubt in my mind that one day you will have everything you want.'

Mary grinned. 'I'm going to miss seeing you every day.'

'Well, if you get that job up at the workhouse I'll maybe get to see you on a Sunday morning before Mass.'

*

Colm had tired of Alana Walsh after only a couple of months so we spent as much time together as we could. I went out on the milk round every morning, and after I'd helped Mammy in the cottage, we spent the rest of the day together. We walked the fields with Buddy and we sat down on the quayside and watched the boats.

One day we were sitting on the rocks under the lighthouse when I said, 'Do you know if I ever had a daddy, Colm?'

'Sure, everyone has a daddy.'

'That's why I'm asking, because there doesn't seem to be any sign of mine.'

'Well now, Cissy, I can't help you there. I was only about six years old when your mammy went into the workhouse and you'd only just been born. No one has ever spoken of it that I can remember.'

'It's okay, I was just wondering is all.' I shrugged my shoulders. 'What you've never had, you don't miss.'

'Why don't you ask your mammy?'

'Because I don't know how she'll take it; she has a fearful temper and a sharp tongue, she said so herself.'

'I guess it depends how much you want to know. I mean, is it worth bringing the wrath of the mammy down on your head for?'

'I'll think about it.'

We stood up and walked down to the water's edge. Colm picked up a flat stone and threw it into the sea. It bounced across the surface four times.

'Can you teach me to do that?' I asked.

Colm found another flat stone. He stood behind me and showed me how to hold it in my palm so that it skimmed the water. I could feel his breath on the back of my neck and I wanted to put my arms around him and hold him close. Instead, I dropped the stone and walked away back up the beach. Colm caught up with me.

'Giving up already?' he said.

I turned to face him. 'Will you miss me when I'm gone, Colm?'

'I will, of course.'

'I'll miss you too.'

'You won't have time to miss me, Cissy. You'll be too busy living the high life with the highbrows up on the hill.'

'I'll never forget you, Colm.'

'What's this all about?'

'You might forget me.'

'You're only going up the hill, Cissy, you're not taking the next boat to Liverpool.'

'Am I being silly?'

Colm put his arm around my shoulder. 'I'm afraid so. Anyway, you'll see me every morning and on your Sundays off, we'll see your little friend Nora.'

'I wish Nora could get a job with the Honourables but Mrs Foley said she wouldn't be strong enough for all the heavy lifting. Unless I get a house of my own, I don't think that Nora will ever get out of that place.'

'Does she want to get out?'

'I've never asked her, it might make her sad if I asked.'

'You have a kind heart, Cissy.'

'I hope the granddaddy will manage without me. He's getting very old, Colm, and I worry about him.'

'I'll keep an eye on him, so don't you be worrying yourself about that. And every time I've seen Nora, she seems happy enough. It's time you started thinking about yourself and stopped worrying about everyone else.'

'I only worry about the people I love, Colm Doyle, and I'll worry about them for the rest of my life,' I snapped.

Colm held his hands up. 'I'm glad to see you have the fighting spirit, that might come in handy when Miss Baggy Knickers comes home from school.'

'Why did you have to remind me about her?' I said, punching his arm.

'Truce?' he said.

'Truce,' I said, laughing.

One afternoon I was helping Mammy clean the potatoes.

'How old is Granddaddy?' I asked.

'I don't even think he knows himself,' she said, smiling.

'That's not a proper answer,' I said.

'He's always seemed old to me, Cissy. A mean, bigoted old man.'

'But he's not so bad now, is he?'

Mammy looked at me and smiled. 'You're right, he's not and I'd say that is because of you. You reached into that icy old heart of his and you warmed it with your chatter and your smiles. You made him love you, Cissy, whether he wanted to or not.'

I took another potato out of the water. 'Can I ask you something, Mammy?'

'Ask away.'

'Promise you won't be cross?'

Mammy smiled. 'I promise I won't be cross.'

'Do I have a daddy?'

Mammy was quiet for a minute, then she wiped her hands on a cloth. 'Come and sit with me, Cissy,' she said.

The granddaddy was outside on his chair so Mammy sat beside the fire and I sat at her feet.

'I wondered when you were going to ask me,' she said softly.

'I don't need to know, Mammy, not if it's going to make you sad,' I said quickly.

'You have a right to know, child, and telling you won't make me sad.'

'Was he nice, Mammy?'

'He was lovely.'

'How did you meet him?'

'There was a ceilidh down at the church. A ship had docked in the quay and a bunch of Norwegian sailors came into the hall.'

'Norwegian?' I said, amazed.

'Yes, Cissy.'

It took a minute to take this in. 'I'm not just Irish, then?'

'No, love, you are definitely half Norwegian.'

'What happened?'

'Well, they started to dance with us girls. The local lads weren't happy about it and a fight broke out. The sailor I'd been dancing with hurried me away. His name was Stefan.'

'My daddy's name was Stefan?'

'That's right.'

'We spoke different languages but somehow we understood each other in all the ways that mattered. He was handsome, Cissy, your daddy was so handsome.'

Mammy touched my hair. 'His hair was the same colour as yours and… oh, his smile! I fell in love that night and I thought that he fell in love with me too. We saw each other every moment we could and then it was over. We had no time to say goodbye, his ship sailed away during the night. When I got down to the quay the next morning he was gone and I was never able to tell him that I was carrying his child. We'd been together for just a few months but when he went away, part of me went with him.'

'And you had to go into the workhouse?'

'I had brought shame on my parents. My father nearly killed me and I know he would have killed Stefan if he could. He threw me out into the street with nothing but the clothes I was wearing. The workhouse was the only place I could go.'

I could feel the tears running down my cheeks. 'I'm sorry, Mammy.'

'You have nothing to be sorry for, child. I knew what I was doing but I was foolish enough to think that he would come back.'

'Did he know about me?'

'I didn't know myself until it was too late. By the time I did, he was long gone. I know they say that sailors have a girl in every port, but Stefan was different. In the short time I knew him, I grew to trust him and I would like to think that if he knew I was having his child, he would have come back.'

I stared into the fire. 'Are you ashamed of me?' I said.

Mammy stood up and gently lifted me to my feet. She put her arms around me and gently kissed the top of my head.

'Never, Cissy,' she said. 'Never.'

I thought about how hard it must have been, to be all alone and expecting a baby when Mammy had no husband to look after her. She must have been so frightened.

'You're growing up fast, Cissy, and you are beautiful. One day you will fall in love, but I want you to do it right. I want you to be married when you bring a baby into this world.'

'I want to make you proud and I promise never to bring shame on you.'

Mammy took my face in her hands. 'You are Cissy Ryan, daughter of Moira Ryan and granddaughter of Malachi Ryan – and you are loved,' she said.

CHAPTER SIXTEEN

At the break of dawn, on a dark rainy September morning, Colm and Blue pulled up outside the cottage to take me to the big house. I hadn't slept well and I felt too sick to eat anything. I'd packed my bag the night before, all I had to do now was say goodbye. I knew that I would see them all again on my day off but I felt empty inside as though this was the end of something. I remembered the day I'd arrived and how angry the granddaddy had been and how he'd wanted to throw me out into the street, just like he'd done to Mammy, in nothing but the clothes I was standing up in. I remembered thinking he was the Devil himself and how I'd tried to see his tail but we'd grown to love each other and I would miss seeing him every day. I looked at him now, crouched over the fire; Buddy was on his lap and he was stroking his fur. He'd got up early to see me off. I wished he hadn't because I knew I was going to cry and there wasn't a lot of crying done in our little cottage. I wished someone would speak.

'I'd better go,' I said, breaking the silence.

The granddaddy just nodded his old head.

'I'll be back on Wednesday.'

He nodded again and I looked at Mammy, who gestured to me to go over to him.

I knelt down at his feet and stroked Buddy. 'Be a good boy, Buddy,' I said, 'and look after my granddaddy for me because I love him even though he smells like a dead ferret.'

Granddaddy smiled at me and touched my cheek with his bony old hand.

'You'll be grand, Cissy,' he said. 'You'll be grand.'

I stood and picked up my bundle. Mammy came to the cottage door but she didn't see me off, she just said, 'Thank you for taking her, Colm.'

'You're more than welcome, Mrs Ryan, and I'll bring her home to you on Wednesday.'

Mammy nodded at him, then looked at me. 'Be a good girl, Cissy, and do your best and you'll be fine.' Then she went into the cottage and closed the door.

I looked back at the little cottage where I had been so happy. I would miss being there with Mammy and Granddaddy, but I knew that it was time to move on.

'Ready?' said Colm.

'I suppose I am,' I said.

'Best foot forward, Blue, for today is a very special day.'

'Is it?' I said, looking doubtful.

'It is of course. Come on, Blue, let's get this girl of ours off to Bretton Hall.'

I liked that Colm had said 'This girl of ours' – it made me feel warm inside, as if I belonged, as if I was important to him.

As we trotted through the town and out towards the strand, there was a bitter wind coming off the sea and I was freezing cold. Colm had put a blanket around my shoulders but my nose felt as if it was going to drop off. The water looked dark and menacing in the half light of morning, its blackness broken only by the bright beam from the lighthouse window, radiating backwards and forwards across the heaving waves and lighting up the craggy rocks beneath its base. In the daytime, the lighthouse wasn't scary at all. The granddaddy said it had saved many a ship from being crushed on the rocks and many a sailor from a watery grave. I shivered and pulled the blanket closer around me.

'Penny for them,' said Colm.

'I was thinking that the sea looks awful scary this morning.'

'The sea has her moods, just like the rest of us. On a good day she is gentle and calm but if she's upset, she lets us all know about it.'

'A bit like the mammy,' I said, grinning at him.

Soon we were trotting through the big iron gates of Bretton Hall. I was feeling sick again. Colm jumped down from the trap, then took my hand and helped me down too. He handed me my bundle. 'You'll be fine, Cissy, and if I don't see you in the morning, I'll collect you on Wednesday and take you home.'

I smoothed Blue's back and buried my face in his soft coat, then I put my arms around Colm. I felt like crying. I knew I was being silly because I'd see him when he brought the milk and I'd see him on my days off, but I didn't want to be here in front of this strange house. I wanted to be home in the little cottage getting the granddaddy his tea.

'I think I'd rather work in the laundry with Mammy,' I said. 'At least then I could sleep in my own bed at night.'

Colm smoothed my hair away from my face and kissed my cheek. 'The next time I see you, you'll be full of it, telling me tales of how the other half live and being too grand for Paradise Alley.'

'If there's one thing I'm sure of, it's that I'll never be too grand for Paradise Alley.'

'May God go with you,' said Colm, giving me a gentle shove.

I walked away from him and up the drive. I didn't turn back because I knew if I did, I might lose my nerve and beg him to take me home.

I walked around the side of the house and knocked on the kitchen door. As I stood there, waiting for someone to answer, the strangest feeling came over me and I knew with certainty that once that door opened and I stepped inside, my life would change forever.

Eventually the door did open and I found myself looking at a large lady with a ruddy face and a mass of unruly hair. She wasn't fat, just big, more like a man than a woman. The mammy would have described her as big-boned: she seemed to take up the whole of the doorway so that I couldn't see the room behind her.

'You must be Cissy Ryan,' she said, smiling. 'I'm Mrs Hickey.'

'Good morning, Mrs Hickey,' I said.

'Come in, child, you look frozen and terrified.' She stepped aside and I went into the warm kitchen.

'Take off your shawl and stand by the stove, you'll soon get some heat into your body.'

I stood in front of the stove and stretched my hands out towards the flame; it was lovely.

'I bet you could use a nice cup of tea. I was just about to have one meself.'

Just then Annie came into the room, causing a blast of cold air to rush into the kitchen.

'Door!' yelled Mrs Hickey.

'Sorry, Mrs Hickey,' said Annie, slamming the door quickly behind her.

'The child was born in a barn,' said Mrs Hickey to no one in particular.

'It's terrible cold out there,' said Annie, blowing on her hands to get some warmth into them.

'Make us all a cup of tea, Annie. Make one for Bridie as well, she'll want one when she's done the fires.'

'Yes, Mrs Hickey, I'll do that right away, so I will.'

'And while the kettle's boiling, you can take Cissy up to your room and show her where she's to sleep.'

'You're to sleep beside me,' said Annie, grinning. 'It's been terrible lonely up there without Rosie.'

'Your uniform is hanging on the wardrobe door, Cissy. I hope it fits okay, Rosie was about your size.'

'Thank you, Mrs Hickey,' I said. 'I'm sure it will be fine.'

I followed Annie up the stairs to the top of the house. The room was tucked under the eaves. There wasn't much furniture in there, just a couple of beds, a wardrobe and a chest of drawers. The room was at the back of the house overlooking the gardens. When I looked out of the little window the view nearly took my breath away. The lawns sloped right down to the sea. It was growing light now and the water looked less threatening. A thin sun was breaking through the clouds, glistening on the tips of the waves rushing towards the shore. It was the most beautiful sight I had ever seen.

'I have the top three drawers and you can have the other three, is that okay?' said Annie.

I turned around and smiled at her. 'I don't think I've got enough clothes to fill three drawers,' I said.

'Me neither,' said Annie, grinning.

Annie was a skinny little thing but with a smile that warmed my heart.

I sat on the bed and started to undo my bundle. 'I don't remember seeing you in the workhouse, Annie,' I said.

'I only went up there about three years ago when my mother died.'

'I'm sorry.'

'I was desperate sad, Cissy. Relatives took in my younger brothers and sisters but nobody wanted me.'

'Well, I can't think why,' I said, smiling at her, 'because I think you're lovely.'

'I'm not all there though, am I?'

'Who told you that?'

'Pretty much everyone. I can't do the reading and the writing or me numbers.'

'That doesn't mean you're not all there. Do you want to learn?'

'I'd love to be able to read a book but I don't think I'll ever be able to.'

'I can teach you if you want.'

'Really?'

'Let's prove them all wrong, shall we?'

'Yes, let's,' said Annie, grinning.

'Do you know my friend Nora?'

'That was terrible sad, wasn't it?' she said, her eyes filling with tears.

'What was terrible sad?'

'That she passed away so young.'

'What are you talking about, Annie? Nora hasn't passed away.'

'She has, Cissy. I was up there only yesterday to collect a few bits I'd left behind. Mrs Foley was in a terrible state. She said that during the night Nora had been taken up to heaven in the arms of the angels.'

I heard the words coming out of Annie's mouth but I couldn't believe what she was saying. 'You're wrong,' I shouted. 'You're wrong.'

Annie was staring at me with a horrified look on her face. 'Oh, Cissy, I'm sorry, I'm sorry.' Tears were rolling down her cheeks. 'I shouldn't have said. I didn't think! Oh, Cissy.'

I put my head in my hands and cried as if my heart was breaking. My lovely friend Nora was gone, I'd never see her sweet face again in this lifetime. 'Why did God have to take Nora?' I sobbed.

Annie sat beside me and took me in her arms. 'I could cut me tongue out, I could. I could cut me tongue out.'

I wiped my eyes. 'You've done nothing wrong, Annie. I would have found out anyway.'

'I'll be your friend, Cissy, I will. I'll be your friend.'

I nodded. 'That would be nice, Annie,' I said, but I knew in my heart that no one could ever replace Nora, not ever.

Everyone was so kind to me that day but it meant nothing; it didn't help, it didn't bring Nora back to me. I was unhappy for a long time after Nora died, it felt like a little bit of me had died too.

I loved working up at the big house though and I threw myself into my work. Mrs Hickey said she'd never met such a hardworking girl and she was delighted with me, but it was the work that took my mind off my sadness. Every task I was given I did the best I could as if I was doing it for Nora. I hoped she was looking down on me and feeling proud. I spoke to her all the time as I lit the fires and polished the floors and then one day I found myself thinking of her and smiling instead of crying. Mrs Hickey noticed the difference in me.

'It's nice to see you smiling again, Cissy. Maybe now you can go a bit easier on the polishing, for it's a wonder there's any varnish left on the surfaces.'

I smiled at her. 'I'll try, Mrs Hickey.'

I hadn't gone on the milk round since losing my best friend and I knew that Colm would understand.

We were walking out the wood road when I told him. The trees and hedges were white with frost and we could see our breath like steam rising in the freezing air. Everywhere looked beautiful, like a million diamonds sparkling away in front of us, behind us and all around us, as if we were being held captive in a giant glass cage. Our boots crunched beneath us as we walked over the hard, crisp ground and the sky above us was the brightest of blues. I tucked my hands into my shawl and hugged my body to try and get some warmth. I loved walking in this magical place with Colm by my side. It was at times like this that my heart felt lighter and my soul felt at peace.

Buddy was running along in front of us, snuffling away at the undergrowth and chasing anything that dared to move. He was such a big dog now and not the little runt of the litter that I had fallen in love with. I had accepted that he was the granddaddy's dog but I liked to think that he loved me too. I bent down to ruffle his fur as he laid a frosty stick at my feet.

'Why not come with me on your next day off, Cissy?'

I stood up and threw the stick for Buddy to chase. 'I'm not ready, Colm.'

'I'm not saying you should go inside the place but…'

'But what?'

'Wouldn't you like to visit Nora's grave?'

'I do want to, but…'

'It will make it real?'

I nodded.

'There will never be a right time, Cissy, but seeing where she is laid to rest might give you some comfort.'

Mary had got the job at the workhouse helping Mrs Foley with the little ones and she visited Nora's grave whenever she could and kept it tidy and said a prayer. Maybe Colm was right; maybe it was time to go myself, otherwise Nora would be wondering where I was.

'Okay, Colm, on my next day off. We'll go then.'

'Good girl,' said Colm, putting his arm around my shoulder. 'I think that's a good decision.'

As we started walking back through the woods, small flakes of snow started falling down around us. It was as if Nora was sending angel dust down from heaven and saying: '*Yes, please come and visit me, Cissy. I've been waiting for you.*'

CHAPTER SEVENTEEN

The following Sunday, I got up early and went downstairs. It was so cold in the cottage that there was ice on the inside of the windows. It affected Granddaddy the most because of his poor old legs. We let him sleep, with Buddy lying across his feet.

I crouched down in front of the fire and held my hands out towards the flames. The cold had never bothered me much but now I was spoilt. Bretton Hall was always warm, with fires in all the rooms and the giant stove in the kitchen belting out heat as if it was mid-summer. Of course when it *was* summer the heat would be almost unbearable and we'd have to have the door open all the time but right now as my teeth chattered, I longed to be in the kitchen with Mrs Hickey and Annie and Bridie, feeling toasty and warm.

'It's a good job you have a fine coat now,' said Mammy. 'It was decent of them to give it to you.'

'It belonged to Rosie, the girl who was there before me. She left it behind when she was dismissed.'

'Well, let's hope she doesn't come back for it.'

'Bridie said she wouldn't be brazen enough to show her face at the Hall ever again, so I think the coat's mine.'

Mammy put a bowl of steaming porridge on the table. 'Sit and eat,' she said. 'The food will keep the cold out and I've warmed some water for your wash.'

'Thank you, Mammy.' I'd been dreading breaking the ice on the bowl of water and I was grateful to her for being so kind. 'I wasn't looking forward to it,' I said, spooning the porridge into my mouth.

After I'd helped the mammy clear up, I washed and dressed and waited for Colm to take me to the workhouse.

As Blue trotted through the town and up the hill I started to feel awful sad again. Colm seemed to know how I was feeling; he reached across and held my hand.

Mr Dunne opened the big iron gates and Blue walked inside.

'I'm sorry for your trouble, Cissy,' said Mr Dunne. 'She was a sweet child and we all miss her.'

'I miss her too,' I said.

'I remember the two of you wandering around the house and getting into all sorts of mischief. You had poor Mrs Foley demented at times, trying to find you.'

I smiled, remembering.

'Are you going round the back?'

'Yes.'

'Do you want me to show you the way?'

'I know the way, Mr Dunne. Me and Nora used to put flowers on the babies' graves.'

'I'll leave you to it then.'

'And I'll wait for you,' said Colm. 'Unless you want me to come with you?'

'I'd rather go on my own.'

'That's grand then, meself and Blue will be here when you're ready.'

I jumped down from the trap and walked around the side of the house to the gardens, then followed a path through a wooden gate and into the graveyard.

I stood for a moment and looked out across the field at the rows and rows of wooden crosses. These poor souls had ended their days here. Some had been here all their lives and never lived in the outside world or knew what it was to have a family of their own or to be loved. I thought it was the saddest of places.

It took me a while to find Nora because all the graves looked the same. None of them had headstones, just the simple wooden crosses to mark the spot. Nora's grave was under a tree, away from the rest. That made me feel happy – as if Nora was special. I knelt down on the ground and traced the name that was written on the cross: *Nora Foley.* Nora Foley? She had the same name as Mrs Foley, now wasn't that strange? I'd never even known Nora's surname. Come to that, I hadn't known my own when I lived in the workhouse. But to have the same name as Mrs Foley was nice because Mrs Foley had always loved her. Sometimes I thought she loved her more than she loved me. Maybe they were related in some way? I'd ask the mammy, she might know.

I sat on the hard, frosty ground and stared at the little cross. I knew that Nora wasn't really there because she would be up in heaven with Holy God and all the saints and angels but in this place of silence I felt her near to me. I closed my eyes and I could almost feel her warm breath on my cold cheek. 'I miss you, Nora,' I whispered. 'I wish you hadn't left me, for I always had a dream that one day I would come for you and we would live together for the rest of our lives. I know that God must have wanted you to be with him but I need you too and I'll never forget you.' I put my fingers to my lips and touched the cross. 'I'll come again, Nora, I'm not frightened any more. Sleep peacefully, my friend. I love you.'

I was quiet as Colm drove back through the town and he seemed to understand that I was too full of emotion to speak. He dropped me outside the cottage and carried on up Paradise Alley.

The granddaddy was out of bed and in his usual place beside the fire. Mammy helped me off with my coat and hung it on the hook behind the door.

'Are you glad you went, Cissy?' she asked.

'I am, Mammy, it's made me feel better. I don't know why I was so scared of going.'

'You're a sensitive girl, Cissy, and there's no harm in that.'

I walked over to the granddaddy and knelt down in front of the fire. 'I've been to see Nora,' I said, holding my hands out towards the flames.

Granddaddy nodded his old head. 'Yes, your mammy said.'

'And I wasn't scared.'

'You have nothing to fear from the dead,' he said. 'It's the living you have to worry about.'

'I think you're right,' I said, smiling at him.

I stood up and went across to Mammy. 'I found out the strangest thing in the graveyard,' I said, sitting down at the table.

'And what was that?'

'Nora has the same name as Mrs Foley. Don't you think that's strange?'

Mammy didn't answer me; it was as if I hadn't spoken.

'Did you hear what I said, Mammy? Nora's name is Nora Foley. Don't you think that's strange?'

Mammy turned to face me. 'Mrs Foley was Nora's mammy, Cissy.'

I stared at her. 'Nora's mammy? Nora had a mammy and it was Mrs Foley?'

Mammy nodded.

'Did Nora know that Mrs Foley was her mammy?'

'She didn't, she never knew.'

I felt the stirrings of anger in my chest. 'But that's not fair, she should have told her. Nora would have loved to have known she had a mammy. She died not knowing. I think that's the saddest thing I ever heard.'

'It wasn't Mrs Foley's fault, Cissy. She wasn't allowed to tell her. The head of the workhouse said it would cause jealousy among the other children.'

'Then I think the head of the workhouse is cruel and mean and I hate him for it, Mammy. I do. I hate him for it.'

'Nora didn't suffer because of it, Cissy. Mrs Foley loved that little girl with all her heart, even though she could never lay claim to her.'

'Bastards, the lot of them,' muttered Granddaddy from his chair by the fire.

'Didn't stop you sending us up there though, did it?' snapped Mammy.

The granddaddy made a sort of snorty sound like the pigs up at Collins's farm but didn't answer.

Mammy sat down at the table. She reached across and held my hand.

'Kate Foley and meself went into the workhouse on the same day. You and Nora were born only hours apart, maybe that's why you were always so close.'

'Did you look after me in there?'

'I was allowed to care for you until you were weaned and then I was moved to the women's section. It broke my heart to leave you, Cissy. I saw you as often as I could when you were little and only because Kate Foley sneaked me in but I knew that I was going to get her in trouble if I was caught so I bided my time until we could be together. The day I laid claim to you as my own and we walked out of those gates was the happiest day of my life.'

I could feel the tears behind my eyes. I had never known that Mammy had taken care of me, that I'd been held in her arms and loved. Her heart must have broken to leave me. I was beginning to understand why she got so cross.

'What about Mrs Foley?'

'Nora didn't thrive, so Kate was allowed to stay with her longer. At that time the nursery was run by a gobshite of a woman called Mrs Riley. But she died, so Kate took over, on the understanding that no one should know that she was Nora's mother.'

'It's still sad though, isn't it?'

'It is, but at least Nora was with her mother even if she never knew it.'

'We both loved Mrs Foley.'

'I know you did and that made leaving you less hard because I knew that she would look after you. Kate was, and still is, a good, kind woman.'

'Do you think I should go and see her?'

'I think she'd like that, Cissy.'

CHAPTER EIGHTEEN

Christmas at the Hall was magical. There was a great big tree in the hallway and another in the drawing room, hung with silver and gold and glass and wooden ornaments, filling the house with the smell of the woods and pine and growing things. Huge garlands of winter foliage were wrapped around the banisters and draped across the marble mantelpiece. Tradesmen were coming and going all week, bringing hams and turkeys, oranges and sweetmeats. The butcher's boy carried the turkeys into the kitchen by their scrawny necks, swinging them towards Annie, making her squeal in terror.

Mrs Hickey never stopped moving or giving orders. She had the girls from the village come to help make sausagemeat and mincemeat, butcher the joints, prepare brandy butter and other treats, and peel and blanch vegetables and fruit. She spent hours up in the drawing room with Mrs Bretton devising menus and then adding extra ingredients to the lists she'd pinned up all around the kitchen so that there would always be plenty to eat for everyone, for no matter what time of day or night someone might be in need of a little refreshment.

The kitchen itself smelled of cinnamon and fried meat and pastry. Pies and puddings were lined up in the pantry on trays ready to be cooked and served. There were terrines and pastes in jars, potted shrimp and gentleman's relish with a thick layer of butter on the top to keep it fresh. Mrs Hickey was constantly baking bread and mince pies. Her face grew red and shiny as she knelt in front of the oven, sliding trays of food onto the shelves. There was a permanent circle of sweat under her armpits staining her grey dress. Every time she was called upstairs she had to change into a clean one, which made her mumble under her breath about only having one pair of hands. Every now and then she burnt herself on the oven or a hot tray and she took her anger out on whichever poor soul was closest to her.

It was hard work but I loved the bustle of it all. I loved the glow of the candles that were lit in the drawing room after dark and how they were reflected in the grand mirrors and the silverware and the baubles that hung from the branches of the tree. You could feel the excitement. Parties were being planned, and guests would be coming. The men would be bringing their valets and chauffeurs. During the rest of the year, the Brettons only kept a small staff to run the house but at Christmas, as well as the girls from the village, extra staff was taken on; waiters and grooms to look after the horses. Some guests came by car but many would still be coming by horse and carriage.

On Christmas evening, once our duties were over, there was going to be a party downstairs for all the staff. In between baking and cleaning, the girls giggled and talked about what they were going to wear and how they should do their hair and who it was they hoped would grab them for a kiss under the mistletoe. All of this chatter and gossip was driving Mrs Hickey mad; she had no inclination to be kissed under the mistletoe or anywhere else for that matter, all that concerned her was the amount of food she was able to churn out before the big day.

In the cellar, the best bottles of wine were dusted off and the brandy and port were all ready to be decanted. Mr Bretton kept his cigars locked in a cabinet in the smoking room and they were taken out. I confess I liked the woody smell of them although of course the women didn't smoke. Bridie explained that their lungs weren't made the same as men's.

We prepared all the bedrooms, making up the beds for guests and keeping them aired with bedpans. We polished the woodwork and the mirrors and got down on our hands and knees to make sure the floors were spotless. We could not have worked harder if we'd tried, and we didn't mind it for a moment because we were all full of the spirit of Christmas and we were as cheerful as the little robins that sat on the handle of the gardener's spade while he was digging up the winter veg.

Two days before Christmas, a tall young man walked into the kitchen. Mrs Hickey wiped her hands on a tea towel and stood beaming at him.

'What do they feed you at that school of yours? I swear you've grown a foot since I last saw you,' she said.

'The truth is, Mrs Hickey, they starve me. I intend to eat you out of house and home.'

'Oh, Master Peter, it's good to have you back,' she said, laughing.

'And it's good to be back.'

I stared at him – yes, I could see it now; those kind eyes and lovely smile. But he didn't look like a boy any more, he looked like a man and oh, he was handsome, with his brown curly hair and blue eyes! I couldn't take my eyes off him.

Mrs Hickey saw me looking at him.

'Master Peter,' she said, 'this is Cissy.'

'Oh, Cissy and I are old friends, isn't that right?' he said, winking at me.

I could feel my face burning up as I remembered the last time I saw him and what I had called his sister.

'Old friends, eh?' said Mrs Hickey, looking a bit confused.

'We met when we were children. If I remember rightly, you were delivering our milk.'

'Yes, Master Peter, I was.'

'And now you're all grown-up and quite the young lady.'

I didn't answer; it was as if someone had sewn my mouth up.

'Is your sister home yet?' asked Mrs Hickey.

At the mention of Miss Caroline, I could feel my face starting to redden again.

'She's arriving this afternoon and I expect we shall all know about it. Well, I just came down to wish you a very happy Christmas, Mrs Hickey.'

'Oh, and a very happy Christmas to you as well, Master Peter.'

At the door he turned back and smiled at me. 'Happy Christmas, Cissy,' he said. Then he was gone and the kitchen was suddenly a very dull place indeed.

CHAPTER NINETEEN

I'd worked all my days off in the weeks leading up to Christmas, so Mrs Bretton said that I could go home on Christmas Eve and attend Midnight Mass as long as I was back at the crack of dawn on Christmas morning to help Mrs Hickey prepare for the big day.

Me and Annie were sent off to collect logs from the woodshed. As we opened the kitchen door, Mrs Hickey screamed at us.

'Jesus Mary and Joseph!' she yelled. 'Would you ever close that door?'

'I don't know how she thinks we can go outside without opening the door first,' complained Annie, shutting it quickly behind us.

It was bitterly cold outside with a wind coming off the sea that would take your nose off you and yet I stood still, looking out over the garden. The grass was covered in crisp white frost that crunched under our feet and sparkled in the thin morning light. It spread out before us like a glistening blanket tumbling down to the water's edge. The black branches of the trees stood stark against the whiteness of it all.

'What are you doing, Cissy?' scolded Annie.

'Just looking,' I said.

'Sure, this is no time to be taking in the view. We'll have Mrs Hickey on our backs if fires aren't lit before the family wakes up.'

'But don't you think it's beautiful, Annie?'

'I don't have time for such things,' she said, bending down and lifting a heavy log into the basket.

'Give me your hand,' I said.

'Oh, Cissy!'

'Come on, give me your hand.'

Annie sighed, but reached towards me and I helped her up. We stood together looking out over the garden. Our breath was like wispy clouds floating around us and drifting off into the cold air.

'Well?' I said.

'It's nice, alright,' said Annie. 'I'll grant you that.'

I closed my eyes and breathed in the sharpness of this December morning and I remembered a poem in one of the books I'd borrowed from Colm's father.

'A thing of beauty is a joy for ever,' I recited, 'Its loveliness increases; it will never pass into nothingness…'

And then a voice joined mine, a deep voice.

'But still will keep a bower quiet for us, and a sleep full of sweet dreams, and health, and quiet breathing.'

I opened my eyes to see Master Peter standing in front of me, smiling. 'Mr Keats, Cissy, my favourite poet… but where did you learn that?'

It seemed that every time I saw Master Peter, I was making a fool of myself. Who was I to be spouting poetry when I should be knowing my place and helping Annie with the logs? 'Out of a book,' I mumbled.

I glanced at Annie, who looked as if she wanted the ground to swallow her up.

Master Peter nodded his head. 'We should all take the time to look at the beauty around us but we are mostly too busy to appreciate it.' He smiled at me. 'I'm glad that you do, Cissy.'

I didn't know what to say except, 'I have to get the logs in.'

'I'm keeping you from your work. Have a nice day, Cissy,' he said, walking away from me.

'Blimey, Cissy,' said Annie, 'imagine Master Peter talking to you like you were a proper person!'

'I am a proper person, Annie, and so are you.'

'We're not like them, though, are we?'

'But we're like us and that's the way we are meant to be.'

'I suppose so,' said Annie reluctantly.

I could barely feel my fingers as I lifted the cold heavy logs into the basket, then taking a handle each, we carried them upstairs. We were sweating by the time we reached the drawing room, where we cleaned out the ashes from the grate and lit the fire. We held our cold hands out towards the flames, slowly getting some warmth back into them. By the time we had done the same in all the bedrooms we were more than ready for our breakfast. There were more people than usual sitting at the long wooden table and amidst the chatter and the laughter I was able to think about what had happened in the garden without anyone commenting on my silence. Maybe I hadn't made such a fool of myself. Master Peter had looked pleased that I knew that poem and it was nice to think that we had a mutual friend in Mr Keats.

After lunch, Bridie came rushing into the kitchen. 'Quick, Cissy,' she said. 'Miss Caroline has arrived. I need you to help with her bags.'

My heart sank as I followed Bridie out to the front of the house. A big shiny car was standing on the drive and a gorgeous young girl was being helped out of it.

'Welcome home, Miss Caroline,' said Bridie, reaching for one of the many bags.

'Thank you, Bridie.'

'This is…' said Bridie, gesturing towards me.

The girl glared at me. 'I know who *she* is,' she said, before brushing past and climbing the steps up to the front door.

'Jesus!' said Bridie. 'What in heaven's name was all that about?'

I reached for one of the bags. 'She remembers me,' I said, 'from before.'

'From before what?'

'From before we grew up, from when we were children. Don't you remember, Bridie? Don't you remember when I called her Miss Baggy Knickers?'

Bridie nodded her head. 'Oh dear! Well, it looks like you've got yourself an enemy there.'

I couldn't get Miss Caroline out of my mind for the rest of the day. I'd hoped she wouldn't recognise me but she had, of course she had, and now like Bridie said, I'd made an enemy and I knew I must do my best to stay out of her way as much as I could.

Once I'd finished work, I ran up to my room. Annie came in just as I was changing out of my uniform.

'You're awful lucky, Cissy,' she said, sitting down on the bed. 'I wish I had a home to go to.'

I sat down beside her. 'Maybe one day you'll have a home of your own, Annie.'

'And what chance do I have of that ever happening?'

'We never know what's going to happen in the future, none of us do. I bet you never thought you'd ever leave the workhouse and get this fine job, did you?'

'You're right, I didn't and I'm grateful but sometimes I long for a place to call my own. A little cottage with my own front door and my own hearth to sit beside. I dream of it all the time.'

'I'll light a candle for you tonight when I go to Mass and I'll ask the Blessed Virgin to look down kindly on you and ask her son to grant your wish.'

'Thanks, Cissy. You're a good friend, my best friend.'

I put my arms around her and kissed her cheek. 'You never know, Annie, tomorrow night at the party some young man might sweep you off your feet and carry you away to your own little cottage.'

'And pigs might fly,' she said, grinning.

'So they might. It's Christmas and at Christmas anything can happen. Anyway, I'll be back first thing in the morning.'

It was pitch-black as I walked down the drive towards Colm.

'Let's get you home,' he said, taking my hand and helping me up beside him.

'Thanks for getting me,' I said.

'You're more than welcome. Your mammy and granddaddy are only longing to see you. It's been weeks since you were home.'

'You wouldn't believe how much work there is to do, Colm. Christmas is a very grand affair at the Hall and you should see all the food. There's tons of it and it's not like the food we eat, even the potatoes are different. They get them shipped over from England and you'll never believe this, but they peel the skins off them! They do, they peel the skins!'

'Well, they are very welcome to their English potatoes, Cissy, for I've never eaten a finer potato than the ones we grow here.'

'Oh, I wasn't meaning theirs are better, just different.'

Colm didn't speak all the way home and I was feeling cross. I'd only mentioned the English potatoes, for God's sake! You'd think I'd said something awful about the Pope, not a sack of potatoes.

'Why are you so cross, Colm Doyle?' I said.

'Who says I'm cross?'

'I do, and I don't know why. Are you so possessive of the Irish potato that you begrudge the Brettons eating a bag of English ones?'

We looked at each other and both burst out laughing at the foolishness of it all.

When we got to the cottage Mr Collins was coming out the door.

'Merry Christmas, Cissy, and to you, Colm,' he said, waving at us.

'And a merry Christmas to you, Mr Collins,' I said.

We opened the door and I was nearly knocked off my feet by Buddy, then Mammy threw her arms around me and Granddaddy was smiling. Suddenly I didn't care about all the food at Bretton Hall or the trees or the lights because I was home among my family and it was the only place I wanted to be on this Christmas Eve. I took off my coat and hung it behind the door.

'What was Mr Collins doing here?' I said.

'He came by to see Buddy,' said Mammy.

Then there was a snort from the granddaddy: 'He did in his eye,' he said.

CHAPTER TWENTY

I had always loved Midnight Mass. I loved everything about it: the candles, the carols, the smell of incense and Father Kelly in his gold and white Christmas vestments. I loved seeing the Baby Jesus in the manger and the Virgin Mary looking so tenderly down at him and Joseph standing beside her, but this year I just felt a great heaviness in my heart. I remembered another Christmas with Nora kneeling beside me, her little face so lovely in the glow of the candles and now she was gone, taken up to heaven when she was still just a young girl. I tried to make myself feel better, knowing she was with Jesus and the angels and that now she'd know that Mrs Foley was her mammy, but it didn't help. I wanted her here with me, I needed her more than Jesus did.

The next morning, I got up early – I wanted to spend some time with the mammy before I went back to the Hall. It felt like the middle of the night when I came downstairs. Mammy was at the stove stirring the porridge and, to my disbelief, Granddaddy was piling peat onto the fire. The room felt grand and warm. Buddy ran to me and I bent down and ruffled his soft fur.

'What are you doing up so early, Granddaddy?'

'I thought I'd see you before you were off to the Hall and your mammy has a surprise for you.'

I looked across at Mammy, who was smiling at me. She reached into the cupboard and brought out a parcel, wrapped in brown paper and tied with string.

'Happy Christmas, Cissy,' she said, handing it to me.

I sat at the table and unwrapped the parcel. My eyes filled with tears as I stared down at the beautiful pale blue dress in front of me. I lifted it carefully out of the paper and held it up against me.

'Oh, Mammy,' I said, jumping up from the table and putting my arms around her. 'Thank you, oh, thank you.'

'I hope it fits, child, I had to take a bit of a guess. You know Mrs Quirk down at the laundry?'

I nodded.

'Well, her daughter is a dressmaker and I got her to run it up for me. Now, away and try it on.'

I kissed her cheek and ran upstairs. The dress felt like silk as I slid it over my head, letting it fall in soft folds to just below my knees. It fitted like a glove.

Mammy and the granddaddy were waiting as I came into the kitchen.

Mammy nodded. 'It's as lovely as I hoped it would be. It brings out your eyes.'

'Granddaddy?' I said, spinning around in front of him.

'You look grand,' he said.

'I have nothing for you, Mammy.'

'It's enough that you're here, Cissy.'

Colm was soon at the door to take me up to the Hall. As we trotted through the town, he reached down and handed me a paper bag.

'For me?'

'Who else?'

I opened the bag and inside was a brooch. It was so dark that I couldn't make out the colour but it sparkled and it felt smooth and cold in my hand.

'It's only glass,' said Colm, 'but one day, when I'm rich, I'll get you a proper one.'

'I wouldn't want another, Colm,' I said, reaching across to touch his hand. 'I only want this one.'

'That's grand then. Happy Christmas, Cissy.'

'Happy Christmas, Colm.'

*

There was so much activity in the kitchen that I don't think anyone saw me arrive. I ran upstairs to the bedroom. Annie was trying to squash her unruly hair into her cap.

'I wish I had hair like yours, Cissy,' she said, 'and not a bloody bush on top of my head!'

'You have lovely hair, Annie. Sure, people would die for those curls.'

'Thanks, but I think you're just being kind because you're my friend.'

'Not at all, your hair is beautiful.'

Annie turned away from the mirror and put her arms around me. 'Happy Christmas, Cissy.'

The kitchen smelt of spices and berries and winter greenery freshly cut from the garden to decorate the table. Mrs Hickey was yelling at everyone and her face was shiny from the heat of the ovens; she kept mopping it on the sleeve of her shirt.

Everyone seemed to have a job to do. A couple of lads who'd been taken on to serve at table hurried past with trays of glasses that sparkled like diamonds in the dim corridor. Everything was exciting and different and I couldn't wait to get caught up in it all.

Mrs Hickey spotted me and Annie in the doorway. 'Don't just stand there gawping like a couple of eejits! Annie, come here and get cracking on the veg and you, Cissy, help Bridie upstairs with the breakfast or am I expected to do everything myself?'

'Yes, Mrs Hickey,' said Annie. 'I mean, no, Mrs Hickey. I mean, I'll do it right away, Mrs Hickey.'

I grinned at Annie and ran up to the breakfast room, smoothing my apron as I went. Bridie was taking the lids off the breakfast trays. 'Mrs Hickey sent me to help,' I said.

Bridie smiled at me. 'Thanks, Cissy. Did you enjoy seeing your folks last night?'

'It was lovely but it was hard saying goodbye this morning.'

'You're going to be so busy this day you won't have time to think about anything but serving the Brettons.'

'I'm sure you're right, it's pretty mad down in the kitchen.'

'Now, all you have to do is pour the tea and coffee, they'll help themselves to the food – and tuck your hair into your cap.'

I pushed the stray bits of hair under my white cap and waited for the family to arrive.

'They'll be guests you won't know, Cissy, strangers, but don't let that worry you, just pour the tea and coffee and look pleasant.'

'What if they speak to me?'

'They'll be too busy feeding their faces to be speaking to the likes of us.'

'That'll suit me fine.'

Bridie was right, it was as if the pair of us were invisible. They piled their plates with bacon and liver, kidneys and black pudding, eggs and soda bread as if they hadn't eaten in a year. The smell of the food was making my mouth water. It seemed like hours ago that I'd eaten the thin porridge and I was feeling hungry.

I heard her before I saw her. She flounced into the room on the arm of a young boy, giggling and looking up at him, tossing her shiny, golden hair over her shoulder. She stopped dead when she saw me. I kept my eyes down, I didn't want any trouble.

'Tea or coffee, Miss Caroline?' asked Bridie quickly.

I could feel Miss Caroline's eyes burning into me. I could feel beads of sweat prickling under my armpits.

'Orange juice. And *she* can carry it to the table.'

I knew she meant me.

'I'm sure Cissy has better things to do than wait on us.'

I looked up and Master Peter was smiling at me.

'Isn't it her job to wait on us, Peter?'

The boy who'd come in with Miss Caroline was looking awkward. 'I'll take it to the table for you, Caroline,' he said.

'Good man,' said Peter.

Caroline looked furious. She hated me, that was for sure. If I was going to keep my job, I would have to stay out of her way as much as I could.

'Don't worry, Cissy,' whispered Bridie. 'She'll be back to school soon and anyway, it looks as if you have your own protector in Master Peter.'

I nodded in agreement. 'He's awful nice, isn't he?'

'It's hard to believe they have the same parents. There's no airs and graces about that boy, there never has been.'

I looked across the room and watched as Master Peter ate his food and talked to the people beside him. He had a lovely easy smile that drew people to him. I'd never tire of looking at that face. Just then he looked up and caught my eye. I could feel a rush of heat to my face as if I'd been caught doing something I shouldn't. I lowered my head, what was I thinking? I had no right to be going red and shy and lowering my eyes like a proper lady. I was a servant for God's sake and he was an Honourable, but then I remembered Colm saying, 'You're as good as anyone else, Cissy,' and that made me stand a little taller.

I was glad when breakfast was over and I could go back downstairs, where I belonged.

The kitchen was a hub of activity. A couple of girls were garnishing trays of shiny pink salmon, whose dead eyes stared up to the ceiling, with very thinly sliced circles of cucumber, overlapping them slightly so it looked as if the salmon had cucumber scales. The girls were concentrating hard on their work; one had the tip of her tongue stuck out of the corner of her mouth. Another girl was decorating an enormous trifle, carefully slicing pieces of red and green angelica into diamonds and arranging the shapes on top of the cream. A fourth was stirring the gravy. A woman from the village with great big arms was carving into a whole leg of cooked ham, slice after slice of pink meat falling onto the plate in front of her as she sawed at it with a knife as long as my leg. Great big pans full of root vegetables – potatoes, carrots, parsnips and swede – were bubbling on the hob. Steam filled the air, and a mixture of different smells, some sweet, some savoury; all of them delicious. A row of tureens was lined up on the table, lids off, insides gleaming, waiting for food to be put inside them, their lids put on, and then taken to the dining room, where they would stand on the hot plate on top of the sideboard. Girls were running up and downstairs, laying the table, putting out the best silver cutlery that had been polished to a fine shine and the finest glassware. Bottles of wine had been left outside to keep cool.

Mrs Hickey was sliding food into the oven, ladling hot steaming soup into silver tureens, yelling orders, screaming for the back door to be opened and screaming for it to be closed.

It was mad, it was hectic, it was noisy and crazy and busy, but it was fun. Even for those of us working, it was fun. We all pulled together. Everyone did their bit to make this Christmas Day the best it could be.

Once dinner was over and everything cleared away, we were all able to take a break. Mrs Hickey nodded off beside the fire on her old chair with her feet resting on a stool. She'd worked hard, she deserved a rest.

'I'm going for a bit of a sleep,' said Annie. 'Are you coming up, Cissy?'

'I think I'll go for a walk.'

'Out there? Jesus, it's freezing!'

I smiled at her. 'I think I'll survive.'

I went into the boot room and took my coat down from behind the door, then I wrapped my shawl around my head and went outside. At first the cold air took my breath away but it was lovely after the heat of the house. I started walking, following the path down to the sea. Snow still sat on the trees, and every so often the wind moved the branches, sending a flurry of soft white powder around my shoulders. Everything was so white and shiny that my eyes were dazzled by the brightness of it. As I got closer, I could hear the waves gently lapping the beach, smell the seaweed and taste salt on my lips. I jumped down onto the wet sand and walked towards the shore. My boots sank into the wetness, leaving footprints behind me as I walked. I stood still and looked along the coast. The tall spire of the church rose above the town like a needle piercing the steel-grey sky and above the church I could just make out the hazy outline of the workhouse. How different my life was now from the world inside those thick stone walls. Now I was free to walk along this beach and watch the little waves trickling into the shore. I could run if I wanted to, I could do anything I had a mind to do. If only my dear friend Nora could be with me this day, then my happiness would be complete.

I thought about Mammy and the granddaddy and hoped that they were having a nice time. Mr Collins was coming to dinner and bringing a fine fat turkey with him. Part of me wished I was there with them in the little cottage in Paradise Alley, helping Mammy with the cooking and chatting to the granddaddy, maybe walking up the lane to wish Colm and his daddy a happy Christmas and giving Blue a carrot. I put my hand in my pocket and took out the brooch that Colm had given me. I held it up to the light: I could see now that it was ice blue, like the sea and the sky and the snow on the trees and the frost on the water. I knew that every time I looked at it, I would remember that Colm had given it to me on this Christmas Day. I pulled my shawl closer around my head and began to walk back to the Hall.

CHAPTER TWENTY-ONE

The living room and dining room of the big house were separated by a partition wall that could be folded back to make one big room. This was where the party was to be held. The carpets had been rolled up in each room, most of the furniture removed, the fireplaces and window ledges decorated with boughs of holly and ivy. Mistletoe had been hung from the doorframes and beams, and swags of gold and white fabric caught with glass baubles hung around the walls, giving the party room the feel of an ocean liner, or something else, something really grand. The curtains were tied back, so that the windows could be opened later, if necessary.

I stood at the door to the room, gazing at it in admiration. The fires had been lit earlier, but allowed to die down so as not to make the room too hot for dancing. Small tables and chairs had been placed around the edges so people could have a sit down if they so wished. The grand piano was at the far end of the dining room, polished to a glossy shine and covered in candlesticks. I didn't think I'd ever seen a room look so romantic.

I'd heard someone mention that the floor was special, sprung for dancing. I stepped forward. It didn't feel any different to me but then I was no floor expert and no dancing expert either. I closed my eyes and tried to imagine how it might feel to dance in the arms of a handsome young man. Just as I was about to be carried away in this daydream, I heard voices from the Hall behind me and I scuttled back out and hid behind a thick velvet curtain, just in time. The first guests were arriving, coming through the front door, out of the dark winter night, bringing with them a rush of cold air. They gasped in amazement as they saw the tree standing in the hall beneath the stairwell and it did look beautiful with its streamers and candles and baubles. They said good evening to one another and to the staff and then they took off their coats and gave them to one of the hired boys, who took them upstairs to hang up in the spare bedrooms. More guests were arriving all the time.

I glanced at my reflection in the big hall mirror. I was wearing a little white cap on my head, and a white apron over my dress. My eyes were bright, my cheeks slightly flushed. I looked tidy and neat, professional.

I tucked a stray hair behind my ears and went over to the side-board, where a young man dressed in waiting clothes was pouring champagne into flutes that were already organised on silver trays; twelve glasses to a tray. I picked up a tray of full glasses, the bowls of the glasses clinking on their narrow stems, the honey-coloured champagne fizzing and dancing. Walking as carefully as I could, putting each foot down flat, one in front of the other, I carried the tray to the living room door and I stood beside it and as each guest passed me I asked: 'Would you like a glass of champagne, Madam? Sir?'

They all smiled at me, said thank you and took a glass. It was wondrous to see them, the ladies especially. Oh, those dresses! Silk shimmering in the light, velvet stoles with fur collars, the brilliant, tiny beads sewn into the bodices. The older ladies had darker, more complicated dresses with embroidery and lace and sequins, but it was the younger ones – their shoulders bare, skin creamy white, jewels at their throats and ears – it was the younger ladies who held my eye. They wore light colours, bright colours, dresses that clung to their hips and chests, and their hair was all beautifully fashioned and pinned with flowers and beads and jewels too. The men were smart, I'm not saying they weren't, with their moustaches oiled and their hair all shiny and dark, their shoes polished, their trousers creased. The men, scented with cigar smoke and cold air, were one thing, but those beautiful, perfumed young ladies, gathering in the living room with their glasses of champagne and chattering like a flock of exotic birds, those ladies were something else altogether. I wondered what the mammy would make of it all. I had a feeling she wouldn't be that impressed. My mammy wasn't impressed by finery and jewels but I couldn't help but be wide-eyed with wonder at it all.

My tray was empty in no time and I returned to the sideboard to fetch another.

'Thirsty work, socialising,' said the wine waiter. He winked at me. I picked up the tray; I could hardly wait to get back to my position.

As I walked carefully across the room, head down, balancing the tray, I was suddenly knocked off my feet. I went one way and the precious tray of beautiful crystal glasses went the other, crashing and smashing, spurting golden liquid across the beautiful polished floor. I heard gasps from the guests as I hit the floor.

'You want to watch where you're going,' said a familiar voice.

I looked up into the mean eyes of Miss Caroline Bretton sneering down at me. She'd done it on purpose, I knew she had, and I felt like tearing at her beautiful hair and scratching at her face. I wanted a real fight, a rolling-around-the-floor sort of a fight, but I couldn't, could I? Because she was gentry and I was nobody – and I'd lose my job.

She swept away, her dress almost touching my face as she went. I started to pick up the pieces of glass. I'd probably have to pay for the damage, so I was relieved to find that not all of the glasses had broken.

People were having to step around me, I felt such a fool. Tears of anger burned behind my eyes. Everything had been so lovely and now it was all spoilt because of that horrible girl. I hated her, I did. I hated her! Father Kelly said we should love our fellow man; well, Miss Caroline Baggy Knickers wasn't a man, she was a devil so it didn't count, did it?

And then Master Peter was kneeling beside me.

'Don't worry, Cissy,' he said gently. 'You won't be in any trouble. I saw what happened and I shall tell my parents.'

'I don't want to make a fuss.'

'You're bleeding.'

I looked down at the blood dripping onto the floor, mingling with the champagne.

Master Peter took a hankie out of his pocket and wrapped it gently around my hand. 'Now go downstairs and get it seen to, I'll get a boy to clean this up.'

'But…'

'Don't worry about anything, it's only a few glasses.'

'Thank you,' I said, standing up. 'I'll wash your hankie and return it to you.'

'Keep it,' he said, grinning at me.

Oh, he's kind, I thought as I ran downstairs. He might be an Honourable but he didn't look down on me. He made me feel as if we were the same, like he was talking to a friend. I'd like to be Master Peter's friend, I really would.

'That young madam needs to be taught a lesson,' said Bridie, as she held my hand under the running water.

'Master Peter gave me his hankie,' I said.

Bridie looked at me. 'Be careful, Cissy,' she said.

'Why?'

'I think you know why. He's a lovely boy but no good will come of it. I've seen it before and it always ends bad. I don't want you getting hurt, girl.'

'I won't, I just thought it would be nice to be his friend.'

'Folks like him can never be friends with folks like us.'

'But we're all equal in God's eyes, Bridie.'

'It's not God's eyes you need to worry about, Cissy, it's the Brettons' and Caroline in particular misses nothing.'

Once the festivities were over and the guests had retired to the lounge it was time for our own little party in the kitchen. Me and Annie were in the bedroom, getting ready.

'I wish I had something pretty to wear,' said Annie, scowling at her reflection in the mirror. 'I wish I had a pretty dress like yours; you look lovely, Cissy.'

I smoothed down the skirt of the blue dress that Mammy had given me. I almost felt beautiful in it but it made me feel bad that Annie didn't have a lovely dress as well. I opened the drawer and took out the velvet ribbon. I was just about to tie it in my hair when I looked at poor Annie standing there in her grey dress.

'Kneel down in front of me, Annie,' I said. She did as she was told and I wound the ribbon into her curly hair and tied it with a bow, leaving two strands floating down the back of her head. 'There now,' I said.

Annie spun around, grinning. 'Oh, thank you, Cissy.'

'You're welcome,' I said, smiling at her. 'Now let's go and join the party.'

CHAPTER TWENTY-TWO

The kitchen was full of people, maids and grooms and valets, all smiling and laughing, out to have a good time after working so hard all day. A young lad I'd never seen before was playing the accordion and one of Mr Bretton's grooms was playing the tin whistle. The long wooden table had been pushed back against the wall to provide a space for the dancing. It was so wonderful. Annie hung back. 'Come on, Annie,' I said, catching hold of her hand. 'There's nothing to fear here.'

Annie looked doubtful. 'I don't know half these people, Cissy,' she whispered.

'And they don't know *you* so we're all in the same boat, aren't we? Anyway, I'm here and I'm not going anywhere.'

Annie didn't look convinced but she followed me into the room. There were jugs of orange juice on the side for the women and beer for the men. I poured some juice for me and Annie and found two chairs for us to sit on.

'Better?' I said.

Annie nodded her head. 'As long as you don't leave me.'

'Now why would I be doing that?'

'Some young man might whisk you away from me.'

I thought of Colm with his dark hair and warm eyes. 'I'm not for being whisked anywhere, Annie.'

Some of the girls had started to dance in the middle of the floor, lifting their skirts, showing their petticoats and boots.

'These village girls are very brazen,' said Annie.

'Sure, they're only having a good time. It's harmless enough and anyway, it's Christmas.'

'Well, they look no better than they should, Cissy, and just because it's Christmas, that's no excuse to be showing off your undergarments to the whole world.'

A few brave boys joined the girls. I wished I could dance, I'd maybe have a go myself.

'Can you dance, Annie?'

'I can, as it happens,' she said, smiling. 'When I was young, my mammy and daddy taught us all to dance. Sure, we used to have a grand time in our little cottage. I wish I was back there now,' she said softly.

I reached across and held her hand, 'But you will always have your memories, Annie, no one can take those away from you.'

Annie brightened. 'You're right, I don't know what's wrong with me tonight.'

'I think Christmas takes a lot of people like that, it makes you think of happier times, but maybe we should just enjoy what we have now and be grateful for it.'

'Um, excuse me?' said a voice.

There was a boy standing in front of us, smiling down at Annie.

'Would you like to dance?' he asked, shyly.

'Go on, Annie,' I encouraged.

She looked petrified, so I gave a her a little nudge. 'Yes, she would,' I said to the boy.

Annie glared at me but she stood up and walked onto the floor with him.

I watched as the boy spun her around, her eyes sparkled and her cheeks were flushed. She looked across at me and grinned. She was having a lovely time and it made me so happy.

It was getting hot, so I fetched my shawl and made my way outside for some fresh air. I didn't wander far beyond the back door as it was pitch-black but it was nice to lean against the wall with the light from the windows and the sound of the music and laughter close by.

Just then the door opened. 'Not dancing?'

I did a little bob. 'I came out for some air,' I replied.

Master Peter smiled. 'There's no need for that, Cissy.'

I didn't answer; I didn't know what to say.

'It looks like they're having a great time in there.'

'I think they are,' I said.

He guided me away from the door. 'I have something for you,' he said, handing me a small parcel.

I couldn't believe that Master Peter was giving me a present. I undid the wrapping. Inside was a book but it was so dark, I couldn't see the title.

'The Collected Poems of our friend, Mr Yeats,' he said.

'I can't take it,' I said, trying to give it back.

He pressed it into my hands. 'Happy Christmas, Cissy,' he said, gently kissing my cheek.

'Happy Christmas, Master Peter.'

'Please, just Peter. At least when we're on our own,' he added quickly.

He was standing so close to me, we were almost touching. I'd felt chilly when I'd stepped out of the kitchen but now I felt as warm as if it was a summer's day.

'Well, I'll let you get back to your party,' he said, and walked away.

I touched my cheek where he had kissed me and I hugged the little book to my heart.

I was glad it was dark. I was glad that I was on my own for surely anyone could see my face that I knew was flushed and my eyes that I knew sparkled. I leaned against the wall. 'Happy Christmas, Peter,' I whispered.

That night in bed, I hugged my pillow and pretended that it was Peter. I thought of the little book he had given me and how he had kissed my cheek. He must like me, he must. I closed my eyes and drifted off to sleep with his handsome face filling my dreams.

Things seemed rather dull at the Hall once the festivities were over, except for one thing. Master Peter didn't have to go back to school for another week but I supposed that meant neither would Miss Caroline.

'Isn't Miss Caroline getting a bit old for school, Bridie?' I asked, as we were putting clean linen on the beds.

'Oh, she's not going back to school, Cissy.'

My heart dropped. 'She's not staying at home, is she?'

'She's going to a fancy place in Switzerland to be finished off.'

'What do you mean, finished off?'

'She has to be taught all the social graces before she gets presented into society.'

'What will they teach her?'

'She'll be taught how to walk and stuff like that.'

I giggled. 'She already knows how to walk, doesn't she?'

'I know, it's daft, isn't it? They'd be better off sending her somewhere that would teach her how to be kind.'

'I don't think she'll ever be kind, Bridie.'

'Neither do I, but once she gets presented at court she'll hopefully find herself a feller who's foolish enough to take her on, then she can go and live with him and stop plaguing us with her spiteful ways.'

'Well, that can't come soon enough for me; she's never forgotten what I called her.'

'And I don't think she ever will, Cissy.'

'What about Peter? I mean, Master Peter,' I said quickly. 'Will he have to be finished off too?'

'No, but you can be sure that once his studies are over, he'll be attending all the balls so that he can be introduced to the right sort of girl that will be acceptable to the Brettons as his future wife.'

I busied myself tucking in the corners of the sheet but inside I felt sick. I realised I was falling in love with a boy who could never be mine.

Bridie noticed my silence. 'You must know that's the way it works.'

'Yes, yes, of course I do.'

'But you don't really believe it?'

I shrugged my shoulders.

'I know you like him, Cissy, but he could never walk out with you and if he did, the Brettons would cut him off without a penny to his name. He has to marry into a family like his own, a family with status and money.'

I could feel my eyes filling with tears because I knew that what Bridie was saying was true. I was being a foolish girl to think that a book of poetry and a kiss on the cheek meant anything to him.

'Stick to your own kind, girl, or there'll be trouble ahead, mark my words. I always thought that maybe you and Colm…?'

'So did I, Bridie.'

After we'd finished the beds, there was an hour before lunch had to be served.

'Is it okay if I go for a walk?'

Bridie smiled at me. 'I always think of you as a sensible girl, Cissy. You go for a walk and put the boy out of your mind.'

I knew that she was right and I knew that she was only trying to protect me. 'Don't worry about me,' I said.

It was warmer today as I made my way down the path to the beach. It was still slippery underfoot but the snow had melted. I thought about everything that Bridie had said and I knew I must stop these foolish thoughts and accept what she was saying. I'd been hoping that Peter and me could spend some time together before he left, but now I couldn't wait for him to go.

I heard footsteps behind me. 'Wait up,' called a voice.

I turned around to see Peter running down the path.

'I hope you don't mind me joining you,' he said, grinning. 'I saw you from the drawing room window and I could do with a walk myself.'

I didn't answer him.

'What's wrong?' he asked, falling in step beside me.

'Nothing,' I mumbled.

He caught hold of my arm and stopped me walking.

'Yes, there is. Have I done something, Cissy?'

'What would your parents say if they saw us going for a walk together?'

'But they won't.'

'But if they did? What would they say?'

Peter seemed to be having trouble looking at me.

'I know what they'd say and I know they wouldn't approve and so do you.'

'We'll just have to make sure they don't see us then, won't we?'

'I can't take that chance, Peter. They might tell you off but they'd probably throw me out. Have you thought of that? No, you haven't, have you?'

'I'm sorry, Cissy, but I like you. I like your company, I enjoy being with you.'

'I enjoy being with you too, Peter,' I said sadly.

'Look, we're only young, why can't we just be friends? No one need know, we'll be careful. Please, Cissy. I'd never hurt you, you must know that, don't you?'

'You might not mean to hurt me, Peter, but I fear that you will.'

'I've never met anyone like you before,' said Peter, taking my face in his hands. 'I've been so happy since you came to work for us. Why can't we be friends? It will be our secret, no one need know. Please, Cissy, please.'

I looked into his eyes and I was lost. 'Just friends then, Peter, just friends,' I said. But I knew in my heart that what I felt for Peter was much more than friendship and it scared me.

CHAPTER TWENTY-THREE

And so we became friends and I lived for the times when Peter was home. We became clever at finding secret places where we could be together, away from the prying eyes of Bretton Hall, away from Bridie and Annie and Mrs Hickey. If there were moments when my head told me that this was wrong and that no good could come of it, I brushed those thoughts away; we weren't hurting anyone. If we held hands as we walked beside each other or Peter put his arm around my shoulder, I told myself that this was what good friends did. It was only at night when I closed my eyes that I could admit to myself that friendship was not what I felt when I thought about him. I loved him. I did; I loved him, and I knew what I was doing and I knew it couldn't last, but if friendship was all he could offer then I'd take it and be grateful for it.

If Peter was at home on my days off I told the mammy that I was needed at the Hall. I'm not sure that she believed me. I knew that Colm didn't, but I wanted to spend as much time with Peter as I could.

'Are you going to tell me about it?' he said one day, as we were sitting on the rocks under the lighthouse.

'Tell you about what?' I said.

'I've known you long enough to see that something has changed.'

I stood up and walked towards the water's edge. The sea was calm and still on this lovely spring day. I could feel Colm beside me even before he spoke.

'If it's none of my business then tell me but sometimes it's better to share a worry than carry it on your own.'

'Who says I'm worried?' I snapped. 'There's nothing wrong with me and I haven't changed and I don't need to talk to you about anything, Colm Doyle, so I suggest you keep your own counsel and leave me to mine.'

Colm put his hands on my shoulders and turned me around to face him.

'I care about you, Cissy, and I don't want you to get hurt. If I'm wrong then I'm sorry, but I have a feeling this has something to do with Master Peter Bretton.'

I pulled away from him and started to walk back up the beach.

'And what if it is?' I shouted. 'What is it to you? I'm almost sixteen, I'm not a child any more and I don't have to ask your permission to be friends with Peter.'

'Friends, is it?'

'Yes, friends.'

'Then good luck to you, Cissy Ryan, and I hope it stays fine for ya.'

We walked back home in silence and with every step I took, I felt worse and worse. Colm was my dearest friend, he was like my brother and I'd been mean to him and rude too. I was sorry but I couldn't tell him that because I was full of anger and I needed someone to be angry at. I remembered a time when he had been my whole world, when I only had to see his face to be happy, a time when my dearest wish was to be his wife. Where had those feelings gone?

We parted without saying goodbye and there were tears in my eyes as I opened the door to the cottage.

Mammy was kneeling beside the granddaddy.

'Go for the doctor, Cissy! Get Colm to take you in the cart.'

'What's wrong?'

'It's your granddaddy. Hurry now, hurry!'

I ran out the door and tore up the lane, screaming Colm's name. He ran round the side of the house.

'What's wrong?' he said.

'It's the granddaddy, Colm. We have to get the doctor, we have to get him now.'

'You go back home, Cissy. I'll get the doctor.'

'Please hurry.'

'I'll be as quick as I can, now go home.'

I ran back down Paradise Alley and into the cottage. 'Colm is getting the doctor, Mammy.'

I ran over to Granddaddy's chair. His eyes were closed. Buddy was lying at his feet and he looked up at me as if to say, 'Please help.'

'What's wrong with him, Mammy?'

'I don't know, child. At first I thought he was sleeping but then Buddy started to whine and I knew something was wrong. I can't wake him up, Cissy.'

I took hold of his hand; it felt cold and clammy and his face didn't look right.

'What's wrong with his face?'

'I don't know!'

'He's not going to die, is he?'

Mammy shook her head as if to clear it. 'I don't know, Cissy.'

It felt like forever before Doctor Cassidy pushed open the door. 'Why don't you wait outside, Cissy?' he said.

'But I…'

Colm put his arm around my shoulder. 'Come on, let's give the good doctor a bit of space to do his work.'

I let myself be led outside. 'He can't die, Colm, he *can't.*'

'Now who said anything about dying?'

'I love him.'

'I know you do so I think we should say a little prayer. You never know, Himself might be looking down on us and grant your grandfather the strength to overcome this illness.'

I walked across to Blue and leant my face against his solid back, then I closed my eyes and I begged the Blessed Virgin Mary to ask her son to look down kindly on Malachi Ryan in his hour of need.

Just then Doctor Cassidy pushed open the door and came outside.

'We need to get him up to the infirmary. Can you drive us, Colm?'

'Of course, Doctor.'

Between them they lifted the granddaddy into the cart.

'I'm going with him,' I said.

'So am I,' said the mammy, snatching up her shawl.

Doctor Cassidy rode up beside Colm, and me and the mammy sat either side of the granddaddy. They'd covered him with his old smelly blanket and his face looked calm and untroubled as we sped along.

'What did the doctor say?'

'He thinks your granddaddy has had a stroke, Cissy.'

'What's that?'

'He says it's to do with the brain.'

'But he won't die? He'll get better?'

Mammy looked pale and worried as she looked at me. 'He might be better off dying, child.'

My eyes burned with unshed tears. 'No, he won't because I'll look after him. I will, Mammy. I'll look after him.'

Mammy reached over and held my hand. 'I know you will, love, but I'm not sure that's what he would want.'

'Well, he's not going to die and that's that.'

'Then maybe he won't, Cissy, maybe he won't.'

I smoothed his old head and whispered in his ear, 'I need you, Granddaddy. Please don't leave me.'

As we started to race through the town I saw Buddy running behind us.

'Stop, Colm! I have to get Buddy.'

'Whoa, Blue!' said Colm and we stopped to let Buddy jump up onto the cart.

The infirmary was attached to the workhouse and we were soon going through the big iron gates. Doctor Cassidy ran inside to get help. Two men came out with a stretcher and carried the granddaddy inside.

'The dog won't be allowed in there, Cissy,' said the doctor.

'Don't worry,' said Colm. 'I'll look after him, you all stay as long as you need to.'

I looked at Colm and I felt a rush of gratitude. For as long as I could remember he had been there for me and I knew he always would be. Peter Bretton was as far from my thoughts as he could be. These were the people I loved; these were the people I would always love.

My granddaddy didn't die but he wasn't the man he used to be. He couldn't talk so well and one of his old legs didn't work any more.

'He can't be left, Cissy,' said the mammy. 'Doctor Cassidy thinks he'd be better off in the workhouse, where he can be taken care of properly.'

'No,' I said. 'He has to be here at home, he'll die if he goes in there.'

'But he has to be looked after.'

'Then I'll look after him.'

'How can you do that, girl?'

'I'll leave my job.'

Mammy shook her head. 'I know you love him and I know you want to care for him and I'm proud of you for that, but you wouldn't be able for it. He will need everything doing for him, personal things. It's not a job for a young girl, however much you want to do it.'

'He'll die up there, Mammy.'

'We didn't die, did we?'

'No, but he's old and he'll be among strangers and he won't have Buddy. He'll surely die of a broken heart.'

'Then it's our job to make sure he doesn't. We have to make him believe that he is loved so that he doesn't feel like he's been abandoned.'

'I can do that. I can visit him every evening after work.'

Mammy smiled at me. 'And if he gets the care he needs, then maybe one day he will be well enough to come home again, but for now we have to trust in the goodness of God and those that will care for him.'

'I thought you didn't believe in God, Mammy.'

'I think we all find ourselves believing in Him when death knocks at our door.'

I looked across at Buddy, who had taken to sitting in the grand-daddy's chair. He looked so lost and alone.

'Could we bring Buddy in to see him? He must miss him something terrible. I think if he could see Buddy, it would help him to get better.'

'Didn't the doctor say that no dogs were allowed in there?'

'Buddy's not just a dog, Mammy, he's the granddaddy's best friend.'

Buddy whined as if he knew we were talking about him. 'Poor little feller,' said Mammy. 'He must wonder where he's gone.'

'So can we take him for a visit? Mr Dunne had a dog and no one seemed to mind about him and he smelt as bad as the granddaddy.'

'Perhaps if your granddaddy goes into the workhouse, then Buddy can visit. Maybe it's just the infirmary that don't allow dogs.'

I didn't want the granddaddy to go in there but if it meant that he could see Buddy then maybe it wouldn't be so bad. I went across to the chair and knelt down in front of the little dog. There seemed to be so much pain in those lovely brown eyes that I felt like crying. I smoothed his silky ears and kissed his little nose. 'Don't worry, you'll see him soon, if I have to hide you under my shawl.' Buddy licked my face as if he knew what I was saying.

CHAPTER TWENTY-FOUR

As the year went on and the seasons changed there was little change in my granddaddy. Colm collected me every evening from the Hall; he always had Buddy with him.

I grew to hate going through those big gates. It broke my heart to see Granddaddy sitting in a chair by the window, gazing out but seeming to see nothing. He knew it was me because he held my hand tightly as if he didn't want to let it go. Buddy would jump up onto his lap and the granddaddy would absentmindedly stroke his fur. He tried to speak, but it all came out in a jumble of words that I couldn't understand. When he looked at me, his eyes had a desperation about them as if he was trying to tell me that he didn't want to be there. I talked to him like I used to when I'd first come to the cottage. He hadn't answered me then just like he didn't answer me now. I told him about the goings-on at the Hall and about Miss Baggy Knickers getting finished off in Switzerland. I told him how Buddy sat in his chair by the fire, waiting for him to come home. I even told him about Peter and how much I liked him. It was nice to talk about that, knowing my secret would be safe within these old grey walls. Sometimes I would read to him from the little book of poems by Mr Yeats. He seemed to enjoy listening to me; he'd close his eyes and his face would become calm and peaceful. I always told him how much he was loved so that he wouldn't feel abandoned by me or the mammy.

It was hard to get Buddy off his lap when it was time to leave. He'd whine all the way home and couldn't be comforted. I knew how he felt because there were times when I wanted to scream and shout at the unfairness of it all. What sort of God would leave my granddaddy in that state? He might have made some mistakes in his life but I knew he was sorry for them. He didn't deserve what he'd got. Maybe the mammy had been right when she'd said it would have been better if he'd died. I understood now why she'd said it; she was wiser than me. I'd wanted the granddaddy to live for my sake, I hadn't thought about what *he* might have wanted. I had a lot of growing up to do. Sometimes what *you* want isn't the most important thing in the world.

I was seeing less and less of Peter because I spent every spare moment up at the workhouse and he didn't like it. One day he followed me out to the clothes line. It was a beautiful autumn day and he wanted us to go for a walk in the woods later on.

'What's the point of me coming home to see you when you're never here?' he said.

'You know why I can't see you, I have to visit my granddaddy.'

'Every day?'

'Yes.'

'And I wish you wouldn't call him your granddaddy, Cissy, it sounds so… so…'

'So what?' I asked.

'Common,' said Peter.

'Well, maybe that's because I *am* common. It's never bothered you before.'

'I don't think I've noticed it much before but honestly, Cissy, he's all you ever talk about these days.'

'And what do you want me to talk about? Us?'

'Well, it would certainly make a pleasant change.'

I picked up the empty basket and started walking back to the house. 'There is no us,' I said, 'and I'm sorry that my granddaddy's illness is causing you so much inconvenience.'

He pulled at my arm. 'Don't go in yet, stay a bit longer.'

I shrugged him off. 'Some of us have to work for a living, Master Peter. We can't all hang around, doing nothing.'

'Look, I'm sorry. It all came out wrong.'

I stared at him. 'Did it?'

'I'm sorry about your grandfather, I am, but I miss you. Surely we can find some time to be together?'

He did look sorry and if I was truthful, I'd missed him too. 'I'll try and get back early,' I said.

Peter smiled. 'Thank you, Cissy, and I didn't mean it when I said you were common, truly I didn't.'

I went into the kitchen. Mrs Hickey was making pastry; her hair was white from all the flour that was floating around her. She stared at me and then spoke. 'What did Master Peter want with you, Cissy? It looked as if the two of you were arguing.'

I could feel myself blushing under her stare. 'He was just passing the time of day, Mrs Hickey,' I replied.

'Well, that's not what it looked like to me and forgive me, but why would Master Peter be needing to pass the day with you at all?'

'I don't know,' I mumbled.

Mrs Hickey was pummelling away at the pastry as if her life depended on it. 'People notice more than you think,' she said.

'I told you, we were only talking.'

'It's what you were talking about that bothers me.'

'Thank you for your concern, Mrs Hickey, but I can look after myself.'

'I hope you can, child, I hope you can,' she said, more gently now.

Mrs Hickey was kind, she wasn't a gossip. 'I didn't mean to be rude,' I said.

'And I didn't mean to be nosy, but it's because I care about you. I don't want you getting hurt.'

And all of a sudden I was blubbing and Mrs Hickey's arms were around me, covering my uniform with flour.

'Sit down there, love, and I'll get us both a good strong cup of tea,' she said gently.

I sat down and rested my head on the table. It was all too much. The granddaddy and Peter and then Mrs Hickey's kindness had unleashed something in me that I'd been trying desperately to keep inside.

'Better out than in,' said Mrs Hickey, placing a steaming cup of tea in front of me. 'You can always talk to me, Cissy, and I will do my best to help you.'

'Thank you, but this is something I have to work out for myself.'

'Well, I'm here if you need me is all I'm saying.'

Just then Annie came into the kitchen. Her face was covered in soot and she looked so funny, it broke the ice and me and Mrs Hickey burst out laughing.

'What's so funny?' said Annie, looking confused.

'You,' said Mrs Hickey. 'And God bless you for it, child, it was just what we needed.'

'Glad to be of service to ya,' said Annie, grinning.

I tried to put Peter out of my mind for the rest of the day and I was relieved when my work was finished and I ran down the drive to meet Colm. Buddy was all over me as I climbed up onto the cart.

'You know where you're going, don't you, boy?' I said, ruffling his ears. Buddy licked my face as if he understood what I was saying.

My heart sank as we went through the gates. Buddy was down from the cart as soon as we stopped. I left Colm chatting to Mr Dunne and walked slowly along the dark brown corridor to the ward. I hated it here. I hated the smell of the place; it smelt of despair and dying things and hopelessness. It filled my nose with a stench that was worse than the granddaddy. I could hardly breathe. My poor granddaddy was stuck here when I knew he wanted to be at home in his old chair covered with his smelly blanket.

'Could I bring his blanket into him, Mammy?' I'd asked one day. 'It might make him feel more at home.'

'That old blanket gives Buddy comfort and I don't think they'd want it on the ward,' she'd said.

As I pushed open the ward door, I felt sick. I felt like running away from this place and never coming back, but Buddy was wagging his tail and making little squeaking noises. He couldn't wait to get to his beloved friend.

As I walked into the room, a nurse came up to me.

'He's not so well today, Cissy, I'm not sure you should be visiting.'

'Tell that to Buddy,' I said, as the little dog ran to find the granddaddy.

'Don't stay long then,' said the nurse.

He wasn't in a chair today, he was in bed. I hardly recognised him. His hair, which was usually stuck up all over the place, had been smarmed down on his head. Buddy was already cuddled up beside him but the granddaddy didn't seem to know that he was there. He was as still as anything. His two old hands were resting on top of a grey blanket. He looked too tidy, too still. He didn't look like my granddaddy and he didn't smell like my granddaddy – it was as if this place had taken him away from me. My eyes filled with tears as I took one of his hands and brought it up to my cheek.

'Granddaddy?' I whispered. 'It's me, Cissy, and Buddy's here too.'

I sat beside him, willing him to open his eyes and smile at me and stroke Buddy's soft fur, but he didn't move. The only sound was a kind of rattle as he breathed in and out. I got up and walked across to the window that looked out over the graveyard. Was this what Granddaddy stared at as he sat in the chair?

I watched the leaves falling from the trees and settling on the graves like a patchwork blanket of reds and golds. I loved autumn. It reminded me of walking through the woods with Colm but today the beauty of it seemed all wrong. There should be a storm raging outside; there should be wind and rain battering the windows, not this calmness, not this beauty.

And then Buddy whined. I turned back towards the bed. Granddaddy's eyes were open and he was staring at me. I hurried to his side. 'I'm here,' I said. 'Cissy's here.'

I held his hand and he gripped it with a strength I didn't know he had in him and then he mumbled something. I put my ear close to his mouth. 'I'm listening,' I said gently.

'I want...' he said. 'I want...'

'What do you want, Granddaddy? What do you want?'

He was struggling to get the words out. 'To know,' he said.

'What do you want to know?'

He shook his head and gripped my hand tighter, he was getting agitated.

'Try again,"I said, gently.

'To go,' he said.

'Home? Do you want to go home?'

He closed his eyes again. 'No,' he said softly.

I looked at this dear man whom I had grown to love so much and my heart felt as if it was breaking in two. I knew he couldn't live forever. I knew that, but I wasn't ready to say goodbye, not yet, not yet... and then Buddy put his paw on my hand. Tears ran down my cheeks as I looked into Buddy's deep brown eyes. His love for this old man went far beyond his own needs; he knew it was time and he loved him too much to want him to stay in a world that he'd had enough of.

I lay my head on my granddaddy's chest. 'It's okay,' I whispered. 'You can go now. Me and Mammy and Buddy will be alright. You don't have to fight any more, just go to sleep. Holy God is waiting for you; he knows you're a reformed man and I'm sure he's forgiven you all your sins. Your poor wife might give you a bit of a hard time but she knows you're sorry for being such a bad husband and I'm sure that once you're sat together on a nice white cloud, you can sort things out.' I kissed his old face. 'I love you, Granddaddy, and I'll miss you something terrible but I'll carry you in my heart wherever I go and I won't ever forget you. Go to sleep now, go to sleep.'

I sat beside him listening to his chest rising and falling until he gave one last breath and left me.

CHAPTER TWENTY-FIVE

Granddaddy had lain in the cottage overnight. Neighbours had come in to say goodbye to him and Buddy hadn't left his side. Just before the lid of the coffin was closed, I picked his old blanket off the chair and tucked it around him.

'To keep him warm,' I said.

Mammy smiled and nodded.

All our neighbours in Paradise Alley walked behind the coffin as Colm and Blue made their way slowly through the town. Colm had tied a black ribbon around Blue's neck. Other people joined us as we headed for the church.

I was surprised to see Mr and Mrs Bretton and Peter standing at the entrance as we pulled up. Colm, his father, Mr Collins and Mr Tully from the alley carried the coffin into the church on their shoulders and placed it in front of the altar. Me and Mammy and Buddy walked slowly behind.

The church was packed, but that was what the town was like. Mammy said you could always be sure of a good send-off in Ballybun. As we followed the coffin down the centre aisle of the church I spotted Mary and Mrs Foley sitting together. Mary smiled sadly as we passed.

I held Mammy's hand as we sat side by side in the pew. It hurt to look at the coffin, I couldn't bear to think of my granddaddy in that box. As Father Kelly sprinkled holy water over it, a ray of light streamed through the stained-glass window above the gold crucifix. That kind of made it feel special, as if the granddaddy was some sort of saint even though I knew he wasn't.

Father Kelly stood in front of the altar and smiled down at me and Mammy.

'We have come here today to say goodbye to our friend, Malachi Ryan,' he began. 'A good man, at times a stubborn man, but a man who recognised his failings and atoned for them. In his last few years his greatest joy has been his family: his daughter Moira, his grand-daughter Cissy and his little dog Buddy. He was, in his own way, a man of God, even if he liked to protest that he wasn't. But God knows Malachi Ryan for he has looked into his heart and seen goodness there. So let us kneel and pray for his soul, knowing that he is now in the arms of the Lord for all eternity and that his sins have been forgiven.'

The Mass seemed endless and I was relieved when Father Kelly said, '*Ite missa est.*' Go in peace, the Mass has ended.

It was a beautiful day. The sun was shining and there was a warm breeze lifting the fallen leaves and scattering them among the graves, giving colour to the stark grey headstones and the old Celtic crosses. Father Kelly prayed for my granddaddy's soul as he was lowered slowly into the ground. It felt as if part of me was going down with him. I was glad I'd tucked his old blanket around him to keep him warm.

Eventually, people started to move away, heading back to their families and their lives. They chatted to each other as they walked across the grass. Nothing had changed for them; they had shared in the grief of losing an old man who was not their own. They had been good neighbours, they had done their duty.

Mary and Mrs Foley came and stood beside us.

Mary bent down and stroked Buddy. 'I'm sorry about your granddaddy,' she said.

'I'll miss him, I surely will. Thank you for coming, Mary.'

'We have to go now,' said Mrs Foley.

'It was good of you to come, Kate,' said Mammy, putting her arms around her.

Mrs Foley nodded. 'Take care, Moira,' she said.

I watched them walking across the grass. Mary turned back and waved.

Mammy touched my shoulder. 'We should go,' she said. I didn't want to go. Buddy cried and pawed at my leg, he didn't want to go either. Father Kelly walked over to us.

'How can I leave him all alone under the ground, Father?' I said.

'Sure, he's long gone, Cissy, that's just an old body down there. Malachi Ryan is in a far better place than you or I and I'd say he's running around like a young feller up there and having a grand old time.'

'Is he, Father?'

'You can depend on it.'

It made me feel better to think of him running around on two good legs and when Colm came across, I held his hand and we walked towards the gates. The Brettons' car was behind Colm's cart.

'Thank you for coming,' said Mammy.

'We are sorry for your loss,' said Mr Bretton, tipping his hat.

'Thank you,' she said.

Peter was leaning against the big shiny car, glaring at me. I didn't know why, and then I realised I was still holding Colm's hand. Well, Peter was just going to have to put up with it, wasn't he, because Colm was as close to me as if he was my brother and he had always been there for me. I held his hand even tighter. This day wasn't about Peter Bretton, this day was about saying goodbye to my granddaddy and being with those I loved. Did that mean it wasn't love that I felt for Peter? Well, maybe it wasn't, maybe I was learning the true meaning of love. Maybe it wasn't about secret meetings and poetry books, maybe it was about loyalty and being there through the good times and the bad, and maybe it was about caring for someone more than you cared for yourself. I was beginning to think that Peter Bretton wasn't able to do that.

I was dreading going back to the cottage and I knew that Mammy was feeling the same way. Colm must have known.

'My father has put on a bit of a spread up at the house,' he said, 'if you'd like to come up?'

Mammy looked relieved. 'We would,' she said, 'and thank you.'

'That's grand then,' said Colm.

It was lovely to see so many people in the big kitchen. Since the granddaddy had taken to sitting outside the cottage he had made friends with a lot of his neighbours and they were truly saddened by his passing. It was lovely to hear them speaking kindly of him.

'He was a clever man, your grandfather,' said Mr Tully. 'He might not have had an education but he had a fine brain. I'd say there wasn't much that he didn't know.'

It made me feel proud to know that my granddaddy was so well thought of.

I looked across the room. Mr Collins was sitting next to Mammy, his hand resting on her arm. I was glad that he was here to give her comfort for I could see her smiling as they spoke quietly together. I remembered him telling me that she'd been the prettiest girl in town when she was young. Well, she was still pretty. I hoped that maybe she could find some happiness after being alone for so long. If anyone deserved to be happy, it was my mammy.

It was lovely to see so many people paying their respects but the room felt stuffy and I felt the need to get away. I was finding it hard to breathe and I pulled at the collar of my dress.

Colm noticed. 'Would you like to take a bit of a walk, Cissy?' he said.

I nodded. 'I would.' I told Mammy that I would see her back at the cottage and I called Buddy.

We walked down Paradise Alley and out towards the wood road. Buddy ran ahead of us, snuffling in the hedgerows and rolling in the leaves that had piled up under the trees.

'He's going to miss Granddaddy,' I said, watching the little dog. 'Especially when Mammy's at work and he's alone in the cottage.'

'How about I take him on the milk round and keep him up at the house until your mam gets home?'

'Would you?'

'Of course I would. I'd say old Blue would be glad of the company.'

We walked side by side along the path that led through the woods.

Once we got to the clearing we sat down on the big old log that had been there for as long as I could remember. Colm put his arm around my shoulder and we sat together, not speaking. It had always been that way with me and Colm, we didn't always need to talk. Peter was different, he seemed to want to talk all the time.

Colm was my home, my safe place. But Peter? There was nothing safe about him. Was that why he made me feel so alive? So full of excitement for something I knew I could never have?

I lay my head on Colm's shoulder and looked up at the perfectly blue cloudless sky above the trees. *Tell me what to do, Granddaddy.*

CHAPTER TWENTY-SIX

It had been almost a year since we'd buried my granddaddy and the pain I thought would never leave me had eased. I could think of him now and smile. Colm and Mr Collins had whitewashed the inside of the cottage and Mammy had finally parted with his old chair.

'Do you mind, Cissy?'

'It's just a chair,' I'd said. 'He won't be needing it any more.'

'I thought you might be upset.'

I shook my head. 'I don't need to see an old chair to remember him.'

'And I don't need the smell of it,' she said, laughing.

I didn't worry about her being alone in the cottage because she had Mr Collins and I didn't worry about Buddy because he spent most of his time with Colm these days.

Peter was now at Trinity College in Dublin. We still met whenever he was home. One evening we were sitting down on the rocks.

'What do you want to do once you've finished your schooling?' I said.

'I'm studying law, Cissy. I like the idea of putting some lowlife behind bars. I think it would give me a great deal of satisfaction knowing I had helped get some rogue off the streets.'

'But how can you be sure they're guilty? Wouldn't you be scared of making a mistake?'

'Not my problem. It's winning that matters, I wouldn't be losing any sleep over it.'

'That doesn't sound very kind, Peter,' I said.

He laughed. 'You people are all heart.'

'What do you mean, "you people"?'

'Well, you Catholics with your confessional boxes and talk of forgiveness. It seems to me that as long as you go into a wooden box on a Saturday night and say you're sorry for your sins, you can do any damn thing you like for the rest of the week.'

I stood up and walked away from him and looked out over the water. I suppose he was right, I had grown up to believe in a merciful God, but on his lips the words sounded mean and unkind, as if he was making fun of me.

'Well, it's true, isn't it? Isn't that what you do?' said Peter, joining me.

'I'm one of those people you're looking down on, Peter. It makes me wonder why you want to spend time with me at all.'

He held me away from him and put on his 'poor me' face. It was supposed to make me laugh and it usually did, but today I didn't feel like laughing.

'Forgive me, little Cissy,' he said. 'I've hurt your sensitive little heart, haven't I? Don't be cross with me or I shall throw myself into the sea.'

I liked Peter and I disliked him in equal measures but even when I disliked him, I was drawn to him by some force I couldn't resist. Colm didn't have the same effect on me, even though in my heart I knew he was the better man.

We kissed and went our separate ways so that we didn't arrive back at the Hall together. I watched him walking up the path and felt again the pain of separation I had every time we parted. I got this awful feeling of loss as if I was never going to see him again, as if the hole he left inside me could never be filled by anyone but him.

It was almost Christmas and this year was going to be even more exciting than usual. Caroline was home for good and there was to be a grand coming out ball to celebrate her getting finished off in Switzerland.

'God forgive me but there are times when I wish someone would finish her off permanently,' said Bridie, as we polished and cleaned the drawing room.

'Why do good things happen to bad people?' I said.

Bridie was rubbing away at a smear on one of the beautiful mirrors. She stood back to see if she'd removed it. 'When you've got money I suppose you don't have to worry about being good.'

'But it doesn't seem to have affected Master Peter.'

'I wouldn't be so sure about that, Cissy. I've noticed that he's got a few airs and graces these days. He's not the sweet boy he was.'

'Oh he is, Bridie!'

Bridie stopped polishing. 'Are you sure you're not blinded by love, Cissy?'

'Don't be silly. We're just friendly and he's always been kind to me.'

'Sometimes we can't see what's under our noses and I'd say your nose is blocked at the moment.'

I didn't answer her.

'I've seen you together, Cissy, and if I've seen you, then others will have seen you too.'

'That's just gossip, you know how people gossip.'

'I'm not talking about folk who gossip, I'm talking about your friends who worry about you.'

I wasn't exactly lying to the people who cared about me but I wasn't exactly telling them the truth either and I felt guilty and ashamed. My friends deserved better but I had to keep this a secret, because if I didn't, it would surely put an end to our meetings and I couldn't bear the thought of that. 'Please don't worry about me, Bridie,' I said. 'I'm too canny to be taken in by the likes of Master Peter.'

'I'm pleased to hear it, Cissy.'

But I wasn't, was I? I wasn't canny at all where he was concerned and now several people had noticed our closeness. I knew that I would be dismissed if it reached the ears of the Brettons. I had to stop seeing him if I wasn't to bring shame on my mother. I had to tell him before it was too late. I'd known this friendship, or whatever it was, couldn't last. I'd tell him when he was home for Christmas. I would. I'd tell him.

'And will they be eating English potatoes this year?' asked Colm, as we walked through the woods, collecting holly to decorate the cottage.

I laughed. 'I haven't a clue and I don't much care.'

'Listen to you, Cissy Ryan, are you not in awe of the Brettons anymore?'

'Don't make fun of me, Colm.'

'Sorry,' he said, handing me a bunch of mistletoe to add to our pile. 'But you have been a bit obsessed by them.'

'Not any more.'

'And what has brought this on?'

I shrugged my shoulders: 'Age,' I replied.

'Listen to the old woman,' said Colm.

I laughed and threw the mistletoe at him.

He held it over his head. 'You're supposed to kiss me under it, not throw it at me,' he said, grinning.

I looked fondly at this boy who had always been so kind to me and my family. This boy that I'd asked to wait for me. I moved towards him and looked into his lovely brown eyes. He smelt sweet and earthy, like the woods we were standing in. I wasn't a child any more, I wanted him to see me as a woman. Without taking my eyes from his face, I slowly put my arms around his neck. He seemed to hesitate for a moment and then he leaned down and gave me the sweetest kiss. His lips were soft and warm and I felt so safe in his arms. He was solid and he was real. No secrets, no hiding, this was my Colm who I'd known almost all my life.

He held my face in his hands. 'Happy Christmas, dearest Cissy,' he said softly.

I was trying hard to avoid Peter. It shouldn't have been too difficult with the amount of work I had to do, but he seemed to appear out of nowhere wherever I happened to be. One morning, I was lighting the fire in his bedroom and Bridie was changing the bedclothes when he came into the room.

'I need to see you, Cissy,' he whispered urgently.

I looked across at Bridie. 'I can't talk to you here,' I whispered back. 'Go away, Peter.'

'Not until you promise to meet me.'

Bridie was piling the dirty linen on the floor.

'Okay, tonight.'

'Where?'

I was trying to think of somewhere we wouldn't be seen. It would be too dark to go down to the beach. 'Behind the woodshed,' I said.

'Okay, behind the woodshed,' he said, touching my arm before leaving the room.

I could sense Bridie looking at me so I picked up the linen and went downstairs to the laundry room. It wasn't long before she joined me.

'I know what you're going to say, Bridie, but I've decided to tell him that we can't carry on meeting.'

'I can't tell you how happy I am to hear that, Cissy, but don't be surprised if Master Peter has other ideas on the matter.'

'I can handle him,' I said, sounding more sure than I felt.

'I hope you can, girl.'

The day dragged and I kept going over and over in my mind what I was going to say to Peter. I'd planned to tell him that we couldn't see each other any more at Christmas but this was as good a time as any: I'd tell him tonight.

After I'd finished my dinner and helped clear away the dishes, I went upstairs and changed out of my uniform. I tiptoed past Mrs Hickey, who was sitting in her chair by the fire with her eyes closed. I grabbed my coat and went outside, closing the door quietly behind me. It was pitch-black and cold. I put my hands in my pockets and walked round the side of the house to the woodshed. Peter was waiting for me.

'Let's go inside, it will be warmer,' he said, taking my hand and opening the door.

'No,' I said, looking inside the dark shed.

'We'll freeze out here,' he insisted.

'I want to talk to you, Peter,' I said, 'and I'd rather do it outside.'

'Sounds serious.'

I took a deep breath. 'I can't meet you like this any more, people have seen us.'

'What, the servants?'

'They are my friends.'

'They'll keep their mouths shut then, won't they?'

'But if they've seen us then other people will have seen us too and it won't be long before your family hears of it.'

'So what?'

'I'll lose my job and I'll bring shame on my family. You must understand,' I said, 'we have to stop meeting.'

And then his mouth was on mine. I knew this was wrong, I tried to push him away. He didn't smell like Colm, he smelt of another world – a world that I could never be a part of.

I struggled in his arms but his lips were on me again, only this time I didn't resist. There was a tingle going through my body such as I had never felt before. I put my arms around him and allowed him to pull me closer. This was the most wonderful feeling I had ever felt in my life and I didn't want it to end.

We stayed a little while longer, just holding each other.

We kissed again and he was gone, leaving me feeling confused and alone.

CHAPTER TWENTY-SEVEN

I needed to talk to someone, so on my Sunday off, I went to Mass, hoping to see Mary, but when the people from the workhouse came down the hill she wasn't with them. I found Mrs Foley instead.

'I was hoping to see Mary,' I told her.

'Sure, Mary doesn't work here any more,' said Mrs Foley.

Well, this was news to me. 'Where's she working?'

'Out at the Green Park Hotel.'

'Well, that's a surprise,' I said.

'Well, it was no surprise to me, Cissy. The young ones don't seem to stay long.'

'I thought she was doing alright at the workhouse.'

'She was, and she's a nice girl. I was sorry to lose her but there you are, it's not for everyone.'

'I suppose not. I'll call in at her house and see if she's there.'

'Give her my love and tell her she's missed.'

'I will, Mrs Foley.'

I watched them all troop into the church, then made my way to Mary's house.

I knocked on the door and one of Mary's sisters let me in. 'I've come to see Mary,' I said.

I could see Mrs Butler washing one of the babies in the sink. 'Who is it?' she shouted

'It's Cissy Ryan, come to see Mary,' said the girl. She looked like a younger version of Mary; she had the same green eyes and lovely thick hair.

Mary came running down the stairs and gave me a hug.

'Could we go somewhere and talk?' I said.

'We could go to Minnie's cafe for a cup of tea and a cake. Have you got any money on ya?'

I nodded.

'Is it alright if I go to Minnie's with Mary, Mammy?'

'I thought you had a belly ache?'

'I'm feeling a lot better now, Mammy.'

'Isn't it strange, Mary, that you are well enough to go to Minnie's but not to Holy Mass?'

'It's a mystery alright,' said Mary, winking at me.

'Away with you then.'

'Thanks, Mrs Butler,' I said.

Mrs Butler smiled at me. 'And how are things up at the Hall? I hear there's to be a grand ball at Christmas for Miss Caroline.'

'There is, everyone is very excited.'

'Have a nice time at Minnie's, then.'

'We will.'

We walked through the town and out towards the strand. There was a cold wind blowing in from the sea.

'Jesus, it's bloody freezing!' said Mary.

'At least it will be warm in Minnie's.'

'It better be,' said Mary, pulling her coat tighter around her.

'Did you really have a belly ache?' I asked, blowing on my hands.

'No, but it's me day off and I had to go to Mass every bloody Sunday when I worked up the hill. I'll confess me sins to Father Kelly on Saturday.'

That made me think about what Peter had said. Maybe he was right after all.

'I shouldn't think missing Mass once in a blue moon is a hanging offence,' said Mary.

'I can't believe you left the workhouse.'

'I couldn't stand it another minute, Cissy. There were days when it felt as if the walls were closing in on me. It was like being in a prison.'

Listening to Mary describe the place as being like a prison made me feel sort of sad because I had been so happy growing up there and all my memories were good ones.

'Didn't your mammy mind you leaving?'

'I got a job at the hotel before telling her, so she's fine about it.'

'Imagine, working in a hotel! Do you like it?'

'I love it, Cissy. You meet so many people, every day is different. Up the hill every bloody day was the same.'

'What do you do?'

'I make beds, I clean rooms, I help with the laundry. In fact, I do everything I told you I wouldn't do!'

'As long as you're happy, Mary, I'd say that's all that matters.'

'Jesus if I don't get in out of the cold in a minute my toes are going to fall off!' said Mary, quickening her step.

I couldn't feel my feet either by the time we got to Minnie's and was delighted when we opened the door and were greeted by a rush of warm air.

'Come in, girls, come in!' said Minnie the owner. 'There's a grand big fire over there and a nice table right in front of it. Take off your coats so that you feel the benefit when you go back outside.'

'It's desperate cold out there, Minnie,' I told her.

'And I've had very few customers because of it, so you are very welcome, girls.'

'We'd like two teas and two pieces of your apple cake, please,' said Mary.

I stood in front of the fire and held my hands out towards the flames while Mary waited for the tea and cake.

'You go and sit down,' said Minnie, 'and I'll bring it across to you.'

'It's great to see you,' said Mary, sitting down.

'It's great to see you too,' I said. And I meant it. She was looking lovely and she seemed so happy. This is what I needed, to spend time with my friend and to laugh together as we used to.

'I'd be lying if I said you looked great, Cissy,' said Mary.

'Do I look that bad?'

'You look as if you lost a shilling and found a penny.'

Minnie came over to the table, carrying the tea and cakes. 'Now you enjoy that, girls, and if you want more tea, give me a shout.'

'Thanks, Minnie,' I said.

'So what do you want to talk to me about?'

'Have you ever kissed a boy, Mary? Not just a peck on the cheek but a real grown-up kiss?'

'I kissed Frankie Slattery once.'

'Did you like it?'

'Holy Mother of God, he nearly ate the face off me!'

'You didn't like it then?'

'It was like kissing a wet sponge. Have you kissed someone then? Is that what you want to talk to me about?'

I nodded.

'Well, go on, I'm ageing here.'

'I kissed Peter.'

'Peter?'

I nodded.

Mary looked completely blank then I could see it dawning on her who I was talking about.

'Jesus, Cissy, are you talking about Peter the Honourable?'

I nodded.

'You kissed *Peter the Honourable?*'

'Don't sound so shocked, it wasn't the Pope I kissed.'

'It's nearly as bad, no wonder you wanted to talk to me.'

I rubbed the back of my ear. 'He's not the only one I kissed, Mary.'

'I hope you don't mind me saying, but you're getting very blowsy in yer old age, Cissy.'

'Oh, don't.'

'Minnie!' she shouted. 'We need more tea over here, lots of it. So who else did you kiss? Mr Bretton?'

I giggled. 'God, no!'

'Who, then?'

'Colm. I kissed Colm in the woods.'

Mary bit into a piece of apple cake. Some apple dribbled down her chin and she wiped it away with the back of her hand. 'Well, now you're talking sense,' she said. 'You have every right to be kissing Colm. I wouldn't mind having a go at him meself. Was it lovely?'

'Yes, it was, but that's not the point, Mary.'

'Well, what is the point?' she said, sipping the tea.

'I shouldn't have kissed him, I led him on.'

'And you didn't lead the Honourable on?'

'It was different, Mary.'

'Colm I can understand, but not the other feller.'

'You're going to tell me he's out of my class, aren't you?'

'I wasn't, but he is, Cissy, and no good can come of it.' Mary reached across the table and held my hand. 'But you don't need me to tell you that. You have to finish it, you know.'

'But why must I?'

'Because you'll be thrown out on yer ear and while you're bringing shame on your family, he'll be coming on to the next silly girl who's daft enough to fall for his charms.'

'I can't finish it, Mary, because he makes me feel so wonderful. When he kissed me I felt this tingling from my head down to my toes. Oh, Mary, I can't begin to tell you how he made me feel.'

'I've a fair idea, Cissy, and I believe it's called sex.'

I stared at her. 'Sex?'

'It's as old as time,' she said, as if she was an expert on the subject.

'How do you know about sex?'

'I live in a two-bedroomed cottage and I have seven brothers and sisters. I'll leave the rest to your imagination. Now my advice to you, Cissy Ryan, is the next time you see the Honourable Peter Bretton, you tell him you're not interested in his advances, then run as fast as you can in the direction of Colm Doyle. Do I make myself clear?'

'Perfectly,' I said.

'Okay, now eat yer apple cake before I do.'

CHAPTER TWENTY-EIGHT

It was two weeks before Christmas and things had reached fever pitch up at the Hall and we were all exhausted. Mrs Hickey's lists were getting longer and longer and her temper was getting shorter and shorter. Poor Annie spent most of the day in tears.

'I try really hard to please her, Cissy, but I can never seem to get it right. If I leave the door open, she's too cold and if I close it, she's too hot.'

'She's not really mad at *you*, Annie, she's mad at Christmas and all the things she's got to do. I expect that if we were in her position we'd be mad as well. As long as you do your best then it doesn't really matter what Mrs Hickey thinks. Now dry your eyes and think of the servants' ball on Christmas evening. That boy you danced with might be there again.'

'Do you think he will?'

I nodded. 'But even if he isn't, there will be another fine lad who won't be able to keep his eyes off you.'

'You're kind, Cissy.'

'Now get yourself away before Mrs Hickey explodes all over the kitchen.'

'You are a one, Cissy,' said Annie, giggling.

I watched Annie walk away. There was something about the slope of her shoulders that touched something in me, raising a lump in my throat. She had no one of her own to love her and tell her that they were proud of her. I had my worries alright, but at least I knew I was loved.

People had been coming and going all week. The two tall Christmas trees had been placed in the hall and the drawing room and hung with glass baubles and tinsel that glittered under the crystal chandeliers. Holly and winter foliage was twined around the staircase and draped over the fireplace and the pictures. The whole house was filled with the scent of pine and Christmas and outdoor things.

Frazzled-looking dressmakers ran up and down the wide staircase, followed by their assistants, struggling under the weight of large bales of material.

One morning, me and Bridie were supposed to be cleaning Miss Caroline's room. This was a task I never enjoyed, on account of the fact that she was dreadfully untidy and didn't take care of anything, but if something ended up broken or damaged it was always us that got the blame. That morning was different. The dressmaker had brought a selection of materials for Miss Caroline's approval. They were lovely, draped across the bed like a beautiful rainbow. The cornflower-blue satin reflected the light like water. Touching the blue was a rich plum velvet and the third, my favourite, yellow silk, embroidered with tiny green daisies that reminded me of soft April sunlight. As I knelt down to sweep the dust from the floor into the dustpan, the hem of the satin dress touched my cheek, and the smell of it was lovely, new and fresh. I gave a little sigh.

Bridie came to stand beside me. She gazed down at the bed, at the textures and colours of the fabrics. They were so different to anything she or I ever wore.

'You be careful with that bucket of water,' I told her, 'or we really will be in trouble.'

'Oh, but they're lovely. Wouldn't you love to touch them, Cissy?' said Bridie.

I didn't have to touch them to know how they would feel. How the silk would slide over my skin, how it would shimmer as I walked, how soft the velvet would be around my shoulders. How I wished just for a moment to be a proper lady dressed in silks and satins, waltzing around the floor under crystal chandeliers.

'Didn't you hear me?' said Bridie. 'I said, wouldn't you love to touch them?'

'Sorry, I was miles away.'

Bridie shook her head. 'It's *where* you were that worries me.'

As we stood gazing at the blues, purples and yellows spread over the bed, the door opened and Miss Caroline walked in. The pair of us couldn't move; it was as if we were nailed to the floor. We just stood waiting for the wrath of Miss Baggy Knickers to come thundering down on our heads. Instead, she smiled at us. I didn't know what was worse, her yelling at us or smiling at us. At least when she was yelling we knew what to expect.

She was looking directly at me as she ran her hand over a piece of pale pink taffeta. 'It's lovely, isn't it?' she said.

I nodded.

'What would you choose if you were me, Cissy?'

I looked at Bridie, who nodded her head as if to say, *for heaven's sake pick something, anything*, but I didn't do that. Instead, I looked Miss Caroline up and down. I looked at her beautiful blue eyes and heart-shaped face, her fair hair that tumbled around her shoulders and her pale skin and then I pointed to a piece of material that looked like liquid gold.

'I'd choose that one for you,' I said.

'Good choice, Cissy,' she said, fingering the beautiful piece of fabric. 'And for yourself? What would you choose for yourself?'

Jesus, she'd be asking me to pick something out for Mrs Hickey next! I wasn't sure whether this was her idea of fun. Well, I wasn't going to play into her hands.

I was just about to speak up when Peter tapped on the door and walked into the room.

'You needed my help to pick out some frippery, sister dear,' he said.

'You're too late, Peter. Cissy has already chosen for me and was just about to choose something for herself.'

'What are you up to, Caro?'

'Nothing at all,' she said innocently. 'But now that you are here perhaps you could choose something.' She looked at Bridie as if she had only just noticed that she was there. 'You can go!' she snapped.

'But we haven't cleaned the room yet,' stuttered Bridie.

Caroline glared at her. 'I said, leave us.'

I looked at Bridie's retreating back in panic and wondered if I dared just walk out after her.

'Come on, Peter, what would you choose for her?'

Peter cast his eyes over the lengths of materials. 'The blue,' he said. 'To match her eyes,' he added, smiling at me.

It occurred to me then that we were both playing into her hands and this was just what she wanted.

She didn't speak for a moment and then she said, 'Yes, I can see her in that. She'd pass for a lady as long as she didn't open her mouth. What do you think of my brother's choice, Cissy?'

I didn't answer her, I just stared at the floor.

'Oh, come on, girl! Surely you would love to be dressed in such finery? Isn't it what you dream about in your little bed at night? Gliding around the floor in my brother's arms? You'd be the belle of the ball, wouldn't she, Peter?'

'Shut up, Caro.'

'Oh, forgive me but isn't that where your tastes run these days, little brother?'

'I said shut up. Cissy, go about your business.'

I ran out of the room with her laughter echoing in my ears but instead of going into the kitchen, I sat on the stairs. She knew, she knew about me and Peter – and Miss Caroline Bretton was a dangerous person to hold such knowledge.

CHAPTER TWENTY-NINE

It was three days to Christmas and on my day off, Colm met me at the end of the drive as he'd done ever since I'd started working at the Hall. Lately, I'd managed to avoid him, but I knew I had to face him now.

'Hello, stranger,' he said, as I climbed up onto the cart.

'I've been run off my feet,' I said quickly.

'That's what I thought. Here, wrap this around you,' he said, handing me a blanket.

I tucked the blanket around my knees. 'Thanks.'

'You're welcome. There's a fierce wind coming in off the sea, I thought you'd need it.'

We started down the hill. Things had always been so easy between us but I couldn't think of one thing to say. My heart was heavy and my head was all over the place. It was cold, alright, as Blue trotted along the strand road. The wind had ruffled the water into white peaks that topped the waves like little hats.

'Are you tired, Cissy, or is there something on your mind?' said Colm.

I didn't answer.

'So there's something on your mind, then? And is that why you've been avoiding me?'

I could feel my eyes starting to fill with tears. 'Oh, Colm,' I said.

Colm eased Blue to a stop by the lighthouse. 'Are you going to tell me what it is,' he asked, turning to face me, 'or do I have to guess?'

'I don't know how.'

'Maybe I can help,' he said. 'Would it have something to do with a certain kiss?'

I nodded.

'Regrets?'

I didn't want to hurt him, I didn't, but I was in love with someone else and I mustn't lead him on. He had to know that sweet as the kiss had been, it couldn't lead anywhere.

'Some,' I said softly.

He was quiet for a while and then he said, 'You're letting me down very gently, Cissy, and there's no need. You can be as honest as you like, because you see I'd rather know where I stand.'

'I'm sorry, Colm.'

'So am I, Cissy, so am I. I thought that maybe…' He shook his head. 'But it seems it's not to be. Am I right?'

'Will we still be friends?'

'Always,' he said, picking up the reins. 'So let's say no more about it.'

I knew I'd hurt him, I could tell by the way he spoke, but at least now he knew and he could maybe find a nice girl who would love him like he deserved to be loved. I looked at his lovely face. Yes, of course some girl was going to come along for him and wasn't that what I wanted? Of course it was and yet the thought of him kissing someone else made me feel sort of empty inside.

He dropped me off outside the cottage and as I watched him and Blue going up the alley, I suddenly felt as if I'd lost something precious and I had the urge to run after him and say I'd been wrong.

The mammy was sitting next to the fire on a couch that I'd never seen before.

'Where did that come from?' I said.

'Didn't Mr Collins and meself take a trip to Cork city and buy it.'

'You went to Cork city with Mr Collins?'

'I did.'

'It's lovely, Mammy.'

'It is, isn't it?' she said, stroking the seat. 'Come and sit beside me and try it out.'

I walked across to her and sat down: the couch felt soft and comfortable.

'What do you think?'

'I think it's gorgeous altogether.'

'And there's a new bed upstairs for you. It's a wonder your granddaddy's bed didn't walk out of the cottage of its own accord.'

'What's it like?'

'Go upstairs and look.'

'Not the bed, Mammy! Cork city, what's it like?'

'Oh, it's a wonderful place, Cissy. Meself and Mr Collins walked along beside the River Lee and watched the big boats coming in from England. The quayside was full of people welcoming their loved ones back to Ireland, it brought a tear to me eye.'

'You like Mr Collins, don't you?'

'I do, he's a good man.'

'Do you like him as much as you liked my father?'

Mammy gazed into the fire. 'I knew very little of life beyond this town when I met Stefan. He was so different from the clodhopping eejits I usually came across, he even looked different. We talked about everything. He told me about his homeland; he described the forests and the mountains and the little wooden house he grew up in so clearly that I felt as if I was there. And oh, we laughed, Cissy. His English was good but he didn't always understand my Irish humour. For a very short, wonderful time he opened a door to a world beyond the boundaries of Ballybun and when he was gone, it seemed a very dull place indeed.'

'I'm sorry, Mammy.'

'Nothing to be sorry about. I have you and I have my memories.'

I could see that she didn't want to talk about it any more. She stood up and put some peat on the fire. 'Anyway, you must ask Colm to take you to Cork one day.'

'I don't think Colm is going to be taking me anywhere ever again, Mammy,' I said sadly.

'Sure, you haven't fallen out with him, have you?'

'It was my fault.'

'Has he taken up with Alana Welsh again? Is that what's wrong?'

'No, it's not that.'

'Are you going to tell me or am I to prise it out of you?'

'He kissed me – well, I kissed him first – in the woods while we were gathering the holly.'

'And you didn't like it?'

'Oh, I liked it, alright.'

'So what's this all about then?'

'I kissed another boy, after I'd kissed Colm.'

'You've been very busy with the kissing, Cissy.'

'I suppose I have.'

'And did you like kissing this other boy better?'

'I did.'

'And have you told Colm?'

'I told him just now.'

'Well, at least you've been honest, it would be cruel to keep a lad like Colm hanging on.'

'That's why I told him… but… but now I don't feel so good about it.'

'And are you going to tell me who this other feller is that has taken up residence in your heart?'

'He's just a lad from the Hall.'

'And does this lad from the Hall have a name?'

My mind had gone blank. For God's sake, I must be able to think of one feller's name. I looked around the room and my eyes rested on the picture of Saint Anthony.

'His name's Anthony,' I said, knowing I'd have to go to confession and tell Father Kelly that I'd lied to the mammy. It was a blessing that he had to abide by the seal of confession or I'd be in deep trouble.

'That's a good strong name, Cissy. And you can take comfort in the knowledge that he'll never lose you, for he's the Saint of

Lost Things. Not that I set much store by stuff like that,' she added quickly.

In the afternoon, the pair of us took Buddy for a walk along the river. He tore away on his sturdy little legs.

'Is the River Lee better than our own Blackwater?' I asked.

'Not better exactly, but definitely more exciting, there's more going on. I expect if I saw it every day it would lose its appeal. I hope that's not what's happening with you and Colm?'

'Maybe it is and maybe I'm making the worst mistake of my life but I can't help what my heart is telling me to do.'

Mammy smiled and put her arm around my shoulder. 'Sometimes, out of our worst mistakes come our greatest joy.'

'Can I bring Annie home on Christmas Eve?' I asked as we walked back to the cottage. 'She has no home of her own and she'll be stuck at the Hall.'

'Of course you can and she's very welcome. I'll ask Mr Collins to bring a fine chicken and we'll make a night of it.'

'Thanks, she'll be delighted.'

'And you'll have to introduce me to this lad of yours, Cissy.'

Now what was I supposed to say to that?

CHAPTER THIRTY

'As if Christmas isn't stressful enough, we have a ball on our hands,' said Mrs Hickey, rolling up her sleeves to reveal arms that looked more like a wrestler's than a cook's. 'Are all the rooms ready for the guests, Cissy?'

'We have two more to do but we're waiting for clean linen.'

'Those village girls are desperate lazy little madams! They talk and giggle more than they work. You'd think they'd be glad of the money. If they don't buck up soon, I shall be threatening to speak to their mammies.'

Just then there was a tap at the kitchen door.

'Get that, Cissy. It'll be Colm with the milk.'

Even though I'd hurt him, Colm had still brought me back to Bretton Hall after my day off, but things had remained awkward and it was a silent little journey.

'Do I have to, Mrs Hickey?'

'Now what's wrong? Have you had a falling-out?'

'Not exactly.'

Mrs Hickey raised her eyes to the ceiling. 'As if I haven't got enough to do! Alright, go and see if those sheets are ready.'

'Thanks, Mrs Hickey,' I said.

As I made my way to the laundry room I felt so muddled in my head about everything. I strode into the room and demanded the clean linen.

'Jesus, Cissy!' said Geraldine Toomey, a young girl from the village. 'Keep hold of yer hair! Bridie's already been in for it.'

'Sorry, Gerry, I've things on me mind. I didn't mean to yell at you.'

'Well, as it's Christmas Eve I'll forgive you,' she said, grinning.

I returned her grin. 'Thanks.'

The whole day was madness and we were all running round like headless chickens, polishing silver, washing glasses until they were gleaming, lighting fires, laying fresh towels in all the rooms and eating on the run. There was enough food to feed an army and it was still coming in. Greengrocers were bringing boxes of vegetables, butchers' boys were delivering the meat. Succulent hams, sides of beef, pork, goose and turkey filled the pantry shelves ready for the oven. By the end of the day, we were dead on our feet and Mrs Hickey looked as though she was about to be carted off to the hospital with exhaustion. I'd worked with this woman for nearly two years and yet I knew nothing about her. I didn't know if she had a family, or a home of her own, I didn't know how long she'd been at Bretton Hall or what she'd done before she came here.

'I'm not doing another thing,' she said, collapsing into her chair. 'If it's not done now, it won't be done.'

She was the same every year but part of me thought she actually enjoyed it all. She was queen of the kitchen and that's the way she liked it. God help anyone who was daft enough to interfere.

I still hadn't told Annie that she was coming home with me that night. I hoped that she would like the idea, maybe I shouldn't have just assumed that she would.

'Mind you're both back good and early in the morning,' said Mrs Hickey, when I told her, 'or I'll be coming into town to fetch you.'

I laughed, thinking of Mrs Hickey marching down Paradise Alley and hauling us out of bed.

'Don't worry, Mrs Hickey, I promise we'll be back on time.'

'It's good of you to think of her, Cissy.'

'We'll enjoy having her.'

I hadn't been alone with Peter since we had last kissed. I longed to be in his arms again, but after the scene with Baggy Knickers I knew we must be even more careful than usual. I knew it was wrong, but I had to see him – I *had* to.

I washed up a couple of cups that were on the side, then ran upstairs to the bedroom. Annie was sitting on the side of the bed, rubbing her feet. 'They're killing me,' she said. 'I've decided I hate Christmas.'

'I'm sure you don't mean that, Annie.'

'I do, what have I got to look forward to? At least you're getting away from here for a few hours.'

I sat down next to her and put my arm around her thin shoulders. 'Would you like to come with me?'

'What, home? To your house?'

I nodded. 'If you'd like to.'

Her eyes filled with tears and I felt so guilty. I should have thought of this before. I was a selfish girl, alright.

'Oh, Cissy, I'd love to,' she said, putting her arms around me. 'Are you sure it's alright with your mammy?'

'She'll be delighted to have you, Annie.'

'I was just about to go to bed but now I'm not tired at all.'

I smiled at this young girl, who didn't have anyone to love her and no home of her own. 'We'll have a great time. Now get yourself dressed. I don't know about you but I can't wait to get away.'

Mrs Hickey was snoring her head off as we tiptoed past and escaped out the back door. I was caught up in Annie's excitement and we were giggling as we ran down the drive. I could see Colm waiting at the gates. I was glad that I wasn't alone, it would make things easier.

'Well, you two sound on fine form,' said Colm, as he helped Annie up onto the cart.

'We couldn't wait to get away,' I said.

'Cissy invited me home for the night,' said Annie, her face alight with excitement.

Colm smiled at her. 'Then we'd best get you there,' he said, giving her a blanket. 'Wrap yourselves up in that, girls, it's a chilly old evening.'

We were soon going under the stone archway that led into Paradise Alley. Colm took my hand as I climbed down from the cart. 'I'll fetch you in the morning, Cissy,' he said.

Mammy and Buddy were at the door as if they'd been waiting for us. 'Welcome home, girls,' said Mammy. 'Come in out of the cold. Thank you for bringing them home, Colm.'

'You're welcome, Mrs Ryan.'

'Will you come in?'

'I have my dinner waiting for me up at the house, Mrs Ryan, but thank you for your offer.'

Buddy was jumping all over me, clawing at my legs for attention. I knelt down and ruffled his ears and he pushed his wet nose into my hand.

'Ah, he's lovely, Cissy,' said Annie. 'Will he let me give him a stroke?'

'He will of course, he loves the attention.'

Buddy was delighted as Annie knelt beside me and stroked his tummy.

'You'll have him ruined between you,' said Mammy, smiling.

'He deserves it,' I said. 'Don't you, boy? You deserve to be spoilt because you're the best little dog in Ballybun.'

'I wish I had a dog, Cissy,' Annie sighed.

'Maybe one day you will, Annie,' said Mammy, smiling at her.

'I don't think so, Mrs Ryan,' she said sadly.

'Never say never,' said Mammy. 'Now take off your shawl and make yourself at home.'

There was a grand fire burning in the hearth and the little room was lovely and warm. In front of the window was a little Christmas tree, and the smell of pine mingled with the aroma of peat and roasting chicken. I could feel the tension of the past week leaving my body as the little cottage wrapped itself around me like a pair of warm arms.

'It's all so lovely,' said Annie, looking round.

'The new couch helps,' said Mammy.

The couch was indeed lovely but I missed the granddaddy sitting in his old chair by the fireside. I wished with all my heart that he was here with us on this Christmas Eve.

That night as I lay in bed with Annie beside me and Buddy at my feet, I thought about the holly and berries that Mammy had draped across the branches of the little Christmas tree. I remembered the day that me and Colm had gathered it and how we had kissed and how much I missed the way we used to be, before the Honourable Peter Bretton came into my life.

CHAPTER THIRTY-ONE

I felt as if I'd hardly slept when Mammy gently nudged me and said it was time to get up. Annie was snoring softly beside me, her mouth slightly open. She looked so peaceful lying there that I didn't want to wake her but Colm would soon be here and we had to get back to the Hall early.

Mammy had lit the fire so that it was nice and warm in the little room as we sat down at the table.

'Did you sleep well, Annie?' asked Mammy, putting two bowls of hot porridge in front of us.

'I did, Mrs Ryan,' said Annie, rubbing the sleep from her eyes. 'That's a mighty comfortable bed you have up there, I didn't want to leave it.'

'I'm glad,' said Mammy, putting two parcels down in front of us.

Annie looked wide-eyed. 'For me?' she said.

'Happy Christmas, Annie,' said Mammy, smiling at her.

'Oh, and a happy Christmas to you, Mrs Ryan.'

I stood up and hugged my mammy; I was so touched that she hadn't left Annie out. 'Happy Christmas,' I said.

'Happy Christmas, my love.'

Inside the parcel was a blue knitted scarf and a pair of gloves. Annie had the same but hers were red.

I could see Annie's eyes filling with tears. 'Thank you, Mrs Ryan, they're gorgeous altogether.'

'You are very welcome. Now eat up, Colm will be here in a minute.'

We had on our coats and our new scarves and gloves by the time Colm pulled up outside the cottage.

I kissed Mammy goodbye. 'You won't be alone today, will you?' I said.

'No, I shall be spending this day with Mr Collins.'

'Wish him a happy Christmas from me, won't you.'

'I will, of course.'

Me and Annie climbed up into the cart and Buddy jumped up behind us.

'Did you have a nice time, Annie?' said Colm, as Blue trotted through the town.

'Oh, I had a wonderful time and look what Mrs Ryan gave me,' she said, showing him the red scarf and gloves.

'They look grand and warm, Annie.'

I was thankful again that I wasn't alone with Colm. It was easier with Annie there, and she chatted all the way back to the Hall.

When we stopped at the end of the drive, Colm helped Annie down. 'You go on,' he said. 'Cissy will be up in a minute.'

'Alright, happy Christmas, Colm, and thanks for the spin.'

'You're welcome, Annie.'

I didn't know why Colm had sent Annie off on her own and I could feel my tummy going into knots. I dreaded hearing what he had to say.

'Don't look so worried,' he said, reaching into the cart and handing me a parcel. 'It's not much, but I thought it might please you. Happy Christmas, Cissy.'

I leaned against him and felt the safety I always felt when I was in his arms. 'Happy Christmas, Colm,' I said.

I opened the kitchen door and felt like I'd walked into the Fires of Hell. The kitchen was filled with steam. Mrs Hickey's face was shiny with sweat and her hair was sticking up on her head.

'Happy Christmas, Mrs Hickey,' I said, as I ran past her and upstairs to change into my uniform.

'Don't be long, Cissy, we've a ton of work to do,' she called after me.

Annie was stuffing her hair under her cap as I went into the bedroom.

'She's already yelling at me, Cissy,' she said. 'I'll be glad to see the end of this day.'

'Cheer up, we've got the servants' party to look forward to later.'

'If I'm still able to stand.'

'Come on, best foot forward, we can do this.'

'Alright, Cissy,' she said, grinning.

The morning flew past. Bridie was already lighting the fires in the bedrooms so I went downstairs to do the same in the drawing room and hall.

Once breakfast was over, we collected the dirty crockery from upstairs to pile in the sink for poor Annie to wash up, then we all had a much-needed cup of tea before starting on the dinner.

Serving dishes filled with meats, vegetables and gravy were carried upstairs by the hired staff, who were brought in to wait on table. Once the main meal was over, plum puddings and sweetmeats were added to the menu. Compliments were sent down to Mrs Hickey, who could at last relax in her chair while the rest of us washed and dried the dishes.

In the afternoon, I went outside for some fresh air. It was chilly but there was no wind, so I followed the path down to the beach and walked along by the water's edge. I loved it down here. However sad or worried I was, this place calmed me, making my troubles seem somehow less important against the vastness of it all. I hadn't seen Peter all day but I hoped that I would see him that evening. Every time he came into my mind so did Colm, I couldn't seem to think of one without thinking of the other. Peter made my heart race with longing but when I thought of Colm I felt a sadness for all he had been to me and for a love that refused to go away.

As the time for the ball grew closer, carriages and cars were pulling up outside the front door and young ladies and their maids were stepping down onto the drive.

Me and Bridie helped carry cases up to their rooms. Some of them thanked us but mostly, they just chatted and giggled as if we were invisible. The maids unpacked for them, laying beautiful gowns on the beds for them to change into. It was a different world to the one I lived in, full of excitement and glamour and lovely clothes and people at hand to do your every bidding. I thought of Annie and I wondered if these young women ever thought of the people who waited on them, or what their lives were like. I don't suppose they did.

Bridie and I were serving drinks as the guests arrived. A band was playing at the far end of the room and candles were burning on every surface. The girls seemed to have congregated at one end of the ballroom and the young men at the other. Once a few drinks were consumed, the men relaxed enough to venture to the other side of the room and ask their chosen girls to dance. I watched as they floated past me in their beautiful dresses, their eyes sparkling with happiness as they were whirled around the room.

Bridie had said that this was called the 'season', where young men and young women from good families were invited to balls all around the country in the hope of finding suitable husbands and wives. I felt sick when I thought of Peter falling in love with someone of his own class and leaving me behind. I wasn't silly, I knew it was going to happen – I just didn't know when.

Caroline entered the room with a posse of girls behind her. She was the belle of the ball and she knew it. She outshone every other girl in the room. Caroline Bretton was indeed beautiful and I'd never seen her more beautiful than she looked that night. I held tight to my tray of glasses for fear she would knock them out of my hands again. She might be beautiful on the outside but she was a holy terror on the inside. Pretty soon she had a crowd of young men around her, all eager to take her in their arms. I almost felt sorry for them because in Miss Baggy Knickers's case, beauty really was only skin deep.

I was nearly out of drinks so I went over to the bar to get some more and that's when I saw Peter. He walked into the room with his arm around a girl's shoulder. She was pretty and petite, all bouncing curls and smiles. She was gazing adoringly up at him, her head thrown back in laughter at something he'd said. I shouldn't have been surprised, I knew it was going to happen. This was his world and this was the kind of girl that he would one day marry; the kind of girl that his parents would approve of. I felt awful and wanted to run out of the room but I had to stay and serve the drinks. After all, I was a servant and I had no right to be thinking that Master Peter would ever marry me.

CHAPTER THIRTY-TWO

It seemed like forever before I was allowed to go and get ready for our own little party down in the kitchen.

'Thank God for that,' said Bridie, 'another bloody Christmas over!'

'Will you be at the party?'

'No, I'll be in my bed.'

'Ah, Bridie, just come down for an hour.'

'No. I've been missing my bed ever since I crawled out of it this morning and that's where I'm going.'

'Well, have a nice rest.'

'I intend to,' she said, laughing.

'Can I borrow your ribbon again?' asked Annie when I went into the bedroom.

'No, sorry,' I said. 'I thought I'd wear it myself.'

Annie looked flustered. 'Oh, of course, Cissy, of course you must.'

'Besides,' I said, handing her a little bag, 'I thought you might prefer this one.'

Annie looked at the pale pink velvet ribbon and threw her arms around me. 'Oh, thank you, Cissy, thank you,' she said. 'It's gorgeous altogether.'

'I'm glad you like it, Annie.'

'I love it.'

Once she was ready, I tied the pretty ribbon into her hair. 'You look beautiful,' I told her.

'Are you coming down, Cissy?'

'You go, I'll be down in a minute.'

I opened the drawer and took out the parcel that Colm had given to me. I knew it was a book by the feel of it. I removed the paper carefully, folded it and put it back in the drawer. The book was called *Little Women* by Louisa May Alcott. I opened the first page and inside it said: *To dearest Ellen, Happy Christmas, with all our love Mammy and Daddy x* and written underneath was: *To dearest Cissy, Happy Christmas with all my love Colm.*

I lay down on my bed and held the little book close to my heart. I didn't feel like going to the party, I didn't feel like being with people and pretending to be jolly when I didn't feel jolly at all. I could feel my eyes getting heavy. Maybe I'd sleep for a while and go down later. I closed my eyes and saw Peter's face as he looked down at the young girl earlier on this evening.

I was shivering when I woke up. I had no idea how long I'd slept, it could have been the middle of the night for all I knew. I stood up and stretched. I needed to be with people, I'd go mad if I stayed here on my own, thinking of Peter with his arms around the pretty girl. I splashed some water on my face, put on my best dress and went downstairs. The party was in full swing. Someone was playing on a fiddle, another boy was on the bodhrán; everyone was having a grand time. I spotted Annie being whirled round the room by one of the grooms. She waved to me and I smiled. I was glad she was enjoying herself, she deserved to let her hair down on this Christmas night. I poured myself a glass of orange and stood by the kitchen door, watching the dancers. I didn't want to join them but it was nice to see everyone having a grand time, I was glad I'd come down. This was where I belonged, among my own kind, where I could call my granddaddy 'Granddaddy' without being told I was common and I could go out with a boy and not have to hide it from the world.

The kitchen was hot at the best of times but with so many people crammed into the small space, it was boiling. The heat and the music and the noise were beginning to make me feel dizzy, I needed to get some air. I fetched my shawl and went outside. There was a couple leaning against the wall with their arms around each other and as I grew accustomed to the darkness, I could see other couples in the shadows doing the same. Well, good luck to them and long may they enjoy each other.

I walked away from the house and leaned against the woodshed. The sky was completely black and full of stars, twinkling over my head like a blanket of diamonds and although I was freezing cold and full of worries, I couldn't help but think how beautiful it was.

'So there you are!' Peter was standing in front of me, swaying slightly. I could tell that he was drunk. 'I've been looking all over for you,' he said.

'Why aren't you at the ball with your own kind? What are you doing here?'

His words were slurred as he said, 'Come on, be kind to me. I was bored, I needed to find my little Cissy.'

'Well, you've found me, now I think you should go back to your *little* girlfriend, Peter.'

It looked as if he was finding it hard to focus on my face. 'What are you talking about?'

'I'm talking about the girl you had on your arm.'

He laughed. 'I've had lots of girls on my arm this evening, how am I expected to know which one you are referring to? Let's not fight, Cissy, you know that you are the only girl for me.'

I wanted to believe him. 'Am I?' I said.

He came closer. I could smell the drink on his breath, not like the smell of the Guinness on Granddaddy's breath, but a sweet smell. 'I love you, Cissy. And I want you,' he said.

He'd said *I love you*, he'd never said that before. I should have been happy but I couldn't be sure that it wasn't the drink talking. I took a deep breath. 'Well, you can't have me, Peter Bretton, so there.'

'Cissy, it's freezing.' Peter pushed open the shed door. 'It'll be warmer in here.'

'Do you really think that I'm such an eejit that I'd go in there with you when you're drunk?'

'Oh, come on, Cissy, it's Christmas.'

'Yes, Peter, the day of our Lord's birth, not the day to be canoodling in the woodshed.'

We could hear the sound of laughter as someone approached and Peter almost pushed me into the shed. I listened as the laughter died away. 'I think they've gone,' I said, moving towards the door.

Peter pulled me back. 'Can't we stay awhile? I need you, Cissy.'

'No, you don't, you just need someone to tell you how wonderful you are and how irresistible you are and...'

I didn't finish the sentence because Peter's lips were on mine, hard and urgent and he was breathing very fast. I could have pushed him away, or brought my knee up under him, as Mary said I should do if someone was taking liberties but I didn't. I couldn't, because I was feeling that same thing that I had told her about, that thing that only someone blowsy should feel. Instead, I allowed myself to be swept away by him. Maybe he did love me, maybe he really did. He put his hand over my mouth as I cried out with the pain but I didn't want him to stop, I didn't want him to ever stop. Something so wonderful couldn't be wrong, it couldn't.

Afterwards, he held me gently in his arms. 'That wasn't such an ordeal, was it?' he said, kissing my forehead.

I didn't answer him.

'Oh, Cissy, I'm going to be sick,' he said, rushing for the door.

I could hear him retching outside. And then it hit me. What had I done? I felt as dirty as the logs that had been digging into my back. I'd broken my promise to Mammy and what would the granddaddy think if he was looking down on me? I was going straight to hell. I couldn't even confess my sin to Father Kelly because I would be too ashamed to tell him what I'd done: I deserved no forgiveness.

I walked outside. Peter had gone; he'd just left me there. The smell of vomit made me feel queasy. I wrapped my arms around myself and tucked my chin down. I stepped carefully over the mess and walked back towards the house, staying close to the shadows in case I was seen. Doing what we'd just done was supposed to be such a big thing, but it didn't feel big to me now. It felt small and dirty and insignificant. That's what I felt, humiliated and ashamed and angry, not just with Peter but with myself. Peter had enchanted me with his big blue eyes and talk of poetry and now the spell was broken. I realised the only person in the world I wanted was Colm. I wanted to be in his arms, I wanted to feel clean again and safe and loved. How was I ever going to be able to face him now?

CHAPTER THIRTY-THREE

I'd only seen Peter in passing since that awful night and I was glad. I was ashamed of what we had done, but much as I regretted it, it had somehow freed me. I didn't want to see him any more, I didn't even want to work at Bretton Hall any more. I was going to ask Mary if there were any jobs going at the hotel. I could live at home again and see Mary in the evenings and spend time with Colm. I felt as if there was a future for me away from this place, maybe even a future with Colm. I found myself smiling just thinking about it.

On my next day off, I was surprised to see Mr Collins waiting for me at the end of the drive. He jumped down from the cart as I approached. He was wearing a thick dark coat and he was rubbing his hands together and stamping his feet.

'Where's Colm and Blue?' I asked.

'Blue has taken a bit of a turn and Colm won't leave him.'

'What's wrong?'

'We're not sure. His belly is swollen and he's awful restless. Colm's out of his mind with worry.'

I knew how much Colm loved that horse and how devastated he would be if anything happened to him. 'Well, it was good of you to come in his place, Mr Collins, but I'm sure I could have managed.'

'It would have been a long cold walk on a night like this and Colm didn't want you walking home alone in the dark, so I said I'd get you.'

'Well, thanks, it was kind.'

'You're welcome, Cissy.'

'Can I come up to the house and see Blue?' I asked.

'I'm sure that will be fine. Colm's father is with him and he knows a thing or two about horses, I'm happier knowing he's not alone.'

We were soon going under the stone archway into Paradise Alley. We stopped outside the cottage. 'Come up when you like, Cissy,' said Mr Collins, helping me down. 'I'm sure Colm will be glad to see you.'

I wasn't so sure about that but I hoped he wouldn't mind if I went up to see Blue.

Mammy was at the door, as if she'd been waiting for me. 'Come in out of the cold, Cissy.'

'Where's Buddy?' I said, expecting the little dog to be jumping up at me.

'He's up at the Doyles'. I imagine you've been told about Blue.'

'It's a worry alright, I said I'd go up and see them.'

'I think you should,' agreed Mammy.

There was a grand fire burning in the hearth and the room was lovely and warm, and cosy, with its little Christmas tree, and the green folliage draped over the mantle.

'The tree is so pretty, I haven't the mind to take it down,' said Mammy.

'You've a few days left until Twelfth Night,' I said.

'That's grand then.'

Mr Collins joined us for dinner.

'How's Blue?' I said.

'Not great, I'm afraid.'

I didn't feel a bit like eating the delicious dinner that Mammy had made. I was worried about Blue and I was worried about Colm.

'Do you mind if I go up to Colm's, now?' I said.

'Away you go and tell him I'm sorry for his trouble.'

'I will, Mammy.'

'I'm sure he'll be glad to see you,' said Mr Collins.

I hoped he would, as I started walking up the alley. I went around the side of the house and pushed open the old stable door. Buddy immediately ran to me, pawing at my leg for attention. I knelt down and ruffled his ears. 'Hello, boy,' I said.

Colm and Mr Doyle were either side of Blue, walking him round the stable. Colm was talking to Blue as they walked. 'There's a good feller, we'll soon have you feeling better.' He said it as if he was reassuring a sick child.

'Do you know what's wrong with him?' I asked.

'Pretty sure it's colic,' said Mr Doyle.

'Is that serious?'

'It can be if it's not caught quick enough. We have to keep him moving, Cissy, there's not a lot else we can do. Time will tell is all I can say.'

Colm was gently stroking Blue's neck as they walked. There was a strength in him but also a gentleness that he wasn't afraid to show. My feeling were always so mixed-up when I was with him.

'Now you're here, Cissy, I'll get us some tea and a sandwich. Will you help Colm walk Blue?'

'I will of course, Mr Doyle.'

I took Mr Doyle's place beside Blue and together, me and Colm walked him slowly around the stable.

'Thank you for coming, Cissy.'

'I was glad to come.'

'Did you have your dinner?'

'I had no stomach for it.'

'I'm the same. Blue is never sick, I hate seeing him like this.'

'He'll be alright, Colm, I just know he will. Do you think it might help if we prayed?'

'I'm not a great believer in the power of prayer meself but you go ahead if you want to. I'd say stranger things have happened and right now we can do with all the help we can get – I'm not about to rule out divine intervention.'

'I'll give it a go then.'

I smoothed poor Blue's back and talked to the Blessed Virgin Mary, who I always thought had a bit of clout where her son was concerned. *Dear Mary*, I said in my head. *Please help Blue get better.*

I know he's only a horse but he is one of God's creatures and deserves as much help as any poor soul who is in need of succour. He's a good horse, Mary, and he has the colic right now and Colm is desperate scared that he's going to die. You rode into Bethlehem on a donkey and that's almost a horse and I'm sure you were glad of the ride, seeing as how you were heavy with child. I will leave this problem in your gentle hands, Mary. Amen. Oh, and by the way, Colm needs Blue to help deliver the milk so would you mind getting a move on and having a quick word with that son of yours. Amen.

'I asked the Virgin Mary to intervene on our behalf,' I said.

'Well, let's hope she's in a generous mood and can see her way clear to helping.'

'Oh, I'm sure she will, I told her it was urgent.'

Mr Doyle came back with tea and sandwiches and now that I was here with Colm and Blue, I found that I was ready for some food.

'Shouldn't you be going home, Cissy?' said Mr Doyle.

'I'd like to stay,' I answered.

'I'll take Buddy home and tell your mother that you are staying here. I'll look in later, call me if things change.'

We continued to walk Blue round and round. I was beginning to feel tired and my legs were aching. Colm noticed. 'Have a rest, Cissy,' he said.

'I'll just lie down for a bit, will you manage on your own?'

'I'll be grand, you lie down.'

I don't know how long I slept on the cold floor but when I woke up, Colm was lying beside me.

'Is he better?' I asked.

'My father says that the worst is over.'

'Thanks be to God,' I said. 'The Blessed Virgin must have been listening to me.'

'Maybe she was,' he said, smiling.

I felt so at peace lying there, breathing in the sweet smell of hay and feeling the warmth of Colm at my side. It was where I belonged, next to the boy who had always been there for me, next to the boy that I loved. Suddenly all the worries and confusion of the last couple of years melted away. I sat up and looked down at Colm's lovely face. 'I love you,' I whispered. 'I love you, Colm Doyle.'

He stared at me for a moment and then I was in his arms and he was kissing me and we were both laughing and crying.

I had come home.

CHAPTER THIRTY-FOUR

Everything had changed: the sky was bluer and the grass was greener and there was a feeling inside me that made me want to shout out to the whole world that I was in love. I went about my work with a spring in my step and joy in my heart.

'Have you suddenly been blessed with a vocation, Cissy?' asked Mrs Hickey. 'Are you about to leave us and join the nunnery?'

'I'm in love, Mrs Hickey.'

I could see her face cloud over.

'With Colm,' I said quickly.

'Ah, Colm,' she said, smiling. 'Well, in that case I wish you all the happiness in the world for you couldn't have chosen a finer boy.'

'I know, it just took me a while to realise it.'

'Better late than never, child. I'd say your granddaddy is keeping an eye out for you.'

'I'd like to think so, Mrs Hickey.'

Bridie was delighted. 'I've been awful worried about you, Cissy,' she said. 'I thought your head was full of Master Peter and God alone knows where that bit of foolishness was going to end up.'

'It was for a while but not any more. Anyway, he's gone back to Dublin and to tell you the truth, I'm glad.'

'Well, thanks be to God for that.'

'My feelings exactly,' I said, nodding.

Every morning I made sure that I was at the kitchen door when Colm came with the milk. If there was no one around, we snatched a kiss, which kept me happy for the rest of the day. We spent as much time together as we could. We'd been friends for so long and yet I was still discovering things about him that I hadn't noticed before. Like the way his hair curled around his ears, the little beauty spot on the back of his neck and the way his hands always moved as he spoke.

'If you cut them off, he'd be struck dumb,' said Mr Doyle, laughing.

We walked in the woods even on the coldest of days and we sat on the rocks under the lighthouse, cuddling up together for warmth, then we'd walk across the road to Minnie's and sit by the fire and drink gallons of tea. Nothing we did was particularly exciting, but we had each other and that was exciting enough.

A few weeks later, I caught a bug in my tummy – that's what Mrs Hickey said it was every time I dashed outside to be sick.

'It's the smell of the food, Mrs Hickey,' I said. 'Every time I walk into the kitchen, I feel sick.'

'It'll pass, Cissy. Be sure to drink plenty of water to flush it out of your system.'

I tried doing what Mrs Hickey said but the sickness wouldn't go away. People started to comment on it.

'You're awful white-looking, Cissy,' said Annie. 'You're not going to die, are you?'

'For God's sake, Annie, you'd frighten the Devil himself away with your talk of dying. I have a bug, that's all. Mrs Hickey says I have to give it time to work itself out of my system.'

'I just don't want you to die.'

'Have you never been ill yourself?'

'Plenty of times. I had a terrible toothache once and Mammy tied a string to the door handle, then round my tooth. She slammed the door shut and nearly took my head off.'

'Well, there you go then.'

Mammy and Colm were worried about me as well. One morning, Mammy gave me a tot of brandy. It tasted like poison but it seemed to ease the sickness for a while.

'If you don't get better soon I think you'll need to see the doctor. You've been poorly for weeks now, I've never known a tummy bug go on this long.'

'I just want to feel well,' I said. 'I'm terrible tired from all this vomiting.'

'Why don't you take a few days off work?'

'I can't do that, Mammy. I'm needed, they might replace me.'

'That wouldn't surprise me. You have a fine position up at the Hall, girls would be hammering down the door to step into your shoes.'

'I'm sure I'll be well soon.'

'Well, if you're not, it's down to the doctor with you.'

I was leaning against the shed door after a particularly bad bout of sickness. Sweat was pouring down my face and running down the inside of my dress. I slumped onto the ground. Maybe Annie was right after all, maybe I *was* dying; I certainly felt as if I was.

'Well, well, well…'

I looked up to see Miss Caroline staring down at me with a strange sort of smile on her face. I wasn't up for a fight with Miss Baggy Knickers so I stood up, intending to go back to the house.

'Not so quick, Missy,' she said, as I started to walk away.

'I can't talk to you now,' I said. 'I have a desperate tummy bug.'

I watched as she started to laugh, her mouth open and her head thrown back.

'Tummy bug, eh? Is that what they call it these days?'

I didn't for the life of me know what she was talking about.

'Has it not occurred to you that your little tummy bug is, in fact, a baby? Or are you so ignorant that it hadn't crossed your mind?'

I stared at her and shook my head. 'I'm not having a baby,' I shouted. 'You're just trying to cause trouble as usual.'

'I'd say it's you that's brought on this little bit of trouble, wouldn't you?'

I stared at her mean face and my stomach clenched in fear.

'And who is the lucky father, Cissy?'

Her face had changed, she wasn't laughing any more. 'Because if you think you can lay this at my brother's door, you are sadly mistaken.'

'You're wrong,' I shouted. 'You're wrong.'

'We'll see,' she said, walking away from me.

I felt sick and dizzy. I placed my hands on my tummy. There was a curve there that I hadn't noticed before. I couldn't be having a baby. When did I last have the bleed? I couldn't remember, I couldn't remember. Dear God, she was right: I was going to have a baby. My life was ruined! My legs felt wobbly and weak. I slid down onto the ground. I didn't want a baby, not like this, not with Peter. I was only sixteen, I'd thought myself grown-up, but I wasn't. How could I bring a child into the world when I wasn't much more than a child myself? I was shaking with fear.

I had to talk to someone. I couldn't talk to Mammy, I couldn't bear to see the look on her face or the disappointment in her eyes. Colm? He would leave me. The only person I could talk to was Mary – she would know what to do.

On Wednesday morning, Colm met me at the end of the drive. I could barely look at him.

'Are you still feeling bad, Cissy?' he said, touching my cheek.

'A bit better, I think.'

'Well, that's good, you'll soon be right as rain. Where shall we go today?'

'Do you mind if I go and see Mary? She was upset about some boy the last time I saw her, I want to know if she's alright now.'

'Of course I don't mind, do you want me to drive you out to the hotel?'

'I think I'd like to walk, Colm.'

'Good idea, the fresh air will do you the power of good. Shall I just drop you in town?'

'That'll be grand.'

I walked through the town and out towards the strand. It was still pretty early and I was sure Mary wouldn't get a break until dinner time. I went down to the beach and stared out across the water. It was February and still cold but the ocean always calmed me. Why hadn't it occurred to me that I might be having a baby after what me and Peter had done? I was a foolish girl indeed. I couldn't stay in Ballybun and bring shame on my family and I couldn't hurt Colm, but where could I go? I had very little money. Even if I could afford the boat fare to England, what would I live on once I got there? Tears started running down my cheeks. I brushed them away; feeling sorry for myself wasn't going to help. I stayed on the beach for as long as I could and then went across the road to the Green Park Hotel. My dream of working there had been ruined, everything had been ruined and all because I'd thought I was in love with Peter bloody Bretton, who hadn't so much as passed the time of day with me since that night: he'd got what he wanted and moved on.

I went into the foyer and asked the young girl behind the desk if Mary Butler was around.

'I can't leave the desk,' she said importantly. 'I have to check in any guests that arrive.'

'Are you expecting any, then?' I asked. Mary had told me that the hotel was pretty empty in the winter.

'Well, someone might walk in off the street.'

'I'll keep an eye on it for you while you fetch my friend. Will that do?'

'Well, this is very unprofessional but alright, ask them to take a seat until I come back, but don't strike up a conversation with them.'

'Oh, I won't.' Silly mare, I thought. I didn't have to wait long before she was back, with Mary walking behind her.

'Cissy,' she said, grinning. 'What are you doing here?'

'I need to talk to you, have you got the time?'

'I just have one table to lay and I'll be with you. Go along to Minnie's, I'll be five minutes.'

Just seeing Mary made me feel hopeful. If I didn't talk to someone about it soon I'd burst.

'Two teas please, Minnie,' I said. 'Mary will be here in a minute.'

'Two teas coming up, Cissy.'

I sat by the fire and traced the pattern on the flowery cloth that covered it. I was desperate to speak to my friend. I was relieved when she came through the door, bringing a gust of cold air with her. 'I've ordered tea,' I said.

'Grand,' she said. 'My bloody feet are hanging off me. I'm going to land up with those great knobbly veins at this rate. So what's up?'

I could feel hot tears welling up behind my eyes.

'Two teas,' said Minnie, putting them down on the table.

'Cissy, what's wrong?' said Mary.

I had such a lump in my throat I couldn't get any words out.

'It can't be that bad.'

'It's worse, Mary.' I took a deep breath. 'I'm going to have a baby.'

She stared at me as if she couldn't believe what she was hearing. 'You're having a what?'

'A baby, I'm having a baby… What am I going to do, Mary? I don't know what to do.'

'Well, I'd say the first thing to do is tell Colm. Sure, he'll probably be delighted and he'll have you down that aisle before you know where you are. He's always loved you, Cissy. He'll stand by you. Sure, everything will work out just fine.'

'It's not Colm's,' I said quietly.

Mary looked shocked. 'Jesus, Cissy, whose is it then?'

I didn't answer her.

'Not the Honourable's?'

All I could do was nod.

'You're having the Honourable's baby?'

'Yes. You have to help me, Mary. I have no one else to turn to.'

'Of course I'll help you, Cissy, just let me think.'

I chewed on my lip while I waited for Mary to come up with a plan.

'We'll go and see Father Kelly, your secret will be safe with him. If anyone can help, he can.' Mary reached across the table and held my hand. 'Oh, Cissy, I'm so sorry this has happened to you. God forgive me, I know I shouldn't be saying this but couldn't you just tell Colm the baby is his?'

'Unless it's an immaculate conception, then no, because I've never laid with Colm.'

'Father Kelly is our only hope, then. Have you got Sunday off?'

'Yes.'

'We'll approach him after last Mass and hope to God that he can come up with something.'

CHAPTER THIRTY-FIVE

I had never known a week to drag on like this one. What if Father Kelly refused to help me? What if he felt it was his duty to tell Mammy?

'You look as if you've lost a shilling and found a penny,' said Mrs Hickey one morning. 'Are you still feeling under the weather?'

'A bit,' I said.

She stared at me. 'You can always talk to me, you know.'

Kindness was the last thing I needed. I covered my face with my hands and cried. Mrs Hickey led me to her chair and eased me down into it.

'Oh, Cissy,' she said gently.

'I've been a foolish girl,' I sobbed.

Mrs Hickey took a hankie from up her sleeve and handed it to me. 'Colm?' she asked.

I shook my head.

'That's what I feared. Will you tell your mother?'

'She mustn't know, Mrs Hickey,' I said frantically. 'Promise me you won't tell her.'

She touched my shoulder. 'Not unless you want me to.'

'I don't, she can't know.'

'Do you have someone you can talk to?'

I nodded. 'My friend Mary, she suggested that I speak to Father Kelly on Sunday.'

'I'd say that was good advice. Can he be trusted?'

'Mary says he's bound by the seal of the confessional, even if I don't go into the box. He's a kind man, Mrs Hickey.'

'Then let's hope he can help you, child.'

'I've been such a fool.'

'What you've done is as old as time. You're not the first to find yourself in this predicament and God knows, you won't be the last. You're not a bad girl, you just fell under the spell of a spoilt little boy.'

'I thought he was nice.'

'He always was, but he's taken advantage of you. I could twist the head off him, I could. Will you tell him?'

'No, I won't. I want nothing more to do with him and anyway, what's the point? He's not going to ask me to marry him, is he?'

'I'm afraid he's not, love, but I imagine you've always known that.'

'Miss Caroline knows.'

'I bet she does, nothing much gets past her beady little eyes.'

I took a deep breath and dried my eyes. I'd got myself into this and now I was going to have to get myself out of it.

I hadn't said anything to Annie or Bridie; the fewer people that knew, the better. I had Mrs Hickey and Mary, I wasn't alone.

Colm picked me up on Sunday. It was so hard to pretend that nothing was wrong. 'Can you drop me off at the church?' I said. 'I'm meeting Mary.'

'Will I see you later?'

Oh, how I wanted to see him, to be in his arms, to feel safe again; to pretend none of this was happening. 'Mary might need me,' I said.

'Is she still heartbroken?'

'A bit.'

Mary was sitting on the wall as we pulled up outside the church. I kissed Colm's cheek and climbed down from the cart.

'Cissy?'

I turned around. 'Yes?'

'Nothing,' he said, smiling. 'I just wanted to see your face.'

But he wouldn't want to see my face if he knew. He wouldn't want to see any part of me, ever again.

Mary jumped down off the wall. 'We'd best do some desperate praying while we're in there, Cissy,' she said.

'Praying's not going to change anything, is it?'

'Well, you never know, it's worth a try.'

The Mass went right over my head. I stood, I sat down and I genuflected in all the right places. I'd been doing it since I was a child so it had become automatic but all I could think of was what Father Kelly was going to say when I told him that I was going to have a baby.

We waited till everyone left the church, then we tapped on the vestry door. I felt sick and judging by the look on Mary's face, she was feeling the same. It had seemed like a good idea at the time but now I wasn't so sure.

'Hello, girls,' said Father Kelly.

'Can I talk to you, Father?' I asked.

'You can, of course. Come in, come in. Sit down while I take off these vestments.'

He went into the little side room and me and Mary sat on a bench.

I was trembling all over. 'I'm not sure this is such a good idea, Mary.'

'Can you think of a better one?' she said.

I shook my head. 'I can't.'

'Well, there you go.'

'Now what can I do for you?' asked Father Kelly, coming back into the room.

I stared at the floor.

'Am I that frightening, Cissy?'

'No, Father,' I said.

'Then take your time.'

'If I tell you, Father, you won't tell anyone else?'

'Whatever you tell me will remain within these walls.'

'I'm...' I started.

'Go on, child.'

'I can't.'

'Would it be easier if you closed your eyes and pretended that you were in the confessional box?'

I nodded and closed my eyes. I took a deep breath. 'Forgive me, Father, for I have sinned, it is two weeks since my last confession. I'm, I'm…' I still couldn't say the words.

'She's having a baby, Father,' said Mary.

Father Kelly didn't say anything right away but he looked sad and I felt so ashamed.

'Will the father stand by you, Cissy?'

'No, Father.'

'I see. Have you thought about what you want to do?'

'I'm at me wits' end, Father, that's why I've come to you. I need help.'

'Then I will do all I can. I take it you haven't told your mother?'

I shook my head.

'I thought not.'

'No one must know, I have to get away.'

'Do you want to keep this child?'

'How can I keep it, Father? I have no money.'

'So you would be willing to give this child up for adoption?'

'I have to.'

'Have you really thought this through, Cissy? Your mother is a good woman, I can't see her turning you out.'

'I made a promise to her that I would be a good girl and I've broken that promise. I have to somehow find a way to deal with this myself.'

'Can you help her, Father?' said Mary.

He nodded. 'I have a friend in London, Father Sullivan. He is affiliated to a mother and baby home run by the Sisters of Mercy. He has helped another poor girl of this parish. I will write to him.'

'Thank you, Father.'

'In the meantime, Cissy, I want you to think very carefully. You need to be sure that this is what you want to do.'

'It is, Father.'

'Then we'll leave it in the hands of God and Father Sullivan and I will let you know as soon as I hear back from him.'

'Will you grant me forgiveness, Father?'

He gestured for me to kneel down in front of him and then he placed his hand on my head. 'I forgive you in the name of the Father, the Son and the Holy Ghost. Amen.'

'That wasn't so bad, was it?' said Mary, as we walked down the lane towards the town. 'And isn't it great that he's able to help?'

'London, though,' I said. 'I've never been further than Ballybun in my whole life. Even Mammy's been to Cork city, for God's sake! I'll be like a country bumpkin.'

'Not at all! You're grand-looking and you'll fit in a treat. You'll be coming home with an English accent.'

'It's alright for you, it's not you that's going.'

'I wish I was, I'd do anything to get out of this place.'

'How much have you saved for your passage to America?'

'I'd say another year and I'll be off.'

'Oh, Mary, I'll miss you when you go, you're my closest friend.'

'And you're mine but it looks as if it's *you* that's going to be leaving *me*.'

'Except that the difference is, you want to go to America; I don't want to go to London.'

'We'll both be fine, Cissy.'

'I hope so.'

'I wonder who the girl is?'

'What girl?'

'The one Father Kelly was talking about. He said she was from this parish. It's bound to be someone we know, there's not many people we don't know in Ballybun. She must be a bit on the racy side to have got herself in trouble.'

I stopped and stared at Mary. 'Are you saying that I'm racy, Mary Butler?'

'Oh God, Cissy, no! I don't think you're racy at all, you were just caught up in the moment, sure it wasn't your fault.'

'Whose fault was it then?'

'The Honourable's, he should have known better.'

'Oh, Mary,' I said, 'I don't know what I'd do without you.'

'It could be Alana Walsh, except I think she's more blowsy than racy.'

'I thought they meant the same.'

'Blowsy means flirty but racy… well, you can imagine what racy means. Anyway, I don't remember Alana Walsh going away for nine months. Wouldn't you just love to know, though? You could ask her what the place was like.'

'It looks like I'll be finding out for meself if Father Sullivan agrees to help me.'

'Oh, he'll agree alright, I can feel it in me waters. Did Father Kelly give you a penance to do after hearing your confession?'

'He didn't.'

'I expect he thought you had enough on your plate without burdening you with ten Hail Marys and a Glory Be.'

I looked at my friend. She always managed to make me feel better, whether it was taking me to see a pile of puppies or standing beside me when I needed her most.

'Come on,' she said, linking her arm through mine. 'Let's go to Minnie's, all that talk of confessions has given me a desperate appetite.'

It was two long weeks before Father Kelly received a reply to his letter.

'He is willing to help you, Cissy,' he said.

'Thank God for that,' said Mary, who had again come with me. 'Sorry for that, Father, I didn't mean to take the Lord's name in vain, it was a slip of the tongue.'

'I'm sure he'll forgive you this once, Mary.'

'How will I pay for the boat, Father?' I said.

'I could let you have some of my America money,' said Mary.

'I couldn't take that money from you, it's taken you years to save it up.'

'That was a very kind offer, Mary,' said Father Kelly, 'but you won't need to. We have a small fund put away for desperate cases and I'd say this qualifies as one.'

'Oh, she's desperate alright, Father,' said Mary.

'What will I tell the mammy?'

'Ah, now that's a tricky one, Cissy. Being a Man of the Cloth and a good Catholic, I can't be telling you to lie to your mother.'

'Of course not, Father.'

'I can only tell you what I'd do. Now, I'd say that I'd been offered a grand job in London for a year and it's a great opportunity for me and I'd love to go. This is hypothetical, you understand, but that is what I would do if I found myself in the same situation.'

'Which is highly unlikely, Father,' said Mary, grinning.

'Indeed.'

'Thank you for everything,' I said. 'I'll never forget what you have done for me.'

'I'll keep you in my thoughts and in my prayers, child. As soon as your mother knows, I will arrange your passage to England and may God go with you.'

PART TWO

1911

CHAPTER THIRTY-SIX

I waved to Colm as the boat moved slowly away from the quayside. My heart was breaking as he became smaller and smaller. I saw other people crying as they drifted away from the railings, but I stayed where I was, until the green hills of my homeland became a mere strip of land in the distance.

It had only been this morning and yet it seemed like years ago that I had stood in the cottage with my case at my feet, saying goodbye to Mammy. I wandered if she had guessed the real reason for my sudden departure. Nothing much got past my mammy. She may not have had much of an education but she was no fool. The shape of my body was changing although I'd done my best to hide it from her. Had she guessed?

'I'll miss you, child,' she'd said, taking me into her arms.

'I'll miss you too, Mammy, but I'll be back before you know it and I'll be sure to write.'

She held me away from her and stared into my eyes as if memorising my face. 'Never forget who you are,' she'd said. 'You are Cissy Ryan, beloved daughter of Moira Ryan and granddaughter of Malachi Ryan, and you are loved.'

'I won't forget, Mammy, I'll never forget.'

'Then be gone with you before I make a desperate fool of meself.'

I knelt down and buried my face in Buddy's soft fur. 'Take care of the mammy until I come home.'

He licked away my tears and put his paw on my knee, then walked across to Mammy and sat by her feet as if he'd understood every word I'd said.

Colm hadn't wanted me to go; he couldn't understand why I was leaving him. I wanted so much to tell him the truth, but I couldn't bear to see the look on his face when I told him that I was carrying someone else's child.

'What if you don't like it over there in England?'

'Then I'll come home.'

'You might forget me, Cissy.'

'I'll never forget you, Colm, that's one thing I'm sure of. I'll be back in a year and then we'll be together forever, I promise. But I need to do this, for me.'

'I have something for you,' he'd said, handing me a little bag.

I went to open it, but he stopped me. 'Open it on the boat.'

I put it in my pocket. 'Thank you,' I'd said.

The wind was blowing all over my face as I stood looking out over the water. The boat groaned and creaked as it made its way through the grey choppy sea. It would be hours before I got to see land again; I was told the boat would sail to Wales.

I put my hands in my pockets for warmth and found Colm's gift. Inside the bag was a Saint Christopher medal on a silver chain and a note. *'Dear Cissy,'* it read. *'As you know, Saint Christopher is the patron saint of travellers and, as I can't be with you meself, I'm relying on this feller to keep you safe. Wear it and think of me as I will be always thinking of you. Colm x'*

I felt my eyes filling with tears. I wanted to run to the captain and demand he turn the boat around and take me home. Maybe Colm would forgive me, maybe the mammy wouldn't be ashamed, maybe, maybe, maybe…

I couldn't face Mrs Bretton so I wrote her a letter saying that I wouldn't be working for her any more and asked Mrs Hickey to give it to her. It hadn't been so easy saying goodbye to Annie.

'Where are you going, Cissy?' she'd said.

'To England.'

'But why?'

Her eyes were filling with tears so I took her into my arms. 'It's just something I have to do.'

'I'll miss you, Cissy, you're the only friend I have.'

'I'll still be your friend, Annie, and I won't be gone forever,' I'd said.

'You'll freeze to death out here,' said a voice, interrupting my thoughts.

I looked up at the young sailor. 'I don't mind.'

'Sad to be leaving Ireland?'

I nodded.

'I was sad meself the first time I left and between that and the sickness I was all for running home to me mammy.'

I smiled at him; he looked no more than a young boy. He was probably my age, maybe even older, but I didn't feel young any more. I was only sixteen but I wondered if I would ever feel young again. 'But it got better?' I said.

'Once I got me sea legs it did and sure, now I wouldn't want to be doing anything else.'

'Where is your home?'

'Kerry, and there's no finer place in all of Ireland.'

'I've never been there.'

'Oh, you'd love it, the hills and the lakes, sure I could go on forever. I'll settle back there one day, find meself a sweet Irish girl and never leave its shores again.'

'I'm going away for a year but right now it seems like a lifetime.'

'It'll soon go by. What part are you going to?'

'London.'

'You'll love it. I have a brother in London, working on the building sites. He says it's a grand place altogether, although the streets aren't paved with gold as he was told they were.'

'I hope so,' I said, shivering.

'Come on, let's get you inside in the warm.'

I followed him through a door. 'Do you want to go into the lounge or do you want a bit of a sleep?'

I didn't want to face people. 'I think I'd like to lie down for a bit.'

'Do you know where your berth is?'

I showed him my ticket.

'Take those stairs and you'll find it. Will I help you down with your case?'

'No, thanks, I'll be fine.'

'Grand so, I might see you later.'

I smiled at him. 'What's your name?'

'Eddie, and yours?'

'Cissy.'

'Right then, Cissy, have a good rest and before you know it, we'll be there.'

The stairs were narrow, and it was difficult to get down them with my case banging against the wall. I found the right door and went inside. The room was full of bunks, one on top of the other. I'd thought I would have a little cabin all to myself but already there were a couple of girls laying down. I didn't know which bed to choose.

'Take whichever one doesn't have a case on it,' said a young girl with curly red hair.

'Jesus, I feel sick again!' said her friend.

'She has a terrible weak stomach,' said the red-headed girl. 'She once saw a calf being born and she was sick for a week. I'm Laura, by the way, and me friend here is Oona.'

'I'm Cissy.'

'From Cork?'

I nodded. 'How did you know?'

'The accent's a dead giveaway.'

'Is it?'

'It's very sing-songy.'

'Is that bad?'

'Not at all, it's lovely. Are you going to London?'

'Yes.'

'So are we, unless she passes away during the journey.'

'Laura Hurley! I'll kill you with me bare hands once this feckin' ship stops rolling around.'

'I'd say that will be in about seven hours.'

Oona groaned. 'I want me mammy.'

'You were all for nailing her to the front door this morning.'

'I wasn't sick this morning.'

I chose a bunk and lay down. Mammy had told me I'd probably feel terrible ill, but I didn't feel ill at all. In fact, I loved the feel of the ship rolling beneath me. I placed my hands on my tummy and slept.

I was woken by the sound of someone retching. The room felt hot and stuffy and I had a desperate thirst on me. I got off the bunk and went out into the corridor. The boat was lurching from side to side and I had to grab onto the rails as I staggered along. I went back up the stairs and was just about to go into the lounge when the young sailor I had met earlier stopped me.

'I shouldn't go in there, Cissy,' he said. 'It's full of drunken Irishmen, drowning their sorrows in glasses of Guinness and singing at the tops of their voices. It's no place for a young lady like yourself. What are you after?'

'A glass of water.'

'I'll get it for you. Would you prefer a mineral?'

'Just water, please.'

'Sit there and I'll be right back.'

Up on deck it was chilly. There was a cold wind blowing off the sea. I pulled my shawl closer around me and waited for Eddie to return. Everything was blackness as far as the eye could see. I had no idea if we were anywhere near land. It felt as if I was the only person in the world, I had never felt more alone. I closed my eyes and thought of Paradise Alley and the people I loved. Right now, Mammy might be sitting by the fire on the new couch. Perhaps Mr Collins would be beside her. Would she be thinking of me? Would Colm be thinking of me, or was I already forgotten?

'Let's move to a more sheltered spot,' said the boy, coming back with a glass of water.

We moved to a bench that was out of the wind and sat down.

'Are you feeling sick?' he said.

'Not a bit.'

'Your father must be a sailor.'

'He was,' I said, 'but I never knew him.'

'You might not have known him, but he's given you a fine pair of sea legs.'

The boy had a cheeky grin and a head of red hair. He was nice, and I was grateful for the company. I sipped my water and felt a bit better. Mammy and Colm loved me, I wouldn't be forgotten so quickly.

'Look,' said the boy.

'What?'

'The lights of Wales.'

I stared into the darkness. 'I can't see anything.'

He pointed across the water. 'Over there, can't you see those lights twinkling away in the distance?'

I stared into the blackness. 'Now I see. Are we nearly there?'

'It won't be long. Are you ready for your grand adventure, Cissy?'

Is that what he thought? That I was going on some grand adventure? I nodded. 'As ready as I'll ever be,' I said.

CHAPTER THIRTY-SEVEN

It was way past midnight when the train pulled into Paddington station. I wished it had been summer, at least I would have seen what England looked like. As it was, I had only seen my own reflection staring back at me through the window.

The journey from Ireland had been long and tiring, and I felt dirty and shabby. I was wearing the only coat I owned. I'd been fourteen when I'd first been given it, but I was sixteen now and I'd grown. The sleeves were too short; my thin bony wrists stuck out the ends. It hadn't mattered in Ireland, but suddenly it did. I must have looked just how I felt: a poor Irish girl in trouble.

I knew I was being met by two nuns, at least they would be easy to recognise in their black robes. A kind man on the train had shared his sandwiches with me and I was grateful for them as I was desperate hungry.

He lifted my case down from the rack and put it on the seat. 'Is someone meeting you?' he asked.

I nodded. 'A couple of nuns.'

'As long as you're going to be alright.'

I thought it was nice that a complete stranger cared enough to make sure I was okay.

'I'll be fine,' I said. 'And thank you for the sandwich.'

'I can wait with you, if you like,' he said, looking down at me.

'No, I'll be grand, but it was good of you to ask.'

'You're welcome and good luck.'

I almost said, 'I'm going to need it,' but I thought that might give away my circumstances, so I just waved goodbye to him.

I stepped down from the train and looked around me. The place was huge, with a ceiling that seemed to go on forever. What if I didn't find the nuns? What would I do then? I decided to stay by the gate and hope that they would come to me.

I seemed to be standing there for ages and I began to think that I'd been forgotten. I regretted telling the kind man not to wait with me. I felt like crying and my heart was pounding out of my chest. I knew no one in this strange new country. What was I to do? Where was I to go? Just as I was beginning to give up all hope, two nuns with their veils flying behind them came running across the station towards me. I had never felt so relieved in my whole life.

They were out of breath by the time they reached me.

'Cissy Ryan?' asked one of them.

'Yes,' I said.

'You must have thought we'd forgotten you, child.'

'She must have been terrified, standing here all alone,' said the other nun, 'and all because you couldn't find your blessed shoe.'

'Well, I couldn't be expected to tramp across London in the middle of the night with only one shoe on.'

'She's always losing things, Cissy, she has my knees ruined praying to Saint Anthony.'

'I'm okay now,' I said, smiling.

'Of course you are, of course you are. I'm Sister Mary and this buffoon is Sister Luke.'

Oh, they were nice! They were, in fact, so nice that I burst out crying at the niceness of them.

'There, now see what you've done,' said Sister Luke, 'with all your talk of shoes and Saint Anthony when all the child wants is her bed. We'll have you home in no time, Cissy. We'll get a taxi cab to the convent.'

'And where did you get money for a taxi cab?' demanded Sister Mary.

'I took a loan of a few bob out of the collection box, knowing our dear Lord Jesus will forgive me, knowing one of his children is in need of comfort.'

'I hope you intend to confess your little bit of pilfering to Father Sullivan on Saturday.'

'I will, of course. Now let us get this poor child home, she looks all in.'

Sister Luke held my hand as we crossed the station and Sister Mary carried my case. We walked out of the station and waited for a taxi. I'd thought that London would be full of people and cars and carriages but there were very few people around. I felt lost and alone.

'It must all feel very strange to you, Cissy,' said Sister Luke.

My heart was too full to speak so I nodded.

'As soon as a taxi cab decides to put in an appearance we'll have you home.'

'Home?' I wished I was going home.

I hardly noticed my surroundings as I was led up the wide staircase and put to bed. I felt like a child as Sister Mary tucked the blankets around me. Whatever lay ahead, I knew that I was in a safe place with people who would look after me. I felt light-headed as if the floor beneath me still rolled from the motion of the boat. I fell into a deep sleep as soon as my head hit the pillow.

I was woken by the sound of chattering. I felt so warm and comfy that I could have stayed in bed all day. I sat up and looked around me: there were three girls in the room. I felt shy and out of place.

'The Sleeping Beauty has woken up at last,' said one of them, looking across at me. She came over and sat on my bed, the other two followed her.

'Cissy Ryan?' asked one of them.

I nodded.

'I'm Rose.' She pointed to the other two. 'That's May and that's Sally, we're your room-mates, welcome to St Steven's.'

'What time is it?' I asked, shifting myself up in the bed.

'Well, let's put it like this, you've missed breakfast and lunch,' said Rose.

'Which is probably a blessing,' said May, 'as Sister Monica is on kitchen duty all week and she can't bloody cook!'

I laughed. 'I can't believe I slept so long.'

'We didn't disturb you, strict instructions from Sister Luke,' said Sally, grinning.

'We were beginning to think that you would never wake up,' said May.

All three girls were at different stages of pregnancy. May was so big she looked as if she was about to have her baby at any minute. It made me feel a bit sick, knowing that in time I would look the same.

'Yep, we're all in the same boat,' said Rose, as if she was reading my mind, 'and I imagine that's what's brought you here.'

I nodded.

'Then welcome aboard.'

All three girls were so friendly that I began to relax.

'When you're up and dressed, Iggy wants to see you,' said Rose.

'Give the girl a chance to wake up properly,' said Sally.

'Who's Iggy?' I asked, swinging my legs out of bed.

'Mother Ignatius, she wants to see you down in the office.'

'Don't worry, she's okay,' said May.

The three girls looked very different. Sally was a redhead with a scattering of freckles across her nose. May looked kind of anxious, peering at me through round glasses, and Rose was the prettiest girl I had ever seen, with bright blue eyes and brown curly hair.

'Ah, you're awake,' said Sister Luke, coming into the room. 'I hope these three didn't disturb you?'

'Not at all,' I said.

'I'll wait for you downstairs and take you to see Mother.'

'Thank you,' I said, collecting up my clothes that I couldn't even remember taking off the night before.

Mother Ignatius stood up as I entered the room. 'Sit down, Cissy,' she said, motioning to a chair opposite her. 'I hear you had a grand sleep, so I hope that you are well-rested after your journey.'

'I am, Mother.'

'I know that right now everything must seem very strange to you, but you will soon learn our ways and settle in. You are not here to be punished, Cissy, you are here to be taken care of with love and dignity. The other sisters and I will see to your welfare and help you through the difficult times ahead, because make no doubt about it, they *will* be difficult. Father Sullivan has told me that you wish for your baby to be adopted?'

'Yes, Mother, for I have no means of looking after it and I can't bring shame on my family.'

'I understand, child, but even though that is the decision you have made, giving away your baby will be the hardest thing that you have ever done, and we are here to support you in that decision. A good Catholic family will be found for your baby and you will be giving it the chance of a loving home with people who will cherish it. You will be giving them the gift of life, Cissy, and they will be forever in your debt. Now let us pray together for God's guidance in bringing you to us and his strength and wisdom to stand beside you. You are a part of this family now and we will do our best to look after you.'

It suddenly hit me what I was about to do. However kind these nuns were, they were not my people: I would have to go through this alone.

Before I left the room, Mother Ignatius handed me paper, envelopes, a pen and some stamps. 'You will want to write to your family.'

'But I can't give them this address, Mother, they mustn't know that I am in a convent. I told them that I was going to work in a big house.'

'I'm aware of that, Cissy. A lot of our girls have been in the same position as yourself. Luckily, I have a friend of the parish who has allowed us to use her address. She will deliver the answers to your letters when they arrive.'

'That's kind of her,' I said.

'If you look for kindness, Cissy, you will be sure to find it.'

CHAPTER THIRTY-EIGHT

As the weeks went by I began to get used to living in the convent and I became great friends with my room-mates. After we had done our daily chores we could pretty much do as we pleased, we were even allowed to go into the town. I preferred to stay behind, reading and walking in the gardens. I'd gone with the other girls once, but I didn't like the way we were stared at. It was very obvious where we had come from and some of the looks we got made me feel ashamed.

'Ignore them, Cissy,' said Rose. 'That's what I do.'

'I'd rather just stay here,' I said.

'I felt the same as you to start with but now I don't give a fisherman's tit what they think of me, as I'm never likely to see them again once I leave this place.'

'You're braver than me,' I said.

'Oh, it's not bravery, it's survival. I'd go mad if I didn't get out now and again.'

'I just want to get this over with and go home to Ireland.'

'We all want to go home, Cissy.'

Often in the afternoons when my friends had gone into town I wrote to Mammy and Colm. I kept my letters short and tried not to lie too much. I told them about Rose, May and Sally and said they were the girls I worked with. I told them that I was enjoying my job but couldn't wait to come home. Mammy's letters were shorter than mine, I knew she found letter-writing difficult. She said she missed me and that Buddy was fine. She always ended her letters by saying that Mr Collins wished to be remembered to me. Colm's letters on the other hand were full of love and sweetness. He said that I was in his thoughts every moment of every day. He passed on good wishes from Annie, Bridie and Mrs Hickey. His letters always had a heart with an arrow through it at the bottom of the page. I hated lying to them but I knew that it wouldn't be forever. I would soon be home and I could put all this behind me. I was protecting them from the truth and I would keep doing that for as long as I had to.

In the evenings, we sat on our beds chatting and I soon got to know my new friends better. Rose came from Brighton on the South Coast and like me, she had told her parents that she was working as a maid in one of the big houses. May lived in the East End of London and Sally came from Devon. Her parents had sent her to the convent with strict instructions that she should return home without a baby in tow.

'But I don't mind,' said Sally. 'I'm too young to have a child.'

It was May who shocked me the most, though. She looked like such a timid little thing and yet this was her third pregnancy.

'She's a brazen hussy,' said Sally, smiling fondly at her.

'I can't help meself,' said May. 'I think it's a sickness I have.'

'It's not a sickness,' said Rose, 'it's your inability to hang onto your halfpenny that's the matter.'

'Do you like babies, then?' I said.

'She doesn't keep any of them,' said Rose.

'So you give them away?' I said.

May nodded sadly.

'And you've had them all here?'

'Iggy keeps the bed warm for her,' said Sally.

'And she doesn't mind?'

'Oh, she minds alright,' said May. 'I have a dressing-down every time I come back. She keeps threatening to close the doors on me but I think she's decided that I am her burden to bear and she offers her suffering up to God. She says the sisters are worn out, praying to Saint Jude.'

'The Saint of Lost Causes?' I said.

'That's the feller.'

'Not that he's managed to come up with the goods yet,' said Rose.

'When is your baby due, May?' I asked gently.

She shrugged. 'When it comes, I suppose.'

A week later, I was woken up by screaming. Rose jumped out of bed and turned on the light. May was on all fours on the floor, clutching her stomach.

'Quick, Cissy, get one of the nuns,' said Rose. 'She's having her baby.'

I felt sick as I ran along the corridor to the nuns' quarters. I banged on the door and waited. It seemed like forever before it was opened by Sister Gertrude, who was standing there with a little white cap on her head and a nightgown that came down to her ankles. I had only ever seen her in her nun's habit and a part of me thought that I shouldn't be seeing her in this state of undress.

'Is it May?' she said.

'Yes, she's having her baby, Sister, please hurry.'

'I'll fetch Sister Theresa and we'll be right along. Keep her calm, Cissy, and tell her that everything will be alright.'

I ran back to the room.

Rose was rubbing May's back and Sally was holding her hand. 'Did you find someone?'

'Sister Gertrude and Sister Theresa are on their way,' I said.

May let out another piercing scream. 'Holy Mother of God, I can't do this!' she sobbed.

'Of course you can,' said Rose gently. 'You're a strong brave girl and you can push this baby out.'

'I can't, I can't,' moaned May.

'There now,' said Sister Gertrude coming into the room. 'Let's get you somewhere more comfortable.'

'I can't do this, Sister,' cried May. 'It hurts too much this time.'

'And that pain will be gone as soon as your baby is born. Now lean on me and Sister Theresa and we'll take you upstairs.'

'Do you need help, Sister?' asked Rose.

'We can manage, can't we, May? Slowly now, there's a grand girl.'

Rose squeezed May's hand. 'We'll come and visit you as soon as we're allowed.'

After they had left, we all sat on Rose's bed and covered ourselves with the blankets.

'She's no more than a child herself,' said Rose angrily.

I looked at Sally; there were tears rolling down her cheeks.

'She's not a hussy, is she?' I said softly.

'No, she's not, Cissy.'

'It's okay, you don't have to tell me.'

Rose took a big breath. 'It's her father,' she eventually said.

I didn't understand. 'What's her father got to do with it?'

'He's the one that gives her the babies,' said Sally.

I stared at her, I couldn't believe what I was hearing. 'But can't someone do something to help her? Can't the nuns put a stop to it?'

'I felt exactly the same as you when May told us,' said Rose. 'I went barging into Iggy's office and demanded that she went to the police about him.'

'So why didn't she?'

'Apparently, every time May gets pregnant, her father drops her off at the convent and when she's had the baby, he fetches her home again. Iggy said that if she interfered or made him angry, he wouldn't bring her here again and she'd end up having the child on the kitchen floor. At least when he brings her to the nuns they are able to look after her properly.'

I could feel my eyes filling with tears. 'Poor May,' I said.

'The awful thing is,' said Sally, 'she thinks it's normal.'

'Normal? How can she think it's normal?'

'I suppose it's all she's ever known, poor little cow,' said Rose. 'I wish I could help her.'

'We all wish that we could help her, Cissy, but I don't know what any of us could do.'

'Ruby was all for finding out where he lived and setting the house alight while he was asleep,' Sally smiled. 'She would have done as well if me and Rose hadn't talked her out of it.'

'Who's Ruby?'

'The girl that was here before you. She grew very fond of May, she would have done anything to save her from her pig of a father,' said Rose.

'I wish I'd met her,' I said.

'She was a great girl, one of the best. She even went against her family and refused to give her baby up for adoption.'

'And did her family let her home with the baby?'

'Well, she left here with the child in her arms, so I don't suppose she gave them much of a choice,' said Sally.

'Ruby said she would rather live in a cardboard box than give her baby to strangers.'

'She sounds like a grand girl altogether,' I said.

'She certainly had guts,' said Sally, grinning.

I lay awake thinking about poor May and how awful her life must be. How I longed to be home in the little cottage in Paradise Alley. How I yearned to walk up to the grey house and hold Colm in my arms and how I wished with all my heart that I had never met Peter Bretton and been such a foolish girl.

'Are you awake?' whispered Rose.

'Yes.'

'Me too,' said Sally.

'How long does it take to have a baby?' I said.

'Not long, I hope,' said Rose.

'I'm bloody terrified,' said Sally.

'Have you thought about keeping your baby?' I asked.

'I've thought about it,' said Sally, 'but we live in a small village and my mum said that the family name would be forever tarnished if I came back with a baby and no husband. I'm not as strong as Ruby and, even if I was, I couldn't do that to them.'

'How about you, Rose?'

'I don't let myself go there. If I did, I think I'd go mad. I trust the nuns to find a good home for it and that's all I can do. How about you, Cissy?'

I panicked every time I thought about this child that I was carrying 'Oh no, I can't keep this baby, I just can't,' I said.

Rose put her arm around my shoulder, 'It's okay, Cissy, nobody is judging you here. We all have our own story to tell and our own road to walk.'

Just then Sister Gertrude put her head round the door. 'Are you awake, girls?'

'We are, Sister,' I said.

'I thought you would like to know that May has delivered of a beautiful baby boy and thanks be to God they are both fine. Now try to get some sleep and you can visit her in the morning. Good night, girls, and God bless.'

The three of us were in tears on hearing that May was okay. We knew that not everyone survived childbirth and we were just relieved that dear May had and couldn't wait for morning when we could see her.

CHAPTER THIRTY-NINE

The next day the three of us rushed through our chores and were soon eagerly going up the stairs to visit May. The door was opened by Sister Theresa. 'Good morning, girls,' she said.

'Can we see her, Sister?' said Rose.

'Of course you can but don't stay long because she is very tired after all her hard work.'

We walked over to May's bed and sat down. She was asleep, but it was nice just to be near her. Sally held her hand and after a while she opened her eyes.

'Hello, sleepyhead,' said Sally gently.

May didn't answer, she just smiled.

'Are you okay?' asked Rose.

'I had a little boy,' she said.

'We know,' said Sally. 'Sister Gertrude told us.'

'I've called him Billy.'

'That's nice.'

'I named him after the grocer down the end of our road, he's always been kind to me. He punched my dad once, knocked him clean out. I thought for a minute he'd killed him but he came round. I never have any bloody luck!'

'Did it hurt much?' said Sally.

'It was like passing a block of flats,' said May.

Sally shuddered at the thought of what she was going to have to go through. 'You'd think there'd be an easier way, wouldn't you?'

'I wish Ruby could see him,' said May. 'I'd love that.'

'Why don't you write to her?' I said.

Rose shook her head.

'I never learned,' said May.

'Learned what?'

'To write,' said Rose, glaring at me. 'May has never learned to write.'

'They wouldn't take her at school because she was so clever that she'd show the other kids up. Isn't that right, May?' said Sally.

May giggled.

I felt awful. 'I'll write it for you,' I said. 'Would you like that?'

'Yes please, Cissy.'

'I'll get her address from the nuns.'

Rose looked round the room. 'Where is the baby?'

Just at that moment Sister Theresa came into the room carrying a tiny bundle in her arms, tightly wrapped in a small white blanket. I could see a little arm waving like a starfish. May's face lit up as she hoisted herself up in the bed and Sister placed the baby in her arms.

'He's a little angel. God bless him,' Sister Theresa told us.

'Does he have all his fingers and toes?' said May.

'Look for yourself,' said Sister.

May gently folded back the blanket and the baby started to kick his little chubby legs. 'Hello, Billy,' she said. 'I'm your mummy.'

I had a lump in my throat that was threatening to choke me, and I could see that Rose and Sally were struggling not to cry as well.

As May gazed down at him he looked back at her and never in my life had I seen two people who loved each other so much. How was she going to be able to part with him? Without thinking, my hands went down to my own belly and cradled it.

'Isn't he beautiful?' said May, a look of awe on her tired face.

'Beautiful,' I repeated.

'Are you hungry, darling?' said May. 'Are you?'

She pushed down her nightdress so that her breast was set free and she helped her baby, guiding his mouth to her nipple. I watched, transfixed, as the baby's lips settled and then he began to suck, making funny hungry little noises. His tiny hand rested on May's breast, his fingers so small it was hard to believe that they were real. Still he gazed up at May and she gazed down at him, stroking his cheek with the back of her finger.

'You're doing a good job, May,' said Sister Theresa.

May looked up at her and smiled. 'I know what I'm doing, Sister.'

'Yes, you do, you're a grand little mother.'

May nodded and looked down again and then she reached up her hand and wiped the tears from her eyes with her wrist.

'Time to go, girls,' said Sister Theresa. 'May needs her beauty sleep.'

As we walked back downstairs, I said, 'I didn't know we had to feed them, I just thought they'd take them away.'

'We have to look after the babies until a suitable family is found for them, Cissy. It could take weeks, even months. The nuns are hardly going to be paying for bottles of milk when we have it on tap.'

So I wasn't going to be able to go home as soon as the baby was born? I felt sick to my stomach and at the same time I felt ashamed of myself for not wanting to feed my own child. But I couldn't help it, I wanted to go home as soon as possible and forget that any of this had happened. I'd marry Colm and we'd have a baby of our own, a baby born out of love, not a quick fumble in the woodshed.

'We all have to do it, Cissy,' said Sally. 'We don't get away with it that easily.'

'But I thought…'

'I know what you thought but it's not the way it works. May here has had to do this three times. She's had to give up three babies, Cissy, and she's still able to smile.'

I could tell that Sally was disappointed in me and she was right to be, I was a selfish girl. I thought of May smiling down at her little boy with such love in her eyes. But I wasn't May, I couldn't let myself love this child inside me. I told myself that it was better this way. My child would have a good home with parents who wanted it, they would love it even if I couldn't.

CHAPTER FORTY

The three of us were sitting on the grass at the back of the convent trying to come up with a plan to save May.

'We could hide her?' suggested Sally.

'He'd have the place turned upside down,' said Rose, 'and he'd probably get the law in.'

'But she can't go back there,' I said.

'No, she bloody well can't!' said Sally.

We sat in silence, each with our own thoughts. A warm breeze touched my skin and lifted the hair from the back of my neck. It was hard to believe that on this beautiful day there were homes like the one May lived in, full of fear and sadness and pain.

My thoughts went back to Bretton Hall. The daffodils would be in full bloom, covering the lawn and sweeping down to the sea like a blanket of gold. It felt like a million years ago that I had first stepped through those doors and a million years since I was in Peter Bretton's arms. I never wanted to see that place again and I never wanted to see Peter again. Yet I wondered who had taken my place and I hoped that whoever she was, she would be a friend to Annie.

'We should try talking to Iggy again,' said Rose. 'She must be as worried as we are about May.'

'How long will she have to feed Billy?' I said.

'About six weeks, unless they find a family for him sooner.'

'Hello, girls,' said Sister Luke, walking towards us.

'Hello, Sister,' we chorused.

'It's nice to see the three of you enjoying this beautiful God-given day. Have you been up to see May this morning?'

'We were just about to go, Sister,' I said.

'Well, say hello to her for me, won't you?'

'We will, Sister,' said Sally.

'Sister?' said Rose.

'Yes, child?'

'Do you think we could have a word with Ig… I mean, Mother Ignatius?'

'Mother is at prayer now but I will tell her that you would like to speak to her. Is it concerning May?'

'It is, Sister.'

'The poor child is in our prayers.'

As we watched Sister Luke walk away, Sally made a face. 'Lot of bloody good prayers are going to do her!'

'It's worth a try,' I said.

'It's not prayers she wants, it's an escape route.'

When we walked into May's room there was a girl sitting beside the bed.

'Ruby!' screamed Sally.

Sally and Rose threw their arms around her.

'You two haven't changed,' said Ruby. 'You're still as fat as ever. Another partner in crime?' she said, looking at me.

'This is Cissy,' said Rose, 'visiting us from Ireland, she fancied a little holiday with the nuns.'

'I thought I'd come and see my old mate here,' said Ruby, gazing fondly at May.

'Wasn't it good of her to come all this way to see me and Billy?'

'I'm glad you're here, girls,' said Ruby, suddenly looking serious. 'I have something to put to May.'

We pulled up some chairs and sat down.

'May,' said Ruby. 'I've told my parents all about you and they would like you to come and live with us. If you would like to.'

'Of course, it's what she'd like,' said Sally, jumping up.

'Oh, Ruby,' said Rose, 'we've been trying to think of a way to help her and now you've come up with the best plan ever!' She grinned at May. 'Imagine, May, you can go and live with Ruby, you won't ever have to go home again.'

Instead of looking happy, May had a look of absolute horror on her face. 'No!' she screamed, 'No!'

'What's wrong, darling?' asked Ruby, holding May's hand.

Tears were running down May's face. 'I can't live with you, Ruby, I have to go home, I *have* to.'

'But why? Can you tell me why?'

May had her head in her arms and she was sobbing. None of us could understand why she was so upset by what should have been wonderful news.

'It's alright, love,' said Ruby gently, 'It's alright.'

The four of us sat staring at May. There was something very wrong here and May wasn't telling.

'We'll leave you with Ruby,' said Sally.

Ruby nodded. 'I'll find you,' she said.

We closed the door gently. Sister Luke was waiting for us at the bottom of the staircase.

'Ah, girls,' she said, smiling. 'Mother is waiting for you in her office.'

'Thank you, Sister,' said Rose, almost absent-mindedly.

I waited until Sister Luke walked away. 'I don't understand,' I said.

'Neither do I,' agreed Sally. 'It's the perfect solution. Ruby lives in Cornwall, May's old git of a father would never find her there.'

'Then why won't she go?' I said.

'She looked terrified, there must be one hell of a reason why she won't take Ruby up on her offer,' said Rose.

'Maybe Iggy knows, come on.'

Mother Ignatius listened while we filled her in on what had just happened. She fingered the crucifix around her neck sadly and shook her head.

'It makes no sense, Mother,' said Sally.

'And yet it makes perfect sense to May,' said Mother Ignatius, standing up and walking across to the window.

She didn't say anything for a minute and then she turned to face us. 'May has three younger sisters at home.'

'But what's that got to do with anything?' I said.

'May says that if she doesn't go back, they won't be safe from her father. She believes she is protecting her sisters, girls, and she won't be persuaded by any other course of action.'

So that was it, she was sacrificing herself for the people she loved. Poor, brave May.

'Going to live with Ruby is the best chance she's got, Mother,' said Rose. 'There must be a way to make her see sense.'

'Do you think we haven't tried over the years, Rose?'

'Of course, Mother, I'm sorry.'

'We've offered her a job here with us, helping with the babies, but no, she just goes back home until the next time he delivers her to our door. The Sisters' hearts are broken every time she leaves us, knowing what is ahead of the poor child, but what can we do to help her if she refuses to help herself?'

'You have to find a way to help her this time, Mother, you *have* to.'

Mother Ignatius sat back down and faced us. 'Myself and the Sisters will pray to our Blessed Lord to intervene and cause May's bastard of a father to have a slight accident, rendering him dead.'

The three of sat staring at her with our mouths open.

'Don't look so shocked, girls. The word is used liberally in the Bible and never has a word been more appropriate than in the case of May's father.'

CHAPTER FORTY-ONE

Six weeks later, we were standing on the platform saying goodbye to May and Ruby. Fate had stepped in and given May her freedom: she was on her way to a new life in Cornwall with her dear friend. Sister Gertrude had come with us and was holding little Billy in her arms.

'You saved me,' said May, 'and I'll never forget you all.'

'I'd say it was a higher power than us that saved you,' replied Rose.

'Keep in touch,' said Sally.

'I will.'

Whistles were blowing, and doors were slamming as the train prepared to leave the station.

'Come on, May,' said Ruby gently. 'It's time to go home.'

The three of us held May in our arms and Sally pulled Ruby into the circle. We reluctantly let them go and they stepped up into the carriage. Sister Gertrude handed the tiny baby boy to May.

'Be happy, child,' she said, dabbing at her eyes.

'I will, Sister,' said May, reaching for the baby. 'Thank you for everything.'

'It's our Blessed Lord and Saviour you have to thank, May, for he does indeed work in mysterious ways, his miracles to perform.'

'Ruby?' said Sally.

Ruby stepped back down onto the platform. 'Take care of them both,' said Sally.

Ruby smiled at us. 'I promise you girls that as long as I live, she will never know fear like that ever again.'

May and Ruby were hanging out of the window as the train moved slowly out of the station. We waved like mad until their faces disappeared in a cloud of smoke.

'Fancy a cup of tea before we go back?' said Rose.

'That would be grand,' I said.

'Sister?' said Rose.

'I'm off to St Steven's to see how May's sisters are settling in. You enjoy your tea.'

We walked across to the waiting room and ordered tea and buns. I was full of joy to see May starting out on her new life away from London and away from all her pain and suffering. I didn't even care when a couple of snooty women tutted at our swollen bellies.

The waiting room was clean and cosy and although it was spring, there was a lovely fire burning in the grate.

'Well, that's our May gone,' said Sally, biting into a bun. 'I'm going to miss her.'

I took a sip of tea, it was milky and sweet. 'Do you really think that it was Iggy's prayers that caused that container to fall on her dad's head?'

'Nah, just coincidence,' said Sally.

'I wouldn't rule it out,' I said. 'I once prayed to Our Lady to make a horse well and she did.'

'I bet you also prayed to get the bleed, and it's pretty obvious she didn't answer your prayers that time. Now, either she was busy that day or she thought more of the horse than she did of you.'

I grinned. 'So it wasn't divine intervention then?'

'No,' said Sally. 'Just a stroke of good luck.'

'I wonder what Ruby's parents are going to say when she turns up with May and Billy?' I said.

'Well, they didn't send Ruby back with her baby, Susan, so I doubt they'll send Billy packing.'

'I liked Ruby a lot,' I said.

'She's one of the best,' said Sally. 'I wasn't a bit surprised when she decided that May couldn't leave Billy behind. Once Ruby makes her mind up about something, she sticks to it. Thanks to her, May is able to keep at least one of her babies.'

'Fancy another bun, girls?' asked Rose.

But Sally wasn't up for anything right then. She was white as a sheet and bent double over the table.

'Bloody hell, Sally! You're not having the baby, are you?'

'Of course I'm having the baby, you silly cow!'

'But it's not due for weeks,' said Rose.

'Tell that to the baby,' said Sally, groaning.

'What are we going to do?' I asked, feeling sick and worried for Sally.

'We're going to have to take a taxi back to the convent.'

'Who's going to pay?' gasped Sally.

'We'll worry about that when we get there,' said Rose.

CHAPTER FORTY-TWO

This was a spring like no other, with a sky so blue that it looked as if it had been painted. Everywhere were signs of new growth: daffodils, crocuses and tulips pushing up through the soft earth, vying with each other to be the brightest and the best.

A spring promising hope and new beginnings.

This was not a day to bury a child, who would never feel the warmth of the sun on her cheeks or the cool breeze ruffling through her hair. A child whose soul was as pure and white as the snowdrops scattered among the old gravestones.

Sally had laboured for two days; we could hear her screams all over the house. In the end, they had to call for the doctor but he couldn't save her little girl. Sister Gertrude said that they had almost lost Sally as well. Everyone was beside themselves with grief.

Sally stood between her parents as the little coffin was lowered into the ground. She hadn't cried, not once, not even when she was told that her baby had died.

We helped her pack her bags as her parents waited downstairs to take her home.

Rose and I didn't know what to say, we could find no words that would comfort her. The longer we didn't speak, the worse the silence got, until the silence itself screamed louder than any words.

Sally walked across to the window and stood looking down onto the graveyard. She seemed so alone but something stopped us from moving towards her; it felt as if she was lost to us and then we saw her shoulders heave and a guttural noise that didn't sound human rose up from the very depths of her. She was looking down at the wet patch on her blouse. 'I need to feed my baby,' she sobbed. 'Please let me feed my baby. *Oh please*, she'll be hungry.'

We were on our feet in an instant, holding her, stroking her hair and whispering words of comfort. They might not have been the right words but suddenly it didn't matter. She slid down onto the floor and we fell with her, rocking her like a child and letting her cry out all the sadness that she'd been keeping inside. We held her until the crying ceased, not speaking any more, just holding her. We stayed like that for so long that our three bodies seemed to become one.

Later that day, we stood on the steps and watched her walk down the drive with her parents. When she got to the gate she turned back and gave a small wave.

After Sally left, it felt awfully strange with only the two of us in the bedroom.

When I'd first arrived at the convent I'd thought there'd be loads of girls there and was surprised to find only three others.

Sally had explained. 'The nuns only take in six girls at a time, because they also run St Steven's, the orphanage down the road.'

I was worried that once Rose left, I'd be on my own but a couple of weeks later, we were joined by two sisters from Kilkenny. Their names were Agnus and Orla and they were like two peas in a pod, with fiery red hair and bright blue eyes.

'What the hell did your parents say when they found out the pair of you were pregnant?' said Rose.

'The mammy nearly lost her reason,' said Agnus. 'The poor woman had to take to her bed and the parish priest was a permanent fixture in the house. It was like a bloody mausoleum in there.'

'And he felt the need to sprinkle holy water over everything, including us. The eejit of a man had me hair bloody ruined,' said Orla.

'What about your father?' I said.

'He took to the drink.'

'Not that he hadn't taken to it before our disgrace, our downfall just gave him a good excuse to keep throwing it down his throat,' said Orla, smirking.

'But both of you?' said Rose. 'At the same time?'

'I know, aren't we desperate sinners?' said Agnus.

'We went to a local dance down at the town hall,' explained Orla. 'Some of the lads from the country had smuggled in some poteen.'

I'd heard of it, but Rose hadn't. 'What the bloody hell's that?' she said.

'It's Irish whiskey,' said Agnus, 'they make it up in the hills.'

'It's deadly stuff,' said Orla. 'It'd take the throat off ya.'

'Or in our case, our virginity,' said Agnus.

'Were the lads nice?' I said.

'I can't remember much about my one,' said Orla. 'But the boots on her feller looked like a couple of clodhoppers. I swear to God they still had bits of straw stuck to them.'

'I don't know what we were thinking,' said Agnus.

'I've a pretty good idea,' said Rose, grinning.

The pair of them were like a breath of fresh air and helped Rose and I deal with the sadness we were feeling over our friend.

'God, that was a desperate thing to happen,' said Agnus when we told them about Sally.

'And did you say it took two days to be born?' said Orla.

I nodded, feeling queasy at the thought.

'Jesus, I thought they just popped out like peas! That's what our friend Bernadette said anyway.'

'Well, I'd say your friend Bernadette was having you on,' said Rose.

'I'll kill her when we get back,' said Orla.

Some mornings I woke up and looked across at the beds, expecting May and Sally to be tucked up in them only to remember that it was Agnus and Orla asleep under the blankets.

My body was changing, and I hated it: it was a daily reminder of what I'd done. My breasts had always been small but now they were straining out of my clothes like a couple of overripe watermelons.

'You need to talk to one of the nuns about getting some smocks, they'll be more comfortable and give the baby room to grow,' said Rose.

I hadn't even thought about giving the baby room, I couldn't quite imagine a real baby inside me. I suddenly felt ashamed that I felt this way about an innocent child that had as much right to be loved as any of God's creatures but my growing belly was a constant reminder of Peter and my foolishness. I wanted this child to be born, I wanted to forget about its father. And I wanted to go back home where I belonged.

CHAPTER FORTY-THREE

A few weeks later, I was summoned to Mother Ignatius's office.

'What do you think she wants?' I asked Rose.

'I don't know, but I'd say you're about to find out.'

'Thanks for the help,' I said.

'Well, I'm not a bloody fortune teller, am I? Perhaps she thinks you're such a holy girl, you might want to join the good nuns as a postulant.'

'Very funny.'

'I'll wait in the garden for you and you can tell me what she wanted.'

I splashed some water on my face, put a comb through my hair and ran downstairs.

'Ah, Cissy, sit down, child,' said Mother Ignatius.

I sat and waited while she shuffled through some papers on the desk.

'Now this is a little unusual,' she said. 'We had a family all ready to take Sally's baby and their hearts are broken that the poor child died. I took it upon myself to mention you and that you were soon to give birth. I said I would speak to you first and if you are willing, these good people would like to adopt your child. Like I said, these are unusual circumstances and I will understand if this is not something that sits happily with you.'

I hadn't expected this, that my child would be a replacement for Sally's child. 'I don't know what to think, Mother,' I said honestly.

'Do you want to talk it over with Rose before you give me an answer?'

I nodded. 'Yes, please, I think I would.'

I stood up and went towards the door. 'Are they good people?' I asked, turning around.

'I've only met Mrs Grainger, Mr Grainger is away in America, working. She's a lovely woman, Cissy, and she longs to be a mother. Your child would be going to a good Catholic home. But don't be rushed into making a decision, talk to Rose and let me know.'

'Blimey!' said Rose, when I joined her on the bench. 'I don't know what to think either. Your child would be living the life that Sally's child should have lived, now that's strange.'

'Mmm, that's what I'm thinking.'

'On the other hand, they never met Sally's baby, they wouldn't be comparing them, would they? Your baby wouldn't be second best. At the moment they are mourning a child they never knew or loved.'

'Do you think I should agree, then?'

'You're certain you don't want to keep the baby?'

I wished people wouldn't keep asking me that question. I'd made up my mind and I wasn't going to change it. Keeping this baby would mean I could never return home. Ballybun was a small town, Peter Bretton would be sure to find out but even more importantly, I couldn't do that to Colm or the mammy. 'I don't have a choice, Rose,' I said.

'Then I think you should say yes.'

'I wonder why Iggy chose my baby and not yours; you're due before me.'

'Mine is already spoken for, Cissy.'

'You never said.'

Rose shrugged her shoulders. 'Iggy had them picked out as soon as I came here.'

I had to keep strong, I couldn't waver now. 'I suppose I'll say yes then.'

'You might as well, because if it's not this couple, it's going to be another and that will mean staying here longer, until they find someone else.'

That made my mind up, because the sooner I got back to Ireland, the better.

Rose's baby arrived the next day. She never even made it upstairs, she had her little girl in the refectory, after a good dinner of beef stew and sponge pudding, which she brought up all over the refectory floor. The nuns were running around like madwomen, fetching towels and blankets, all the time reassuring Rose that everything was going to be alright and not to start pushing just yet. But Rose's baby was waiting for no one and Sister Gertrude only just caught the little girl, otherwise she would have slid under the dining room table. They wrapped her in a towel and handed her to me, while they helped Rose. I couldn't believe what had just happened. One minute we had been chatting over dinner and the next I was watching Rose give birth.

'Can I see her?' asked Rose softly.

I held the baby towards her. She moved the towel away from the baby's face and gently touched her cheek. 'Is she alright, Cissy?'

I could feel hot tears burning behind my eyes. 'She's perfect, Rose,' I said.

I followed them upstairs, carefully holding the baby. She was making little mewing noises, like a kitten, and she felt warm and surprising heavy in my arms. Rose looked back at me and smiled. 'Mind you don't drop her, Cissy.'

'I'm not a complete eejit, I think I can carry a baby up some stairs,' I said, smiling back at her.

Sister Gertrude took the baby from my arms. 'I'll give her a little clean up and I'll bring her right back to you, Rose.'

Sister Theresa settled Rose in the bed. 'You have a little rest, and then we'll give you a refreshing wash,' she said, leaving the room.

I sat down next to the bed and held Rose's hand. 'Well, that was a bit of a shock, wasn't it?' I said. 'You never said you were in pain.'

'I wasn't,' said Rose, 'I just felt a bit sick. I thought it was the stew.' She didn't say anything for a while, then she said: 'Is she pretty?'

'She's lovely, Rose.'

Rose lay back against the pillows and closed her eyes. 'You can tell Agnus that her friend was right after all. Jenny popped out like a pea.'

'Is that what you're calling her, Jenny?'

'Yes, do you like it?'

'It's lovely.'

'It was going to be John if it was a boy but do you know what, Cissy? I always thought of my bump as Jenny. Have you got a name for yours?'

I felt my face redden. 'No, I haven't.'

The truth was that I'd never really thought about this baby as a proper person. I was sure that Mrs Grainger would love it, because she wouldn't be plagued with nightmares about how it was conceived. I wanted nothing to do with Peter Bretton and my growing belly was a constant reminder of him. I had to believe that my child would have the loving home that I wasn't able to give it.

To start with, Rose was determined not to fall in love with Jenny, but of course she did – we both did. I watched as Rose fed her; she seemed to know from the start what she was doing. Sister Luke said she was a natural mother and I agreed with her.

Jenny became our world and we couldn't wait to race upstairs every day to see her. Everything about her fascinated us, from her bright blue eyes to her wispy fair hair. I helped Rose to bathe her and we both giggled as she kicked her chubby little legs and screwed up her face when the water splashed over her. Jenny was beautiful, just like her mother, and I dreaded the day when she would be taken away.

Rose and I had become even closer since May and Sally had left. I admired her so much – she always seemed so strong, so sure of everything. I didn't know her story and she didn't know mine, and that was fine. We had made it an unwritten rule between us to keep our stories to ourselves. It had been different in May's case because she'd needed our help and thankfully, she had trusted Rose enough to confide in her. I wanted to ask Rose if she had prepared herself for saying goodbye to Jenny but because she didn't speak of it, I didn't feel that I could. One night, I woke to hear her sobbing so I got into bed with her and held her in my arms. I didn't ask her why she was crying, I didn't have to.

CHAPTER FORTY-FOUR

'I think these clothes were knitted with love,' I said, as I watched Rose do up the pearl buttons on the little white cardigan.

She smiled and nodded, her sadness filling the bedroom. 'Will you come with me, Cissy?'

'Of course I will.'

Tears were pouring down her cheeks as she picked up the tiny baby and held her against her heart. 'You won't remember me, little one,' she said. 'But I'll never forget you. I hope you have a wonderful life, my darling girl.'

I could barely see for tears as I watched Rose kiss the baby one last time before handing her to the young woman sitting nervously in Mother Ignatius's office. The woman's husband stood up and took Rose's hand. 'You have given us a gift, Rose,' he said, 'and we will be forever grateful to you.'

The young woman was staring down at the baby. 'She's beautiful,' she said, looking up at Rose. 'Have you given her a name?'

'Jenny,' said Rose.

'I think Jenny suits her. What do you think, Andrew?'

'I think Jenny is a lovely name, dear,' he said.

'Do you mind if we keep it?'

'That would make me happy,' nodded Rose.

The young man put his arm around his wife's shoulders. 'Jenny it is then,' he said, smiling down at her.

The young woman looked up at Rose. 'Thank you, Rose,' she said.

Tears were running down Rose's cheeks; she brushed them away with the back of her hand. 'Take good care of her,' she said.

'We will,' said the man. 'I promise you that we will.'

I put my arm around Rose as we stood on the convent steps and watched them drive away, then she broke away from me and ran down the drive after the car. I called after her and was about to follow when Mother Ignatius put her hand on my arm. 'Leave her,' she said sadly.

'But will she be alright?'

'Yes, she will, but not today, Cissy.'

I turned to go back indoors.

'I'd like to talk to you.'

'Of course,' I said, following her into the room and sitting down.

'I just wanted to tell you how pleased and grateful Mrs Grainger and her husband are that you have decided to let her adopt your baby.'

'I'm glad she's pleased,' I said.

'She did ask me to put one thing to you.'

'What is it?'

'She has requested that you don't feed the child yourself. How do you feel about that, Cissy?'

How did I feel about it? It meant that I could go home as soon as the baby was born. 'I don't mind, Mother,' I said.

'That's settled then. We will bind your breasts once you've had your baby and your milk will soon dry up.'

'How long will it take for my milk to dry up, Mother?'

'Two or three weeks, but it can vary.'

'Is that all, Mother?' I asked, standing up.

'Do you have any worries, Cissy? Anything you want to talk to me about?'

'Nothing,' I said. 'I'm fine.'

'Well, I'm always here if you need me, as are the other nuns.'

'Thank you.'

'The same applies to Rose. I know she is suffering. She comes across as a strong girl, but she doesn't have to bear this pain alone. Let her know we are praying for her.'

'I will, Mother.'

That night Rose and I squashed up together in her little bed.

'Do you have a dream, Cissy?'

'What sort of dream?'

'About the future.'

'Sort of, but it's not very exciting.'

'What is it?'

'To marry a boy called Colm and live happily ever after in Paradise Alley. Like I said, not very exciting. Do you have a dream, then?'

'Not one that's ever going to come true.'

'Tell me?'

'I want to go to Rome and Venice and Florence.'

All I knew about Rome was that His Holiness the Pope lived there. 'To visit the Pope?' I said.

'Don't be so bloody daft! Why would I be wanting to visit the Pope?'

'Why do you want to go there then?'

'To see Michelangelo's *David* and the ceiling in the Sistine Chapel and... Oh, I don't know, just to be there and see those things.'

I didn't know what she was talking about and when I didn't comment, she said, 'Art, Cissy. Sculptures and paintings and stuff like that.'

'Blimey, can you paint then?'

'Not really, although my teacher at school said I had some talent. She told me about her travels and she let me borrow books. Rome looks wonderful, but like I said, I doubt I'll ever get to see it.'

'Never say never, my friend.'

'It's just a dream, I'll probably go back and work with me mum in the knicker factory.'

'Well, we all need knickers,' I said.

We lay there for a while not speaking and then Rose said, 'Did you think they were nice, the young couple who took Jenny?'

'They seemed very kind, Rose. I thought they had kind faces.'

'They did, didn't they? I miss her, Cissy. I can still feel the weight of her in my arms.'

I held Rose's hand. 'Iggy said she's there if you want to talk to her.'

'What is there to talk about? She's gone, talking's not going to bring her back, is it?'

'No, no, it's not.'

'Goodnight, Cissy.'

'Goodnight, Rose.'

As I lay beside Rose I thought about Colm and Ireland and all the people I'd left behind in Paradise Alley and I longed to see their faces and I longed to be in Colm's arms. We continued to write to each other and that brought me some comfort but where Colm's letters were simple and honest, mine were full of lies.

I had got so fat, I could hardly walk. Mother Ignatius noticed me struggling with a bucket of water.

'What in the name of heavens are you doing, child?'

'I'm going to wash the hall floor, Mother.'

'You are not,' she told me. 'You are going to rest. It's a grand day, I suggest you sit in the garden and watch the world go by. You're not long off your time now, Cissy, and you need to take it easy,' she said, relieving me of the bucket. 'Away with you now.'

I walked out into the garden and sat down on a bench. It was so peaceful here, you couldn't help but feel at rest. There were a couple of nuns walking along, heads down, reading their Bibles. I suppose there was a lot to be said for the life they had chosen, not that it would have suited me. But they had nothing to worry about, did they? No rent to pay, no food to buy – in fact, nothing to worry about at all.

I closed my eyes and raised my face to the sun. Mother had said that this baby would soon be born.

I prayed that once it was all over I could put it behind me, I could be a young girl again. It had all been a dreadful mistake – a moment of foolishness that I regretted. I wouldn't let it ruin the rest of my life but would I ever be able to forget? I wanted to return to Ireland and never leave its shores again. I could almost feel Colm's arms around me, I was almost home.

CHAPTER FORTY-FIVE

I covered my ears with my two hands in an attempt to block out the screams that were coming from the baby. She hadn't stopped yelling from the moment she'd been born. All I wanted to do was sleep but her continuing cries wouldn't let me. The nuns hadn't bandaged me yet and the front of my nightgown was soaking wet.

'We've got a big one here,' Sister Gertrude had said as she'd eased the baby from my body.

'Ah, but she's lovely! Look at the grand head of hair on her, Cissy.'

But I didn't want to see her grand head of hair, I was in agony and she was the cause of it. Sister Gertrude had wrapped her in a towel and laid her on my tummy. I'd turned my face to the wall.

'Come on now, Cissy, hold your baby before she falls onto the floor.'

'Please take her away,' I begged.

'You'll feel better once you've had a bit of a sleep,' said Sister Theresa, taking the baby from me and placing her in the cot beside the bed.

I'll feel better when I'm on the boat back to Ireland, I'd thought.

Sister Theresa washed me gently with warm water. 'Now isn't that better?' she said.

'It is, Sister. Thank you.'

'Are you sure you don't want to hold her? She's a lovely little thing.'

I shook my head.

'Ah, Cissy, if you could just see her.'

'I don't want to see her!' I snapped. 'I'm not keeping her, am I? I'm not even feeding her!' That was the mistake that Rose had made, she'd bonded with Jenny and it had broken her heart to give her away. Well, that wasn't going to happen to me.

'You may regret it later, Cissy. Mother Ignatius encourages our girls to hold their babies, so that when they are gone from here they will remember.'

'But I don't want to remember, Sister. I want to go home and forget that I ever had her.'

I could see the disappointment in the Sisters' eyes but I couldn't change my feelings.

Suddenly there was a commotion outside the door, followed by Sister Luke bursting into the room.

'Come quickly, Sisters! Orla has fallen down the stairs.'

'Oh, dear God!' said Sister Gertrude. 'Is she badly hurt?'

'We don't know.'

'I'm sorry, Cissy, but we're needed. We'll be back as soon as we can, you just rest for a while.'

I couldn't believe that they were leaving me alone. I didn't know what to do with this screaming baby. And the more she screamed, the more milk oozed out of me.

I leaned across and patted the little bundle but that seemed to make the cries increase.

I got out of bed and leaned over the cot. I'd never seen anything so angry in my life. Her little face was bright red and sweaty and she was trying to kick her way out of the towel.

'Alright, alright,' I said, picking her up and getting back into bed. Every bit of me was hurting and my lower regions felt as if they'd been kicked by a horse. As soon as I'd settled her into my arms she started sucking at my wet nightie. This angered her even more and the screaming reached a whole new level.

I knew I shouldn't be feeding her but surely this once wouldn't hurt. Anything to stop the noise. I undid my buttons and she immediately latched onto my breast. A pain like I'd never felt before shot through my body, making me cry out. I moved her head and positioned her better and at last the screaming stopped as she sucked away. I looked out of the window. All I wanted was for this nightmare to stop, for someone to come in and take her away. I was aware of her pawing at my breast like a little kitten. Finally, I looked down at her. Her eyes were wide open and she was looking at me. 'Hello,' I said softly. I held her tiny hand and she grabbed hold of my finger so tightly, it was as if she never wanted to let me go. As I looked down at her little face I could feel something change in me. It was as if I'd been asleep and I was suddenly wide awake. My heart that had been frozen for so long began to melt, as I held my baby close. When she'd been in my belly all I'd been able to think of was Peter Bretton; in my head that was all I could imagine. She was just a thing that had invaded my body, not a real baby at all, just an unwanted extension of him.

How could I have imagined this perfect little being? I gently smoothed her soft downy hair – dark, like the mammy's – and when she stared up at me I felt for all the world as if I was looking into the granddaddy's eyes. I could see nothing of Peter Bretton in her, but even if I had it wouldn't have made any difference to the way I felt. If her father had been the Devil himself I would have loved her just as much.

'I'm sorry,' I whispered. 'I didn't know it was you.'

I watched as her eyes closed, her dark lashes brushing her pale cheeks. I lifted her up and kissed her milky lips. I breathed in her baby smell, feeling as though I couldn't get enough of her.

The late September sun streamed through the window, bathing us in light and warmth. I leaned back against the pillows, holding my child close to my heart. Whatever happened from now on, we would face it together; together we would find a way. I was filled with a strength I never knew was in me and in that moment I knew that I would fight anyone who tried to take her from me. 'It's just you and me now,' I said, smiling down at her.

I didn't have to think what I would call her. I kissed the top of her head and whispered, 'Your name is Nora, Nora Ryan, and I will love and protect you all the days of your life.'

CHAPTER FORTY-SIX

'Will you take Nora back to Ireland, Cissy?'

I shook my head. 'No, Mother, I can't do that.'

'Then have you thought about what you *will* do?'

'No, Mother. I only know that I can't give her up, I *can't.*'

'I know, and I wouldn't try to persuade you otherwise. This decision has to be yours and yours alone.'

'I thought maybe I could work somewhere where they would let me keep her with me.'

'I will make enquiries but I have to tell you that it's unlikely. Is there no one you know in England that would take you both in?'

'No one, Mother. What little family I have is in Ireland.'

'Wouldn't it be an idea to write to your mother and explain about the baby? She is, after all, her granddaughter.'

'It's not that she would turn us away, Mother, it's not that. She's a good woman, she would never turn her back on me or Nora.'

'Then isn't that your best chance? Wouldn't she in time accept the child? If she loves you, wouldn't she also grow to love your child?'

'Mother, when my mammy had me she wasn't married, we had to go into the workhouse. She didn't want me to take the same path that she had taken, she wanted a better life for me and I promised her that I would be a good girl. I can't let her down, I can't bring shame on her.'

'I do understand, but I'm not sure that you are in a position to be so caring of your mother's feelings. You are not your mother, Cissy, and you are not responsible for her past mistakes.'

'There is someone else that I can't hurt.'

'And who is that?'

'Colm. We were to be married as soon as I got back home, he knows nothing about the child.'

'So, I take it that he is not the father?'

I would never tell anyone about Peter Bretton, no one must ever know. 'No, Mother, he is not the father, I only wish he was.'

'Then I will make enquiries. In the meantime you will stay here with us.'

'Thank you, Mother. Have you told Mrs Grainger that I have changed my mind?'

'I have and she was very gracious about it. She is of course very disappointed but she understands and respects your decision. She's a good woman, Cissy.'

'She sounds nice.'

'A few prayers might help, we could do with the Lord on our side.'

'I can do that, Mother, and I'll earn my keep.'

'I know you will, child. Now off you go while I try to find a place for the two of you.'

'Thank you, Mother, for everything.'

'Get praying, Cissy, get praying.'

Nora became my world and I became hers. I loved walking in the gardens, holding her in my arms, her little cheek pressed against mine. We'd sit under a big old tree and while the autumn leaves fell down around us, I'd talk to her, just as I used to talk to the granddaddy. I told her about Paradise Alley; I described the old stone archway leading to the six white cottages and I told her about the granddaddy and Mammy and Colm. 'And oh, you would love Blue,' I said. 'I was frightened of him at first but sure, he's the gentlest of creatures. I'm sorry that you won't meet him.' I missed my home and I missed the people I loved, but something had changed in me now: all that mattered now was Nora.

Agnus and Orla were as fascinated by my baby as I was.

'She's only gorgeous, Cissy,' said Agnus, smiling down at her. 'Like a little angel, she is.'

'I can see why you couldn't give her up,' said Orla. 'I hope I don't fall in love with mine.'

'You've no need to worry about that ,Orla,' said Agnus. 'Because yours will be as ugly as sin, just like its daddy…'

'Well, that's where you're wrong, Agnus Cohan, because Sister Luke said that my baby could have died when I fell down those stairs, instead it was saved by our Blessed Lord, which means he has something special mapped out for it.'

'Like what?' asked Agnus.

'Oh, I don't know, maybe it's destined to be Pope, or a film star. Or…'

'A farmer,' butted in Agnus. 'Like its gobshite of a father!'

'Well, if mine's going to be as ugly as sin then yours is going to be even uglier. Now I come to think about it, your feller had a terrible spotty face, like great festering boils, they were.'

'Enough, girls!' I said, laughing. 'All babies are beautiful and I'm sure yours will be gorgeous altogether.'

'Don't be holding your breath, Orla,' whispered Agnus, grinning mischievously.

I could have stayed quite happily at the convent forever. I worked hard to pay for my keep and once my work was done, I spent all my time caring for Nora. I had no desire to go anywhere else. Maybe Mother Ignatius would let me stay here? A week later, she called me into her office. 'Bring Nora with you,' she said.

When I walked into the office there was a woman sitting at the desk. She stood up as I entered.

'Cissy, this is Mrs Grainger.'

The women was shorter than me. She was wearing a black fitted suit with a long and narrow skirt, ending just above her slim ankles. The jacket was nipped in at the waist and there was silver button detail on the cuffs. She looked very rich and very sure of herself.

My arms tightened around Nora. 'I haven't changed my mind,' I said quickly.

'That's not why I'm here, dear,' she said gently.

'Sit down, Cissy,' said Mother Ignatius.

I sat down and waited for someone to speak.

'Mrs Grainger came to see me last week and she is offering to help you.'

'In what way?' I said.

'She is willing to give you a position in her house.'

'But what about Nora?'

Mrs Grainger smiled at me. 'Cissy, I was of course very sad when I heard that you had changed your mind about letting me adopt your baby.'

'I couldn't help it,' I said. 'I'm really sorry.'

'There is no need to be sorry, you fell in love with your baby and there is nothing more natural than that. Mother Ignatius explained the position you are in and I would really like to help.'

'And Nora?' I said again.

'She will be taken good care of in the nursery.'

'So, you see, Cissy, Mrs Grainger is offering you a job and your baby will be looked after until such time as you can care for her yourself.'

I couldn't take it in. I mean, this was what I had hoped for, wasn't it? To find a job where they would let me keep my baby? So why wasn't I dancing round Mother Ignatius's office full of relief and joy?

'Can I hold her?' said Mrs Grainger, suddenly.

I didn't want to hand Nora over, but I nodded and passed the sleeping baby into her arms. Her eyes filled with tears as she looked down at her. 'She's beautiful, Cissy,' she said, so softly I could barely hear her. I watched as she smoothed Nora's little head. 'I really would like to help, you know.' She handed Nora back to me. 'Take your time, Cissy, please don't think I'm rushing you.'

After she'd left the room, I walked across to the window and watched as the chauffeur helped her into the car and drove away down the drive.

I know I should have jumped at the chance. It was a godsend, a way to keep Nora, but I couldn't understand why anyone would be so kind to someone they didn't know.

'Well, what do you think?' said Mother Ignatius, coming back into the room.

'Why would she do this for me?'

'Because she's a kind lady, Cissy, who has known heartache.'

'What sort of heartache?'

'She has lost three babies, she carried the last one to seven months. She and her husband have had to accept that they will never have a child of their own. She has made a commitment to our Blessed Lord to help those less fortunate than herself.'

I looked down at Nora, who was still fast asleep. We would both have a home, we would be safe. I wished Rose was there to talk to.

'Well?' said Mother Ignatius.

'I'll think about it, Mother.'

'Good girl,' she said, smiling. 'Now pass me that beautiful baby, I'm in desperate need of a cuddle.'

CHAPTER FORTY-SEVEN

I looked around the bedroom one last time. There was a part of me that didn't want to leave. I'd been happy here, I'd been loved and taken care of. I hadn't expected to make friends and yet Rose and May and Sally had become dear to me and I'd never forget them. I had also grown fond of Orla and Agnus. I was walking into the unknown and I was anxious and worried.

But alongside that fear was the thought that today I would at last have my child in my arms again. I would see her little face and breathe in the sweetness of her.

I hadn't seen Nora for a week and when I'd handed her over to Mrs Grainger it had felt as if someone had put their hand inside my heart and ripped it from my body. She'd arrived and taken Nora away. I knew that I would see her again but that was no comfort to me. I had held my baby every single day since she'd been born, I could still feel the beat of her heart against mine. I was lost without her. To think that I'd never wanted her, how could I have thought that? How could I have not known that this tiny scrap of a person would become my whole world?

Mrs Grainger had been adamant about me not feeding her. I tried giving Nora a bottle, even though my breasts were full and aching, but she wouldn't take it and she screamed and wriggled in my arms.

'It's because she can smell your milk, Cissy,' said Sister Gertrude. 'I'm afraid the Sisters will have to feed her.'

I broke my heart crying in Mother Ignatius's office. 'I don't understand, Mother,' I said. 'What difference does it make to Mrs Grainger whether I feed Nora or not? And why couldn't I leave with Nora?'

'I know it seems harsh, Cissy, but she doesn't want the staff to know that you have had a baby out of wedlock. She doesn't want them gossiping behind your back and making things difficult for you. If you and Nora had arrived at the house on the same day, they might well have put two and two together and realised she was your child. Mrs Grainger is a good woman and her only thought is to protect you. You have to trust that she has yours and the baby's best interests at heart.'

'But aren't they going to wonder why there is suddenly a child in the house?'

'They had been made aware that Mrs Grainger was adopting a baby, so it will come as no surprise to them. This is your best chance, Cissy, and I for one am very grateful to her. You don't come across unconditional kindness like this every day of the week.'

Maybe I was a wicked girl but I couldn't help but think that Mother Ignatius had never had a child of her own and had no idea what I was feeling.

'But doesn't that mean that she is passing off Nora as her own baby?' I said.

'Oh no, I'm sure that is not the case. We must have faith, Cissy.'

Sister Luke came into the bedroom. 'Are you all packed and ready, Cissy?'

I took one more look around the room. 'I am,' I said, picking up my case.

'Good girl, we should get going then.'

I followed Sister Luke downstairs and my eyes filled with tears when I saw the Sisters gathered in the hallway to say goodbye. Mother put her arms around me and held me close. 'Our thoughts and prayers go with you, Cissy, and remember we are here if you need us.'

'Thank you for everything that you and the Sisters have done for me. I'll never be able to repay you for your kindness.'

'Your happiness will be payment enough, child.'

Agnus and Orla came in from the garden.

'We thought we'd missed you,' said Agnus.

'You nearly did,' I said, grinning.

'Have a grand time at your big posh house,' said Orla, 'and give that baby a big hug from us.'

'I will, and good luck to the pair of you.'

Agnus hugged me. 'Sure, we'll be fine, Cissy, you just take care of yourself.'

'Stay away from the dances,' I said, kissing them both on the cheeks.

There was a taxi waiting on the drive. 'Have you been at the collection box again, Sister Luke?' I whispered.

'All above board this time, Cissy,' she said, grinning.

I climbed into the cab and waved out the back window until the Sisters and the convent were out of sight.

I felt sick with excitement as the car drove through London. I would soon see Nora and I could hardly wait. The Sisters had told me that Mrs Grainger lived in a place called St John's Wood. I'd never heard of it but as we started passing terraces of tall elegant houses I guessed it was going to be very posh indeed, although not as posh as Bretton Hall and I was glad of that.

'This is it, Miss,' said the driver. 'If you don't mind me asking, are you going to be working here?'

'I am,' I said.

'Then you'd best go below stairs and not use the front door, you don't want to be getting off on the wrong foot.'

I thanked him and stepped out onto the pavement.

'Good luck, girl,' he said with a nod.

I watched him drive away and stood looking up at the house. Behind one of those windows was my baby. I counted four stories as well as the basement. I took a deep breath and went down the narrow steps.

I knocked on the door and it was opened immediately by a young girl. 'Oh,' she said, 'I thought you were the butcher.'

'Sorry,' I said.

She smiled at me. 'Then you must be Cissy. I'm Maggie, come in out of the cold.'

There was an older woman rolling out some pastry on the kitchen table. 'It's Cissy,' said the girl. 'And there was me thinking it was the butcher,' she added, giggling.

'Right, Cissy. Well, you've met the mad one, I'm the sane one, Mrs Dobbs.'

'Pleased to meet you,' I said, shaking her hand.

'Maggie, put the kettle on,' said Mrs Dobbs. 'I don't know about you but I'm parched.'

'A cup of tea would be grand,' I said.

'Sit yourself down then, girl.'

I put my case on the floor and sat at the table.

'Mrs Grainger tells me you have come across from Ireland to better yourself.'

Is that what she's told everyone? I thought. 'Well, I don't know about bettering myself, that suggests there was something wrong with me before.'

Mrs Dobbs threw her head back and roared with laughter. 'You'll do,' she said. 'And you'll need some of that when you meet Mrs Cornish.'

'Who's she?'

'The housekeeper.'

'She's an old battleaxe,' said Maggie, placing a steaming cup of tea in front of me.

'Just do your job and you'll be fine,' said Mrs Dobbs.

It was lovely and warm in the kitchen and I felt comfortable sitting there drinking my tea and watching Mrs Dobbs roll out the pastry. The room wasn't as big as the kitchen at Bretton Hall but that made it feel more cosy. I'd taken to Maggie and Mrs Dobbs right away and I'd deal with Mrs Cornish when the time came – she couldn't be any worse than Caroline Bretton.

'What will my duties be, Mrs Dobbs?'

'A bit of everything. It's not a big household, Cissy, and Mrs Grainger isn't much of a one for entertaining. Mrs Pullet comes in daily to do the heavy cleaning. You'll help Maggie here with the beds and the fires, and you'll both give me a hand in the kitchen.'

'Does anyone else work here?'

'Nanny Price looks after the nursery and she's helped by Betsy, God love her.'

'There are children then?' I said, crossing my fingers behind my back.

'Just Charlotte.'

I was confused. 'Charlotte?' I said.

'The prettiest baby you ever saw,' said Mrs Dobbs. 'She has a head of dark hair and skin like porcelain.'

'What's porcelain?' Maggie chimed in.

'It's good china,' said Mrs Dobbs.

'You make her sound like a doll,' said Maggie, laughing.

Mrs Dobbs smiled. 'She's not far off one, bless her little heart.'

'Is there just the one baby?' I asked.

'Yes, just the one. What makes you ask?'

I had to be careful. 'It's just that you said there were two people working in the nursery.'

'More like one and a half,' said Maggie.

'Now that's not kind, Maggie,' said Mrs Dobbs. 'What she means, Cissy, is that Betsy is… well, how can I explain Betsy?'

'She's not quite all there,' said Maggie.

'Child-like,' said Mrs Dobbs. 'That's how I would describe Betsy. She's child-like.'

Just then a woman came into the kitchen. I stood up.

The woman reminded me a bit of Mrs Hickey, except that her uniform was posher. She had on a long black dress, the sleeves were long too and there was a belt around her ample waist which held an assortment of keys, making a jangling sound every time she moved.

'Cissy Ryan?' said the woman.

'Yes, Miss,' I said.

'You can call me Mrs Cornish, I'm the housekeeper.'

'Yes, Mrs Cornish,' I said.

'Mrs Grainger would like to see you in the drawing room and then Maggie will show you your room.'

I followed Mrs Cornish up the stone steps leading from the kitchen. Her rather large rear end swayed to and fro in front of me. We then walked across the highly polished wooden floor of the grand entrance hall and I waited while she knocked on the door.

'Come in,' said a voice from within the room.

Mrs Cornish went in ahead of me. 'Cissy Ryan is here, Mrs Grainger.'

'Thank you, Mrs Cornish, you can leave us.'

'Come and sit down, Cissy,' she said, beckoning towards a sofa. 'You found us alright, then?'

'The nuns paid for a taxi,' I said.

'That was good of them.'

'They've been very kind to me.'

'Indeed, they have. I imagine Mrs Dobbs has filled you in on your duties?'

'She has.'

'Then I hope you will be happy with us.'

Mrs Grainger was wearing a pale blue dress that looked as if it was made of silk. She crossed her ankles and relaxed back in the chair.

'Can I see my baby now?'

'I'm sorry, Cissy, but that won't be possible. She has a sleep at this time. Nanny Price will be very cross with us if we interfere with Charlotte's routine and we don't want the wrath of Nanny Price to come down on our heads, do we? The nursery is her domain and we have to respect that.' She was smiling at me but her smile couldn't hide the hardness behind those pale blue eyes.

I stared at her, feeling angry inside. The nursery might be Nanny bloody Price's domain, but the baby was mine. 'My baby's name is Nora, Mrs Grainger, it's not Charlotte.'

'Oh, I'm sorry, Cissy, I should have mentioned this before. When I thought that I was going to adopt your baby, I shared my joy with the staff and I told them that her name would be Charlotte. They would think it very suspicious if I suddenly changed it to Nora. You do understand, don't you?'

I felt so angry I couldn't speak.

'Good,' she said, as if I'd agreed with her.

I was beginning to feel desperate. The room suddenly felt hot and stuffy, I could feel sweat beginning to form under my armpits. 'Mrs Grainger, I haven't seen her for more than a week, I need to see her now.'

This wasn't what I had expected. It was all very well for Mother Ignatius to say I had to trust Mrs Grainger but right now I didn't trust her one little bit.

A stony look came over her face; she wasn't smiling at me any more. 'Like I said, Cissy, this is not a good time.'

'When is a good time?'

She stood up to let me know that the conversation was over. 'I'll let you know. Now I expect you want to unpack.'

'You'll let me know?'

'Yes, Cissy, didn't I say that I would?'

Yes, you did, I thought, *but I don't believe you*. I had the sudden urge to rush up to the nursery, pick up my baby and run as fast as I could and away from this house.

CHAPTER FORTY-EIGHT

I was right, Mrs Grainger never let me know when I could see Nora. I decided to bide my time and not do anything to anger her. I needed this job, I had to make enough money to somehow take care of Nora myself. I resolved to go back to the convent and talk to Mother Ignatius, I needed her advice.

Maggie and I shared a bedroom at the top of the house. I worked out that the bedroom was directly above the nursery, and it reassured me to know that Nora was so close.

It was tearing me apart being so close to my baby but not being allowed to see her. I wished I could confide in Maggie, it would be such a comfort to talk to someone.

'Are you happy working here?' I said.

'Are you kiddin'? If you saw where I came from, you'd understand why I'm happy workin' here. There was sixteen of us livin' in three rooms.'

'Sixteen?'

'I have two brothers and a sister as well as me mum and dad.'

'But that's only six.'

'The other ten residents are rats,' she said, grinning.

I made a face. 'Jesus, I have a terrible fear of them! They make me skin crawl.'

'You get used to them, they've been living with us for so long they're like family. My little brother has names for them all.'

I shuddered. There were plenty of rats in Paradise Alley but I had never got used to them.

The granddaddy had said that I was so genteel in my ways that I was destined to be a lady. Fat chance, I'd thought.

I'd been working at the house for a month and I was happy enough with my duties. The work was easy, easier than at Bretton Hall, and I did it to the best of my ability so that Mrs Cornish could find no reason to scold me.

I still hadn't seen Nora and when I passed Mrs Grainger, she looked through me as if I was invisible. She had tricked me alright and I grew to hate her. This was a different woman to the one who had been all sweet and kind in front of Mother Ignatius. She'd fooled us all. Mrs Dobbs had told me that Mr Grainger was away working in America, I wondered if things would have been different with him here.

One day, Mrs Dobbs asked if I would mind taking Nanny Price's dinner up to her. 'Betsy is sick so she won't be down for it.'

My heart leapt with joy, I was going to see Nora. 'Of course I will, Mrs Dobbs,' I said.

She smiled at me. 'You're a good girl, Cissy, but you're not a happy one, are you, dear?'

'I'm fine, Mrs Dobbs,' I assured her.

'I'm a good listener,' she said, 'and I'm no gossip.'

I waited while she handed me a tray. 'The nursery is two floors up. I'd do it myself, but my legs aren't what they were.'

'I'm glad to do it, really I am.'

'Then off you go and would you ask Nanny Price what she'd like for her supper?'

'I will, of course.'

I was so full of excitement and joy and nerves I don't know how I made it up the stairs without dropping the tray. I took a deep breath and opened the door.

A very overweight woman was sitting in a chair. Her eyes were closed and she was snoring. Her head was bent forward, resting on about three chins.

I put the tray down as quietly as I could and looked around. The nursery was beautiful. Three long windows took up most of one wall, bathing the room in warmth and light. Covering most of the floor was a thick gold rug, which matched the pale yellow walls. I could never give my baby all these fine things but I could give her something that no amount of money could buy, I could give her a mother's love.

I checked to see that the woman was still asleep and walked over to the cot. Nora was wide awake. She stared up at me as if to say, 'Where have you been?' I reached down and lifted her into my arms. Oh, the joy of holding her close, feeling her cheek next to mine and smelling her sweet baby smell! I pulled a little button off her cardigan.

'Put that child down at once!' screamed the woman. 'Who are you? What are you doing in my nursery?'

I wasn't daft enough to make an enemy of this woman. 'I'm so sorry, Nanny Price.' I said. 'I'm Cissy Ryan, I've just started working here. I brought up your dinner tray. The baby was whimpering and I saw that she was trying to put a button in her mouth... I was frightened that she was going to choke on it.'

'A button?' she said, horrified.

I opened my hand and showed it to her. 'Did I do wrong?'

'No, no, you didn't do wrong, girl.'

'I didn't mean to interfere but I thought...'

'You thought right. Now I think we should keep this to ourselves, don't you? After all, there was no harm done. We don't want to worry Mrs Grainger, do we?'

I placed Nora back in the cot. 'You can trust me,' I said. 'After all, it wasn't your fault that the button was loose.'

'We understand each other, Cissy. Thank you for your quick thinking.'

'Mrs Dobbs asked what you would like for your supper.'

'I'd like a boiled egg and some toast and maybe a piece of fruit.'

'How's Betsy?'

'She has the bellyache, Cissy – and between you and me she always has the bellyache.'

'It must be hard having to cope with the baby all on your own.'

'And nobody appreciates it, Cissy. It's nice to have a sensible girl like yourself in the house.'

'I'll bring your supper up later then.'

'It will be lovely to see you and I hope I can trust you with our little secret.'

'My lips are sealed, Nanny Price.'

I was smiling as I walked back down the stairs. Not only had I not made an enemy of her, she thought I was her partner in crime. The granddaddy would have been proud of me this day. I knew now that I would be welcomed into the nursery any time Mrs Grainger was out of the way. I'd missed my vocation, I should have been an actress.

Oh, the joy of holding my child again.

CHAPTER FORTY-NINE

Christmas at St John's Wood was nothing like Christmas at Bretton Hall. There was a tree in the hallway that Maggie and I decorated and that was fun. We giggled as Maggie balanced on a ladder to put the star on the top. In the morning, all the staff gathered in the drawing room to receive presents from Mrs Grainger.

'Happy Christmas, Cissy,' she said handing me what turned out to be a bar of soap.

'Thank you, Mrs Grainger,' I said, smiling at her. 'And a happy Christmas to you too.'

I could see that she had great difficulty looking me in the eye but I had to let her think that I was fine with the arrangements and that I enjoyed working for her. I would make my escape when I had somewhere else to go and until that time I would make as many visits to the beautiful nursery where my baby slept as I could. I knew that she was warm and fed and that's all I cared about, but I had to find somewhere else that would take me and Nora in. There must be an alternative.

Sometimes I thought about going home and facing the music. Me and Nora would be safe there, but what if the Brettons laid claim to her? They had money, any judge would choose them to bring up Nora over me. I was writing home less and less because I didn't know what to say to them any more; everything I wrote was lies.

Mrs Grainger dined alone. I thought it was a bit strange that Mr Grainger hadn't joined her for Christmas. In the afternoon she visited a friend, taking Nora with her. I'd hoped she'd leave Nora behind so that I could spend some time with her, but I heard a car pull up outside and saw Mrs Grainger get into it, with Betsy holding Nora, wrapped in a blanket.

The rest of the day was our own to do as we pleased. Maggie was visiting her family and Mrs Dobbs said she was going to sleep the day away. I decided to go and see Mother Ignatius, to tell her the truth about my situation and beg for help.

It felt strange walking up the drive. I'd been gone for almost three months and it felt like a lifetime ago. I rang the bell and the door was opened by Sister Luke, who gave me the biggest hug,

'Well, if it's not yourself, Cissy Ryan, and aren't you a sight for sore eyes? Happy Christmas to you, child.'

'Happy Christmas, Sister. I hope you don't mind me calling on you this day.'

'Mind? Sure, everyone will be delighted to see you, and why have you not brought your lovely baby with you?'

'Oh, that I could have, Sister,' I said sadly.

'So I take it not everything in the garden is rosy up at St John's Wood?'

'You could say that, Sister.'

'Are you wanting to see Mother Ignatius?'

'As long as I won't be disturbing her.'

'Enough of that. Come in, come in. We are all in the sitting room, Cissy, but I take it you would rather see Mother in private?'

'I would, Sister, and thank you.'

She put her arms around me again. 'This will always be your home, Cissy, and you will always be welcome here.'

I'd forgotten how kind the nuns were; they made you feel as if you were family. I'd heard horror stories about places run by nuns who were cruel to the young girls in their care but I'd been lucky. These women practiced the word of God in everything they did, without a word of judgement passing their lips.

I waited in Mother Ignatius's office while Sister Luke fetched her from the sitting room. I stood at the window looking down on the garden. There were a couple of young girls I didn't recognise huddled together on the bench. They reminded me of my friends and how we used to be. I hoped they were all happy now.

'Ah, Cissy,' said Mother Ignatius, coming into the room. I walked towards her and she held me in her arms.

'What a lovely surprise and on God's birthday too. Sit down, sit down.'

As I sat down, I could feel hot tears stinging behind my eyelids.

'You are troubled, child,' said Mother Ignatius. 'Are you not happy in your new job?'

I rubbed at my eyes. 'It's not the job, Mother, it's Mrs Grainger.'

'Is she not kind to you, Cissy?'

'She won't let me see Nora.'

Mother Ignatius shook her head, 'She won't let you see your baby?'

'No, I have to sneak up to the nursery when she's not around. I would never have gone there if I'd known.'

'And I wouldn't have sent you. You have me very surprised, Cissy, she seemed to genuinely have your best interests at heart.'

'I have to get away from there, Mother. I have to get away as soon as ever I can.'

'Yes, I can see that and I will do what I can to help you. Can you bear to be patient while I make enquiries?'

I nodded.

'Is Nora safe, Cissy?'

'Yes, Mother, she has a nanny looking after her and a lovely nursery with yellow walls and a gold rug. But it should be me looking after her, shouldn't it?'

'Yes, it should. She is depriving you of your child and in my book that is cruel beyond belief. And it is not what we agreed. Our convent is full to bursting at the moment but if Nora wasn't safe, I would fit you in somewhere.'

'She's safe, Mother, or I wouldn't be there.'

'Leave it with me, Cissy. I promise that I will find somewhere for you and Nora.'

'Thank you, Mother. Thank you.'

'Take heart now, child, and with God's help we will get you out of there as soon as we can. Shall we go into the chapel and light a candle?'

I nodded. 'I'd like that, Mother.'

I felt at peace, kneeling next to Mother Ignatius, watching the candles flickering away in front of the statue of the Blessed Virgin Mary. *You're a mother*, I said in my mind, *so you will understand what I'm going through. Please help Iggy to find a safe place for me and Nora. It doesn't have to be a posh place like St John's Wood, or Bretton Hall. Just a place where we can be together every day. Happy Christmas, Mary, and a happy birthday to your son. Amen.*

Winter gave way to spring and I still hadn't heard anything from Mother Ignatius, but I knew that she would be looking for a place for us to stay. The change in the weather gave me an unexpected opportunity to see Nora since now that the weather was warmer, Betsy took her out in her pram every afternoon.

I had to wait until my day off to 'accidentally' bump into them. I saw them leave, then followed them to the park. Once Betsy was settled on a bench by the swings, I went over to Nora. My eyes were on the cream pram that she was absent-mindedly rocking to and fro. Every nerve in my body was screaming at me to reach into the pram and pick my baby up, but I didn't want to alarm either of them.

'Hello, Betsy,' I said. 'Didn't expect to find you here.'

She looked up. 'Oh, hello, Cissy.'

'Taking the baby for a stroll?'

She nodded. 'Mrs Grainger says that Charlotte needs to get out into the fresh air as much as she can. Nanny Price can't take her because of her legs.'

'It's nice for you to get out though, isn't it?'

'It's nice for me to get away from Nanny Bloody Price, the lousy old dragon!'

'Don't you get on with her then?'

'She has it in for me, Cissy. I can't do anything right. She says I'm stupid and I'll never amount to anything. I wish I could work in the kitchen. I like Mrs Dobbs, she's always been kind to me.'

'Have you spoken to Mrs Grainger about it?'

'I couldn't do that, I'd lose my job for sure. It's not everyone that would take me on, I was lucky to get this position. I don't even like kids that much.'

Just then Nora started to whimper. Betsy ignored her. 'I'll take her for a walk around the park if you like, give you a bit of a break,' I said.

'Would you?'

'Of course.'

Suddenly Betsy looked doubtful. 'I've been given strict instructions never to let her out of my sight.'

'I expect they were worried about strangers taking her, but I'm not a stranger, am I?'

'Of course you're not, but don't go far, will you?'

'I'll just go for a little stroll.'

I stood up and took hold of the pram before she changed her mind. 'You have a rest, Betsy,' I said, smiling at her.

'Thanks, Cissy.'

I wheeled the pram away from her and once she was out of sight, I took Nora out and sat down on the grass. 'Hello, my beautiful girl,' I said, gently touching her face. A thought went through my head to run with her now, but then I thought of Betsy, who would certainly lose her job. And I needed a proper plan. If Nora was being neglected, it would be different – I'd take her and not give Betsy another thought – but she wasn't, she was growing and she was being cared for. No, I'd wait until Mother Ignatius found us a place. I just hoped it would be soon.

CHAPTER FIFTY

Two weeks later, Mrs Dobbs walked into the kitchen with a face like thunder; she had been called upstairs to see Mrs Grainger.

'What's wrong?' I said.

'You'll find out soon enough, Cissy. She wants to see you next.'

I washed my hands, took off my apron and went upstairs, wondering what this was all about.

Mrs Grainger was standing by the window. She turned and smiled at me as I entered the drawing room. 'I got Mrs Cornish to bring us some tea and biscuits,' she said. 'You would like a biscuit, wouldn't you, Cissy?'

She hadn't offered me tea the last time I'd been summoned to the drawing room, let alone a biscuit. In fact, I couldn't remember the last time she'd spoken to me and here she was offering me tea and biscuits as if we were best friends. I hoped she wasn't going to ask me to give Nora up because if she was, she could keep her tea and biscuits, thank you very much. 'That would be lovely,' I replied.

'Sit down, dear.'

I sat on the sofa and waited while she poured the tea into two china cups. 'Help yourself to a biscuit, Cissy.'

I didn't feel a bit like eating but I thought I'd better take one. 'Thank you,' I said.

'Yesterday, I was privy to a very unfortunate incident.'

'Were you?' I asked feebly.

'Nanny Price and Betsy were having a heated argument in the nursery and Charlotte was crying and very obviously upset by it. I spoke to Nanny Price and told her in no uncertain terms that this was not acceptable behaviour in front of the baby. Her response was that she couldn't work with Betsy another minute and was threatening to walk out if something wasn't done about it. I then spoke to Betsy, who said that Nanny Price bullied her and she expressed a wish to work in the kitchen. So, what I am suggesting, Cissy, and only if you are agreeable of course, is that the best way forward would be for you girls to swap positions.'

My heart was thumping out of my chest. 'You mean I would work in the nursery?'

'You like children, don't you, Cissy?'

I was beginning to think that Mrs Grainger was mad or daft or both – had she forgotten that Nora was mine? 'Yes, Mrs Grainger,' I said. 'I like children very much.'

'That's settled then. I suggest you pack up your things and take them to the nursery, where you will sleep from now on.'

I stopped halfway down the stairs and leaned against the wall. I was going to be able to see Nora every day, every single day; it was a dream come true. I remembered that when I had gone back to visit the convent I had lit a candle to the Blessed Virgin Mary. This was exactly what I had asked her for, to be able to see my child every day. 'Thanks, Mary,' I whispered, running down the stairs. 'It was awful good of ya.'

When I walked into the kitchen, Mrs Dobbs was complaining bitterly to Maggie. 'I'm to be given that fool of a girl who's neither use nor ornament and I'm to lose Cissy.'

'Betsy likes you, Mrs Dobbs,' I said gently.

'And I like her well enough, but at a distance, not in my kitchen.'

'I'm sorry.'

'You have nothing to be sorry about, Cissy. This is not your fault and I have to say I'll miss you, girl. We were a nice little team.'

'I'll miss you an' all,' said Maggie.

'And you, having to work in the nursery with that puffed-up Nanny Price, who's lazy as the day is long.'

'Mrs Grainger didn't give me much choice, Mrs Dobbs, and I can't afford to lose my job.'

'Of course you can't and she shouldn't have put you in that position.'

'I'll get my things and move them to the nursery,' I said, trying to look upset about it.

'Bloody hell!' said Maggie. 'I'm going to have to share a bedroom with *her*?'

'I suppose so,' I said. 'I'm really sorry, Maggie.'

'Like Mrs Dobbs said, it's not your fault.'

And so, my life changed. Nanny Price was delighted to let me take over Nora's care and I couldn't have been happier. I washed her, I fed her and I got up to her during the night. Those quiet moments when the house was silent were precious. As she stared up at me in the half-light of dawn, I talked to her about Ireland and the mammy and the granddaddy. I told her about Colm and Blue and my dog Buddy and I described the little white cottage in Paradise Alley.

She stared up at me as if she understood every word I was saying. My baby would never meet the people I loved, or the town where I was born but I wanted her to know where she came from. She was getting to know me all over again and her smile when she saw my face made up for all the months we'd been apart. Talking about my home made me miss it even more. I dreamed about sitting beside the fire in the cottage with Nora in my arms. I knew that Mammy would love her just as much as I did. There were times when I was tempted to write and tell her everything. My mammy was a strong woman, she wouldn't care what people thought, and I knew without a shadow of a doubt she would write back and tell me to come home. Then a picture of Colm's face would come into my head: I couldn't do that to him, I couldn't break the heart of the boy I loved.

'You'll make a lovely little mother, Cissy,' said Nanny Price one day. 'Which is more than could be said for that Betsy girl. It's easy to see that Charlotte loves you.'

I wondered what she'd say if she knew that I was already a mother – and that Charlotte was Nora, and that she was mine.

Day by day, my daughter was growing more beautiful. She was six months old and getting bigger and stronger. Her little hand would reach out for things, like the buttons on my dress. I would lay down with her on the gold rug and watch as she kicked her chubby little legs. I told her stories and recited bits of poetry that I remembered from the book that Peter Bretton had given me. Nora wanted no one but me, she screamed on the rare occasions when Nanny Price picked her up, which made the older woman cross. Sometimes Mrs Grainger came into the nursery and Nora would give her the same treatment.

'I think Charlotte is getting too close to you, Cissy,' Mrs Grainger said one day as Nora screamed and struggled on her lap, reaching her little arms out to me.

'Oh, she's like that with me sometimes as well,' I said.

'Is she?'

'Oh yes, especially when she's tired, she's probably tired now.'

'She's right, you know, Cissy,' said Nanny Price, when Mrs Grainger left the room. 'I've been thinking that myself. You're not going to be with her forever. You have to ask yourself, is it fair on the child?'

'You are probably right, Nanny Price,' I said, but what I thought was, *oh yes, I will, I will be with her forever.*

CHAPTER FIFTY-ONE

It had been a year since I'd left Ireland and I knew that Mammy and Colm would soon be expecting me back. I dreading writing the letter to say that I had decided to stay in England and that I was never coming home. Once they knew, I would stop all contact with them. It was going to break my heart as well as theirs but I had to put Nora first. Mammy had Mr Collins and Colm would soon find someone to love him. He deserved to be loved and if God was good, maybe one day I would be loved like that again, but for now all I needed was Nora.

Nanny Price was delighted to have me in the nursery and I was delighted to be with my baby every day. Once Nora was asleep, I would go down to the kitchen to see my friends. One day, I walked in and was surprised to see Betsy, sleeves rolled up, making pastry.

'Mrs Dobbs is learnin' me how to make an apple pie,' she said, grinning.

'*Teaching*, Betsy, I'm *teaching* you how to make an apple pie.'

'Ain't that what I said?'

'No, Betsy, it ain't what you said but never mind, you're doing a good job.'

'How's Charlotte?' said Betsy.

'Growing,' I said.

'I didn't think I'd miss her, but I do. I don't miss Nanny Price though,' she said, making a face.

'She's not so bad,' I said.

'I don't suppose she hates you like she hated me.'

'I'm glad you're happier down here.'

'Oh, I am, Cissy. You don't hate me, do you, Mrs Dobbs?'

'No, Betsy, I don't hate you. You're a bit of a dilly sometimes but you're a good girl.'

I was glad that Betsy was happier now and that Mrs Dobbs was kind to her. And despite her concerns, Betsy seemed to be working well in the kitchen.

Mrs Grainger continued to be friendly. I still didn't know why she'd changed towards me but I didn't care. Whatever her reasons might have been for this change of heart, I was more than happy to go along with it. I knew that Mother Ignatius wouldn't let me down and I would soon be leaving this house with my baby, never to return.

I was sitting opposite Mrs Grainger now in the drawing room.

'I've been hearing good reports about you from Nanny Price, Cissy. It seems you have a way with children.'

I sat quietly and waited for her to continue.

'That's why I feel confident in asking this of you.'

'Asking what?' I said.

'A dear friend of mine is in need of a nanny.'

'But I'm happy here.'

'I know you are and I am happy to have you here, Cissy, but this wouldn't be permanent, she only needs you for a couple of weeks.'

'Why?'

'The girl she has working for her is Irish. It seems her father is dying and she needs to go home. Mrs Cushman has just had a baby and she is going to need some help. You would be doing her and me a huge favour and I'm assured that you will be well paid for your trouble.'

'Does she live far from here?

'She lives on the coast in Brighton.'

I knew that Nora would be well taken care of while I was away. Mrs Grainger had never charged me for her care, so maybe this was the least I could do for her.

'I'd be happy to help,' I said.

'Thank you, Cissy, she'll be delighted. I will put you on the train myself and you will be met at the other end. Think of it as a little holiday.'

'I will,' I said.

'And thank you, Cissy.'

I ran downstairs to tell the girls. I was halfway down when I met Maggie running up. 'There's a nun in the kitchen, asking to see you, Cissy.'

Sister Luke was sitting at the kitchen table, drinking tea. She stood up and enfolded me in her arms.

'Ah, there you are, Cissy,' said Mrs Dobbs. 'Sister Luke here wants a word with you. You can use my sitting room, it will be more private.'

'Thank you, Mrs Dobbs,' said Sister Luke. 'And thank you for the grand cup of tea, I was parched.'

'You're very welcome, Sister,' said Mrs Dobbs.

'I have news, Cissy,' said Sister Luke, once we were in Mrs Dobbs' sitting room.

'You've found me somewhere to live?'

'How would you like to work at St Steven's?'

'The orphanage?'

'Yes, the Sisters would love to have you both there, Cissy.'

I put my head in my arms and wept but they were tears of pure joy. It was the next best thing to going home, Nora and I would be safe and loved. I felt in that moment that the weight of the world had suddenly been lifted from my shoulders.

Yes, I was grateful to Mrs Grainger for letting me work in the nursery and I loved looking after my baby but I couldn't claim her as my own. I couldn't even call her by her rightful name, it was only in the night when we were alone that I could call her Nora.

Sister Luke put her arms around me. 'God is good, Cissy,' she said. 'God is good.'

'I don't know how to thank you and the Sisters.'

'Mother was trying very hard to find a place that would take you and the child but she was having no luck. It was Sister Mary who came up with the idea of you working at St Steven's. It was the most enlightening thing that Sister Mary has come up with in her entire time at the convent, I think she even surprised herself.'

'Well, I'm grateful to her.'

'I'll be sure to tell her. Now Mother says that you can come to us whenever you are ready. You can come back with me now, if you like. I will talk to Mrs Grainger and explain.'

'I'm going away, Sister.'

'Going away?'

'Just for a couple of weeks, I promised Mrs Grainger that I would look after her friend's baby in Brighton.'

Sister Luke looked worried. 'Mother Ignatius told us of the situation here in the house and we are all very concerned for you. Are you sure you want to do this, Cissy?'

I hesitated. This could be the answer to everything but I'd promised Mrs Grainger that I would help her friend out. 'I can't go back on my word, Sister,' I said.

'When are you leaving?'

'On Friday.'

'Come and see us when you return and we will arrange to fetch you both and bring you to the convent.'

'Thank you, Sister, I will.'

'Did you say it was Brighton you are going to?'

I nodded.

'Rose lives in Brighton, Cissy.'

'I'd forgotten, maybe I could visit her.'

'Do you have her address?'

I nodded.

'Well, if you do, be sure to give her our love.'

'I will, Sister.'

'God willing, I shall see you in two weeks then.'

'God willing,' I said.

CHAPTER FIFTY-TWO

Teddy was a sweet baby and so tiny. It was hard to believe that Nora had ever been this small. Mrs Cushman fed him herself, even during the night, so there really wasn't much for me to do, except take him out for long walks along the seafront while she rested.

'My health hasn't been good since having Teddy and I tire easily,' she explained.

'That's why *I'm* here,' I said. 'I'll help you all I can.'

'You're a godsend, Cissy, it was so good of Mrs Grainger to let you come to me.'

'Have you been friends for long?'

'Mr Grainger was my husband's friend, they worked together in London. I met Mrs Grainger at one of my husband's work do's. I stopped seeing her after her husband went to America to work, but I let her know when Teddy was born and I mentioned recently that I needed help and wondered if she knew a girl who would be willing to stand in while Helen was in Ireland.'

For some reason I couldn't see this kind gentle woman being friends with Mrs Grainger, they were so different. 'So, you just keep in touch by letter?'

'We don't keep in touch at all now, except as I said, to let her know that I had had Teddy. It's my husband who has kept up contact with Mr Grainger, they were good friends. It was he that told us that they had adopted a little girl.'

My heart missed a beat. Why would Mr Grainger be saying that? Surely he was aware that the adoption hadn't gone through? He must have told them before I'd changed my mind, that would explain it. But I didn't want to question Mrs Cushman about it – it would seem a strange thing for me to do.

I was treated like one of the family. I even ate my meals with them; they made me feel more like a friend than a servant. The house was just off the seafront and it was beautiful. It was a lot smaller than the house in St John's Wood, which made it feel cosier. I loved it here but I missed Nora and I was counting the days until I saw her again.

Mr Cushman was as kind as his wife and he adored Teddy. I made sure that the baby was bathed and smelling sweet when he came home from work, and it was a joy to see how his eyes lit up when he held his little boy in his arms.

I fell in love with Brighton and sitting on the pebbly beach looking out over the sea made me think of home. Maybe I could bring Nora here and show her the ocean?

Mrs Cushman said that I could have Saturday off, as her mother was visiting, so I decided to try and find Rose. I had her address written down: Number Fifteen, Standon Street. I asked Mrs Cushman if she knew where it was.

'It's not far from here, Cissy, you can walk there. Take the road opposite the pier and just keep walking. It's a turning off to the right just before the railway station.'

I felt excited as I started walking along the seafront. It was a beautiful day and the sea was calm, glistening under the bright sunshine. The Palace pier looked so grand, jutting out into the sea. Mr Cushman said that if you laid out all the planks end to end, the pier would reach out for eighty-five miles. I was grateful that the nuns had offered me a job and a place to live but that didn't mean I had to stay there forever. Somehow I felt freer here; there was room to breathe with the hills rising up behind the town and the sea stretching out in front of it.

I found the place easily enough. It was a neat little house in a narrow street of identical houses. Number fifteen was halfway along. I knocked on the blue door and waited. A woman answered, and smiled at me. 'Yes?'

'Is Rose in?' I asked.

'Who shall I say wants her?'

I didn't want to give Rose's secret away. As far as I knew, her mother still knew nothing of Jenny.

'My name is Cissy Ryan,' I said. 'Me and Rose worked together in London.'

'Come in,' she said, opening the door wider. 'We'll surprise her, she's talked a lot about you since she came home.'

'I've missed her,' I said, following the woman into the front room.

'So you decided to stay in London, did you?'

'Yes, I did.'

'As you know, Rose got very homesick, city life wasn't for her. Hush, I can hear her on the stairs.'

'Do you know where my red jumper is, Mum?' she said, walking into the room and then she saw me. 'Cissy!' she screamed, flinging herself at me and nearly knocking me off my feet. 'What are you doing here?'

'Visiting you,' I said, grinning.

'Oh, this is great, I can't believe it!'

'Shall I get you some tea?' said Rose's mum.

'No, I'll take Cissy to the tea shop on the pier.'

'That's a good idea, Rose. It will be lovely on a day like today.'

'I can't believe you're here,' said Rose, hugging me.

'Well, I am,' I said, smiling at her.

We linked arms as we walked down the hill towards the pier.

'Save your news until we get there,' said Rose.

We were soon sitting together at a table overlooking the sea.

'It feels like I'm on a boat,' I said.

'Now I want to know everything. I thought you'd be back in Ireland by now.'

'I should have been, Rose, but...'

'You kept your baby?'

'Yes, I kept my baby.'

'I can't say I'm surprised.'

'No?'

'You went on too much about not wanting anything to do with it. I was never convinced. Boy or girl?'

'A little girl.'

She smiled but there was sadness in her eyes. 'The same as me then.'

I nodded.

'So, where is she?'

'It's a long story, Rose.'

'I'm in no hurry.'

And so I told her all that had happened to me since I'd last seen her. When I'd finished talking, Rose had tears in her eyes and she looked angry.

'I don't like the sound of it at all, Cissy. I've got a good mind to get on the next train to London and snatch your baby back for you. Why don't we? There's nothing stopping us.'

'And what would I do then?'

'You'd live here with me and Mum.'

'But what about Nora?'

'Is that what you've called her?'

'Yes, except that Mrs Grainger changed it.'

'What do you mean, she changed it?'

'To Charlotte.'

'She changed your baby's name to Charlotte?'

Saying it out loud like this made me realise just how wrong it was and I was beginning to feel Rose's anger rubbing off on me.

'She had no right to do that, Cissy. You're her mother, although from what you've told me, that mad cow thinks that *she* is.'

'I've been a fool, haven't I?'

'Not a fool, Cissy, never that. Just an innocent girl who didn't know where next to turn.'

'What should I do?'

'Go and get Nora.'

'But what about Mrs Cushman? I'll be letting her down.'

'Jesus, Cissy, that woman is nothing to you! It's time you stopped thinking about everyone else for a second and started thinking about you and your baby.'

'I have to go back to Mrs Cushman first or she'll have the police out looking for me when I don't return home.'

'Okay, go and see her and then get on the next train to London.'

'I will.'

'Promise?'

'I promise.'

'Go and get your baby, Cissy,' said Rose, leaning across the table and holding my hands. 'Go and bring her home.'

CHAPTER FIFTY-THREE

Mrs Cushman was lovely about me leaving. 'I can see that something is very wrong, Cissy,' she said. 'I think I sensed it all along. If you don't feel that you can tell me what it is, just remember that if there is anything I can do to help you, please ask.'

'I've enjoyed working for you, Mrs Cushman, and your Teddy is lovely. I'm sorry to have to leave you when you need someone to help.'

'Don't worry, Cissy, I will get my mother to help out until Helen comes back. She'll be delighted for the chance to spoil her grandson.'

I didn't feel a bit scared as the train raced towards London because I knew at last that I was doing the right thing. I'd been a fool and I'd let Mrs Grainger bully me, but she was rich and I wasn't and maybe I'd thought I deserved what she did to me. I didn't think that now. Talking to Rose and seeing her anger had given me the strength to fight for my child. I had the same rights as Mrs Grainger. She might be posh and live in a big house but I wasn't frightened of her any more.

I had always been told to know my place, from bobbing to the Honourables to always using the back door, and when you are told that often enough you come to believe it. You come to believe that rich people really are your betters even if they are mean like Caroline Bretton or cruel like Mrs Grainger. But Mammy always told me that I was as good as anyone else. Why hadn't I believed her? I wished she was with me, I wished she was here.

I knew my place now: it was with my child and I would teach her to be proud of who she was and where she came from. I would tell her that she was as good as the next person and whether you are rich or poor, respect is not a right, it's something you have to earn. I would teach my child to be as strong and as wise as the mammy and the granddaddy.

As I stood looking up at the house I had never been so determined to get what I wanted. Nothing was going to stop me from leaving with Nora and I'd fight whoever stood in my way. I lugged my case down the basement steps and went to open the kitchen door but I couldn't get in. It was unusual for it to be locked. I pushed at it and when it didn't budge, I knocked. But no one answered. I put my ear to the door but there was only silence on the other side. I left my case where it was and went back up the steps. It wasn't my fault that I had to use the front door. I rang the bell and the door was opened immediately by Mrs Cornish the housekeeper.

'Cissy,' she said, looking surprised. 'I wasn't expecting you back for another week.'

'I tried the kitchen door but it's locked,' I said quickly.

'Oh good,' she said. 'I was just about to check it, that saves me having to go downstairs.'

It was then that I noticed how quiet the house was. 'Where is everyone?'

'Scattered to the four corners of London, I expect.'

'What are you talking about?'

'Don't you know?' She stared at me. 'You don't, do you? She said she'd told you, she said you knew.'

I shook my head, I was beginning to feel sick. 'Knew what?'

'They've all gone, Cissy.'

And then I was running up the stairs, screaming Nora's name.

'What are you doing, girl?' shouted Mrs Cornish, running behind me.

The nursery was empty, the cot was gone and so too was Nanny Price's chair. I turned and faced Mrs Cornish. 'Where's Nora?' I demanded.

'Who's Nora?'

'My baby, where is she?'

'Get a hold of yourself, Cissy. The only baby that was ever in this nursery was Charlotte, as well you know. Are you ill, girl?'

I started to scream like a fishwife down on the quayside in Ballybun. 'Where is she? Where is she?'

Mrs Cornish grabbed me by the shoulders and started shaking me. I pushed her off and slid to the floor. 'She's taken my baby,' I sobbed. 'How could she do that, Mrs Cornish? *How could she take my baby?*'

'I know you were fond of Charlotte, Cissy,' said Mrs Cornish gently, 'but Charlotte is not your child.'

'She *is* my child,' I screamed, 'and her name's not Charlotte.'

Mrs Cornish sat down beside me. We sat there in silence. And then she said, 'I've never taken you to be a girl who's given to flights of fancy. I'm listening, Cissy.'

And so, between bouts of sobbing, I told my story. As I was speaking, Mrs Cornish reached across and held my hand. 'I should have known that she was always going to take her, she fooled me.'

'She fooled us all, she told me I had a job for life. We were all stunned when she gave us our notice. I'm only here to hand the keys of the house back to the agent.'

'She's sold the house?'

'She never owned it, it was rented.'

'Didn't she tell you where she was going?'

'Not a word.'

'She had it all planned, didn't she?'

'It looks like it.'

'You do believe me, Mrs Cornish? For as God is my witness, I am telling the truth.'

'Yes, Cissy, I believe you.'

I was shivering; every bone in my body was icy cold and my heart was breaking in two.

'Let's get you downstairs to the drawing room, the couch is still there.'

My legs were like jelly as Mrs Cornish helped me to stand up. 'Lean on me, Cissy, we'll soon get you warm.'

Mrs Cornish settled me on the couch and wrapped me in blankets, then she put a match to the paper and wood in the grate. She knelt on the floor beside me and smoothed my hair away from my face, all the while murmuring softly that everything would be alright, that we'd find Nora. She was like a mammy, she made me feel calmer. I closed my eyes and gave way to the overwhelming tiredness that was seeping through my body.

When I woke it took me a few minutes to remember where I was and why I was there. Evening had started to fall and the room was dim, most of it hidden by shadows. The only light was the soft glow from the embers of the fire that had almost burned itself out in the grate. I'd been lying on my arm and now it had pins and needles. I sat up and rubbed it and that's when the horror of the day hit me like a stone: Nora was gone and I'd been sleeping. How long had I slept? I shouldn't have slept. How could I sleep when my baby had been taken from me? As I opened and closed my fist to make the pins and needles stop, I felt heavy and helpless. I pushed back the blanket and swung my legs off the couch. It took an enormous effort to stand and walk over to the long window. Outside, the street lamps were being lit, their light flickering along the pavements. London was settling down for the night. I had never felt at home there but on that night, as I gazed out over the houses and chimneys, the streets and alleyways, the rooftops broken up every now and then by a church spire, I felt lonelier than ever.

This wasn't my city, it wasn't my country. It was a cold, grey, heartless place that swallowed up people, along with hopes and dreams.

Somewhere out there was Nora, somewhere within those streets and houses, behind a door, beyond a curtain was my baby girl. I closed my eyes and I remembered the feel of her in my arms, how she felt when I held her up to my shoulder, her warm little head tucked into my neck. I thought of her heart beating somewhere in the midst of this huge, cold city. I put my hands over my face and I knew it was my fault. I hadn't wanted her in the first place. Now I'd allowed her to be taken from me.

I turned as Mrs Cornish came into the room carrying a tray. 'Ah, you're awake. I've brought you some tea and toast.'

'Thank you, but I don't think I can eat anything.'

'You must try. You are going to have to be strong to get through this, Cissy, and if you don't eat, you will make yourself ill.'

I sat down on the couch and nibbled at the bread. It felt like sandpaper going down my throat.

'Good girl,' said Mrs Cornish, 'now drink the tea.'

On the tray was an envelope, which Mrs Cornish handed it to me. 'She left this for you.'

'I don't want to hear anything she has to say to me.'

'Do you want me to open it? It might be important.'

I nodded and watched as she opened the envelope. 'There's no letter,' she said. 'Just money, a lot of money.'

'I don't want her money.'

'Keep it, Cissy. No amount of money can make up for what she's done to you but you may need it in the future.'

'Don't you see? She's bought her, she's bought Nora.'

As we sat in silence, I felt numb and helpless.

'A crime has been committed here, Cissy. I think we should contact the police.'

'What's the point? Even if they believe me, Mrs Grainger will be long gone.'

'What do you want to do, then?'

'I want to be among my own kind, Mrs Cornish. I want to go home.'

I had to accept that I would never see my daughter Nora again.

PART THREE

1912

CHAPTER FIFTY-FOUR

I took the train from Paddington to Fishguard, where I would board the night sailing to Cork. Mrs Cornish saw me off at the station.

'I will continue to investigate Mrs Grainger's whereabouts. The house agent might know something, she may have left a forwarding address for her mail. As soon as I have news, I will let you know. I have your address and you have mine. Keep in touch, Cissy, and have a safe journey home.'

'Thanks for everything,' I said, putting my arms around her. 'I don't know what I would have done without you.'

'I didn't do much, I wish I could have done more.'

'But you were there and you believed me and took care of me. I'll always remember that.'

'God's speed, girl.'

I bought a ticket for a single cabin, courtesy of Mrs Grainger. I couldn't face having to share with anyone. I needed to be where people weren't, so I thought I'd put her money to good use. I'd never had this amount of money in my life but it meant nothing. Just as money doesn't make you a good person, it doesn't make you happy either. It was never going to bring Nora back.

I hadn't expected to sleep but the motion of the boat rocked me into a deep but troubled slumber. I was chasing someone through dark places, tunnels and woods. They were always just ahead of me – a rustling in the undergrowth, the movement of a branch as if someone had just brushed past and then it was me that was being chased. Running, running away from some unknown terror, my legs heavy and slow, hardly able to move at all, a scream for help dying in my throat as the danger came closer and closer.

I woke up sobbing, my heart beating out of my chest. I was hot and sweaty, my hair was sticking to my forehead. I got out of the bunk, splashed cold water on my face and went up onto the deck. The cool morning breeze ruffled my hair and the sea was as calm as a mill pond. It seemed like a lifetime ago that I had sailed to England. There was no baby in my tummy this time and I was filled with guilt that I hadn't treasured her when she was safe inside me.

In the distance, I could just make out the hazy green hills of Ireland. A small thread of warmth found its way into my heart. I was going home, I would soon be with the people who loved me. I had a lot of explaining to do and I wasn't sure that I was ready for it. I was going to disappoint Mammy and break Colm's heart but the worst had happened and whatever lay ahead, I would just have to face it. I'd been a young naïve girl when I'd left Paradise Alley, but I was coming back a woman. I may not have a baby in my arms but I was a mother now and I always would be.

There were lots of people on the quayside as the boat sailed into Cork harbour. I picked up my case and joined the other passengers walking down the gangplank, then boarded the coach that would take me to Ballybun.

The closer we got to home, the worse I felt. My heart was beating out of my chest and I felt as if I was going to be sick. The reality of what I was about to do suddenly hit me. No one was expecting me home, they thought I was still happily working in a big house in London. I was going to have to admit that it had all been a load of lies, that I had given birth to a baby girl. I had deceived them just as Mrs Grainger had deceived me.

When the coach pulled into the town I made straight for Mary's house. I couldn't go home yet, I couldn't face the mammy. The door was open and a couple of the kids were playing ball outside. 'Are you home from England, Cissy?' asked Brenda, one of Mary's sisters.

I couldn't speak and just nodded.

'Mammy,' yelled the girl, 'Cissy's home from England!'

Mrs Butler came to the door. I put my arms around her and cried as if my heart was breaking into two pieces. 'Holy Mother of God, what's wrong, child?' she said, holding me.

'I need to see Mary,' I sobbed.

Mrs Butler led me to a chair and Brenda carried my case into the room.

'Brenda,' said Mrs Butler. 'I want you to run like the wind out to the Green Park Hotel and bring Mary back. Tell her that Cissy is here and she needs her.'

'I will, Mammy, I'll run as fast as I can.'

'The rest of you,' she said, addressing the other children, 'I want you to go across the road to Mrs Daly and tell her that I have a personal problem to deal with and she's to take you in. I've looked after her tribe often enough and tell her she'll have to give you your dinner.'

Mrs Butler didn't ask me any questions as I sat there, she just put a shawl around my shoulders and gave me a cup of tea. 'I've put a pile of sugar in it, Cissy, it's supposed to help with the shock.'

In no time at all Brenda and Mary came through the door. 'Jesus girl, how did you get back so quick?' said Mrs Butler.

'Colm Doyle picked me up on the way out to the hotel, Mammy.'

'You didn't tell him I was here, did you?' I snapped.

Brenda's eyes filled with tears, 'But you *are* here, Cissy, I didn't know I wasn't to say.'

'It's alright, Brenda,' I said. 'It's alright, I'm sorry.'

Mary knelt down in front of me. 'What's wrong, Cissy?'

'Brenda, go across to Mrs Daley's with the others.'

'Aw, Mammy!'

'Go on now. You were a good girl for fetching Mary here so quickly.'

Mrs Butler looked across at us. 'I've a few errands to run so I'll leave you girls to talk.'

'Do you mind, Mammy?' said Mary.

'Not at all, I'll be back later. Whatever is wrong, Cissy, I'm sure it can be worked out in God's own good time. You're home now.'

'Thank you,' I said.

'I'm glad you felt that you could come here.'

We waited until Mary's mammy got her things together and left.

'Oh, Mary,' I said. 'It's so good to see you.'

Mary reached across and held my hands in hers. 'It's good to see you too. Does yer mam know you're home?'

I shook my head. 'I can't face her yet,' I said.

'What has happened to you, Cissy?' she said gently.

'It's a long story.'

'I've all the time in the world… I've probably got the sack now anyway for walking out in the middle of a shift.'

'Oh, Mary, no!'

'Don't worry, I'm leaving anyway. But enough about me, it's you I want to hear about.'

And so I told her my story, from the moment I fell in love with my baby to the moment she was taken from me.

'The bloody bitch!' said Mary, when I'd finished speaking. 'How could she do that? How *could* she?'

'Because in her eyes I was nobody.'

'Is there no way you can get her back?'

'She could be anywhere, Mary, I wouldn't even know where to start. I have to accept she's gone, or I'll go mad.'

'God forgive me but I could strangle her with my own two hands.'

'I'd say you'd have to line up behind a convent full of nuns once I tell them what's happened.'

'I'm so sorry, Cissy, your heart must be broken.'

'It is, and I suppose it always will be. And I've still to tell Colm.'

'Colm's a good feller, I'd say he'd forgive you.'

'He might forgive me but he won't be wanting to marry me, not when he knows what I've done, how I've lied to him.'

There was a tap on the window. 'That'll be him. Oh, Mary, what am I to do?'

'You're going to tell him the truth.'

Mary opened the door and Colm was across the room and holding me in his arms before I could even say hello. I breathed in the smell of him; I never wanted to let him go.

He held me at arm's length. 'Why didn't you tell me you were coming home?' he said, grinning. 'I would have met you off the boat.'

My eyes filled with tears. 'Oh, Colm,' I said.

'What's wrong?' he asked, frowning,

I shook my head.

'Jesus, Cissy, just tell him!' urged Mary.

'Tell me what?'

I wanted to delay this moment, I wanted him to keep loving me. 'Come and sit down.'

'You're worrying me now,' he said.

'I didn't go to England for a job, Colm.'

He stared at me. 'Then why did you go?'

I looked down at the old stone floor. I didn't want to see the shock in his face when I told him the truth. 'I had a child, Colm. I went to England to give birth to a child. There was no grand job. I lied to you, I lied to everyone.'

His face was white as he stood up and stepped away from me. I'd lost him, as I'd known I would.

Tears were pouring down my face. 'I'm so sorry, Colm. I'm so sorry.'

But then his arms were around me again and he was kissing my cheek and smoothing my hair. I looked across at Mary and she was crying too.

I was in Colm's arms, I had come home.

CHAPTER FIFTY-FIVE

I didn't know whether Colm still wanted me, all I knew was that he had been kind to me and for now, that was enough. If all he was offering was friendship, then I would take it with both hands and be grateful for it. I had to have him in my life. I needed him as I had never needed him before. If he walked away now, I would be lost.

We were both quiet as Blue trotted through the town and under the archway into Paradise Alley. We stopped outside the cottage and he helped me down from the cart.

'Do you want me to come in with you?'

I shook my head. 'No, I must do this on my own.'

'She'll understand, Cissy,' he said gently.

I turned back to him. 'When will I see you, Colm?'

'Soon, Cissy.'

'Colm?'

'Go on now.'

Mammy was standing in the middle of the room with her hands stretched out towards me. I dropped my case on the floor and fell into her arms. Oh, the joy of being back home in the little cottage, the joy of being with the mammy! We clung to each other, laughing and crying. 'Nellie Mahon saw you getting off the bus and she made it her business to come all the way down to the laundry to let me know. She was delighted with herself.'

Buddy was on the couch, he hadn't moved. 'He's forgotten me,' I said sadly.

'Give him time, Cissy.'

I held my hand out towards him and let him sniff me and then in a bound he was on my lap, yelping and licking my face. 'Yes, Buddy,' I said, rubbing his ears. 'I'm home, I'm home.'

'Will you eat something, Cissy? I picked up a fine piece of ham on my way back through the town and a couple of grand tomatoes.'

I suddenly realised not only was I hungry, I was starving.

'That would be lovely, Mammy.'

'And then we'll talk, yes?'

I nodded.

We chatted about this and that as we ate the good food, smiling at each other across the table. Once we'd finished eating, Mammy led me across to the couch and we sat down. She didn't say anything right away and then she took hold of my hand. 'Was it a boy or a girl?' she said gently.

I stared at her. 'You knew?'

'You're my child, Cissy. I couldn't believe that you would leave your home and the people you loved for a job in England, I knew there was more to it than that. I went to see Father Kelly a few months ago.'

'And he told you?'

'No, but he looked as guilty as if he'd stolen the food from the mouths of the poor.'

I stared down at Mammy's hands. They felt rough in mine, from years of toiling in the workhouse and the laundry. I looked up at her. 'A little girl, Mammy, a beautiful little girl. I named her Nora.'

Mammy nodded. 'Where is she now?'

She kept hold of my hands as I told her my story and by the end of it we were both crying. 'My poor child,' she said. 'My poor little Cissy.'

'She's gone, Mammy, I'm never going to see her again.'

'Was it Father Kelly who arranged it all?'

'Yes.'

'Then we'll go and see him, we'll let him know what has happened. He may be able to help.'

'It's too late.'

'It's never too late. Didn't you and me find each other again? I'd all but given up hope that I would ever have the chance to be a mother to you and then the old goat changed his mind and offered us a roof over our heads.'

I smiled, thinking of the granddaddy and how he hadn't wanted me here at first. 'I still miss him, Mammy.'

'So do I, although I never thought I would, but there, you never know where life is going to take you. Don't give up hope, Cissy. Your little girl is out there somewhere and she's alive, she just needs to find her way home.'

'She's just a baby, how can she do that?'

'Maybe that God of yours will light her way. He raised the dead, didn't he? I'd say that bringing one small baby back to its rightful mother shouldn't be too difficult.'

I smiled at the mammy but I knew that even God was no match for Mrs Grainger. I didn't want to hope, it would destroy me.

'Is the child Anthony's?'

For a minute I didn't know what she was talking about. 'Anthony?' I said.

'Isn't that what you called him? The lad up at the Hall that you were so keen on?'

I shook my head. 'There was no Anthony, Mammy. I'm sorry I lied to you.'

'Who then?'

I didn't want her to know, she would be up at the Hall battering the door down. I'd been through enough, I wanted nothing to do with the Brettons. 'Would you be angry if I said I wanted to keep it to myself?'

'You are old enough to have a child, so I'd say you are old enough to keep what is private to yourself.'

'Thank you, Mammy.'

We sat together on the couch. Mammy's arms were around me as I told her about the kindness of the nuns and the new friends I'd made. 'So, you see there were some happy times as well as sad ones.'

'It was the same for me, Cissy. I missed you every day when we were in the workhouse but I made a great friend in Kate Foley. I'd never been one for close friendships but when you are thrown together in difficult times you are grateful for the closeness of others. The poet John Donne must have found himself in similar circumstances when he said, "no man is an island".'

I smiled at her. 'I didn't know you liked poetry, Mammy?'

'I don't. I find it frivolous and I have never been one for frivolity, you need money for that, but that stuck in my mind for some reason.'

The mammy was a mystery to me; she always had been, she wasn't like other mammys. She'd never asked anything of anyone; not money or company or even advice, she kept her own counsel. It made me proud to be a part of her, it made me proud to be her daughter. I would never see that pride in my own baby's eyes. I had carried her for nine months, she had sucked at my breast, she had slept in my arms but she wouldn't remember me. My heart was breaking: my own daughter wouldn't even remember me.

CHAPTER FIFTY-SIX

The following weeks went by in a blur of pain and disbelief at all that had happened. I ate what Mammy put in front of me and I lay awake through the long dark nights. Some nights she would sit with me on the couch downstairs as dawn came up over Paradise Alley. I didn't want to see anyone and I didn't want to step outside the cottage. I was safe here, no one could harm me. I couldn't even face Colm. Mammy walked up to the grey house and told him that I needed to be alone for a while.

'What did he say?' I asked.

'He said he will be there when you need him.'

Father Kelly came to Paradise Alley and I told him my story.

'I feel responsible for this, Cissy,' he said, looking concerned.

'Please don't, Father. You helped me when I needed help, you weren't to know what would happen.'

'I will write to Father Sullivan, he may have some news.'

'It's too late, Father,' I said sadly. 'Mrs Grainger's gone and she's taken Nora with her. She must have had this planned all along and she will have covered her tracks. We'll never find her.'

'The Holy Sisters of Mercy wrote to me, Cissy. They hadn't heard from you and they were worried. I told them you were home.'

'I should have written myself.'

'I've put their minds at rest but I'm sure they would love to hear from you.'

'They were so kind to me, Father, you couldn't have sent me to a better place. If there is any blame here, it lies with Mrs Grainger alone and not with you.'

'Have you been to see Mary?'

'I went straight to her when I got off the coach.'

'So you know her news?'

'What news?'

'She's off to America in a few weeks.'

My heart dropped. Mary had said she was going but I hadn't really understood what she meant until now. 'She's really going?'

'She is, you should spend some time with her while you have the chance.'

'She'd have to come here, Father.'

'Wouldn't you like to walk beside your friend in God's good clean fresh air before she leaves you?'

Mammy sat down beside me and held my hand. 'Maybe it's time to face the world, my love,' she said gently.

I looked into the faces of these two people who only wanted the best for me and I slowly nodded.

It was Mary's half day so I met her from work and we walked across the road to the beach. It was a beautiful spring day, the sort of day that would have once made me feel glad to be alive. The afternoon sun sparkled on the water as we sat together on the wall. 'I'm going to miss you, Mary,' I told her.

'I'll miss you too, Cissy. I've been dreaming of this for so long but now it's really going to happen, I'm scared. How am I going to say goodbye to my family?'

'Are you sure this is what you really want? You don't have to go, you know. When I left, I didn't have a choice but you do.'

'I'm all over the place, Cissy. One minute I'm certain it's what I want and the next I just want to say no, I've made a mistake, I can't leave Ballybun, I can't leave everything I know and love.'

We sat in silence looking out over the sea. 'Will America be this beautiful?' she said, linking her arm through mine. 'Will I find a friend that I love as much as I love you? Will I ever get over leaving my brothers and sisters, me mam and dad?'

'All I can say is that the last thing I ever expected to find in England was friendship but I did and you will too, I'm sure of it.'

'Maybe.'

Mary sounded so unhappy that I was beginning to worry about her. 'Have you spoken to anyone else about how you feel?'

'No one. I've been going on about this for years, I'd feel a right eejit if I suddenly announced that I'd changed my mind, with my ticket bought and my case packed.'

'I think it's more important that you are absolutely sure about this than whether or not someone thinks you're an eejit. This is your whole future, Mary, you have to be sure it's what you want.'

'Every time I put something in the case I feel sick. Oh, Cissy, what am I doing?'

'You're going on a great adventure, Mary. There's whole new world out there across the sea, a whole new world called America. This has been your dream for as long as I can remember and dreams don't come along every day of the week. If it's not the dream you hoped for, then you're just going to have to save up again for your fare home.'

She grinned. 'You're right, Cissy, I can always come home.'

'Of course, you can, America isn't going to hold you hostage.'

'What's your dream, Cissy?'

'To hold my child again.'

'Oh, Cissy, I'm sorry.'

'I know you are.'

'I wish I'd seen her.'

'I wish you had too, for she was beautiful.'

We sat again in silence looking out over the sea. Today the beach was deserted, stretching out way beyond the lighthouse and in the other direction, towards the town. This was my home and I never wanted to leave these shores again.

'She is still beautiful, Cissy,' said Mary, 'and if my dream can come true then maybe with the help of God, yours will too.'

'I've kind of given up on God, Mary, or God's given up on me.'

'You know better than that, Cissy Ryan. God never gives up on anyone, even if it takes Him a long time to get around to it. He must have a list as long as your arm of people wanting His help.'

'Well, He's certainly testing my faith this time.'

'I'll pray for you, Cissy. Not that I can promise He'll listen to me, I'm a desperate sinner.'

'You are not!' I said, grinning.

'Anyway, I'll give it a go, sure we've nothing to lose.'

'When are you leaving?'

'In two weeks' time, April the eleventh.'

'From Cork?'

'Queenstown.'

'And how are you getting there?'

'I'm going on the coach, Father Kelly is coming with me.'

'What about your parents? Aren't they going to see you off?'

'Mammy said she wouldn't be able to stand on the quayside and watch the boat leave and Daddy goes along with whatever Mammy says. I'll say goodbye to them all at home. Will you see me off, Cissy? You and Colm?'

'Of course, I will. I don't know about Colm though, we haven't spoken since the day I came home.'

'Why not?'

I shrugged my shoulders. 'I don't know how to face him.'

'Well, if I'm brave enough to get on a boat and sail thousands of miles away across the sea, I'm sure you can walk to the end of Paradise Alley and kiss the face off Colm Doyle.'

I grinned at her. 'I'm going to miss you, Mary Butler.'

'We'll write,' she said. 'We'll write all the time. I'll tell you all about America and you can tell me all about life in Ballybun. I won't forget you, Cissy.'

'Promise?'

'I promise.'

CHAPTER FIFTY-SEVEN

It was as if I'd never been away. Life in Ballybun had gone on without me; nothing had changed except me. Everyone wanted to know about England.

Nellie Mahon cornered me outside the bakery. She stood too close to me and I had the urge to push her away. She had mean little eyes that peered out from under wiry grey eyebrows that looked like a couple of unruly bushes.

'Did your mother tell you that it was me that saw you stepping off the bus?'

'She did, Mrs Mahon.'

'And did she tell you that I went all the way out to the laundry to inform her of your arrival?'

'She did, and she was grateful.'

'Did she say that?' said Mrs Mahon, looking pleased with herself.

'She did.'

'I thought it was my Christian duty to let her know. She looked very surprised, Cissy. Did you not tell her you were coming home?'

'I thought I'd surprise her.'

'I'm not one for surprises meself, I find there's an air of deceit about them. Not that I'm saying you were deceitful, you understand.'

'Of course,' I said, trying to edge away from her.

She caught hold of my arm. 'Is England full of pagans? Did they try to convert you to the Protestant faith?'

'No, they didn't, I found the people to be very kind.'

'You probably didn't notice, Cissy, with you being so innocent but I've heard terrible tales of brainwashing and white slavery.'

'I don't think there was anything like that going on, Mrs Mahon.'

'Well, in my opinion, I think you had a lucky escape. I'd say they are more to be pitied than feared. Our Blessed Lord in His wisdom must have taken care of you.'

I started to walk away when she said. 'Are you home to stay now, Cissy?'

'I think so, Mrs Mahon.'

'Sure, your poor mother will be glad of the company, all alone in that cottage with neither kith nor kin to give her comfort. As you well know, I'm not one to poke my nose in other people's business but I've heard that Mr Collins from up at the farm is around a lot these days. Are they stepping out?'

'I really must go, Mrs Mahon,' I said. 'My mother will be waiting for the bread.'

'Well, it's good to see you home safe and sound, back where you belong. I'll maybe call in for a cup of tea some time.'

Oh please don't, I thought as I hurried home through the town. I couldn't wait to tell Mammy about the white slavery, it would make her laugh. I loved to see the mammy laugh, she didn't do it often enough.

Things had changed between Colm and me. I wasn't the same young girl who had left Ireland. Some days I felt as though I had grown far beyond my years. Colm was six years older than me but it didn't feel that way any more. He'd stayed here in Ballybun, delivering the milk and tending to Blue. Nothing had changed for him but it had for me: I had a child and I would never be the same again.

We took long walks just as we used to, out the wood road and along the strand, with Buddy running between us. I avoided the places I had been with Peter Bretton, those secret places that for a while I had lived for. Being with Colm made me realise what a stupid girl I had been, to think that Peter loved me, or that I had loved him. How blind I had been to the goodness in Colm and how easily I had fallen for Peter's lies.

Ballybun was a small town and I lived in fear of bumping into any of the Bretton family. Had Caroline Bretton told her brother of her suspicions? Did he know that I had gone to England to have his child? Well, he would never hear it from my lips, that was for sure. I might not have had Nora for long but I had held her and seen her sweet smile and loved her, which is more than any of them would ever get the chance to do.

I wrote a letter to Annie to let her know that I was home and I asked Colm to deliver it for me. I suggested we meet on the beach the following evening when she finished work.

The next day I decided to visit Mrs Foley. The workhouse towered above me as I climbed the hill and I remembered how me and Nora used to stare out of the window, waiting for our mammies to come and collect us. It seemed like a lifetime ago. The old building held no fear for me, just a deep sadness for the poor souls that were in there and knew no other life than the one within those stark grey walls.

I rang the bell and waited for Mr Dunne to let me in. He smiled when he saw it was me.

'You're a sight for sore eyes, Cissy,' he said. 'You're looking well, girl.'

'So are you, Mr Dunne.'

'Not me, Cissy. I'm older than God and crippled with the arthritis, but there you go, we all have our crosses.'

'I've come to visit Mrs Foley,' I said.

'She's up at Nora's grave, Cissy, shall I leave you to find her?'

I nodded and walked round the side of the house to the graveyard. I still found it hard to see the rows and rows of wooden crosses that covered the hillside; all those poor souls that had died within these walls. Me and Mammy had been the lucky ones, we had got to go home.

As I opened the gate that led up to the babies' section, Mrs Foley was walking down the hill towards me.

'Ah, Cissy, have you come to visit Nora's grave?'

'I've come to see *you*, Mrs Foley.'

'Well, that's a lovely surprise. Let's go inside and I'll make us a nice cup of tea. I heard you were back from England,' she said, as she busied herself with the cups and saucers. 'Your mother must be delighted to have you home.'

'I'm sorry I haven't been to see you for such a long time,' I said. 'I should have come before.'

'There's no "should" about it, we do things when we are able to and you're here now.'

'I suppose I just couldn't face you.'

'It was a sad time, Cissy, but I visit her every day and I talk to her. It's a great comfort to me.'

'I always thought that Nora and I would live together one day,' I said sadly. 'I didn't realise she was so ill...'

'She was never a strong child, not like yourself, but you made her very happy and I will always be grateful to you for that.'

'I still can't believe she is gone.'

'Neither can I but that sweet girl is at peace now and you and I have our memories.'

Me and Mrs Foley sat at the table and drank our tea and talked about Nora and Mary.

'You'll miss your friend, Cissy, when is she off to America?'

'In a couple of weeks.'

'Nothing stays the same, does it?'

'Maybe it's not supposed to,' I said.

That evening I sat on the rocks and waited for Annie. I could see Bretton Hall up on the hill and my stomach twisted as I was reminded of Peter and what we had done. I wondered if he was there and how he would react if he knew that he had fathered a child. I turned my eyes away from the house and looked out towards the sea. This place had always given me comfort and it still did, even though the windows of Bretton Hall felt as though they were boring into my back.

'Cissy!'

I turned and saw Annie running down the path, her unruly hair flung back from her face. As I stood up and walked towards her, she fell into my arms.

'Oh, Cissy,' she said. 'It's so wonderful to see you. I've been so excited, I thought the day would never end!'

I slipped my arm through hers. 'It's lovely to see you too, Annie.'

We walked together along the shore line towards the town. 'Shall we go to Minnie's for a cup of tea and a bun?'

'Oh, that would be grand, Cissy.'

As the weather was so nice Minnie had put tables outside and it was lovely sitting in the fresh air with the sound of the sea all around us.

'So how is it up at the Hall?' I asked.

'Not the same without you. Mrs Hickey still has me nerves wrecked but she's not a bad soul and I think she likes me.'

'Of course she does, how could she not?'

'And Miss Caroline is getting engaged.'

This was a surprise. 'I feel sorry for the poor feller,' I said, grinning.

'If he's daft enough to fall for that little madam he deserves all he gets.'

I didn't really want to ask but I found myself saying, 'And Master Peter?'

Annie bit into one of Minnie's sticky buns and I waited.

'He's off on his travels, he's been gone a year now. He's nicer than his sister, don't you think so, Cissy?'

'Well he couldn't be much worse.'

We stayed chatting until the light began to fade.

'I'd better get back,' said Annie sadly. 'But oh, it was lovely to see you again.'

'It was lovely seeing you as well,' I said. 'And we'll be sure to keep in touch.'

Annie put her arms around me. 'I'd like that,' she said.

One evening I was up at the grey house sitting on a bale of hay, watching Colm brush Blue's coat.

'Did you know that Mary's going to America in two weeks?' I said.

'The whole town knows,' said Colm. 'It's quite an event.'

'I said I'd see her off. Would you come with me?'

'If you want me to.'

'I do.'

'Then I'll come. I'd like to wave her off.'

'Thanks.'

'You'll miss her.'

'I don't want to think about it. I always knew she was going, she talked about it often enough, but now it's actually happening I feel terrible sad. She's my only real friend.'

'And who am I, a distant uncle twice removed?' said Colm, winking.

I smiled, 'You're more than a friend, you're, um…'

'What?'

'I'm not really sure, but more than just a friend.'

'I'm glad to hear it, Miss Ryan.'

Colm continued to brush Blue until his coat shone like silk. 'Is Blue really well now?' I said.

'Right as rain. He scared the bejeebers out of me, though.'

'I remember.'

He put the brush down and sat beside me. 'It wasn't long after that you went away.'

'I'm sorry, Colm.'

'You could have told me, you know. We could have worked something out between us. You didn't have to go to England.'

'What else was I to do?'

'You could have stayed here with me, would that have been so awful?'

I shook my head. 'People would have talked.'

'And what do we care about that?'

'They would have thought you were the father.'

Colm took my face in his hands and gently kissed my forehead. 'I love you, I always have and it looks like I always will. That funny little girl, waiting on the quayside, all wide-eyed and skinny-legged, found her way into my heart and stayed there. How could I not love a child that was a part of you?'

Why hadn't I trusted Colm? Why hadn't I turned to him and told him the truth? If I'd done that, Nora would be with me now. I leaned into him, trying to hide the tears that were running down my face.

We stayed like that for a while, warm and cosy in the old barn, listening to the goings-on in the alley outside and the sound of Blue breathing and the noises in the dark corners where the little creatures scuttled around.

He held me away from him and wiped my tears with his hand. 'We'll go to England, Cissy. And we'll find out all there is to know about this woman, someone must know something.'

A tiny bit of hope entered my heart. 'Would you do that for me?'

He brushed my hair away from my face. 'I would, of course.'

'You've never asked who my baby's father is.'

'I thought you'd tell me in your own good time.'

'Do you want to know, Colm?'

'I think I know.'

'It's Peter. Peter Bretton is Nora's father.'

Colm just nodded. I wondered what he was thinking, I wished I could get inside his head.

'You must have loved him,' he said quietly.

'I thought I did.'

'And now?'

'No, not now.'

'Then we'll deal with the rest together. We'll go to England and we'll find your baby.'

I put my arms around his neck. I had never loved Colm Doyle more than I did in that moment.

CHAPTER FIFTY-EIGHT

Mary and I were sitting in Minnie's discussing the party that Father Kelly was to throw for her.

'It's awful good of him to hold it at the rectory,' said Mary.

'He's a good man, I've always thought so.'

'Did he hear back from Father Sullivan?'

'He did, but Father Sullivan was as shocked as he was. I don't want to lose hope but isn't false hope worse than accepting she's gone?'

'I don't know, I've never lost a child so I don't know how I would react.'

'Colm has more hope than I have. He says we'll go to England and find out where Mrs Grainger has taken Nora.'

'Will you go?'

'Of course.'

'Does he know who her father is?'

'He guessed, it wasn't hard.'

'A nice pot of tea,' said Minnie, putting a tray down in front of us. 'It's lovely to have you home, Cissy, you were missed.'

'Thanks, Minnie. I missed being away from you all.'

'Let me know if you want the tea topping up.'

'Thanks,' I said.

Mary poured the tea. 'So are you and Colm together?'

'I wish to God I knew. He tells me he loves me but he's told me that since I was a child. I feel like shaking the truth out of him.'

'But he's forgiven you?'

I stirred the sugar into the cup and added a drop of milk. 'He's never actually said as much.'

'Have you asked him?'

'I'm scared to.'

'You should ask him, Cissy, then you'll know where you stand.'

'What should I say?'

'You should say, "Are we just friends, Colm Doyle? Or are you secretly dying to ravage my young nubile body?" and if it's the latter, you can start planning the wedding.'

I smiled. 'You make it sound easy.'

'It is.'

'Maybe I'll ask him at the party.'

'Or maybe *I* will.'

'No! He'll know we've talked about him.'

'What does he think we talk about? The weather?'

'Maybe I will then.'

'What are you wearing to the party?'

'I only have the one good dress but it holds bad memories. I've thought about giving it to Annie.'

'What? Your good dress that yer mammy had made for you?'

'I know, but it's tainted.'

'For God's sake, Cissy, it's a bit of material, wear the bloody thing!'

I thought of my beautiful dress that I had been so proud to wear and then I remembered how it was crushed up against the logs in the shed and I was full of shame. 'I don't want to wear anything that reminds me of Peter Bretton.'

'We're the same size, why don't we swap?'

'Are you sure?'

'Of course, your dress is gorgeous, I'll be the belle of the ball. I might even find meself a feller.'

'Bit late for that, isn't it?'

'It's never too late for a bit of romance, Cissy.'

'Ever the optimist, Mary Butler.'

'I just hope no one brings presents to the party. I've a pile of them at home. Every day, someone just happens to be passing the house with something for the journey. I'll have to take the food to the party.'

'They bring food?'

Mary nodded. 'Ham, eggs, cheese.'

'For the journey?'

Mary nodded. 'It will have gone off before I step foot on the gangplank.'

'Still, it's thoughtful,' I said, grinning.

'I'm taking two small cases, not a feckin' trunk. Why couldn't they bring something useful, like jewellery or lipstick? Then I could land in America in style.'

'You'd look blowsy, they might not let you in.'

'Then I'll come straight back home.'

'Still having doubts?'

'Every bloody day!'

'Oh, I'm going to miss you, Mary.'

'Stop, you'll start me off.'

'Who am I going to tell my deepest secrets to?'

'Colm Doyle, that's who. He's your best friend, he's always been your best friend. Fight for him, Cissy.'

We were just about to leave when Minnie handed Mary a bag. 'A fine batch of sausage rolls for the journey, Mary.'

We managed to hold it together until we got outside, then collapsed in fits of laughter.

'The kids will love them,' said Mary, wiping her eyes.

Mrs Mahon was walking towards us. 'And what are you two naughty girls giggling about? Is it boys?' she said.

'No, Mrs Mahon,' said Mary, politely. 'It's sausage rolls.'

We watched her walk away and started laughing again, hysterical laughter that turned to tears and left me sobbing.

Mary held me in her arms. 'Oh, Cissy, it wasn't your fault that your baby was taken, you're allowed to laugh now and then.'

'It seems wrong.'

'It's what's going to get you through this, my darling friend. Laugh when you can, no one is judging you. God won't keep Nora from you just because you laughed.'

'Promise?'

'I promise, now let's go and try these dresses on. I want the boys in Ballybun to know what they're going to be missing.'

CHAPTER FIFTY-NINE

The front room of the rectory looked lovely; there were candles burning on the dressers and a long table was pushed up against the wall and piled high with food.

'People have been coming in and out all day,' said Father Kelly. 'It takes something like this to bring the town together, everyone wants to say goodbye to Mary and wish her a safe voyage.'

'It looks grand, Father,' I said.

'I'm sorry Father Sullivan couldn't help, Cissy. I really hoped he would know something. He continues to investigate.'

'Thank you for trying, Father.'

'Sure, I did very little.'

'She's gone, Father, and I have to accept it and try to get on with my life.'

'Am I right in thinking that is easier said than done?'

I nodded.

'I'll remember Nora in my prayers.'

I held my tongue and didn't tell him that I'd lost my faith. He put his hand on my shoulder and then walked away.

There were a couple of fellers playing fiddles and one of Mary's brothers playing the bodhrán. Mammy and Mr Collins were dancing together. Mr Collins had his arm around the mammy's waist, and they looked happy and at ease as they circled the room. I was glad that they had found each other and were not alone in the world. By the look on Mr Collins's face as he looked down at her I'd say he still thought that Moira Ryan was the prettiest girl in Ballybun.

Mrs Butler was sitting on Father Kelly's couch weeping, with half the women of the town patting her shoulder and bringing her glasses of sherry. She wasn't going to be able to stand by the end of the night. Mary walked over to me, looking beautiful in my blue dress. She was indeed the belle of the ball, the star of the show, and she was loving all the attention.

'Will you look at her?' said Mary, pointing to her mammy. 'Sitting there like the Queen of Sheba and all the women dancing attendance on her. My father will have to carry her home, providing he can stand himself.'

'She's enjoying it by the look of her.'

'I can't believe this is my last night in Ballybun, Cissy.'

'Are you excited?'

'I'd get on the boat now, if I could. Mammy is going to be weeping and wailing all night and none of us will get a wink of sleep. You'd think she'd be glad to get rid of one of us, wouldn't you? Father Kelly says it's like the parable of the good shepherd. You know the one, where he has a flock of sheep but can't rest until he finds the one that's lost.'

'I'd say the Bible has a parable for most situations.'

'Our lot are more like a pack of wolves than sheep.'

'I'd say you're right,' I said, grinning.

'Your Colm looks handsome tonight, Cissy.'

I looked across at poor Colm, who seemed to have been cornered by Mrs Mahon. 'I'd better rescue him,' I said.

'Ask him.'

'Ask him what?'

'If he forgives you. You said you'd ask him tonight.'

'Did I?'

'You know you did. Go on, I want to know that you two are going to be alright before I go.'

I walked over to him. 'I'm sorry to butt in on your conversation, Mrs Mahon, but Father wants a word with Colm.'

'Will you excuse me, Mrs Mahon?'

'Perhaps we can catch up later, Colm,' she said.

'I hope not,' Colm said under his breath as we walked away. 'What does Father Kelly want?'

'He doesn't want anything, I just used that as an excuse to rescue you.'

'Awful woman, but I supposed she's to be pitied. I don't think there's a soul in the town who wants to be her friend.'

'And that's because she's a desperate gossip. Even Father Kelly says she's better than a telegraph for getting news round the town fast.'

'So she has her uses,' he said, smiling. 'Shall we get some fresh air?'

I nodded. He took my hand and we went through the kitchen and into Father Kelly's neat little garden. We walked down the path and sat on a bench looking out over the fields that led up to the workhouse.

'Do you ever think about your time in there, Cissy?' said Colm.

'Not much, I think of my friend Nora though. I still feel her loss. I wish she could have known a life outside the place.'

'But you named your little girl for her?'

'I did, except that Mrs Grainger changed it.'

'You've been through a lot.'

'It was all my own fault, I have no one to blame but myself. I was a foolish girl.'

'We all do foolish things, Cissy.'

'Can I ask you something, Colm?'

'Ask away.'

'Do you forgive me?'

'For what?'

'For going with Peter. For having his child?'

Colm put his arm around my shoulders. 'There's nothing to forgive. You didn't do it to hurt me, did you?'

'No, but…'

'What?'

I turned and faced him. 'Did it make you feel differently about me? Did it make you stop loving me?'

Colm stared out over the fields. 'I was jealous of him and I was worried for you because I knew you were going to get hurt.' Then he looked at me. 'But I never stopped loving you, Cissy.'

He still hadn't said what I wanted to hear and I almost shouted at him. 'How do you love me though? Like a sister, like a friend? Or do you love me like a… like a…'

'Lover?' said Colm, smiling.

I was glad of the darkness because I knew that I was blushing. 'Yes, Colm, like a lover.'

'Now let me think, Cissy Ryan.'

'You're teasing me.'

'To answer your question, yes, I love you like a brother and I love you like a friend, and I love you like a man loves a woman and I want to marry you if you'll have me.' He held my face in his hands and stared at me. '*Will* you have me, Cissy? Will you take a chance on a feller that hasn't much to give you but would give you the world if he could? Will you walk the road beside me? Will you love me in sickness and in health? And will you stay by my side through whatever shite is thrown our way?'

My eyes were full of tears. 'I will walk beside you, Colm, and I'll be proud to call you mine, for I've loved you almost all my life and I will love you until the day I die.'

We sat together on the bench and I looked across the fields to the workhouse and I remembered the day that me and Mammy had walked out of those gates and into another life, a life that held Colm. A life that held the boy I was going to marry.

CHAPTER SIXTY

Half the town seemed to have turned out to see Mary off. It was desperately sad to see her brothers and sisters clinging to her.

'I think you should get Mary onto the coach,' said Mammy.

'I think you're right, Mrs Ryan,' said Colm.

'Mr Collins and I will just say goodbye to her.'

'Are you alright, Cissy?' asked Colm, holding my hand.

I nodded. 'I'm not sure how I'll be when I watch her sail away though.'

'It'll be sad alright but you're a strong girl and that's what she's going to need from you. You can cry on my shoulder all the way home.'

I knew that it was going to be hard to see my friend go away but with Colm by my side, it was going to be easier to say goodbye: I wasn't alone.

I sat beside Mary and Colm and Father Kelly sat in the seat behind us.

As we pulled away, I held her hand. There were tears pouring down Mary's face as she waved a final goodbye to her family. I was trying to be strong but I felt like crying too. I could find no words to comfort her, so I just kept hold of her hand as we left Ballybun behind us and headed towards Queenstown.

The further we got from the town, the better Mary began to feel. 'That was the hardest thing I have ever done,' she said. 'It all feels so unreal, I can't get my head round the fact that I am going to America. I'm actually going, Cissy, can you believe it? Because I can't.'

'You have so much ahead of you, Mary, so many exciting things to see. I bet when you come home for a visit, you'll sound like a proper Yank.'

'If I can afford to come home for a visit.'

I took an envelope out of my bag and handed it to her.
'What's this?'
'It's so that you can come home one day for a visit.'
Mary opened the envelope and looked inside. 'But I can't take it.'
'Yes, you can, Mary.'
'You can't afford to give me all this.'
'It's blood money so I can do what I like with it.'
'From Mrs Grainger?'
'The very one. If I can't give the money back, then I want to do good things with it. Anyway, I've plenty left.'

Mary put her arms around me. 'I can't tell you what this means, Cissy. It makes going so much easier because now it's not final, I can see my family again one day and I can see you. Thank you.'

When I had first got the money, I was all for throwing it into the nearest fire. It was Mrs Cornish who had persuaded me to keep it and having decided to do so, I was determined to put it to good use. Being able to do this for Mary made me happy.

We had been given so much food by the people in the town that we were able to feed the whole coach and the journey became almost jolly. Before we knew it, we were pulling into Queenstown.

Father Kelly and Colm carried Mary's bags as we walked down to the dock. There were hundreds of people on the quayside; men carrying bags and bundles, women holding tightly onto the hands of their children and porters wheeling trolleys laden with trunks and cases in and out of the crowd.

We stood staring up at the ship, towering above us like an enormous mountain, seeming to almost block out the sky above it.

'Wait,' said Mary. 'I don't think I can do this.'

'That will be the nerves,' said Father Kelly. 'It's natural that you will be nervous, for this is a life-changing thing that you are doing, Mary.'

'But I'm not sure that I want to change me life now,' she said. 'I'm thinking me life was fine as it was. I loved working in the hotel and sitting with you in Minnie's. What was I thinking, Cissy? Why did I think that America held more for me than Ballybun?'

'You don't have to go, Mary. You know that, don't you?'

'But all that food,' she said. Which made us both double up with laughter.

'You'll be fine,' I said. 'Look at the size of it. You'll come to no harm on a ship like that.'

As we looked up at the majestic ship towering above us, we couldn't help but be awed by the size of it.

'But it's so big,' said Mary.

'It needs to be big to carry all these people safely across the sea to America,' said Colm. 'But if you really don't want to go, we can turn around now and go back home.'

'I'd feel like an eejit after having a party and all.'

'They'll forget, Mary,' I said.

We were being jostled by people trying to get past with cases and stray kids dashing around. I took hold of Mary's hand and walked her to a quieter spot.

'I have something to tell you, Mary.'

'What's that?'

'Last night at the party, Colm asked me to marry him.'

'Oh, Cissy, that's wonderful! I am so happy for you, I really am. Now I know you'll be okay without me.'

'I'll still miss you, Mary. Marrying Colm isn't going to change that.'

'And I'll miss you.'

'Are you ready?' I said. 'Or do you want to go home?'

Mary put her arms around me. 'I'm going to America,' she said. 'This is my dream. Look in on my family now and again and write to me. I want letters, lots of letters.'

'I shall look forward to hearing all your news.'

'There's one thing I want to ask of you, Cissy.'

'Anything.'

'Will you take Eddie?'

'For walks?'

'For good. Will you take him and look after him? I'm the only one who bothers with him, he'll starve to death with me gone.'

'Of course I'll take him, Mary, he'll be great company for Buddy.'

Mary kissed my cheek. 'Goodbye, my dearest friend.'

My eyes were so full of tears that I could hardly see. 'Goodbye, Mary,' I said.

Colm had his arm around me as we watched her walk up the gangplank and disappear inside the ship.

'Do you want to wait until she sails?' he asked.

'Yes, I want to wave to her.'

We waited while the crowd began to thin out. It made me feel sad watching men and women walking up the gangplank, hanging onto cases and children and waving to the families they were leaving behind. They were sailing away from these shores for a new life in America. I hoped that it would be everything they hoped it would be.

We watched the gangplank being pulled away from the big ship and scanned the people waving from the decks.

'Can you see her, Colm?'

'There she is,' said Father Kelly. 'She's waving to us.'

I spotted her and waved back. She was mouthing something but I couldn't hear her so I just kept on waving.

'I think someone is trying to get your attention, Cissy,' said Colm suddenly.

'What?'

'There's a young girl in a blue coat, I think it's you she's waving at.'

I didn't recognise her immediately. I knew the face but I didn't know where I knew it from and then I remembered: the girl in the blue coat was Betsy. What was Betsy doing on a ship going to America? She had no money. It was then that I saw her being yanked back from the railings.

'It's Betsy!' I screamed.

'Who?' said Colm.

'Betsy, she helped look after Nora in London, she must be travelling with Mrs Grainger. We can't let the ship leave.'

'Are you sure, Cissy?' said Father Kelly.

'I'm absolutely sure, Father.'

Father Kelly looked around, then grabbed hold of a young sailor.

'This ship must not leave the dock,' he said to him.

'I'm sorry, Father,' said the boy, 'but we are about to go, it's too late to stop it now.'

'Listen,' said Father Kelly. 'A terrible crime is about to be committed if this boat sails.'

I could tell that the young sailor didn't know what to do and then he said, 'Follow me, Father, the First Class gangplank won't have gone up yet.'

We started running along the quayside behind him, pushing through the crowds. The sailor was shouting as he ran: 'Hold the gangplank!'

A man beside the gangplank looked at us as if we were mad.

'These people have to get on the ship,' said the sailor.

'Too late,' said the man.

'Do you want the wrath of God to come down on your head, man?' said Father Kelly.

'No, Father, but you've left it too late. I have my orders.'

'What's your name, son?'

'Sean O'Brian, Father.'

'And are you a good Catholic?'

'I am, Father.'

'Then you will know that there comes a time in your life when you must answer to a higher authority than that of mere men.'

'Of course, Father,' he said, standing aside. 'Please board the ship.'

'Good man, Sean, I shall read your name out at Mass on Sunday.'

'Thank you, Father.'

I clung to Colm's hand as we almost ran up the gangplank. My heart was pounding out of my chest. I wanted to tear the ship apart to get to my baby. I couldn't believe what had just happened. What if I hadn't seen Betsy? I couldn't bear to think of it – Nora would have been lost to me forever.

We followed the sailor down some steep steps and along a corridor.

'I'm taking you to the captain,' he told us.

We stopped outside a door and the sailor knocked on it.

'Enter,' said a voice from inside.

We followed the sailor into the cabin.

'Sir,' he said. 'These people say that a crime is being committed on this ship, so I thought it best to bring them to you.'

'Thank you,' said the captain. 'You did the right thing.'

Father Kelly stepped forward and shook the captain's hand. 'I am Father Kelly from the parish of Ballybun.'

'Please sit down, all of you,' he said, 'and be assured that if there is some wrongdoing here, this ship will not leave until it is sorted out to your own – and my –satisfaction. Now will one of you tell me what is wrong?'

Father Kelly looked at me and I nodded for him to do the explaining.

'There is a woman on board this ship who is travelling with a child that is not her own. She has stolen the baby from this young girl here.'

'You have to believe us,' I pleaded.

'Get the purser,' he said to the sailor. 'I need to look at the passenger list.'

'Right away, Sir,' said the sailor.

'What is the woman's name?' asked the captain.

'Her name's Mrs Grainger,' I said.

'And apart from the child, is she travelling with anyone else?'

'A girl called Betsy, I don't know her other name.'

'Don't worry, dear, if what you say is true, and I am inclined to believe that it is,' he said seriously, 'your baby will soon be returned to you. Is the child a girl or a boy?'

'A little girl, Sir.'

The door opened. 'Ah, Purser, do you have the passenger list?'

'Here it is, Captain,' he said, handing it over.

'I imagine the lady will be travelling First Class,' said Father Kelly. 'If that helps.'

'It does,' replied the captain, running his finger down the list.

'Here we are,' he said. 'A Mrs Veronica Grainger, travelling with her daughter, Miss Charlotte Grainger, and a Miss Betsy Perkins. Do you have any proof that the child is yours?'

I'd carried Nora's birth certificate around ever since Mother Ignatius had given it to me.

I took it out of my bag and handed it to him. He read it and then looked at me.

'This child's name is Nora.'

'Mrs Grainger changed it to Charlotte, Sir.'

He handed it back to me. 'I'm afraid this isn't proof.'

'I've known Cissy Ryan all her life, Sir, and I can vouch for her honesty,' said Father Kelly. 'If you need further proof then you can contact the Sisters of Mercy in London, who allowed Mrs Grainger to take care of the child until Cissy could take care of her herself.'

'I might have to do that. Now I think it's time to speak to the lady in question, don't you?'

There was a time when I would have been afraid to face Mrs Grainger but not today, today I was going to take back my daughter if it meant dragging her from Mrs Grainger's arms.

'Come with me, Purser,' said the captain. 'I may need your help.'

'Yes, Sir.'

Then he turned to the sailor. 'Make sure the First Class gangplank stays in place and keep guard at the top. Don't let anyone leave this ship.'

'Right away, Sir,' said the sailor.

'Thank you for your help,' I said, as he went towards the door.

'You're welcome, Miss, I hope it all works out for you.'

'It will,' I said, finally beginning to feel like there was some hope.

'Right,' said the captain. 'She's in cabin forty-eight.'

'Follow me, Sir,' said the Purser.

We went back up the stairs and through a door marked 'First Class'. The Purser stopped outside cabin forty-eight. The captain knocked but there was no answer.

'This is your captain, Mrs Grainger, I need you to open the door.'

I could hear whispering inside and then Betsy's voice.

'It's the captain, Madam, we have to do what he says.'

'Come away from the door, Betsy.'

'If you don't open this door immediately, Mrs Grainger, I will be forced to get the police on board.'

I could hear the fear in Betsy's voice as she said. 'We have to open it, Madam, he's gonna get the law. What 'ave you done, Madam?'

'I said, come away from the door.'

'You're frightening me,' said Betsy.

'Can you hear me, Betsy?' said the captain.

'Yes, Sir.'

'You need to open this door. You are in no trouble but I need to speak to Mrs Grainger on a very serious matter.'

There was no sound for a moment and then the door slowly opened and we were looking at a white-faced Betsy.

'Good girl,' said the captain. 'Purser, will you look after this girl?'

'Of course, come along with me, lass.'

'Hello, Cissy,' she said softly as she passed.

'Hello, Betsy,' I whispered back.

Mrs Grainger was standing in the corner of the room. She had Nora in her arms and the baby was whimpering.

'You're holding her too tight,' I said, beginning to panic.

'Don't tell me what to do with my own child,' she screamed.

'But she's not your child, Mrs Grainger, is she?' said the captain.

'She sold her to me,' she said, pointing a finger at me.

'You're a liar,' I shouted. 'I would never sell my own child.'

The captain stared at Mrs Grainger. 'So you admit that this is not your child, then?'

'I can look after her better than she can. I can give her a better life, she will want for nothing. What can she give her? Nothing.'

'I might not be able to give her the finer things in life, Mrs Grainger, but I can give her love.'

Nora was whimpering again. It was all I could do to stand there and not make a grab for her.

Colm and the captain moved further into the room. 'Give me the child,' said the captain.

'Get away from her,' screamed Mrs Grainger, red-faced.

'If you don't hand me the child immediately, I will have you arrested and taken off the ship.'

Mrs Grainger slumped down onto the bed. She knew she'd lost. 'Take her,' she snarled and almost threw Nora at the captain, who handed her to Colm.

Colm walked over and gently placed her in my arms. 'Your baby, Cissy,' he said, smiling.

My cheeks were wet with tears as I looked down at Nora. It had been so long since I'd held her in my arms, my heart was bursting with joy. I looked at Mrs Grainger slumped forward on the bed and I felt nothing for her, nothing at all. 'Do you want to press charges, Miss Ryan?' asked the captain.

'Do you, Cissy?' said Father Kelly.

I shook my head. 'I just want to go home.'

Father Kelly shook the captain's hand. 'What will happen to her now?'

'I shall hand her over to the American authorities when we dock. I'll let them deal with her. If you would please leave your details, Father.'

'Of course,' said Father Kelly.

I looked at the captain and smiled. 'Thank you.' I said.

He smiled back. 'I'm glad that I was able to help.'

Once we were back up on the deck I looked down at Nora. She'd changed, she was bigger than when I'd last seen her. Mrs Grainger had stolen those precious months from me. I held her up to my face and kissed her sweet little head. Oh, to have her in my arms again! My heart was bursting with happiness.

'She's beautiful,' said Colm, smiling down at her.

'She is, isn't she?' I said.

The young sailor was still keeping guard. 'Do you want me to carry her down the gangplank for you?' he asked.

But I wasn't ready to hand Nora over to anyone, not even this kind young sailor. 'No, thanks,' I said. 'I can do this.'

'I'm glad you got her back, Miss.'

'You helped,' I said.

'Glad to,' he said, grinning.

Colm steadied me as we stepped down onto the quayside.

There were still crowds of people waiting for the ship to leave.

'Can you see Mary?' I asked.

'No... hang on, there she is,' said Colm.

I spotted her and lifted Nora up.

I could see her laughing and waving at us.

We waited as the great ship pulled away from the quay. I looked at the name on her side: it was a strong name. This ship would carry Mary safely across the ocean to her new life in America. People around us wereweeping, but with Nora in my arms I was too filled with happiness to feel sad.

'Home?' said Colm.

'Can I have a minute on my own?' I said.

'Of course, my love.'

I walked a little away from him and watched as the RMS *Titanic* grew smaller and smaller, carrying with her the hopes and dreams of so many souls.

I looked down at my baby, safe and warm in my arms. 'Your name is Nora Ryan,' I said softly. 'Beloved daughter of Cissy Ryan, granddaughter of Moira Ryan and great granddaughter of Malachi Ryan and you are loved.'

EPILOGUE

I wandered across to the stables with Stevie balanced on my hip. My sweet boy was growing by the day, a sunny-natured little feller who smiled at everyone and was loved by all. At almost fourteen months old he should have been walking, but Mammy said he was too lazy.

'He's like yer granddaddy,' she said. 'We'll be waiting on him until he finds himself a wife.'

But I liked the fact that he still held his chubby little hands up to be carried; that he still wanted to be close to me. I was enjoying his babyhood and I was in no hurry for him to grow up. I'd carry him in my arms for the rest of his life if I could.

'Shall we go and see Nora?' I said, kissing his cheek. 'Shall we see how your big sister is getting on with the horse?'

I walked around to the back of the stable, where Colm was giving Nora her first riding lesson. I stayed out of sight, watching him lead the horse slowly around the yard. I could see darling Blue up in the field, too old now for work, happy to let this newcomer take over from him.

Nora looked so serious up on the little horse's back that I smiled. At only five, she was old beyond her years. Whatever task was assigned to her, she put her heart and soul into it. Life for this beautiful little girl was a serious affair. I often wondered whether her personality had been formed in those first few months of her life when we had been apart.

'I don't hold with that sort of modern thinking,' said Mammy. 'The child is like me and it will stand her in good stead when she has to deal with fools and eejits.'

Mammy loved both the children but it was plain to see the special bond she held with her first grandchild. Nora felt the same about her. The highlight of her week was the time she spent with her nanny and granddaddy up at Collins's farm.

When I was a child, hugs and kisses were few and far between, yet Mammy seemed able to give Nora all the love and affection that I myself was at times denied. I knew that Mammy loved me but she hadn't always been able to show it. It warmed my heart to see her eyes soften when she looked at my little girl.

Mammy had moved into the farm with Mr Collins but the pair of them hadn't felt any urgency to get married.

'People are talking, Moira,' said Father Kelly.

'People are always talking,' Mammy had said.

'Then do it for your grandchildren, or do you want them mocked in the town?'

This of course changed her mind and she agreed to a small ceremony down at the church, as long as there was no fuss and no fancy tea and cakes afterwards. Now at least she had the town's approval and I think she quite enjoyed being addressed as Mrs Collins.

A lot had changed since the day I'd brought Nora home. The shock of losing Mary to the cold waters of the Atlantic Ocean had the town paralysed with grief. For weeks we waited in the hope that she was in a hospital somewhere and that we would hear from her, but as the weeks turned into months, we had to accept that she was gone. Father Kelly held a memorial service for her at the church. It was so packed that there were people kneeling outside on the steps, wanting to pay their respects to one of their own, a young girl who had dreamt of a new life in America.

The one piece of good news in all the sadness was that Betsy had been pulled from the water by a young man to whom she was now happily married. They had made their life in America and she was soon to give birth to her first child.

The day after the service I walked up the hill with Nora in my arms.

I rang the bell and Mr Dunne let me in.

'A desperate sad day, Cissy, I'm sorry for your loss.'

'Thank you, Mr Dunne.'

'And is this your little one?'

'It is, Mr Dunne.'

'She will give you comfort.'

I nodded.

'Are you wanting Mrs Foley?'

'No, I'm going around to the graveyard.'

I walked around the side of the house, through the little gate and up the path to Nora's grave. I sat on the ground, holding my baby on my lap. It was a beautiful spring day and the graveyard looked less grim with the pretty flowers scattered between the wooden crosses.

'Hello, Nora,' I said. 'I've brought my little girl to see you. I named her for you, I hope that makes you happy. Mary should have reached you by now. If she has, will you hold her tight? Because she's had a terrible shock and I'd say she needs the warmth of your arms around her. I miss you both and I will never forget you. Look down on my child and keep her safe.'

Colm and I married a week after we came home with Nora and we moved into the grey house with Colm's father. It was soon after our wedding that Mammy moved in with Mr Collins, which meant that the little cottage was standing empty.

'I'd like to give it to Kate Foley,' Mammy said. 'I want her to have a life away from that place.'

'I think that's wonderful, Mammy, but do you think she might like some company?' I said.

'Who do you have in mind, Cissy?'

'Annie.'

Mammy smiled at me. 'Of course, Annie.'

And so the little cottage in Paradise Alley that held so many happy memories for me gave Mrs Foley and Annie a home of their own.

Buddy and Eddie ran ahead of me as I walked across the yard to Colm, who took Stevie in his arms and kissed his little cheek.

'I'm riding the horse, Mammy!' said Nora.

'You are, my love.'

Colm looked fondly at our little girl, who he'd loved as his own since the day the captain had placed her in his arms. 'She's going to be a fine little rider,' he said.

My heart was full as I looked at my little family: Colm, who I grew to love more every day; Stevie, my beautiful boy and Nora, the child of my heart who I'd almost lost. I was indeed blessed.

A LETTER FROM SANDY

Thank you so much for choosing to read *The Little Orphan Girl*. If you did enjoy it, and want to keep up-to-date with all my latest releases, just sign up at the following link. Your email address will never be shared and you can unsubscribe at any time.

www.bookouture.com/sandy-taylor

I would like to thank all my readers for your on-going support and wonderful reviews.

This story is fiction but it was inspired by my mother, who was born in a work house in southern Ireland.

If you have enjoyed my story I would be very grateful if you could take a moment to post a short review, which may help new readers discover my books.

I have really enjoyed hearing from you and I will always respond to your messages. You can get in touch on my Facebook page or through Twitter.

I really do appreciate you all.

Thank you again,
Love
Sandy x

@SandyTaylorAuth

SandyTaylorAuthor

ACKNOWLEDGEMENTS

As always, there are so many people to thank. My wonderful children, Kate, Bo, and Iain. My amazing grandchildren Millie, Archie and Emma Willow: you are always in my heart. To the wonderful team at Bookouture: Oliver Rhodes, Claire Bord, Kim Nash and my fabulous editor Natasha Harding. Thank you for all the support you give me.

It has been an amazing journey. I would like to thank my brothers and sisters Mag, Paddy, Marge and John and all my nieces and nephews for always believing in my writing. Sending lots of love to my Irish family.

To my amazing friends, too many to mention you all. Angela, Linda, Lynda and Lis: I would be lost without you. To Lesley, Louie and Wenny, thank you for always being there, love ya lots.

And to my wonderful agent and friend Kate Hordern who took a chance on me, thank you for everything Kate.